DESPERATE CHARGE

Callista stood behind Han, gripping the back of his chair. "The Jedi academy is under attack," she said. "We have to help. We need to do whatever we can."

"All right," Han said. "Chewie, full forward shields. Punch it. We're gonna make a straight line."

The *Millennium Falcon* soared beneath the immense *Knight Hammer*. A flurry of TIE fighters blocked their way, flying in a tight formation as they shot a constant pattern of blasts. Han streaked toward them at full speed. Chewbacca roared in alarm.

"Oh, but, sir—" Threepio cried.

"I see 'em," Han said. "They'll move."

The TIE fighters held their position, still firing. The *Falcon*'s forward shield began to weaken, but Han plunged onward, right down their throats. . . .

The sensational *Star Wars* series published by
Bantam Books and available from all good bookshops

The *Empire* Trilogy by Timothy Zahn
Heir to the Empire • Dark Force Rising
The Last Command

The *Jedi Academy* Trilogy by Kevin J. Anderson
Jedi Search • Dark Apprentice
Champions of the Force

The Truce at Bakura
by Kathy Tyers

The Courtship of Princess Leia
by Dave Wolverton

The *Corellian* Trilogy by Roger MacBride Allen
Ambush at Corellia • Assault at Selonia
Showdown at Centerpoint

The *Cantina* Trilogy edited by Kevin J. Anderson
Tales from the Mos Eisley Cantina
Tales from Jabba's Palace • Tales of the Bounty Hunters

The Crystal Star
by Vonda McIntyre

The *X-Wing* Series by Michael Stackpole
Rogue Squadron • Wedge's Gamble
The Krytos Trap • The Bacta War

The *Black Fleet Crisis* Trilogy by Michael P. Kube-McDowell
Before the Storm • Shield of Lies
Tyrant's Test

Children of the Jedi
by Barbara Hambly

Darksaber
by Kevin J. Anderson

Shadows of the Empire
by Steve Perry

The *Han Solo* Trilogy by A. C. Crispin
The Paradise Snare • The Hutt Gambit*
Rebel Dawn*

and in hardcover

The Illustrated Star Wars Universe
by Kevin J. Anderson & Ralph McQuarrie

The New Rebellion
by Kristine Kathryn Rusch

Planet of Twilight
by Barbara Hambly

*Forthcoming

DARKSABER

KEVIN J. ANDERSON

BANTAM BOOKS

TORONTO · NEW YORK · LONDON · SYDNEY · AUCKLAND

DARKSABER
A BANTAM BOOK : 0 553 40880 1

Originally published in Great Britain by Bantam Press,
a division of Transworld Publishers Ltd

PRINTING HISTORY
Bantam Press edition published 1995
Bantam edition published 1996
Bantam edition reprinted 1997

Bantam Books are published by Transworld Publishers Ltd,
61–63 Uxbridge Road, London W5 5SA,
in Australia by Transworld Publishers (Australia) Pty Ltd,
15–25 Helles Avenue, Moorebank, NSW 2170,
and in New Zealand by Transworld Publishers (NZ) Ltd,
3 William Pickering Drive, Albany, Auckland.

Reproduced, printed and bound in Great Britain by
Cox & Wyman Ltd, Reading, Berkshire.

To Lillie E. Mitchell
who does so much of the invisible work on
these books, allowing me the freedom and the
energy to tell my stories as fast as they want
to come out of my head

ACKNOWLEDGMENTS

I would like to pass along my very special thanks to Barbara Hambly, for helping me with Callista and for giving me such a perfect springboard for *Darksaber*.

I am especially indebted to the imagination and artwork of Ralph McQuarrie. Much of this novel is tied closely to work we developed during the creation of *The Illustrated Star Wars Universe,* which provided much inspiration.

Nar Shaddaa and Nal Hutta just wouldn't be the same without the work done by Tom Veitch and Cam Kennedy in their *Dark Empire* graphic novels.

Kenneth C. Flint helped with the Tatooine portion of the story; Timothy Zahn gave me guidance with Pellaeon; Bill Smith and West End Games provided detailed background material on the Hutts and on Crix Madine. The Usual Suspects—Tom Dupree, Lucy Wilson, Sue Rostoni, Allan Kausch—made this project possible in the first place and assisted along the way.

And my wife, Rebecca Moesta, helped far more—in ways both obvious and not so obvious—than I could possibly describe on the rest of this page. I love you.

The time is eight years after the battle of Endor.

Grand Admiral Thrawn and the resurrected Emperor have been defeated and their forces scattered, leaving only bickering warlords to fight over the scraps of Imperial war machinery deep in the Core Systems, far behind enemy lines. The renegade Admiral Daala is believed dead, but with her lone remaining Star Destroyer she has limped back to the shelter of the tattered Empire, where she hopes one day to return to the fight for lost Imperial territory. . . .

On Yavin 4 Luke Skywalker has formed an academy to reestablish the Jedi Knights, former guardians of the Old Republic. He has already taught many students how to use their powers with the Force; more candidates come, while others decide to go forth and help safeguard the fragile alliance of the New Republic.

In recent months Luke has destroyed the automated Dreadnaught, the Eye of Palpatine, and rescued the spirit of the Jedi woman Callista, who was trapped in the Dreadnaught's computer for decades. Luke has fallen deeply in love with her, even as she inhabits the body of one of his lost students. Though Callista is now alive again and free to love Luke Skywalker, she has inexplicably lost all of her Jedi powers in the ordeal.

Luke is desperate to find some way for Callista to get her abilities back. No matter where the search may lead him. . . .

DARKSABER

TATOOINE

CHAPTER 1

The banthas plodded in single file, leaving only a narrow trail of scuffed footprints across the dunes.

Twin suns hammered down on the procession. Waves of heat rippled like cloaking shields, blurring the distance and making an oven of the Dune Sea. Indigenous creatures took shelter in whatever shadow they could find until the firestorm of afternoon trickled away into the cooler dusk.

The banthas moved with no noise other than the muffled crunching of their footsteps in the sand. Swathed in strips of cloth, the Tusken Raiders astride the shaggy beasts looked from side to side, keeping watch.

Wrapped entirely in bandages, yet still uneasy about the disguise, Han Solo looked out through narrow metal tubes designed to shield the eyes from blowing grit. His mouth was covered with a corroded metal filter for the sand; the filter contained a small internal moisturizer to make Tatooine's fiery air more breathable. The other Sand People had tiny ventilators studded around their desert coverings. Only their strongest survived to adulthood, and they prided themselves on it.

Han rode on his bantha, hoping to remain inconspicuous in the middle of the procession. The hairy beast swayed as it walked, and Han tried not to clutch its scalloped, curving horns more often than the other Tusken Raiders did. The bantha's sharp back ridges were covered with matted fur, and the disconcertingly thin saddle made the ride excruciatingly uncomfortable.

Han swallowed, taking another sip of his precious water and biting back a complaint. This had, after all, been his own crazy suggestion. He just hadn't expected Luke Skywalker would be so eager to agree, and now Han was stuck. The mission was vital to the New Republic, and he had to follow through.

With a muttered command, the lead Raider urged his bantha to greater speed. The procession trudged through fine sand, winding along the crest of a shifting dune that stood like a towering sentinel in the arid ocean. Han did not grasp the dune's great size until they had ascended for the better part of an hour without reaching the top.

The suns grew even hotter, if that were possible. The banthas coughed and snorted, but the Sand People were focused on a mission.

Han swallowed, trying to ease his parched throat. Finally, he could remain silent no longer and whispered into the short-range transmitter implanted in his breathmask. "Luke, what's goin' on?" he said. "I've got a bad feeling about whatever they're up to."

It took Luke Skywalker a moment to respond. Han watched the thin rider two banthas ahead of him sit up straighter; Luke seemed far more comfortable in his disguise than Han felt. Of course, Luke had grown up on Tatooine—but the young man's voice now sounded bone weary as it came over the voice pickup in Han's ear.

"Nothing to do with us, Han," he said. "A few of the Sand People have vague suspicions, but they haven't centered on us yet. I'm using the Force to distract anyone who pays too much attention. No, this is something different entirely. A great tragedy . . . you'll see." Luke heaved a long breath through his breathmask. "Can't talk now. Have to concentrate. Wait until they're preoccupied, and I'll explain more."

Up ahead, Luke slumped forward in his Tusken disguise. Han knew his friend was expending an incredible amount of energy to lull the Sand People into ignoring their two unwanted guests. Luke was able to use his abilities to muddle the minds of weak individuals, but never before had Han seen his friend manipulate so many minds at once.

The trick was to keep the Sand People from *noticing* them; then it was easy for Luke to divert a few stray thoughts. If someone sounded an alarm and all the Sand People focused on the intruders, though, not even a Jedi Master would be able to keep up the charade. Then there would be a fight.

Tucked under his tattered robes, Han carried his trusty blaster pistol. He didn't know if he and Luke could take on the entire band of Raiders—but they would make a good accounting of themselves if circumstances ever came to that.

The lead rider reached the peak of the sand mountain. The bantha's wide feet trampled the wind-sharpened edge atop the dune. The air was still, as if stunned. The sands glittered like a billion miniature novas.

Han adjusted the corroded filters over his eyes. The other banthas plodded up, surrounding their leader, who raised his cloth-wrapped arm, brandishing a wicked-looking gaffi stick. Behind the Tusken leader, his single passenger sat slumped and sullen, though it was difficult to understand the body language of these masked and alien people.

Han sensed somehow that this withdrawn passenger was the center of the ceremony. Was some kind of honor being bestowed, Han wondered, or was this man being exiled from the tribe?

The passenger slid off the lead bantha, letting himself drop from the shaggy beast. He clung to the woolly fur as if in desperation, but no sounds came from his bandaged face, not even the guttural grunts and snorts the Tuskens used as language. Head down, his eye tubes pointed toward the churned sand where bantha footprints had trampled the pristine dune, the passenger stood dejected in front of the lead rider.

The leader waited beside his mount, holding the upraised gaffi stick; the other Sand People climbed down from their banthas. They thrashed their own weapons in the air. Han and Luke copied the gestures, trying to blend in.

In his disguise Luke moved slowly and wearily. This mission was taking a heavy toll on the Jedi Knight, and Han hoped they would reach their destination soon.

The forlorn passenger hesitated at the edge of the dune, gazing across the sweeping ocean of loose sands that spread to the horizon. The Sand People stood at attention and raised their gaffi sticks high.

While they concentrated on the intensity of the moment, Luke's voice buzzed in Han's ear. "All right, they're distracted," he said. "I can explain. The lone Tusken Raider lost his bantha three days ago. A krayt dragon killed it, and unfortunately our friend there got away."

"What do you mean, *unfortunately*?" Han mumbled, hoping his voice wouldn't carry over the restless sounds of the Sand People.

"The Tusken Raiders have a very close relationship with their banthas," Luke said. "It is a mental bonding, a symbiosis, almost like a marriage. They become part of each other, bantha and Tusken. When one member of the pair is killed, the other is incomplete—like an amputee." Unconsciously, Luke flexed his cyborg hand. "He has no place in Tusken society, though he is more an object of pity than of hatred. Many believe he should have died beside his bantha, no matter what the circumstances."

"So, are they just going to kill him?" Han asked.

"Yes and no," Luke said. "They believe the spirit of the dead bantha must decide. If the spirit wishes for him to bond with another mount, our friend will find a free wild bantha in the desert, join with it, and return in triumph to the tribe, where he will be fully accepted—even highly revered. However, if the bantha's spirit wants his rider to join him in death, then the outcast will wander hopelessly in the desert until he dies.''

Han barely shook his head. "Doesn't sound like his chances are too hot.''

Luke said, "Probably not—but that is their way.''

The Sand People waited for the exile to make the first move. Finally, with a single anguished cry that might have been triumph or challenge, he plunged down the steep and shifting slope of the dune. The Sand People tilted their heads toward the burning sky and let out a loud ululating cry that made Han shudder.

The Tusken Raiders thrashed their gaffi sticks to wish their companion well. The banthas raised up their squarish, shaggy heads and bellowed in unison, a rumbling, growling cry that shook the Dune Sea.

The lone Raider waded down the steep slope. Dusty golden sand flew up around him as his feet and legs sank in. His robes flapped behind him as he plodded on. He tripped and tumbled, flailing his arms, and finally jabbed his gaffi stick deep into the uncertain surface, one arm thrust out to gain balance, leaving a swath of disturbed sand behind him.

The exiled Raider heaved himself to his feet again. Sand trickled from his flowing cloaks, but still he marched ahead, not looking back. A few of the banthas bellowed again. The sound was swallowed up in the empty vastness. The outcast's drab garments soon made him fade into the landscape.

The lead Raider turned and, with a single energetic leap, mounted his bantha. The other Sand People climbed into their saddles. The banthas snorted and stomped on the loose sand.

Han got back to his seat. Luke was the last to balance himself again, and by that time the lead Raider had already turned the hairy beast to the side and began to plunge down the shallower slope at the back of the dune. The other Sand People followed, marching closely in line to mask their tracks.

Han risked a glance behind him. He could just make out the single exiled Raider dwindling in the distance, moving with slow determination as ripples of heat blurred his tiny figure. Soon he was swallowed completely by the unforgiving jaws of the Dune Sea.

The heat of the day seemed to last forever, and Han rode in a fugue state, barely aware of his surroundings, self-hypnotized by a litany of rocking footfalls. Ahead, Luke continued to sit upright on the bantha saddle, though he wavered from time to time. Han wondered what sort of energy the Jedi Knight was tapping into.

The group camped in a thick maze of rocky badlands punctuated by pockmarked stone needles rising out of the windblown sand. Darkness fell quickly with the double sunset, and the temperature plummeted. For a while the rocks continued to throb with stored heat, but they quickly cooled.

Grunting and chuffing to each other in their baffling language, the Sand People pitched camp. Each knew his or her own duties—Han could not tell whether the individual Tuskens were male or female. Luke had said that only assigned mates were able to see each other with faces un-wrapped.

Two of the younger people encircled a flat area with smaller rocks, and piled bricks of what Han realized must be dried bantha dung, the only fuel source available out in the barrens.

Han and Luke moved about, trying to appear busy. The banthas, not corralled or tied in any way, were simply led to a side canyon where they could rest for the night. Other Raiders broke out packages of stringy dried meat. Han and Luke took their share and squatted on boulders.

Carefully, Han lifted his metal breathmask and jammed a piece of the meat into his mouth. He chewed and wasted several drinks of water as he tried to make the jerky palatable enough to swallow. "What *is* this stuff?" he muttered into the voice pickup.

Luke answered without looking at him. "Dried and salted dewback flank, I believe."

"Tastes like leather," Han muttered.

"It's more nutritious than leather . . . I think," Luke said. He turned his metal eyetubes toward Han, who could detect no expression on the wrapped-up face. Han became disoriented if he swiveled his head too fast while looking through the small holes in the eyetubes.

As the Sand People finished their meal, they gathered around the blaze as a tall Raider hunched near the brighter part of the fire. From the careful way he moved, the slow placement of limbs—not to mention the silent reverence the other Tuskens granted him—Han got the impression that this was a very old person.

"The storyteller," Luke's voice said in his ear.

Other Raiders brought out long poles and unfurled bright clan banners marked with jagged slashes, some sort of violent written language. These must be totems, symbols not seen by the outside world at all.

A young, wiry Raider sat next to the storyteller. Others came back from their bantha saddles with trophies, visual aids for the story. They held out scraps of rough cloth, a bloodied banner. Han saw battered and cracked stormtrooper helmets like the skulls of fallen enemies; a luminous milky gem the size of his fist, which Han recognized with a start as a krayt dragon pearl, one of the rarest treasures ever to come from Tatooine.

The old man raised up his bandage-wrapped hands and began to speak. The other Raiders sat enraptured as stories spilled out in low grunts and barely recognizable sounds that might have been words.

Luke translated for Han. "He's telling of their exploits, how they took an entire stormtrooper regiment many years ago. How they slew a krayt dragon and took the pearls out of its gullet. How they defeated another Tusken clan, slaughtered all their adults, and adopted their children into the clan, thereby increasing their numbers.''

The storyteller finished his tale and squatted lower, gesturing to the young apprentice who glanced around. Two Tusken Raiders stood on either side of the boy, holding their gaffi sticks with the axheads pointing down at the apprentice. The storyteller raised a trembling hand and turned it sideways like a knife blade. The apprentice hesitated for a moment and began to speak slowly.

"Now what?" Han said.

Luke answered. "That boy is being trained as the clan's next storyteller. The Tuskens believe very much in inflexible tradition. Once a story is set down as an oral path, it must remain forever unaltered. This boy has learned the story: he is now telling about a raid on a moisture farmer who attempted to bring peace between humans and Jawas and Sand People.''

"But why the weapons?" Han said. "Looks like they're ready to snuff the poor kid.''

"They will, if he makes so much as one mistake. If the boy alters a single word, the storyteller will chop down with his hand, and the Raiders will kill the apprentice immediately. They believe that speaking the stories in any manner other than the way they were originally told is great blasphemy.''

Han said, "Not much room for mistakes, is there?''

Luke shook his head. The other Tuskens were concentrating completely on the boy's speech. "The desert is a hard place, Han. It allows no room for mistakes. The Sand People are a product of that environment. They have harsh ways, but such harshness has been forced upon them.''

The boy finished, and the old storyteller raised his other hand in a congratulatory gesture. The young apprentice slumped with trembling relief, and the other Sand People muttered their appreciation.

After a while, the fire was banked and began to burn low. The Tusken Raiders settled down for the night.

"I'm going to get some rest," Han said. "You haven't slept in two days, Luke. Can't you wait until they all go to sleep, then catch a nap yourself?"

Luke shook his head. "I don't dare. If I stop monitoring their thoughts, if I release my hold on their minds, they might suddenly realize we're not supposed to be with them. If somebody sounds an alarm, we're lost. Besides, a Jedi can go a long time without rest."

"Whatever you say, buddy," Han said.

"We should reach Jabba's palace by tomorrow," Luke said with weary hope.

"I can't wait," Han said. "I mean, we had so much fun the last time we were there."

CHAPTER 2

The Sand People roused themselves in the frigid darkness before the first of Tatooine's twin suns crept over the horizon. Han shivered, finding no warmth in his bandage wrappings. Luke moved more sluggishly than ever.

Han was worried about his friend. In addition to exhaustion, Luke was suffering from deep frustration at his inability to help Callista—the Jedi woman he loved—regain her lost powers. And now, after days without sleep on the razor's edge of peril, hiding among ferocious desert nomads, Luke's stamina was wearing dangerously thin.

The Tusken Raiders saddled their banthas, and the shaggy beasts stomped impatiently, as if anxious to be off before the day's heat caught up with them. Soundlessly, with gaffi sticks and scavenged blaster rifles ready, the Sand People rode out into the desert as the sky filled with purple, brightening to a lavender shot with molten gold.

When the first sun rose, Han felt the temperature skyrocket after only a few moments. The air smelled flat and metallic through his mouthpiece, but Han endured in silence.

He thought of Leia and their three children back on Coruscant and fantasized about the peaceful life of a small yet successful trader. But Han grimaced behind the bandages: such a quiet life would be a greater torture than any vicious punishment the Sand People could devise.

By midmorning, the Tusken Raiders topped a rocky rise and looked across distended shadows and painted desert to the ruins of Jabba the Hutt's palace. The citadel stood silent and monolithic in the crags. Han shivered at his first glance.

"I told you I'd get us here," Luke said through the voice pickup.

"We're not inside yet, kid," Han answered.

"When I split off, follow me," Luke said. "I'll distract the Sand People so they won't even notice us separating from them. Once we get out of sight, I can release my control—and I'll be glad for the rest."

Far across the rolling ocean of sand, the collected winds made a minor sandwhirl, such as often whipped up in the wastelands—but Luke used it to his advantage.

The lead Raider grunted something and pointed with his gaffi stick, wheeling his bantha about to watch the sandwhirl. The other Sand People turned, inordinately fascinated by the dust whirl. They chattered among themselves, grunting and hooting through their breathmasks.

Luke used the diversion to nudge his bantha to the right, splitting off from the line of Tusken Raiders. Han yanked on the rough curved horn of his mount. He couldn't believe it was going to work, but he and Luke rode side by side, trotting down the sandy slope. Their footprints churning up dust, the banthas crossed the great empty bowl into the rocky canyon that led to Jabba's palace.

Han looked back anxiously, but none of the Tusken Raiders turned in their direction. The Sand People continued to point their sticks and shout toward the sandwhirl as if it were an approaching army.

Luke urged his bantha between the narrow, rust-rock

walls where the canyon shadows fell about them. Heat-broken boulders rose on either side, and the baked sulfurous sand and mud was like duracrete underfoot as the mounts trotted toward the lower entrance of Jabba's palace.

Once they were out of sight, Luke let out a heavy sigh and slumped against his saddle. "We made it!" he said. "They shouldn't remember us at all."

"Yeah," Han said, "and we got all the way from Anchorhead without anybody noticing us—no spies, no witnesses, no records. Now we can check out these rumors and get back home."

A harsh wind whistled down the canyon, moaning through the minarets of Jabba's palace. The high observation towers had open black windows, like gaps in a grinning skull. Han looked up and saw blaster scoring on the fused bricks. A few scuttling lizards ran from a pocket of shade to some other cool, dark crack.

Han could not see enough through the round eyetubes of the Tusken face wrapping. In disgust he peeled the bandages off and removed the metal eye coverings, tossing them to the ground. He drew a deep breath of the dusty air and coughed. "Boy, I'm glad to get rid of that."

Luke's face looked monstrous swathed in his Tusken disguise; but he carefully unwrapped himself, stuffing the rags inside his tattered desert robes.

Han shook his head as he looked at the ruins. Jabba had not been the first inhabitant of the huge palace. It had been built centuries before the Hutt crimelord was born, or hatched . . . or however it was that baby Hutts came to life.

Long ago, exiled monks of the B'omarr Order had found an isolated spot on the backwater world Tatooine and built their towering monastery, remaining mysterious and aloof from the planet's other inhabitants. Sometime later the bandit Alkhara had broken into the monastery and used parts of it as his hideout as he preyed upon moisture farmers. The B'omarr monks didn't seem to care about Alkhara's presence, though—utterly ignoring him.

Since that time, a succession of undesirables had located their headquarters in portions of the B'omarr monastery, the latest of whom had been Jabba the Hutt. After Jabba's death at the Great Pit of Carkoon, a civil war had broken out among Jabba's minions as each scrambled to steal the Hutt crimelord's possessions, ransacking the palace.

With Jabba's crime empire in ruins, the silent and mysterious monks had taken the opportunity to reclaim what had been theirs, destroying those among Jabba's followers who did not flee fast enough. The palace had since remained a haunted edifice, to be avoided by all but the most daring.

Recently, though, some of what Leia called his "scruffy" old friends had passed along disturbing rumors that other Hutts were poking around in the abandoned palace, looking for something—something important enough for them to risk coming back.

Luke slid down from his bantha and patted its woolly side. The bantha snorted in confusion and stamped its feet. Han's bantha snuffled.

The corroded door loomed in front of them, a durasteel barrier pitted with blaster scars, some bright and new, others decades old and worn away. Luke and Han approached together. Over the years, the control circuits had crossed or decayed, and the heavy barrier had raised—and stuck—half a meter from the ground. Drifts of sand had collected in the gap. A cool, musty-smelling breeze leaked out of the shadowy inner corridors.

"We could crawl under, I suppose," Han said without much enthusiasm, running his fingers over the heavy durasteel door.

Luke went up to the lichen-covered external panel. "It might slip and squash us both like it did Jabba's rancor. I think I'll try these controls first."

As soon as Luke touched one of the buttons, a panel

creaked open in the center of the door, and a bobbing
artificial eye extended, swaying on a rusted metal stalk—
Jabba's surveillance system. The machine's words were
garbled and slurred as if its programming had deteriorated.

The scolding tone in its vocal synthesizer was more
than Han, weary as he was, could tolerate. He reached into
the folds of his desert robe, pulled out his blaster pistol,
and blew the thing into smoking shards and sparking
wires. "Oh, shut up!" he said, then turned to Luke with a
roguish grin. "Didn't like the way it was looking at us."

Luke set to work on the door controls, and finally,
with a coughing sound, the door lurched up another meter
and jammed in its tracks. "Think that's good enough?" he
said.

Before Han could reply, the whine of a blaster bolt
spanged against the metal door, creating another bright
silvery scar. "What?" he cried, whirling.

Their two banthas snorted in greeting. Another
blaster bolt shot down the canyon and burned a hole
through Han's draped desert robe, barely missing his
chest. Han held up the drab cloth in shock, looking at the
smoldering hole.

The entire group of Sand People thundered down the
canyon, whipping their banthas to a frenzy and waving
gaffi sticks. They fired recklessly with their blasters. Han
and Luke's two banthas reared.

"Looks like you stopped distracting 'em too soon,
kid," Han said, diving toward the partially open door.
"Must have seen our tracks."

"I guess this door is open enough," Luke said and
scrambled into the shadows beside Han. "Now if only I
can figure out how to close it . . ."

More blaster bolts struck the door, making the musty
corridors echo and thrum. The Sand People jabbered with
rage, and their banthas made loud sounds as they churned
around the door.

Luke found the inner door controls and grabbed at a
bunch of the twisted and corroded wires. A single hope-

less spark flickered out, then the entire control panel went dead.

"Better do something quick, Luke!" Han said, crouching down with his blaster pistol.

One of the Sand People fired into the interior shadows; the energy bolt ricocheted on the flagstone floor, bouncing into the darkness behind Han and Luke. Han fired his own blaster at the bandaged feet he could see. One of the Tusken Raiders yowled and leaped backward.

Luke gave up on the control panel and stood with his hands hanging at his sides. His fists clenched, then relaxed as he concentrated on the Force.

The tracks groaned as he moved the mechanisms holding the heavy door in place. Suddenly, with a thunderous *clang,* it crashed down, belching up clouds of old dust and engulfing the hall in darkness.

"Well, that was fun," Han said. "Don't suppose you remembered to bring along a portable glowlamp?"

Luke reached into the folds of his robe. "A Jedi always comes prepared," he said and removed his lightsaber, pushing the activation button. With a *snap-hiss* the vibrant green blade spilled out, a rod of incandescent light that made Han shield his eyes. "Not the most impressive use I've ever made of my lightsaber," Luke commented, "but it'll do."

The two crept deeper into the winding catacombs of the palace toward Jabba's throne room. They didn't quite know what they were looking for, but both were confident they'd spot something amiss.

"It didn't look that much better when Jabba lived here," Luke said.

"Maybe all the housekeeping droids broke down," Han said.

Inside the abandoned main throne room where the bloated Hutt had pronounced judgment on his helpless victims, Luke's lightsaber illuminated the walls with a glare that made the shadows jump and ripple. Scavengers, small and large, made loud noises in the otherwise tomb-like room. Pebbles trickled from a loose block in the wall.

"Those weird B'omarr monks are still here in this place," Han said. "But they don't look too anxious to reclaim the rooms Jabba used."

"I'm not sure anyone pretends to understand the B'omarr Order," Luke answered. "From what I've heard, when they reach their greatest state of enlightenment, each monk undergoes some kind of surgery that removes his brain and places it in a life-support jar. It keeps them from being distracted by physical diversions, leaving them to ponder the great mysteries."

Han snorted and looked into Luke's pale blue eyes. "Good thing Jedi don't go for nonsense like that."

Luke smiled at his friend. "I seem to remember you called the Force a 'hokey religion' when I first met you."

Han looked away, embarrassed. "Well, I've gotten smarter since then."

Sudden mechanical sounds were as loud as distant explosions in the echoing room. The two whirled: Luke with his lightsaber ready, Han pointing his blaster pistol. The whirring servomotors and articulated legs came closer, many feet clicking like ice picks on the flagstone floors. Han felt his skin crawl with remembered revulsion as he thought of the crystalline energy spiders that lived in the black spice mines of Kessel.

But the thing that emerged was neither entirely a droid nor entirely alive—a set of sharp mechanical legs moving, staggering, as if with poor muscular control . . . an automated steel insect that stumbled into the throne room. And slung under the legs, where the bloated body of a spider would have been, hung a spherical jar filled with clear fluid that bubbled and gurgled, pulsing life-support into the convoluted and spongy form of a human brain.

"Uh-oh!" Han said. "It's one of the monks. Who knows what they're after?" He pointed the blaster directly at the brain jar.

No, came a flat, processed voice—a synthesized word

through a tiny speaker mounted on the set of mechanical legs.

Luke held up his other hand. "Wait, Han . . . I'm sensing only confusion. There's no threat."

Are you . . . friends of Jabba's? the spider legs asked.

"I've got better taste in my friends," Han said. "Who're you?"

The spider legs skittered from side to side as if the brain had stopped concentrating and lost control. *I am Maizor. I was once a rival of Jabba's. We had a . . . confrontation, and I lost.*

The synthesized voice paused, as if processing. *Jabba ordered the monks to perform their surgery on me and place my brain in this jar.*

More thinking, more flat and mechanical words. *I use these legs when I wish to move about. It took me a year to stop screaming in silence and become adjusted to my new circumstances. Jabba kept me around his palace as a joke, so he could laugh at how pathetic I had become.*

The spider legs skittered, though the voice grew louder, tinged with defiance. *But now Jabba is dead. The palace is empty. And I am the last one laughing.*

Han and Luke looked at each other. Han gradually lowered his blaster. "Well, any enemy of Jabba's is a friend of mine," he said. "In fact, we were there at the Great Pit of Carkoon when Jabba was killed."

I am greatly in your debt, Maizor said. Blinking lights flashed around the brain jar's life-support systems.

"Then perhaps you can help us," Luke said. His voice was calm, filled with Jedi power. "We're seeking information. We've heard rumors. If you have been here in the palace, you might have seen what we need to know."

Yes, Maizor said. *Many strangers have come here recently. Much activity. Very mysterious.*

"Can you tell us who they were, what they were looking for?" Han said, amazed at how easy the answer had come. "We need to know what the Hutts are up to."

Hutts, the mechanical voice said. *I despise Hutts. Many Hutts have intruded here. Searching.*

"And what were they looking for?" Han persisted.

Information. Jabba's information. Jabba had much knowledge stored here in secret databanks. He had his spies everywhere, collecting data to use or to sell. Not only was Jabba a crime kingpin, he also knew much about the Rebel Alliance—though the Empire refused to pay him enough to make it worthwhile. Jabba also had many Imperial secrets.

The spider legs bobbed up and down. *Imperial secrets. That is what the Hutts were looking for.*

"Imperial secrets?" Luke said. "But the Empire has fallen. We haven't heard anything from them in years. What could the Hutts possibly want with Imperial information?"

Imperial information, Maizor repeated. *Imperial Information Center, the great database on Coruscant. Jabba knew secret passwords. He could access the Emperor's most heavily protected information.*

Han was startled. "You mean the Hutts can break into our computers? Impossible! We've locked down all of those files."

Jabba had ways of accessing them, Maizor replied.

"Tell me," Luke said, "did the Hutts find what they were looking for when they came here?"

Yes, the spider legs said. *They intend to create their own bargaining force, an invincible weapon. The Hutt crime syndicate will be more powerful than the Rebels or what's left of the Empire.* Maizor flinched. *I hate the Hutts.*

Han groaned. "Oh no, not *another* superweapon!"

"Do you know any details of their plans?" Luke asked, bending closer to the brain in the jar. "Any specifics?"

No, Maizor said. *They have the key they sought, and now they will move on to their next step.*

Han nodded grimly, looking to Luke. "We have to

get back to Coruscant and report to Leia. The New Republic needs to be on their guard.''

Luke switched off his lightsaber, plunging the room into thick, oily shadows, but he reached forward to rub his fingers on the edges of Maizor's brain jar. Fizzing bubbles continued to curl through the nutrient fluids, but the brain hung motionless. ''Is there anything we can do for you?'' Luke asked. ''I might be able to help you find peace in your existence.''

A harsh, hiccoughing sound came from the voice synthesizer. *No, Jedi. The B'omarr monks have already given as much solace as they could. What you must do for me is stop the Hutts' plan. Humiliate them.* The spider legs rocked back and forth. *I will remain here alone—and continue to laugh at Jabba. That is my reward.*

CHAPTER 3

Since their banthas had run off, leaving them stranded at Jabba's palace, Han suggested to Luke that they investigate the vehicle hangars in the lower levels. Together, the two of them might be able to reassemble a functioning speeder so they could make good time away from the ruins. Luke agreed, his mind preoccupied with his real reason for wanting to come to Tatooine.

Under the flickering light of old glowpanels, Han tinkered with the mechanical subsystems of damaged vehicles. The scrapped engines and hull parts were all that remained after the frantic mass exodus of Jabba's minions. Because of rumors and superstitious fear, Jawas and other scavengers had not dared to come steal away what was left, so dismantled skiffs and flyers remained in the maintenance bay, salvaged for parts.

Han and Luke worked together, swapping out components, making modifications from what they had on hand. At last they operated a clanking mechanical side door, letting the wash of yellow sunlight scour the filthy hangar bay. They climbed aboard two battered swoops that reminded Luke of the speeder bikes he and his sister, Leia, had ridden so recklessly through the forests on Endor.

Luke sat on the dented metal seat, trying to be comfortable on the scraps of the petrified leather covering. "It's been a long time since I did something like this," Luke said. "Feels good."

"Just like old times, kid." Han powered up the humming repulsor-lifts. "Let's head back to Mos Eisley Spaceport so we can get out of here."

"Wait, Han," Luke said with a pensive expression. "There's something I have to do first. We'll need to make a side trip, circle around to the Jundland Wastes."

Han looked at him, pursing his lips, then he nodded. "Yeah, I thought you had something else on your mind from the way you were acting. Anything to do with Callista?"

Luke nodded, but gave no details.

"I guess I should know by now that when I'm with a Jedi, nothing's simple and straightforward," Han said.

As events continued around him, Luke forced himself to keep moving, proceeding to the next step, hoping that he would find some clue at his next destination. The news of the Hutts' secret plan alarmed him, but his heart ached at being separated from Callista. He longed to be with her. He longed to help her.

Following threads of the Force, he and Callista had *connected* with each other's personalities from the very first. They had linked like two pieces of a precise puzzle. Callista was right for Luke, and he was right for her. Being Jedi, they knew it in a way that few other lovers could understand.

Though Callista had been born decades before Luke, her spirit had been frozen within the computer of the automated Dreadnaught *Eye of Palpatine*. Luke had fallen in love with Callista's luminous form, until she came back to life in the body of one of his brilliant students, who had sacrificed herself to destroy the Dreadnaught.

Now Callista was physically whole again. Flesh and blood. Beautiful. They could be together.

But in a devastating irony, Callista had lost all her Jedi abilities in the transformation. She was alive again, but not the same, not *completely* there. They could no longer link with each other, mind and spirit. They'd had only those heady days to remember, trapped together aboard the *Eye of Palpatine*.

But it was enough to galvanize the deep love between them and make them keep trying to find an answer. Luke would never give up until he found a way to bring Callista back whole. . . .

He stood anxious and alone, feeling like a prodigal son outside the ramshackle, collapsed hut that had once been the home of Obi-Wan Kenobi.

Han waited by his repaired swoop, drinking the last of their water. Luke had forgone his share, building up his mental energy through concentration. They would be at the Mos Eisley Spaceport soon, no matter what happened at the ruins of Obi-Wan's dwelling.

Luke swallowed and stepped forward, his footsteps crunching in the silence. He had not been here in many years. The door had fallen off its hinges; part of the clay front wall had fallen in. Boulders and crumbled adobe jammed the entrance. A pair of small, screeching desert rodents snapped at him and fled for cover; Luke ignored them.

Gingerly, he ducked low and stepped into the home of his first mentor.

Light slanted in from cracks in the walls. Dust motes drifted like gold dust through the sunbeams. The place smelled of mustiness, empty shadows, and ghosts. Unlike Jabba's palace, however, scavengers had had no qualms about cleaning Ben Kenobi's abode of everything of the

slightest value. The stove and heater units had been removed, leaving only vacant notches in the clay walls.
Ben's sleeping pallet had been stripped down to its splintered frame. Shreds of cloth, long since turned into nests
for rodents and insects, lay wadded in the corners.

Luke stood in the middle of the room breathing
deeply, turning around, trying to sense the presence he
desperately needed to see. This was the place where Obi-
Wan Kenobi had told Luke of the Force. Here, the old man
had first given Luke his lightsaber and hinted at the truth
about his father, "from a certain point of view," dispelling the diversionary story that Uncle Owen had told, at
the same time planting seeds of his own deceptions.

Luke pulled out his lightsaber and gripped the handle, but did not switch it on. After he had lost his father's
weapon on Cloud City, Luke had built a new lightsaber
that belonged to him and no one else—not an artifact from
the past. He had forged his own path in the absence of his
teachers.

It seemed that Obi-Wan and Yoda had begun to prepare him, but had left Luke with so many questions, so
much knowledge unlearned . . . and the insane Joruus
C'baoth could tell him only perversions of what a true Jedi
needed to know. The Emperor had shown Luke dark side
ways, but Luke needed to understand so much more.

He needed to know how to save Callista.

"Ben," he said and closed his eyes, calling out with
his mind as well as his voice. He tried to penetrate the
invisible walls of the Force and reach to the luminous being of Obi-Wan Kenobi who had visited him numerous
times, before saying he could never speak with Luke
again.

"Ben, I need you," Luke said. Circumstances had
changed. He could think of no other way past the obstacles
he faced. Obi-Wan had to answer. It wouldn't take long,
but it could give him the key he needed with all his heart.

Luke paused and listened and sensed—

But felt nothing. If he could not summon Obi-Wan's

spirit here in the empty dwelling where the old man had lived in exile for so many years, Luke didn't believe he could find his former teacher ever again.

He echoed the words Leia had used more than a decade earlier, beseeching him, "Help me, Obi-Wan Kenobi," Luke whispered, "you're my only hope."

Luke waited again, trembling faintly. He had tried everything he knew. Callista had undergone other training in her own years as a Jedi. She knew things Luke had never imagined—but even she knew of no way to tear away the smothering blanket around her, the blindness that prevented her from using the Force.

"Ben, please!" Luke cried. His body shivered with the intensity of his desperation and dwindling hope. The empty hut sat around him holding only memories.

Nothing.

Silence.

Emptiness.

Obi-Wan was not there. The old Jedi teacher would not come. Luke knelt down in the dirt on the floor, scrabbling in the dust for some sign, some other message, as realization sank in.

He would get no help from Obi-Wan after all.

Luke swallowed his despair, vowing never to give up. He lifted his chin and clamped his lips together in a grim, determined line.

Perhaps that was the message: Obi-Wan's silence, proving to him that Luke was a Jedi Knight himself. He could not rely on Ben Kenobi or Yoda or others to help him. *He* controlled his own destiny. He was no longer just a student. Luke would have to solve his own problems.

His resolve hardened within him. No, he had not tried everything. He would search the galaxy with Callista. He would find the answer one way or another.

Luke stood up and clipped the lightsaber to his belt again. He had no need to draw it. He looked around with one last twinge of hope that he might see a glowing outline, the old man nodding to him, reaffirming that Luke's answer was the correct one. But he sensed nothing.

When he stepped back out, the blazing sunlight washed over him like a cleansing flood. He took a deep breath and went to meet Han.

Han Solo stood in the shade beside his floating swoop and wiped sweat from his forehead. "Well, kid?" he asked. "Find what you were looking for?"

"No . . ." Luke said, "and yes."

Han shook his head. "Leave it to a Jedi never to give you a straight answer."

"In this case, there is no straight answer, Han. I'm done with Tatooine," Luke said. "We can go back to Mos Eisley now. We have to warn the New Republic what the Hutts are up to."

CHAPTER 4

A storm of rocks swept across space, colliding and smashing with enough force to crush boulders—or spaceships—to powder.

The Hoth Asteroid Belt was a nightmarish hazard to navigation. A few fragments collided with the Orko SkyMine ship's forward deflector shields, then vanished into bright plumes of vaporized dust.

On the foredeck Durga the Hutt rested on his levitating platform like a slab of raw flesh, watching through the command viewports. Durga saw only one thing as he watched the colliding asteroids: *resources.* Vast untapped resources containing every sort of metal and mineral that could be of use to the Hutts' new secret project.

"Increase deflector shields," Durga said, puffing his cheeks and stretching the smeared birthmark across the left side of his head.

His minions scrambled to do his bidding. Weequays, Gamorreans, human slaves, and others clustered about the expeditionary ship's controls, bickering about how best to implement the order. Durga was not impressed with the intelligence or the free-thinking abilities of his contracted employees—but he had not hired them for those qualities.

Beside the sluglike Hutt, Imperial General Sulamar turned from a status screen and snapped to attention. Always obsessively attentive to protocol, the general kept his uniform trim and pressed, with edges that could have cut Mandalorian iron. The left breast of his uniform was plastered with a treasure chest of medals from previous campaigns he had won (about which he never ceased blabbering). He smiled grimly, a sallow-faced, flinty-eyed man who looked somehow small inside his uniform, as if he were actually no more than a frightened boy trapped in a grown-up disguise.

"Mineral Exploiter Alpha has already begun its hunting and processing routine," General Sulamar said. "Mineral Exploiter Beta has just been unleashed." He clicked his black heels together. "I trust the profits for Orko SkyMine will be up this quarter?"

"They better be," Durga said. "Move us forward so I can observe the mining activities." He gestured with one small, slimy hand.

Orko SkyMine was merely a sham corporation that the Hutt crime empire had put together to disguise their expenses—a false commercial venture that would exploit the untapped Hoth Asteroid Belt. They had wanted a remote location and limitless resources for their secret project. The incredibly complex and expensive Mineral Exploiter was the first step in what would be the Hutts' eventual domination of the galaxy.

"We're tracking Beta, sir," one of the human technicians said. "Moving forward to get within view."

"Make sure you steer clear of those asteroids, Navigator," General Sulamar snapped, making his voice deeper and gruffer, as he always did when issuing orders.

Durga gave a guttural growl. "I am in command of this ship, General. I will give the orders here."

Sulamar bowed in embarrassment and took a step backward. "My apologies, Lord Durga."

Durga narrowed his huge coppery eyes, then turned to the navigator. "You heard the general," he said. "Do as he says!"

As the Orko SkyMine expeditionary ship threaded its way through the colliding rocks, Durga eased forward. He blinked his thick-lidded eyes, trying to spot the metallic blip against the starfield.

As they approached, the mammoth ore-processing unit began to stand out, gleaming and sparkling, a flurry of motion. *A magnificent machine,* Durga thought as he saw the hulk—a giant cargo container with a front end of moving mechanical mouthparts and turbolaser turrets to blast asteroids to rubble. It stuffed the rubble into a giant processing maw, chewed it up, spit out the useless slag, and kept its precious ingots of worthwhile metals. The newly designed automated Mineral Exploiters had a simple mission: sophisticated sensors directed the behemoths to hunt down the highest and purest concentrations of metals out in the asteroid belt and to dismantle the rocks and exploit the treasure.

"They seem to be functioning perfectly," Sulamar said, again snapping to attention after he studied the diagnostic screen. "You have every confidence in their abilities?"

Durga let loose a deep belly laugh. "Naturally! My pet scientist Bevel Lemelisk designed them. Perhaps you've heard of his other work?" The Hutt leaned forward so that his huge head was close to General Sulamar's sallow face. "When he was bonded to the Emperor, Lemelisk was in charge of constructing both the first and the second Death Stars."

Sulamar's eyebrows shot up, showing how impressed he was.

"Bevel Lemelisk designed these Mineral Exploiters, and he will also be hard at work overseeing the construction of our new weapon."

"Sounds like you couldn't have found a better man,"

Sulamar agreed, then faced forward, watching Mineral Exploiter Beta continue its work.

The machine finished devouring a medium-size asteroid and dumped the molten waste slag, which hardened into small flying shards in its wake. The machine's sensors swept the asteroid belt for a new target.

"Beta is picking up a very high concentration of metal," one of the Devaronian diagnosticians said. "It's amazingly pure."

The Mineral Exploiter altered course and increased speed toward its new target. Durga watched with growing glee.

"Must be even more resources out here than we anticipated!" another tech said. "Mineral Exploiter Alpha has found a rich source as well. The target seems to be moving on an odd course for one of these asteroids, but it registers as pure metal. Like nothing we've ever seen out here."

Durga chortled with satisfaction. "If these Mineral Exploiters continue to find such wealth, we might not need the other two we have under construction."

The pilot of the Hutt expeditionary vessel increased shields as they followed Mineral Exploiter Beta through the asteroid belt.

"Alpha is also headed this way," the human technician said.

General Sulamar frowned. "Do you think they could have picked up the same target?"

"Uh-oh," the Devaronian station chief said.

Durga sat up straight on his repulsorsled. He puffed his rubbery cheeks again. "I don't like the tone of that, mister."

"I don't like what I'm seeing," the horned Devaronian responded. He raised his clawed hands in panic. "Alpha and Beta haven't picked up the same target—they've detected *each other*."

"Well, shut them down," Durga said. "An unforeseen programming glitch. We can't afford to lose those two pieces of equipment.''

The Devaronian hammered instructions into his control panels. The other technicians worked frantically—to no avail. The Gamorrean guards stood dumbfounded, blinking at each other in confusion.

The Devaronian pounded his fists on the panel. ''I can't, sir! I don't have the override code!''

Durga bellowed, ''Well, who does?''

''Only Bevel Lemelisk, sir.''

''Get him up here,'' Durga shouted.

''But, he asked not to be disturbed, sir,'' the Devaronian said.

Durga gurgled in rage at the comment and punched a control button on his repulsorsled. Suddenly, the Devaronian technician's chair erupted with electrical fire, deadly voltage arcing across the victim's hands and arms, crawling up his spinal column and skittering around inside his skull. The alien's skin blackened and burned. He opened his fanged mouth to scream, but only blue lightning came out.

In seconds the Devaronian slumped down, a skeletal corpse that steamed as flakes of ash fell onto the floor of the expeditionary ship.

''Now, would someone else like to get Bevel Lemelisk for me?'' Durga boomed. ''Before it's too late?''

One of the human technicians leaped off his chair and ran to the turbolift.

General Sulamar snapped his fingers, and two Gamorrean guards came forward to remove the charred Devaronian body. Lightly tapping the singed skin to make sure that all of the electrical current had gone away, they whisked the crumbling body out of sight.

Despite his outburst, Durga knew they could never rouse the weapons engineer fast enough to do any good. With outrage and horror, he watched as the two gargantuan machines came together, considering each other to be prime sources of metallic wealth. Unthinking, they followed identical programming: (1) grapple target, (2) dismantle with laser cutters, and (3) process all raw materials.

The giant machines were mindlessly murderous, blasting each other's hull plates, ripping metal arms and stuffing them into processing maws—an unconscionable disaster unfolding before Durga's eyes.

The Mineral Exploiters were very efficient. It took less than ten standard minutes for them to rip each other to nonfunctional shreds, drifting hulks of torn-apart components and half-slagged molten ingots. The metal debris drifted apart, taking its own place in the asteroid field.

Durga felt fury boiling inside him, and he hammered his fists on the control panels. He looked around at his technicians, seeking someone worthless to blame—but all of them had leaped out of their booby-trapped seats and stood at attention beside their panels, safely away from their chairs.

CHAPTER 5

Bevel Lemelisk scowled as he trudged along the corridors of the Orko SkyMine ship, huffing with the effort and with his own annoyance at Durga's constant demands. He stepped into the turbolift for the bridge deck, muttering to himself . . . things he would never dare say in front of the bloated Hutt crime lord. Durga always wanted the impossible and wanted it *now*.

The turbolift lurched, yanking Lemelisk upward. He stumbled against the wall, grabbed the railing, and frowned at the controls as if they had intentionally made him lose his balance.

Lemelisk patted his rounded paunch as his stomach growled. He had forgotten to eat midday meal again. He kept losing track of things. He brushed his cheeks, feeling the prickle of long, pale stubble, and realized he hadn't shaved in two days either. He sighed, chastising himself. He usually remembered to take care of personal hygiene before he appeared in front of Durga, but the insistent Gamorrean guard hadn't given him a chance to collect his thoughts. Lemelisk ran a hand through his spiky white hair, making sure it stood up in straight shocks, just the way he preferred it—though he doubted the fat slug boss would ever notice a human's appearance.

The turbolift stopped with a sudden jolt, but this time Lemelisk braced himself. Before the doors opened, he worked up his indignation. He hated to be disturbed while he was concentrating. He had left specific orders that no one was to barge into his chambers; but the rude guard had done just that, lumbering in when Lemelisk was completing final touches on a difficult three-dimensional crystal-lattice puzzle. All of Lemelisk's plans had shimmered and dissolved, plunging him back to square zero.

This time, Bevel Lemelisk vowed he wouldn't be meek and groveling. He strode onto the command deck, drawing in a deep breath so that his chest temporarily looked larger than his belly. "Durga, what is the meaning of this?" he said, letting contempt fill his voice.

The command deck personnel whirled at his words and cowered as if they had just been browbeaten. Lemelisk noticed that not a single one of them remained seated at their stations. He smelled singed meat in the air like badly cooked morning sausages; his empty stomach rumbled again.

General Sulamar hunched forward as he strode toward Lemelisk. The glittering medals and badges on his chest jangled with a dizzying flash of color. Lemelisk ignored him. The Imperial General—with all his blustering talk of military exploits such as the Massacre of Mendicat, the Subjugation of Sinton, and the Rout of Rustibar—was all hot air. Lemelisk himself had, after all, overseen the construction of the Death Star battle station. How could mere military exploits compare to that?

Seeing the weapons engineer, Durga issued a wordless roar of outrage and annoyance that sounded like a cross between a belch and a boiler explosion. Lemelisk stalled in his confident stride. He had never heard such anger in the Hutt's voice before.

Lemelisk blinked his pale eyes, and his attention

flickered to the bridge windows. He saw the spiraling orbits of rocky debris in the asteroid belt. Then he noticed the sputtering remnants of the two automated Mineral Exploiters that had torn each other apart. His throat felt as if it had been filled with quick-drying duracrete. "Uh-oh," he said.

Durga eased his repulsorsled closer to Lemelisk, who stood transfixed, trying to think up an excuse faster than the Hutt could do anything that Lemelisk might regret.

"I am most displeased with your performance, Lemelisk," Durga growled, his birthmark throbbing dark and threatening.

Lemelisk shuddered violently, wincing as the clear and painful memories flooded back to him. The Emperor had said exactly those words just before he had executed Bevel Lemelisk for the first time. . . .

Shortly after the Death Star was expected to crush the Rebel base on Yavin 4, Bevel Lemelisk had been summoned to meet personally with Emperor Palpatine deep within the Imperial palace.

Lemelisk had been flanked by red-armored Imperial bodyguards as they whisked him off on a high-speed shuttle across the skylanes of the planetwide city. The millions of illuminated windows winked like corusca gems. Each point of light seemed to be another torch celebrating his triumph.

Lemelisk rubbed his jowls, pleased that he had remembered to shave this time. The red Imperial guards were a silent lot, standing at attention like statues. Lemelisk hummed and grabbed his jutting knees as the shuttle approached the enormous pyramid of the Imperial palace.

The guards rushed him down the hall so quickly that their flowing scarlet cloaks billowed around them. When the group reached the door to the Emperor's private chambers, the guards stood at attention, their force pikes raised, their smooth plasteel helmets obscuring any expression.

Lemelisk jaunted happily into the vaulted room, pleased to see the black-cowled Emperor waiting for him. Palpatine hunched in his chair, reptilian yellow eyes glowing through the oily shadows cast by his hood. The Emperor appeared to be falling into ill health: His skin was blistered and folded in upon itself like a pasty drapery over his bones, as if decay had set in well before the advent of death.

But Lemelisk couldn't be troubled by unpleasant thoughts right now. He stood on the polished stone floor and made a cursory bow of obeisance. "My Emperor," he said. "I trust you have received word by now that our Death Star has destroyed the secret Rebel base."

"I have received word," Palpatine said and gestured with one long-clawed finger. Lemelisk glanced up at a clattering sound and saw a flexible wire cage released from the vaulted ceiling above. He ducked, but the cage fell squarely down over him, seating itself to the floor as if Palpatine were directing it with invisible powers. The cage was made of fine mesh, the grid barely large enough to stick his smallest finger through.

"Excuse me, Emperor?" Lemelisk said. "Is there something further you wish to discuss with me? Another project perhaps? Anything else I can do for you?" Lemelisk swallowed again.

"Yes, my servant," Palpatine said. "You may die for me."

"Uh—" Lemelisk could think of nothing else to say. "I was hoping for something else, actually," he said stupidly.

Palpatine glowered at him. "I just received word that your Death Star was destroyed at Yavin. A puny band of Rebels with outdated fighters found a weakness in your design—a thermal exhaust port that allowed a single X-wing pilot to strike a fatal blow. *One pilot* obliterated an entire battle station!"

Lemelisk pursed his lips. "Thermal exhaust port, eh?

I knew I must have forgotten something. I'll have to fix that in the next design.''

"Yes, you will," Palpatine said with an icy voice. "But first, you will die for me."

Lemelisk blinked his watery blue eyes and reached out to touch the fine, tough wires of his cage. He looked around, and nervousness raged like a whirlwind around him. Though he had shaved, his neck itched fiercely.

The Emperor sat completely still, yet he must have manipulated a set of controls because with a sharp *snick* at Lemelisk's feet tiny openings appeared in the polished stone floor, orifices that led down to a black unknown. He heard clicking sounds, the scrabbling of sharp, hard feet.

"I am most displeased with your performance, Lemelisk," the Emperor said.

Bevel Lemelisk shuffled aside as something small but iridescent poked out of the opening: a beetle of some kind. The eight-legged, hard-shelled insect shone a deep blue as it clambered into the light and paused to probe the air with waving antennae. From other openings five identical beetles emerged. They fluttered their wing cases, then took flight, buzzing around the enclosed space. Lemelisk swatted at one, but the blue beetle detected the motion and swooped toward him, sinking mandibles with serrated razor edges into the thick flesh of his palm.

"Oww!" Lemelisk flailed his hand until the beetle lost its hold. He stomped on it, cracking its carapace. But the scent of blood attracted the other beetles to him. He watched in horrified fascination as a dozen more of the insects emerged from the floor holes, fluttering their wing cases and buzzing toward him.

"Those are piranha beetles," the Emperor said, lounging back in his swiveling black chair. "They are native to Yavin 4, and I considered them too precious for extinction when your Death Star was expected to destroy the moon. So I rescued them."

The beetles swarmed over Lemelisk now. He slapped

at them, shouting, paying little attention to Palpatine's words. "Stop this!" he yelled.

"Not yet," the Emperor said.

The beetles sliced through his clothing to the skin on Lemelisk's arms, his thighs, his chest, his cheeks. Blood flowed around him, drenching his shredded clothes. He could not keep up with the new injuries. Hundreds more beetles swarmed out, battering themselves against the cage mesh.

"These fine insects are not in danger of becoming extinct after all, though," Palpatine said, "since your Death Star did not work! You have failed me, Bevel Lemelisk," he said, slowing his words. His wrinkled, rubbery lips bent upward in a fiendish grin.

"And now, I'm going to watch these beetles devour you, bit by bit. They are very hungry, you see, and don't get satisfied easily. But if they gorge themselves and begin to slow down, don't worry—I have plenty more." The Emperor let out a glacial laugh, but Lemelisk could no longer hear.

The beetles buzzed in his ears, tearing at his flesh, his hair, his clothes. He struck at himself, throwing his body against the cage mesh. In the process, some of the beetles were stunned, and their own companions fell upon them, cracking through the iridescent shells and chewing to the soft organs within.

Lemelisk screamed and begged—to no avail. The agony went beyond his comprehension, beyond his imagination. His vision turned black after the piranha beetles devoured his eyes—but the pain continued for a long time afterward. . . .

Later, Lemelisk had awakened, blinking his restored eyes, and was completely disoriented. He found himself in the same vaulted chamber, wrapped in a clean, white uniform. His body felt young and strong, without the paunch and the flab from spending too much time working on projects in his mind and too little effort maintaining his health.

Lemelisk bent his arms and looked at his hands, blinking in astonishment. Hearing a small buzz and clatter, he glanced over to find the wire-mesh cage still filled with buzzing, clacking piranha beetles that scampered up and down the walls, snapping their mandibles. Spattered patterns of fresh blood made arcs along the walls of the cage. Inside, he saw a carcass that had been stripped down to gnawed bones and shreds of clothing—the clothing he himself had worn only moments ago.

"You'll grow accustomed to your clone in a moment," the Emperor said, rubbing his knobby fingers over a strange ancient-looking artifact. "I trust that all of your memories have been transferred properly? It is an uncertain skill at best, and the Jedi I stole the technique from was reluctant to give me thorough instruction. But it seems to work."

Lemelisk nodded weakly, wanting to faint but knowing he didn't dare.

"Now don't fail me again, Lemelisk," the Emperor said. "I'd hate to have to think of an even worse execution for next time."

Now, as he faced Durga the Hutt and Imperial General Sulamar, Lemelisk sought some reservoir of strength within himself. The Mineral Exploiters had destroyed each other in a horribly embarrassing debacle.

"We can recover from this," he said quickly. "Yes, I believe I can alter our plans so that our schedule will remain unaffected in the long run."

Durga lurched backward, blinking his large copper red eyes. "What?"

"You have the two other automated Mineral Exploiters nearly completed. This is a tragic loss," Lemelisk said, gesturing toward the window, "but we have to expect a few setbacks. This was poor planning, I admit, but I can program the other machines so that such a failure will not occur again."

General Sulamar squared his shoulders and glared at Lemelisk. "You are absolutely correct," he said. "This will not happen again!"

Lemelisk dismissed him with a wave of his hand, trying to display more self-assurance than he felt. "Consider those two to be test prototypes, Alpha and Beta. Expendable. We know the error now."

But Lemelisk mentally kicked himself for letting such a stupid lack of foresight nearly cost him his life. He began to tremble and clamped down on his muscles, forcing himself to stand firm. He had no wish to be executed again—that had happened enough times already—though he was convinced Durga the Hutt could never be a match for Palpatine's cruelty.

"I promise to rectify the problem, Lord Durga," Lemelisk said with a bow. "But while I'm doing that, you must focus on our main goal. Even before we worry about construction resources, the primary item on our agenda must be to get those plans from the Imperial Information Center."

Durga growled, a low gurgling sound.

General Sulamar said, "It is not your place to dictate—"

Durga smacked the stuffed-shirt Imperial across the chest with one fat-fingered hand. "I have already scheduled an expedition to Coruscant, Lemelisk," he said. "I will have your precious plans shortly."

CORUSCANT

CHAPTER 6

In the plush chambers of the New Republic's Chief of State, Leia Organa Solo hurried to make herself presentable. Beside her, Han Solo fiddled with his shirt fasteners and cursed the tiny glittering insignia he tried to apply to his diplomatic finery.

"I hate this, Leia," he said. "I love you enough to do this—but I don't enjoy getting dressed up even to meet people I *like*." He finally buttoned the insignia then brushed down his shirt front. "And I don't exactly count those overgrown mud worms among the people I like."

Leia placed her hand on his shoulder. "Do you think I like it any more than you do?" Vividly, she recalled her imprisonment by the vile Jabba the Hutt, when he had forced her to wear a humiliating costume and sit chained in front of him so he could caress her with his enormous rubbery tongue. "The Hutts had a death warrant out on both of us not long ago, but this Durga is making some new kind of overture. It's a diplomatic necessity that we receive the fat slug and hear what he has to say."

"Diplomatic necessity," Han scoffed. "I wouldn't

trust one of those blobs of slime farther than I could roll him. Keep a blaster hidden in your robes.''

Leia checked herself in the surround mirror. She looked cool and perfect in her best raiments, impressive and regal. ''I will, Han, don't worry.''

Threepio entered, quiet hums emanating from his servomotors. ''Excuse me, Mistress Leia,'' he said. ''I believe I am prepared for this important meeting of state. I have polished all of my body plates and oiled my gears and brushed up on my programming for protocol and etiquette.''

''Great,'' Han said. ''You can take my place. Okay?''

''Sir,'' Threepio exclaimed, ''I hardly believe that would be wise. Why—''

''He's joking, Threepio,'' Leia said, glaring at Han.

''Sure, Threepio. Just joking,'' Han agreed a little too quickly.

''The children wish to say good night to you,'' Threepio said. ''Mistress Winter is already here and has made preparations to tell them bedtime stories.'' The droid held his golden arms out as if in a mechanical shrug. ''Somehow, the children don't enjoy it when *I* tell them stories. I'm simply at a loss to explain it.''

Leia paid little attention to the litany of the droid's complaints. ''Children are just difficult sometimes,'' she said.

The twins, Jacen and Jaina, were three years old now and beginning to get into everything imaginable. Baby Anakin, now nearly two, remained quiet and withdrawn, sleeping a lot, barely attempting to talk. The dark-haired boy with the large ice-blue eyes lived in his own world most of the time, while the twins insisted on making themselves the center of attention.

''I'm as ready as I'm going to be,'' Han said, brushing his brown hair and letting out a long breath. ''Still can't believe I'm making myself look pretty for a Hutt.''

''I doubt Lord Durga would notice, sir,'' Threepio

added helpfully. "The Hutts have a different standard of beauty, you know. In fact I have learned—"

"Not now, Threepio," Han said and offered his arm to Leia as he escorted her toward the door.

"Some other time, perhaps," Threepio said and hurried after them.

Out in the common room Winter sat on a padded seat with the three children on the floor as she spoke to them, telling a detailed story she had memorized word for word.

Leia's personal servant had helped her through many difficult times, guarding the children during the most vulnerable early years in their Force-sensitive lives. Winter had a flawless memory and never needed to refresh her thoughts, able to recall word for word anything she had heard or read in her life. Despite her calm, emotionless demeanor, Winter carried the deepest and most unshakable loyalty for Leia herself and for the New Republic.

Winter seemed to enjoy her role of watching the three children while Leia and Han kept enormously busy with matters of state. Her new position allowed her to continue advising Leia as an appropriate confidante, yet remain behind the scenes.

Jacen and Jaina leaped to their feet, scuttling over to greet Leia and Han. "Hey!" Han cried and grabbed the twins in a bear hug. Jacen's brown hair was tousled—as it always was—while Jaina's hung straight and neat. Anakin remained quiet and politely seated, patiently waiting for Winter to continue the story. He got up when it was his turn for a hug.

"Winter will watch you," Leia said to the children. "Mommy and Daddy have an important meeting with a Hutt."

The children snickered. Han looked at her with raised eyebrows and a see-I-told-you-so expression on his face. "Come on, Goldenrod," he said to Threepio. "We sure wouldn't want to be late for our 'diplomatic necessity.' "

They left their quarters, and a pair of permanently stationed guards escorted them down the hall. Threepio rattled on as they marched. "Perhaps some background would be of use in your upcoming negotiations, Mistress Leia? I have recently downloaded—"

"We don't know if there are going to be any negotiations, Threepio," Leia said. "The Hutts are the biggest gang of criminals in the galaxy. They took me prisoner and then they tried to kill us all. I don't think we should expect too much kindness."

"Yes, yes, but it would be most useful to have a basic understanding of Hutt philosophy, as I interpret it according to the—admittedly sparse—information I've been able to find," Threepio said.

"The Hutts originally came from a system called Varl, whose star suffered some sort of disaster. And so they were forced to move to another planetary system. They took over an entire planet through devious business dealings, until they managed to evict the former inhabitants and claim the world for themselves. They renamed it Nal Hutta, which, in their own language, means 'glorious jewel.' The moon of Nal Hutta was named Nar Shaddaa, but in common parlance, it is known as the Smugglers' Moon."

"We've been there, Threepio," Han said, bored.

"Oh, yes! I forgot. In any case, the Hutts have an extremely involved clan system, and no one outside is permitted to know the family name of any Hutt—thus, Jabba's own clan name was known only to his relatives."

"Very interesting," Han mumbled as they turned the corner and headed toward the rear of the presidential receiving room. "I sure can't understand why the kids would rather have Winter tell them a bedtime story."

"Why, thank you, sir," Threepio said, missing Han's irony entirely. "Actually, very little is known about how the Hutt clans interact—although certain accidents and disasters have led some to speculate on interclan warfare in which stronger Hutt families wipe out weaker ones."

The guard at a large door leading into the receiving

room stood aside. Leia passed through, shoulder to shoulder with Han. "Thanks Threepio. That'll be all," she said.

"Ah, but I have so much more to tell you," the droid continued.

"Take a hint, Goldenrod," Han said more loudly.

"I . . . take your meaning, sir," Threepio said, then whirred quietly after them into the receiving room.

Leia leaned over and whispered to Han as they passed into the echoing room. "Han, the Hutt crime empire is very powerful, and we'll need to show them diplomatic courtesy. We've got to at least pretend to be civil."

Han rolled his eyes, then pulled his elbow against his side, pressing her hand to his ribs in a warm gesture. "Pretend?" Han said. "Pretending happens to be one of my strong suits. You just watch."

Another set of escorts followed them on either side of inlaid flagstones that formed a promenade to a pair of impressive-looking chairs. Leia didn't like the frivolous display. It seemed too regal, too Imperial—but appearances were very important in public spectacles and matters of state. While the senators and the military leaders formed the backbone of her power, Leia herself was the Chief of State and President of the Senate. She was the visible face on all decisions made for the government, and so she was forced to play her part with grace and charisma.

Leia had had her difficulties with some members of the council, particularly those who wished her to remain at home for her entire term of office and never venture out to the scattered but reluctant planets who expressed interest in joining the New Republic. That just wasn't her style.

Leia seated herself in the Chief of State's chair and tried to collect her thoughts. Han shifted beside her, crossing and uncrossing his arms over his dress shirt, then gripping the scrolled work of the armrests. He looked bored already.

Electronic fanfare sounded from outside the chamber. The doors at the other end of the room groaned open, dragged by sluggish worker droids that were no more than boxy torsos upon which were fastened heavy arms and legs for performing difficult labor.

As the doors opened and Durga's entourage passed into the reception chamber, Leia saw that the Hutt crime lord also knew the value of spectacle.

The bloated wormlike creature reclined on a broad pallet that drifted above the floor on a cushion of repulsorlifts. But Durga moved forward through the plodding efforts of a team of Gamorrean slaves lashed to the floating platform by red velvet bonds. The piglike guards kept their squinting eyes to the polished flagstones. Drips of moisture splattered the floor as the Gamorreans either perspired heavily or simply drooled.

Stooped, lizard servants trooped into the audience chamber in front of the Gamorrean guards. Their triangular heads bobbed low to the ground as they placed electronic music synthesizers to their lips and hissed into the voice pickups. The computer then processed and transmitted the noises as beautiful brassy reception music.

Durga the Hutt heaved himself up, as if to emphasize his importance. If anything, Durga seemed even fatter than Jabba. His sloping head was like a sagging mound of slime, stained by some sort of birthmark like dark green ink thrown in his face; his huge round eyes were like spoiled fruit. His childlike hands seemed out of place on his swollen body.

What made Leia's breath catch in her throat, though, were the dozens and dozens of hairy creatures swarming over Durga and his retainers like large simian lice. The creatures were each about the size of Leia's forearm with grayish brown fur and large curious eyes. Each one had four supple arms that ended in dexterous fingers. The two legs appeared flexible enough to be used as a third set of arms and hands, should the need arise. The creatures constantly shifted position like vermin, blinking their eyes and staring in all directions as if voracious for information.

Threepio stepped forward and spoke his preprogrammed message. "The New Republic gives greeting to mighty Durga," he said, but then his own personality won out. "And—if I might be permitted to ask—what *are* those furry . . . creatures with you?"

"Does a protocol droid speak for you?" Durga said in his deep belly voice.

"I would appreciate an answer to his question," Leia said. "I am Chief of State Leia Organa Solo."

"My immediate apologies for the . . . unsettling dealings you have had with Hutts in the past," Durga said. "My people have been known to carry grudges for a long time, because we are such long-lived creatures."

"Yeah? Well, Jabba didn't live so long," Han muttered. Leia gestured for him to be quiet.

"Times change," Durga continued, clasping his small hands in front of him. "Many of my clan members are disturbed that I should speak to you, but it means a great deal to me. I am willing to let past matters fade to shadows for the profit and improvement of our situations. I would appreciate if you could do the same, at least for the sake of these conversations."

Leia nodded, cool and aloof. "I agree for the moment," she said, "but you still haven't answered my droid's question. I, too, am interested in your furry companions. We haven't seen their like before."

"Ah, please excuse me," Durga said. "These are the Taurill, semi-intelligent creatures, busy workers and good pets. They passed all quarantine scans when we arrived on Coruscant. They are insatiably curious and would like to explore. They intend no harm."

Leia then used a tactic Luke had taught her, urging that even if she did not intend to become a full Jedi Knight, she should at least learn to use her Force sensitivity in diplomatic matters. This was a skill Leia couldn't afford to ignore, and as she sat calm-faced, her mind worked furiously, attempting to sense the real purpose behind Durga's mission.

She detected distant reactions from the Gamorrean

guards—who knew virtually nothing about their own situation. The Taurill were a fuzzy, confusing mass of faint impressions . . . but Durga the Hutt remained a blank wall to her. Somehow, his mind was strong enough to resist her probing, or perhaps the Hutts were genetically shielded, because she remembered that Luke also could not read or manipulate Jabba the Hutt.

"If my pets make you uncomfortable," Durga said in a conciliatory tone, "I would be happy to remove them from my person." He clapped his small hands together, and the Taurill scattered, departing from his platform and leaping on to the shoulders of the Gamorrean guards. Leia guessed there must be at least a hundred of the frenetic little creatures. They scampered across the flagstoned floor examining alcoves, planetary banners, and displays. One ran up and studied Threepio, and the golden droid tried to shoo it away.

"Durga, I must insist that you control—" Leia began.

"Pay them no mind," Durga spoke in a loud, commanding tone. "They'll cause no damage. Now, to the point of my visit."

Beside her, Han flicked his glance nervously around as the Taurill wandered about the room, poking into corners, creeping behind their chairs.

Leia was forced to regain her composure so she could outthink the Hutt crime lord. She thought she knew what Durga was trying to do. He wanted to rattle them, distract her into giving something away—but she wouldn't let him manipulate her. She stonily pretended that the distracting creatures were not there. That would fluster him.

"Yes, Durga," she said. "I am most interested in your mission to Coruscant. What brings a Hutt crime lord to an audience with the legitimate government of the New Republic?"

Durga spread his arms wide. "Madam President, your words wound me. Let us not begin these talks with definitions of crime lords and legitimate governments. We are all trying to do what is best for ourselves. The Hutt *kajidic,* the clan system of business that my brothers and I have established, encompasses a great many worlds—a significant fraction, I daresay, of your own New Republic. The Hutts do not want war—commercial or actual—and I don't believe your fledgling government can afford a drawn-out struggle either. Unlike the Empire, we Hutts have an invisible web of influence and relationships in places you cannot imagine, far more than a simple military garrison you can strike.''

He blinked his heavy-lidded eyes. ''However, I do not come here to make threats, but an overture of peace. Although you called our operations a 'criminal empire,' I'm here to offer an end to all that unpleasantness.

''Our simplest solution is *legitimacy.* I propose that the Hutts form an alliance with the New Republic, become commercial partners. If you legalize our activities, then we are no longer a criminal empire, but a respected commercial venture. Is that not true?'' he said with a gesture toward the ceiling as if to indicate his high hopes.

''We Hutts could carry out our business without the need for secrecy and security, and thereby increase our profits enormously. We would pay appropriate taxes and tariffs, and the New Republic would grow stronger as well. You could then marshal your defenses toward fighting your true enemies, rather than simple business competitors such as ourselves.''

''Is that the only reason?'' Leia said, trying to keep the skepticism from her voice. The Taurill continued their relentless poking and prodding and investigating, but Leia fixed her gaze on Durga the Hutt.

''We Hutts have our pride,'' Durga continued. ''It is our greatest wish to become respectable, true businessmen rather than powerful outlaws.''

''I see,'' Leia said. Using her mask of diplomatic training, she smiled—but in her mind she vowed that all the stars in the galaxy would burn to cold ash before she ever entered into an alliance with the Hutts.

Just then one of the New Republic honor guards, who had tried valiantly to remain quiet during the negotiations, attempted to scare away two of the Taurill that had begun crawling on him like mammalian spiders. They climbed the guard's uniform though he swiped at them to brush them off. He swung his ceremonial blaster rifle, trying to jostle them free.

One of the Taurill grabbed the weapon as if it were a tree branch and pulled himself on to the end. The other Taurill climbed the length of the guard's forearm to the firing button of the blaster and accidentally—though Leia had the odd impression that it might have been *intentional*—pushed the firing stud. The rifle fired, blasting the hapless Taurill at the end of the barrel into a flaming ball of furry cinders.

Durga's wide mouth dropped open like a trapdoor. The other Taurill shrieked in sudden panic. The guard gaped down at his blaster rifle in dismay. "I didn't mean it!" he said.

The hundred Taurill in the reception chamber fled in all directions with an ear-splitting volley of panicked chitters, heading out the door, into the air ducts, hiding behind the chairs and in any shadowy corner.

"Don't let them escape!" Durga howled. "They are my pets, and I would be most displeased to lose any of them." The Hutt glared at the poor New Republic guard as if he wanted to feed him to a rancor.

The honor guards instantly broke formation, rushing around to grab the multiarmed pets. The Gamorreans turned in circles, champing their tusks, clearly not understanding what had just happened. Threepio flailed his golden arms and ran after several of the creatures.

Leia sent for more assistance, but she knew the vast echoing corridors of the enormous Imperial palace offered infinite places for the Taurill to hide.

Han lounged back in his chair with a wry, lopsided grin. "Told you we shouldn't have bothered to dress up," he said.

*   *   *

In the confusion, three of the Taurill easily made it to their
destination, winding through the air ducts, between walls,
and along pipes, descending deep below the former Imperial palace into the shielded secret chambers far down in
the bedrock.

The Imperial Information Center.

The Taurill were a hive mind, a single organism with
thousands and thousands of bodies sharing one collective
consciousness. Each of the individual creatures was
merely an extra set of eyes and ears and hands to do the
bidding of the Overmind that controlled all of its members.

Durga had discovered the Taurill in the Outer Rim
and had paid dearly for information on how to exploit the
scattered mass mind. Durga had then quietly executed the
one explorer and xenobiologist who had uncovered the secret of the Taurill. Now only Durga knew what the cute,
furry creatures were actually capable of.

He had entered into a pact with the Taurill, promising
the Overmind great wealth and power—but what the
Overmind really wanted was to spread itself out across the
reaches of the galaxy, dispersing its members to different
star systems so that it could grow. Durga was only too
happy to comply.

Now, while dozens of the Taurill remained in the diplomatic reception room, creating a diversion and acting
innocently confused and frightened, these three Taurill
commandos slipped into the shielded computer database
compiled by Emperor Palpatine himself.

The room was cold and sterile, smelling of metal.
The doors were guarded by heavily armed assassin droids.
Mechanical slicers hunched over the information termi-
nals, jacked in and focused entirely on their work.

The Taurill emerged from tiny access openings,
scrunching themselves down to make their bodies small
enough to pass through. On nimble feet they pattered

across the cold floor plates, swinging their four arms until the three reached separate access terminals.

The Taurill crawled up and began work at different stations, punching through obscure menus, finding the information they needed. Although the system was heavily guarded and passworded, the Taurill entered the special codes and phrases that had been obtained from Jabba's secret stash of information. Before long, the Taurill had broken through.

One of them inserted a small information cylinder and began downloading the precious plans. Data spilled into the compact new container. After only a few moments, their mission was complete.

The Taurill secreted away their data cylinder, and in unison the three furry commandos scampered back to the access openings.

The Overmind knew exactly what had been accomplished and transmitted that information to Durga through one of the calm and recaptured Taurill bodies up in the reception room.

Durga petted the creature, rumbling with pleasure.

In the reception chamber Leia held her head in her hands, wondering how to salvage the situation—but also trying to stifle a laugh. She didn't particularly care if Durga's dignity had been offended.

One of the reptilian retainers hummed into his musical synthesizer again, sending out a loud and soothing tone that made Leia's teeth throb. It seemed to serve as a summons for the Taurill, though. Cooing and purring, they ran toward the music, as if drawn by invisible leashes. They approached Durga's sled, dozens and dozens of them emerging from hiding places like a swarm of vermin.

"If that was so easy," Leia wondered aloud, "why didn't Durga simply use the musical tones at the very beginning?"

The Gamorreans began counting the Taurill as they

came in, but the stupid guards lost track numerous times until Threepio finally stepped in to help. He rapidly pointed to each of the remaining fuzzy creatures. "Ninety-seven, Lord Durga. That is my count for the Taurill."

The Hutt grumbled. "I came here with ninety-eight, and your man executed one of them—so I believe our tally is intact." He glared at the nervous honor guard. "Perhaps, Madam President, you would consider reassigning your trigger-happy escort, who is given to such disruptive outbursts during a delicate diplomatic negotiation."

"I will consider it, Durga," Leia said. "But perhaps *you* should consider leaving your unruly pets behind if you plan to conduct 'delicate diplomatic negotiations.' And if you simply must bring them, keep them under tighter control when they are in the vicinity of dangerous weapons."

Durga reared up as if offended, then let out a deep belly laugh. "I like you, Leia Organa Solo. I am glad to have such a strong counterpart who does not cower in fear. I wish to continue these negotiations at some time in the future. Allow me to extend an invitation for you to make a visit to Nal Hutta, at your convenience? I would be happy to receive you there."

Leia nodded, noncommittal. "I'll consider it, Durga," she said. "If my rather busy schedule will permit it."

Durga bowed on his repulsorsled and bade them all farewell.

The Gamorrean guards turned the Hutt around and strained against their red velvet leashes, pulling the floating sled back out into the corridor. The worker droids groaned and shuffled as they swung the heavy doors shut.

Leia slumped back in her seat and only then noticed that she was perspiring heavily. Han patted her hand.

"We really should spend more time with the Hutts. They seem like such a pleasant species," he said. "Now how about we get something to eat?"

CHAPTER 7

Callista sat alone in the jungles as night gathered on Yavin 4. Near the horizon, a lambent glow from the setting gas giant streaked the sky; Massassi trees rose tall, spreading their many-branched silhouettes against the deepening purple. Stars poked out, lights twinkling through a cloak of blackness.

She had not gone far from the Great Temple where Luke Skywalker had founded his Jedi academy. The stair-cased pyramid had endured for thousands of years, and stood now like a jagged black cutout surrounded by dusk.

Callista sat with her long legs crossed in front of a campfire she had built from dry brush, concentrating, al-lowing no distractions. Her malt blond hair was mussed and windblown, but her gray eyes were fixed on the flames. The warmth spread out in waves, gentle but insis-tent, driving back the damp coolness that settled over the lowlands.

She stared into the flames and *pushed,* but she felt nothing, not even a flicker of her former abilities. Feathery tongues of fire licked at the logs, lending the bark a soft orange glow. Tiny sparks drifted into the air in corkscrew patterns, like incandescent starfighters crashing to oblivion. Callista grimaced and tried harder to touch the flames with her mind, to nudge the embers.

But nothing happened. She sensed no communion with the fire.

Luke's other Jedi trainees could make the flames dance, pulling them out like flexible sheets to make faces, images, twisting them into braids. It was a simple Jedi exercise. Callista had learned how to do it many years ago; back then she had not even needed to concentrate. But now, try as she might, the flames would not respond. Her Jedi powers had abandoned her.

She stood with a lost sigh of frustration and kicked apart the logs to let the fire die. Sparks showered upward like a rekindled space battle, and the embers fought to maintain their brightness.

Callista trudged back toward the great stone pyramid, wondering when Luke would come back. Behind her, the fire gasped and died into a waning glow.

As Callista readied for bed, alone, she answered a summons at her door, surprised to find the Jedi woman Tionne standing in the corridor.

"I found something in the records," Tionne said, blinking her mother-of-pearl eyes over an anxious expression. She had a narrow face, pointed chin, high cheekbones, and large eyes framed by long silvery hair that gave her an elfin, ethereal appearance. "It isn't much, but I thought you'd like to know." Her voice had a musical lilt, and it was not surprising that Tionne enjoyed singing, accompanied by a stringed instrument of her own devising.

Tionne was not one of Luke's stronger trainees, but she had proven to be his most skilled assistant and teacher at the academy. She had always been intrigued by Jedi lore and legends, and she spent much time studying archives,

compiling a great history of the thousand generations of
Jedi Knights who had served the Old Republic.

"Come in," Callista said, gesturing. "What is it?"

Tionne raised her pale eyebrows. "You might like to
know that at least you aren't alone. Not in history at any
rate."

Callista perked up. "Other Jedi have lost their powers
before?"

"Yes, there was another." Tionne sat down on the
rumpled covers of Callista's sleeping pallet, her mysterious pearlescent eyes widening. She enjoyed nothing more
than retelling the Jedi legends she knew and loved so well.

"Ulic Qel-Droma, a great warlord who fought in the
Sith War on the side of evil with Exar Kun. He betrayed
Kun and led the Jedi Knights here, where they trapped
Kun's spirit in the temples and laid waste to the entire
moon. But by turning to the dark side, Ulic Qel-Droma
damned himself forever, and in a final confrontation he
was stripped of his Force ability."

"But how?" Callista said. "The Force is in all
things. How can one Jedi Knight strip another of the ability to use it?"

"Ulic was not *deprived* of anything," Tionne continued, "in a manner of speaking, he was blindfolded to the
Force. Ulic no longer had access to it."

"But how could I have had such blinders placed upon
me?" Callista said. "Was it just a consequence of my
spirit entering another body?"

"Cray's body," Tionne said with a slight tightening
in her throat. Callista remembered that the silver-haired
Jedi woman had known Cray well, had trained with her—
and now Callista's spirit inhabited the same body, while
Cray herself had died in a suicide mission against the *Eye
of Palpatine*.

"I can't explain it," Tionne said with a shrug. "I can
only tell you what I've learned. Every piece of information
adds more to the solution. Someday"—Tionne rested her

long and delicate fingers on Callista's forearm—"we'll find the answer."

Callista nodded and stood to usher Tionne out the door. The Great Temple had fallen silent with late evening, the other Jedi trainees either sleeping or meditating in their own chambers. Out in the corridor, the little astromech droid Artoo-Detoo puttered along the flagstones, looking lost without Luke Skywalker.

Callista vowed to keep trying, keep searching. There had to be some way. She had waited for so long inside the computer, and now that she had found her love in Luke, she would not let him go without a fight. But she could not be a part of him, true Jedi to true Jedi, until she regained her ability to use the Force. She couldn't give everything to him until then.

Their time had been so brief before they had been snatched apart, left with only their loss, to look into each other's eyes with an invisible barrier between them that neither could breach.

Callista swallowed, but her throat remained dry. Despite her reservations, she could not wait until Luke Skywalker returned to her.

When Luke did return several days later, Callista knew instantly that he had been unsuccessful. She was unable to read him in the way she had once sensed emotions with her Jedi potential—but she could tell by his demeanor and downcast expression that he had not found the answers he sought.

She met Luke on the landing grid in front of the pyramid. The other Jedi students emerged one by one to welcome their Master home. Callista ran to him. Luke moved quickly, delighted to see her. He caught her in his arms, holding her close, but said nothing.

She kissed him, then spoke quietly into his ear. "General Kenobi did not answer your summons?" she asked.

He looked at her strangely, blinking his cool blue eyes, and then smiled. "I keep forgetting you were a Jedi so long ago that you knew Obi-Wan when he was a young military commander."

He averted his gaze. "No, he didn't answer." Then he spoke quickly as if to reassure her. "But that doesn't mean anything. I'm going to keep trying—and so are you," he said.

"You can bet on that," she agreed. "I'd do anything so we can be together."

"So would I," Luke said, "if only I knew *what* to do."

"Let's go greet the others." Callista slipped her arm around his waist. He held her, and the two walked toward the temple. "I'm sorry you didn't find the answer," she said, "but just having you back makes me happy."

"That much I can give you," Luke said, "but I hope we can have more . . . so much more."

"We will," Callista said.

CHAPTER 8

A heavy, warm rain sheared through the jungle, pattering on the glossy leaves. Master Skywalker ignored it, or accepted it, as he led his group of students along the wet pathways through the undergrowth surrounding the Great Temple. Droplets of glittering water danced across their Jedi robes.

Kyp Durron looked up at the open patches of leaden gray sky through the tall trees. The rain caressed his face with pearly fingers that traced the contours of his chin and ran into the hollow of his throat. Others might have taken the gloom and storm as an ill omen, but rain brought life to the jungle moon, and Kyp considered it a healthy change from the humid sunshine.

Cilghal, the Calamarian Jedi Knight, walked directly behind Master Skywalker. Her watery blue robes rippled around her, already soaked, though they looked as if they were designed to be wet. Her salmon-colored skin glistened, and she blinked her large fish eyes in contentment at the rain.

Kyp walked beside the cloned alien Dorsk 81, whose

smooth skin and rounded features made him appear streamlined, with all the sharp edges worn away. Dorsk 81 had pale, olive green skin, wide yellow eyes, and an open innocent face. The cloned alien had been fighting to regain his self-assurance, struggling with generations of identical and talentless predecessors in his genetic line. Kyp and Dorsk 81 had become close companions in the past year. They had opposite personalities—which might have made them clash, but somehow the two filled each other's empty spots.

Master Skywalker led the group of trainees through the hushed underbrush, where even the birds and insects remained subdued, hiding under the shelter of thick leaves from the downpour.

They came down an embankment to the wide river that sliced through the jungle, a broad ribbon of greenish water that teemed with life. The current flowed swiftly; thousands of pockmarks dimpled the surface as rain pounded down.

Across the river and through the rain, Kyp could see the ruins of another Massassi temple, the tall, crumbling Temple of the Blueleaf Cluster. Nearby, the large power-generating station hummed and steamed in the afternoon shower.

Master Skywalker stopped at the bank, his feet squishing in the mud. He spread his hands at his sides as if drawing up lines of Force from beneath the surface. He shrugged back his hood. His pale brown hair had darkened from the falling rain and lay plastered in thick clumps against his head. Raindrops sparkled on his cheeks as he turned toward the other trainees.

"I'm pleased to be marking a passage," he said. "The river flows, as does the Force—never ending, always moving. . . . I brought you to Yavin 4 to begin your instruction. I can only set you on the path of the light side and open your minds to the possibilities of the Force. You must all complete your own training. Each of you must decide when that time has come.

"Since the New Republic needs Jedi Knights to spread peace and stability, we cannot stay here indefinitely in our comfortable academy." Master Skywalker looked at the drenched candidates and at his own soaked robe. "Well, maybe it's not always comfortable," he said. The Jedi students chuckled.

Kyp felt suddenly nervous. Although he had looked forward to this graduation for a long time, he now felt as if he were putting an end to one of the most important times in his life—even if it meant he was about to start an even more crucial or exciting phase.

"Three trainees have decided to depart from the Jedi *praxeum,* the academy where we learn action and learn the Force."

Kyp and Dorsk 81 stepped forward to stand beside Cilghal and turned to face the other Jedi trainees. Cilghal tilted her head to the sky, letting the rain stream across her face.

"They have mastered each lesson I prepared for them," Luke Skywalker said. "They have built their own lightsabers and completed their training."

Cilghal withdrew her own lightsaber handle from her pale blue robe; her weapon was silvery and smooth, with subtle indentations and blisters, as if organically grown, much like the large Mon Calamari starcruisers. Kyp and Dorsk 81 pulled out their own lightsabers. As one, the three graduates flicked on the weapons. Steam sizzled around them as raindrops hissed against the glowing blades.

"You three must go and become guardians for the galaxy, protectors of the New Republic," Master Skywalker said. "You must fight the dark side in all its manifestations. You are Jedi Knights now."

Cilghal focused her round eyes on the humming blade in front of her. "I will return to my homeworld, where I serve both as a Jedi Knight and an ambassador. The Mon Calamari are talented and industrious people.

We can pool our resources to enhance the stability of the New Republic.''

Dorsk 81 blinked his yellow eyes and looked nervously to Kyp, who gave a slight nod of encouragement. The cloned alien said, ''I wish to return to my home planet as well. To Khomm, where our society has remained the same for centuries. Showing them that I am changed—that I have become a Jedi Knight—will shake them up,'' he said. His slit mouth turned upward in a faint smile. ''I believe they need to be reawakened.''

Master Skywalker then looked at Kyp, who drew himself up to seem as tall as Dorsk 81. ''I'll go with him for now,'' Kyp said. ''His homeworld is toward the center of the galaxy, near the Core Systems. I'm really worried that the Empire has been so quiet in the last couple of years. Sure, we've seen the renegade Admiral Daala and the *Eye of Palpatine*—''

Here, Master Skywalker flinched and glanced at Callista who, though she appeared wet and bedraggled in the rain, still glowed with affection for Luke.

''But I still think the warlords must be planning something,'' Kyp said. ''I can't imagine any greater service to the New Republic than for me to find out what's going on. I'll slip in and snoop around the Empire.''

Master Skywalker nodded in approval, then addressed the other Jedi trainees. ''Someday you all will become guardians. Think of where you might go, where you could do the most good.'' He turned back to the newly graduated Jedi Knights. ''May the Force be with you.''

Kyp looked at the others, saw uneasiness or hard determination. Tionne nodded peacefully. Kam Solusar, the hard-edged Jedi, stood unblinking as if nothing could affect him. Kirana Ti, the warrior woman from Dathomir, looked confident in her glittering red-and-green reptilian armor. Beside her, the addle-brained hermit from Bespin, Streen, looked at the raindrops on his hands and flicked his gaze from side to side. Kirana Ti placed a strong hand on his shoulder, as if she could suddenly sense his doubts.

The others reacted in their own ways, agreeing or looking away. Kyp knew Luke's original group of trainees well; others were new arrivals, coming to be trained as the word went out from system to system, and more potential Jedi Knights were found.

Master Skywalker dropped his hands to his sides, relaxing. Kyp switched off his own lightsaber, and the handle swallowed the silvery pure blade. Cilghal and Dorsk 81 also extinguished their weapons.

Luke smiled at them all. "I think I've had enough rain. Let's go back to the temple."

Suddenly, Kyp felt the tension fade from the air, and it seemed as if they were a group of companions on a simple hike rather than in a ceremony laden with galactic import.

Master Skywalker stepped into the milling group of trainees, seeking out Callista. He took her hand, and they smiled at each other as they led the others along an overgrown path back to the Great Temple.

En route to Khomm, Dorsk 81 piloted the small private spacecraft the New Republic had given them. The cloned alien watched the bright spot of his homeworld grow.

"Approaching on standard vector," Kyp said from the passenger seat and toggled the comm system. "Kyp Durron and Dorsk 81 on approach. Request landing coordinates."

Within a moment, the space traffic controller calmly gave Kyp the data he needed. He looked curiously at Dorsk 81. "Are they expecting us?" he said.

The olive-skinned alien shook his head. "No, they just rarely respond to anything in an unusual way."

Kyp looked at the cloned alien, recalling a previous time they had traveled together. While under the influence of Exar Kun, the ancient Dark Lord of the Sith, he had gone with Dorsk 81 to an abandoned jungle temple, Kun's private fortress of solitude. There the black spirit tried to destroy Dorsk 81 on a whim, to demonstrate the power of the dark side; Kyp had saved him, though Dorsk 81 hadn't even known about it.

Since the defeat of Kun, when Dorsk 81 had faced his fears and his inadequacy, the cloned alien had become stronger by accepting his own limitations. Kyp did not push him, but let the smooth-skinned alien follow his own path.

The pale green sphere of Khomm grew larger, filling the viewport. From a distance the planet seemed peaceful and misty, featureless. It had no natural satellites, not even phases of the moon to make regular change. Khomm's orbit was practically circular, the tilt of its axis nonexistent, creating no change of seasons. So close to the galactic center, the moonless sky was filled with bright stars.

"Looking forward to going home?" Kyp asked as Dorsk 81 altered the navigation controls to take them into a low-energy orbit, from which they could begin a smooth descent to the spaceport.

The alien nodded. "I'm eager to see my duplicates again," he said. Because they all came from the same clone stock, obviously Dorsk 81 could not call them his parents or siblings, because they were all genetically the same—something subtle had changed with Dorsk 81, though, giving him an ability to touch the Force that none of the other clone stock had exhibited so far.

"I am particularly looking forward to seeing Dorsk 82," he said. "Grown from my genes, it is likely he has matured since I have been away."

Kyp blinked in surprise. He hadn't known that Dorsk 81 had a . . . child, offspring, younger duplicate. "I'm looking forward to meeting him too."

As Dorsk 81 piloted the ship in for a landing, Kyp looked up at the densely clustered stars that made a broad river of light across the night of space. The Core Systems. He vowed to find out what the Empire had been doing after all this time.

CORE SYSTEMS

CHAPTER 9

True night was impossible in the Core Systems. Stars clustered so closely together that even the blackest regions of space were a symphony of stellar flares and hot ionized gas clumped in regions once considered uninhabitable. In a navigational hell like this, remnants of the Empire hid among uncharted systems where they could wait and recover—and war upon each other.

Admiral Daala walked erect and alone, a proud example of Imperial training as stormtrooper guards provided an armed escort into the fortress of Supreme Warlord Harrsk. Her face appeared to be chiseled from stone, still beautiful but now weathered so that its edges held a bitter sharpness. Faint lines were etched around her mouth from too many years of clenching her teeth, too many months trying to reunite the feuding warlords who squabbled over the Empire's remaining military might like nek battle dogs tearing a carcass.

Shadows haunted Daala's eyes, memories of failure and a snuffed fire of revenge, but the green of her irises flashed molten when she thought of how simple it would be to strike effectively against the clumsy New Republic. Even now, the Rebels still hadn't managed to secure their hold on the galaxy, though the Empire had given them years in which to accomplish it.

The stormtroopers formed a tight and comforting honor guard around Daala as she strode down the fused corridors into the bedrock. Supreme Warlord Harrsk had established his stronghold on a rocky planet that orbited close to a red giant star. Its surface crust remained soft and cracked, seeping lava like an oozing wound.

In orbit, giant solar smelters provided energy and processed raw material to construct Harrsk's personal fleet of *Imperial*-class Star Destroyers. Upon arrival here, Daala's loyal second in command, Kratas, had gone aboard the flagship *Shockwave* to inspect the weaponry. Harrsk had completed construction on twelve of the Star Destroyers so far, using whatever resources he could scrape together by bullying all the systems within reach.

Daala thought of the unexploited military strength in the safe shadow of Harrsk's planet, where ripping rays from the red giant could not damage the ships' systems. Back when she had been ordered to guard Maw Installation, Daala had commanded only four Imperial Star Destroyers—and in her private little war against the Rebels, she had lost three of those ships.

Yes, she could console herself that she had destroyed a Rebel colony, blown up a convoy to a new military base, and attacked and damaged the waterworld of Calamari— but overall her tactics had been woefully outdated and ill-considered. She had allowed dark anger to blind her to the shortcomings of her own schemes. She had suffered from fiendishly bad luck as well—but she had no intention of allowing luck to become a factor again.

Daala had given up everything to limp back to the Empire, surviving in the battle-scarred wreck of her last Star Destroyer, the *Gorgon*. Reaching sanctuary, she had been unimpressed with the weak and childish warlords who now held the future of the Empire in their hands.

Imperial authorities had commandeered Daala's remaining troops, scattering them among other ships in other fleets. They had scrapped the *Gorgon,* taking away the few usable components to rebuild other ships.

Daala, though, did not give them the chance to reassign her to a fighting group, preferring instead to act as a freelance ambassador, a peacemaker visiting the far-flung warlords. Each of them had concocted increasingly ridiculous titles for themselves, trying to top their nearest competitor—from Grand Admiral to High Admiral, to Supreme Commander, to Omnipotent Battle Leader. Admiral Daala had retained her own simple rank, requiring no further medals or titles. Her mission of unification remained incomplete, and she and Commander Kratas traveled from system to system, banking on their reputation and speaking to ears that seemed unfortunately to be filled with duracrete.

Around her now, the air smelled warm and steamy with a sulfurous edge that leaked through the vitrified tunnels. Daala's mane of reddish hair flowed behind her like a comet's tail. She had tried to trim it back to control it, but she disliked the severe look it gave her. Part of her needed to remain free, confined only by the limits of what she knew she could accomplish.

Harrsk's stormtroopers formed up and lined the corridor like a gauntlet for her to pass. Tall synrock doors rose to the ceiling, etched with complex patterns that evoked an Imperial grandeur. A stormtrooper struck his fist against a circular brass plate set into the rock, and sound enhancers piped the single knock through an echo chamber so that it boomed and reverberated like the summons of a powerful deity.

Daala tried to hide her expression of distaste. Elaborate formality and overblown demonstrations of supposed power did not bode well. Supreme Warlord Harrsk seemed to consider himself very important—and in Daala's experience, that meant he probably wasn't.

The synrock doors ground open, and Daala marched

forward without waiting to be announced. Her black boots clicked on the fused stone floor. She saluted. "I give you greeting, Supreme Warlord Harrsk."

In a large chamber Supreme Warlord Harrsk had installed banks of observation panels. He sat on a small floating chair that bobbed as he kicked himself away from the station over to another panel.

"Ah, Admiral Daala," Harrsk answered. The grin stretching across his face was hideous. The entire left half of his head was sizzled, leaving only bubbly pinkish skin, a mass of thick and insensitive scar tissue. His eye had been blinded, but Harrsk had replaced it with a synthetic droid optical sensor that caused his eye socket to glow yellow.

Harrsk had been nearly killed in an explosion during the battle of Endor. His Star Destroyer was crippled, but he managed to escape with part of the fleet to a rendezvous point in the Core Systems just after he had seen the Death Star explode. Harrsk could have repaired his skin with existing medical techniques, but had chosen not to, keeping the hideous scars as a badge of honor—and no doubt, Daala thought, a means of intimidation.

He shifted in his repulsorchair, and the seat bobbed with his motion. The hair on the unscarred half of his head was short and neat and black, and he seemed to show as much meticulous care for the intact side of his visage as he showed disdain for the scarred portion.

"Your reputation precedes you," he said. "I am honored to have such a great war hero among us—and pleased that you have at last come to me after wasting so much time with my weaker rivals."

Harrsk gestured toward the screens on his wall. Daala noted that he had holocams mounted on the hellish planetary surface, as well as remotes in orbit and more distant spy satellites on the fringes of the system. One image showed an ongoing fissure tearing a rock shelf apart as scarlet-orange lava spilled out in an incandescent waterfall. Harrsk nodded to the central screen that showed his dozen Imperial Star Destroyers in shadow where the rocky planet eclipsed the red sun.

"I was just speaking with your Commander Kratas," Harrsk said. "He seems to be most impressed with my *Shockwave.*" He punched a button, and the scene shifted to show Kratas leaning over a station on the command bridge of a new Star Destroyer. His dark eyes glittered, and his heavy eyebrows were upraised.

"Admiral!" Kratas said, snapping to attention. "It feels good to be on the bridge again. This is a fine piece of military machinery. I had forgotten how sleek and maneuverable an Imperial Star Destroyer could be, after all the damage we suffered on the *Gorgon.*"

Daala reminded herself to chide him for showing such glee. Kratas must learn to act more professional. But he had been through enormous ordeals at her side. Kratas had been a solid second in command, a foil for her ideas . . . though perhaps if he had been stronger in his resolve, more willing to show a little backbone, Kratas might have convinced her that her tactics against the Rebels were unwise.

"I'm glad you are impressed, Commander," Harrsk said. "You may continue your inspection. Admiral Daala and I have some things to discuss."

Kratas began to snap a trim salute, but Warlord Harrsk ended the transmission without even acknowledging him. He swiveled in his floating chair to face Daala. She looked at him intently, staring at his one dark eye and one glowing optical sensor. She saw through his scars, paid no heed to his face or his droid eye—only to the mind that drove this collection of hardware that could be put to better use.

"Let us not draw out our discussions," he said. "I know of your mission. You have spent the last year speaking to others, trying to sow the seeds of unification. I admire that. I, too, grow tired of this endless civil war—but, again, your tactics are all wrong. Such techniques might have worked under the frail democracy of the Old Republic, but it is not the Imperial way."

When he stood, she saw that the warlord was substantially shorter than she. "You are a hero, Admiral Daala. Your word carries weight. That's the only reason you have been able to travel unharmed through the hostile territories in the Core Systems. But it's time you ended this game. You must throw in your lot with the most powerful warlord—myself, obviously. With you as my second in command, I will have the power to bring those pretenders to their knees and forge them into a fighting force. We'll need to kill off the traitors, of course, but I suspect that many of their loyal soldiers would welcome the change in command. We're all frustrated, you know."

Daala bristled. "I understand what you're saying, Supreme Warlord, and your fleet is indeed impressive." She gestured to the screen, which depicted the shadowed group of Imperial Star Destroyers. "But I'm not convinced that you could so easily overwhelm your competitors. The moment you became stronger, the others would form alliances, and the struggle would be even bloodier than before.

"Rather, we must all focus the fleets on a common goal. Act independently, if you wish, but meet and discuss overall strategy so that we select appropriate Rebel targets and inject our venom where it will cause the most damage." She raised her gloved fist, glaring with ice-green eyes at Harrsk. "It serves no purpose for Imperials to be at each others' throats."

Harrsk chuckled, but the smile stretched across only the intact part of his face, while the scarred mask remained unmoved. "I see now why your battles were a dismal failure, Admiral," he said. "You are such a naive commander. No wonder Grand Moff Tarkin locked you away where you could cause no harm while the rest of us continued the real fight for the Empire."

Rage erupted like a volcano within Daala—but before her words could break through the barrier of her clenched teeth, the viewscreens began blinking with alarms. One of the distant spy cams mounted high above the ecliptic had detected searing lights, trains of afterburners streaking through space so fast that the sensors could not focus.

Harrsk scuttled toward the screens and pressed his face close against one. The in-system holocams trained on the giant sun showed more trails arrowing in.

The central screen switched, and Commander Kratas was there again. "Admiral Daala—uh, excuse me, Warlord Harrsk—we've detected incoming ships, moving fast." More of the out-system spy holocams triggered alarms, a dozen more ships coming from below the orbital plane this time. "I've spotted seventy," Kratas said in disbelief.

Harrsk shouted, "Sound all alarms!" Battle klaxons ripped through the tunnels.

When the images finally focused, Daala caught her breath as she recognized the fleeting forms of seventy-three *Victory*-class Star Destroyers, smaller warships each about half the size of an Imperial Star Destroyer. But these ships were fast, agile, and bristling with weaponry. Their hulls were made of a crimson alloy so that the Victory ships looked like bloody fangs clamping around Harrsk's Star Destroyers.

"Is this a drill?" Daala said. "Are you trying to impress me?"

"No!" Harrsk said, glaring at her so deeply that even the scarred portion of his face rippled with distaste. "That's High Admiral Teradoc." He shouted to the Star Destroyers. "Lock on any target and fire."

Running lights flashed on, powering up on the bone-white Star Destroyers eclipsed by Harrsk's planet. Green turbolasers shot out, skewering target locations—but the *Victory*-class ships roared by too fast. Five of the crimson ships erupted as they took severe hits, but even those losses were insignificant compared with the sheer number in the attacking fleet.

"Teradoc is trying to disgrace me," Harrsk said.

On screen, Daala could see Kratas snapping to his duty as ranking officer on the bridge, instinctively issuing emergency orders. She was proud of how her second in command instantly took charge. She had trained him well.

"Concentrate all firepower," Kratas said. "Select one target, destroy it, then move on to the next. Scattered fire won't accomplish anything."

Kratas took Warlord Harrsk's flagship to the point of a phalanx formation. The *Shockwave* was larger than the other Star Destroyers, more heavily outfitted with high-energy weapons. The *Shockwave* targeted and fired, obliterating a sixth Victory ship. It aimed again, crippling a target, and the crimson vessel went dim and spun out of control.

Then Daala realized with horror that the *Shockwave* itself was the primary target for the combined assault of a hundred *Victory*-class Star Destroyers. They converged like metal filings drawn to a magnet, firing and firing.

"He's trying to destroy my flagship!" Harrsk said, balling his fists and standing next to his floating chair. "He wants to humiliate me. I told you."

"Cease fire," Kratas ordered his bridge crew. "Route all power to our shields. We've got to withstand this salvo."

The *Victory*-class destroyers came on without pausing. The other Star Destroyers in Harrsk's fleet shot at them, taking a minor toll, but the crimson warships were suicidal, seeming not even to notice the loss of their comrades. The *Victory*-class ships formed a blanket of turbolaser fire, stabbing again and again, pummeling the shields of the *Shockwave*.

"We can't hold out much longer," Kratas said, his voice harsh with strain. "Shields failing." He turned to look out of the screen again. His dark eyes, wide with realization, seemed to be staring directly out at Daala. "Admiral, I—"

Then the screen turned to a fuzz of gray static. One of

the spycam images showed the *Shockwave* cracking apart as geysers of molten white fire shot from breaches in the hull. The engine compartment spewed unleashed energy in all directions. The hull integrity could not hold.

The *Victory*-class Star Destroyers kept firing until finally the *Shockwave* was no more than a glowing cloud of debris and an agonizing memory for Admiral Daala. "Oh, Kratas," she whispered. "I'm sorry."

Achieving their target, the surviving Victory ships—sixty-two of them according to the tally on the data screens—reversed course and streaked toward hyperspace, even as Warlord Harrsk's remaining Imperial Star Destroyers took unsuccessful potshots in their wake.

Daala stood, feeling cold outrage. Commander Kratas hadn't even been part of Harrsk's fighting force. He had been a bystander in a childish squabble between feuding warlords. Daala's lip curled as the rage built inside her, like pressurized steam rushing through her blood.

"We won't stand for this," Harrsk growled. "This time we'll get even, and I have the means to do so with you, Admiral Daala," he said, looking up at her, his golden droid eye blazing.

Daala was startled from her grim reverie. "What?"

Harrsk continued breathlessly. "We must smash that obese coward now with everything we have! I've been gathering my military might for a strike just such as this."

Daala fixed Harrsk with a withering glare. "I have no intention of assisting you in your childish brawl, Warlord Harrsk. You just lost me the best commander I ever had. I will not perpetuate this—"

"Stormtroopers!" Harrsk shouted toward the door. "Come here immediately, weapons ready."

The stormtrooper contingent marched into the large viewing room. Their white boots thundered on the glassy floor as they stood at attention. Cold black goggles and white plasteel helmets smothered all expressions.

"Take Admiral Daala to one of my Star Destroyers," Harrsk said. "She will command our retaliatory strike against High Admiral Teradoc." He scowled at her. "If she refuses, you will execute her immediately for treason."

Daala bristled. "I won't allow you to order me around like that."

"I outrank you, and you have my orders," he screamed. "Do you serve the Empire or do you have your own agenda?"

The stormtroopers brought their blaster rifles to bear, pointing at her. They looked uneasy, but they followed their warlord's orders. Daala could feel aiming mechanisms focusing on vulnerable points in her body.

"Very well, Harrsk," she murmured, still stunned at the loss of Kratas and numb with her own unchanneled anger. She intentionally denied him the title of Supreme Warlord. Her green eyes narrowed to calculating slits.

"Give me full command of one of your Star Destroyers, and I will lead your fleet."

CHAPTER 10

As the forces of Supreme Warlord Harrsk reeled from the attack, Admiral Daala found herself on the command bridge of the Imperial Star Destroyer *Firestorm*.

She surveyed the carnage High Admiral Teradoc's forces had wrought: the smoldering wreckage of the flagship, the frozen bodies of all troops lost in the explosion. Three more of Harrsk's Star Destroyers had also been sufficiently damaged as to require lengthy repairs. She would not be able to use them in her retaliatory strike.

That left eight—twice as many battleships as Grand Moff Tarkin had given her to defend Maw Installation. It would be enough.

Daala stood rigid on the bridge, staring out at the red giant star. Thick filters had been placed across the viewports so she could watch the blazing ocean of hot gas without blinking. The commotion of battle preparations continued around her unheeded.

Inside her, a cauldron of frustration simmered. She did not want to fight Teradoc. She did not want to fight Harrsk. She wanted them both—and all the other squabbling warlords—to fight the cursed *Rebels*! Commander Kratas had died because of their bickering. They were a disgrace to the memory of the Empire; and if this was all the Imperial ideal could offer anymore, then perhaps it was best they failed.

But Daala could not accept that. Tarkin had taught her never to give up. She clasped her hands at the small of her back, squeezing her black gloves so tightly that her bones hurt. There must be a better way, even if she had to force these others kicking and screaming to see it.

Harrsk's magnified image came to her over the comm system. He kept his half-scarred face turned squarely into the transmission range, flaunting both his ugly and his undamaged side. "Admiral Daala, I am aboard the Star Destroyer *Whirlwind* at your flank. You will take the point in our attack. I trust you have already developed a strategy?"

"Warlord Harrsk," Daala said, looking into the blurred image of his face, "I have just begun to study the data your spies gathered on Teradoc's fortress. Give me a moment to assess the possibilities for attack."

"No," Harrsk insisted. "The High Admiral will never expect us to strike so swiftly. We lose our element of surprise with each second of delay. It'll be a full-frontal attack with all weapons blazing. We'll knock him reeling!"

Daala scowled. She took quick, controlled breaths through flared nostrils. "Warlord, I have studied my own failures and realized that many of them can be traced directly to ill-advised actions in the heat of anger."

"Nevertheless," Harrsk said, "you will follow my orders and launch an immediate attack. I don't have the time or the patience to deal with your cowardice and insubordination. If you continue to argue, I will strip you of your rank and place you in the brig."

Daala stiffened. She certainly wanted to be removed from this sham command, but she did not want to be imprisoned and tried for treason. Kratas was gone. Her former crew was gone. Her every connection had dwindled to insignificance. And she must start somewhere to rebuild her capabilities. This was a beginning, and Daala decided to apply her imagination to discover some way to salvage the situation.

"Very well, Supreme Warlord," Daala said, saluting him crisply. "With full command authority of this Star Destroyer, I will do my best to strike a blow for the Empire."

"Good." Harrsk rubbed his hands together. "My personal Star Destroyer will remain off to the side, so as not to draw direct fire. We will confuse them by having you lead the charge. Don't let me down."

"I would never let the Empire down, Supreme Warlord," Daala said.

She gave orders to the navigator, and the *Firestorm* edged to the front line of battleships. The three damaged Star Destroyers remained in eclipse, huddled in the shadow of Harrsk's hot world. The eight remaining ships followed Daala's hyperspace coordinates as she gave the orders to launch for the fortress of High Admiral Teradoc.

A rocky swath of planetoids orbited in a disk around a lavender-and-white gas giant. The crumbling, ice-laden ring system looked beautiful from far away, reflecting distant gold sunlight—but Daala saw it as a tactical challenge. The rubble created tens of thousands of possible targets, all places the High Admiral could have chosen to hide his fortress.

"Let's see if your spies provided good information," Daala said into her comm system linked to Warlord Harrsk's on the *Whirlwind*.

"It better be—we paid enough for it," Harrsk said. "A significant portion of my budget was devoted to bribing other Imperials to get that information."

Daala's expression did not change, though disgust welled up inside her. It should never have been *possible* to bribe Imperial soldiers. That kind of unprofessional behavior had brought the Empire to its knees—corruption, dishonesty, and criminal lack of vision.

"Very well, Warlord," she said. "We are heading directly into the ring systems, on target. All turbolasers are primed and ready."

Like projectiles shot from a gun, the Star Destroyers plunged into the ring plane, swooping toward their target. Large ice shards and reflective rocks cruised around them. The fleet came on at full speed, hoping to pounce before Teradoc could muster his forces again.

Daala imagined that the High Admiral must now be celebrating, his commanders retired and relaxing, expecting no retaliation so soon. They would get a surprise, she thought with a smile—and so would Harrsk.

As Daala led the attackers on their high-speed assault, two of the planetoids in the rings exploded, proximity charges rigged to detect the passage of incoming hostile ships. The flaming debris from the detonations sprayed in all directions, hailing upon Harrsk's Star Destroyers, crippling one and destroying two others.

Five left, Daala saw. What a waste.

"They know we're here, Admiral," her tactical officer said.

Harrsk was shouting over the comm system, his voice reedy with excitement. "Admiral Daala, what happened? Why didn't you predict that?"

Daala blanked the sound on the transmission, enjoying the warlord's livid face as he wordlessly continued to shout at her.

"We are locked on to Teradoc's fortress right now, Admiral," the navigator said.

On a screen in front of her, high-resolution diagrams of the ring system flashed up: one nondescript, medium-size rock blinked to indicate the site of the High Admiral's stronghold.

"*Victory*-class Star Destroyers approaching!" the weapons sergeant shouted.

Daala gripped the bridge rail, studying all components of the situation. She saw that dozens of the small planetoids were in fact garrisons, hollowed-out rocks that served as hangars for the crimson Victory ships. The smaller warships emerged and began their pursuit, some newly refurbished, others still battle-scarred from the recent attack on Harrsk's molten world.

"Do not engage them," Daala said.

The tactical officer sat up, his black eyes glittering and startled. "Excuse me, Admiral?"

"I said, do not engage," she snapped. "Those *Victory*-class ships are not our target. We have a much more important mission to accomplish, and we cannot afford to be drawn away by their amateurish attempts to distract us."

Behind her, in the tattered remains of her phalanx of Star Destroyers, Harrsk ignored her orders and commanded his gunners on the *Whirlwind* to shoot at the pursuing Victory ships. Two other battleships followed Harrsk's lead, but Daala snapped over the open-ship communications. "Cease fire! We need all of our energy for the main thrust." The image of Harrsk continued to bellow in silence with the sound turned off. Daala ignored him.

She turned and looked at the bridge crew under her command. "Tactical officer, I want personal command of the weapons systems."

"Admiral?" the weapons sergeant said. "Are you sure that's wise?"

"Personal control," she repeated. "I intend to fire the first blow myself." Then she feigned a soft smile, banking on her reputation. "I've been working for this a long time." The weapons sergeant nodded briskly.

Blazing spears of turbolaser fire shot at them from Teradoc's fortress. On the enhanced view she could discern camouflaged weapons batteries, and she knew that the High Admiral himself was probably hiding deep in an armored bunker, safe from the battle, while his swarms of Victory ships served as disposable perimeter defenses.

Daala moved to the weapons console, and the gunner surrendered his seat, looking at her in awe. She sat down and glanced at the controls, familiarizing herself in an instant. Daala had spent the last year learning to become a part of the Empire's future rather than staying mired in its past.

"I am siphoning off all power from the turbolaser batteries," she said, "and concentrating our entire first strike on the ion cannon."

The tactical officer coughed and looked at her nervously. "But, Admiral—the ion cannon simply obliterates electrical and computer systems. Are you sure that will be sufficient to accomplish our objective?" He squinted down at the readout of Teradoc's rocky fortress.

"It will be sufficient to achieve my goal," Daala said.

As the Victory ships came in, dodging icy ring-system debris, Daala targeted the *Firestorm*'s ion cannon and placed her finger on the firing button.

"Admiral!" the weapons sergeant cried, "those coordinates are—"

She removed her sidearm and fired a stun blast at the sergeant. Glowing blue arcs engulfed him and he tumbled into a crumpled mass on the deck. Before the others on the bridge could react, Daala fired the ion cannon.

The *Firestorm*'s weapon belched out a disruptive blast that washed over the bridge tower of Warlord Harrsk's Star Destroyer *Whirlwind*. Lightning bolts traced a thousand wicked fingers across the hull, shutting down his command systems, his computers, his weapons.

The *Firestorm*'s bridge crew leaped to their feet in an uproar, and Daala stood quickly. She raised her voice to shout down the objections. "I am in command of this ship, and you will follow my orders!"

She leveled her blaster pistol and flicked its switch to the KILL setting. "Anyone who questions my orders will be executed on the spot for mutiny against the rightful commander of this vessel. Do you understand?"

She gave them only a second to look at her in cowed

silence. "Drop back. We will parallel the *Whirlwind*. Harrsk's ship is dead in space, so increase our shields to protect him in case any of Teradoc's ships come after us."

As the others moved sluggishly to respond, loud thumps reverberated through the *Firestorm*. Two of the three remaining Imperial Star Destroyers began firing on her ship.

"They are loyal to Warlord Harrsk," the navigator said.

"They don't know what they're doing," Daala responded. "If any of you bore love for the Empire, you would have done this long ago."

"Our shields are on full, Admiral," one member of the bridge crew said, voice trembling. "We have covered both ourselves and the *Whirlwind,* but the shields are diffuse. We cannot withstand a full-fledged attack if the *Victory*-class ships—or our own—decide to take us out."

"Open a channel," Daala said. "All bands. I want to make sure our Star Destroyers are listening as well as Teradoc's—and Warlord Harrsk himself."

She stepped into the transmitting area and drew a deep breath of the processed air on the bridge. Good Imperial ships smelled sharp and clean and metallic. It reinforced Daala's strength to follow her convictions.

"This is Admiral Daala," she said, "in command of the Imperial Star Destroyer *Firestorm*. I serve the Empire. I have always served the Empire, and I will never fire upon any other loyal Imperial." She swallowed grimly.

"I have made a preemptive strike on Warlord Harrsk's Star Destroyer to prevent him from attacking another Imperial stronghold. Harrsk's attack is in direct response to hostile action taken by High Admiral Teradoc. I condemn that action as well. I can no longer tolerate wasted effort and squandered resources that could be better applied to destroying Rebel bases.

"Many of you may have heard of my attempts to destroy the Rebel Alliance, when I had only four Star Destroyers, outdated information, and no support from the Empire.''

With a stuttering burst of static, Warlord Harrsk's image broke in. Daala was surprised, but momentarily pleased, that he had been able to get his comm system working again so quickly.

"Don't listen to her! She's a traitor and a renegade!" Harrsk said. "I order the loyal crew on the *Firestorm* to take Daala by force and execute her. Her crimes are obvious."

Daala continued to hold the blaster pistol, but she let it dip down as she swept her gaze at her bridge crew. "*Is* my crime so obvious?" she asked. "My only aim is to stop this civil war so we can fight our true enemy. Do you honestly believe Warlord Harrsk has the greater interests of the *Empire* in mind—or is he merely interested in his personal power?

"I am not taking over. I do not want personal power or political leadership. All I ask is a military command. I will serve under any leader who will devote his forces to defeating the Rebel Alliance once and for all."

Working the comm controls, Daala broke through the jammed transmission and spoke to all ships again. She noticed that the crimson *Victory*-class ships had swarmed around them, dozens strong, their weapons sufficient to obliterate Harrsk's Star Destroyers—but they held their fire.

Daala went to the command station on the *Firestorm*'s bridge, turning her back on the crew to demonstrate a measure of trust. She remained extremely tense, but refused to let it show. Out of the corner of her eye she watched the navigator slowly rise from his seat and begin to withdraw his blaster sidearm. Daala prepared to turn and shoot him without warning, but one of the operations chiefs placed a hand on the navigator's forearm, making him hold his fire. Daala trembled with relief.

She punched up the command systems for the *Firestorm,* keying in her access code, glad that she had forced

Harrsk to give her full computer privileges before agreeing to run the attack on Teradoc's fortress. Harrsk had suspected nothing, and now she had the final say on every decision.

The *Firestorm*'s computer recognized only Admiral Daala. She punched in a command she had dreaded even to consider on her own ship, verified it, then pressed the COMMIT button.

She spoke again into the transmission field. "If this is what my Empire has become, I no longer wish to serve it. I have just initiated the self-destruct countdown on the Star Destroyer *Firestorm*."

The bridge uproar was more subdued this time, as if the crew were still stunned from her first mutinous action.

"The countdown is set. Warlord Harrsk's ship is powerless and trapped within my deflector shields. Self-destruct will take place in fifteen standard minutes unless Harrsk issues an immediate command ordering all hostilities to cease."

Seated in the cramped bridge station of the *Victory*-class Star Destroyer 13X, Vice Admiral Pellaeon studied this unexpected new development, both pleased and perplexed. His cap fit snugly against his gray hair. He tugged at his long pale mustache as he sifted through the implications of the broadband message.

If the enemy had continued its headlong surprise attack, the fleet of Imperial Star Destroyers would certainly have caused severe damage to High Admiral Teradoc's fortress. Pellaeon's Victory swarm could have mopped up the remaining ships, but only at great cost to themselves.

Now, though, the leader of this sudden and unexpected retaliation had turned upon one of her own ships. Not surprisingly, Warlord Harrsk had not led the charge, cowering instead in one of the rear Star Destroyers.

But this Admiral Daala . . .

Pellaeon leaned back in his padded seat. He had

heard of her, two years after the defeat of Grand Admiral Thrawn had left Pellaeon in personal disgrace. Daala had come out of nowhere and begun a single-handed attack against the Rebels. With such a small fleet she had no hope of ultimate victory, but Daala had seemed interested only in causing significant damage *now,* with no overall strategy, just a desire for destruction.

Pellaeon had admired her efforts to take action—the other Imperial commanders seemed to prefer internal arguments. He looked about him on the small control deck of a *Victory*-class ship, the smallest craft he had commanded in a long time. He did believe in High Admiral Teradoc's plan of building up a huge fleet of smaller, more versatile ships—but still he missed the grandeur of commanding the *Chimaera.*

As he brought his fleet closer, weapons ready but not firing, Pellaeon hovered over the stalled Imperial Star Destroyers and looked down at Admiral Daala's ship, at how she had incapacitated Warlord Harrsk's *Whirlwind.* Her turnabout had been an interesting, desperate, and inexplicable tactic—but Pellaeon admired its purity of purpose. Daala was someone who, like Thrawn, was able to focus on an objective and devote resources and tactics to that end. High Admiral Teradoc and Warlord Harrsk both seemed little more than ill-behaved children bullying each other about.

He heard Daala's impassioned speech begging for a unified front against the true enemy. Several crew members on Pellaeon's own ship softly murmured in agreement. He kept his own feelings to himself, though he agreed as well. As he looked at Daala's image, he wondered what kind of artwork she might like.

"Vice Admiral Pellaeon," his navigator said, "perhaps we should back off, if her self-destruct threat is genuine. If both of those Star Destroyers blow, we'll be caught in the shockwave and severely damaged, if not destroyed."

Pellaeon sat rigidly for a moment, then stiffly shook his head. "No, we'll stay right here. Open a channel."

His bridge crew looked at him in amazement. "A channel to the *Firestorm,* sir?" the comm officer said.

"No, open band. I want all ships to hear this." The comm officer blinked, then nodded and carried out Pellaeon's order.

He rose slowly from his padded black chair. "This is Vice Admiral Pellaeon, commander of High Admiral Teradoc's fleet, issuing a specific order to my own ships to maintain position." Several crimson ships had begun to edge away from their confining net. Harrsk's Star Destroyers had already backed away, gaining distance.

"As a gesture of good faith and out of respect for Admiral Daala's request, I hereby order an immediate cessation of hostilities on our part."

Almost immediately a red light flashed on the 13X's comm panel. The officer turned to Pellaeon. "I have an urgent message from High Admiral Teradoc, sir." The comm officer raised his eyebrows, clearly intimidated and awaiting orders.

"I'll speak to him here on the bridge," Pellaeon said. He squared his shoulders. "You may all listen."

Teradoc's image came through, red-faced and puffing. The man's girth had increased threefold in the last year or so. "Pellaeon, what do you think you're doing?" he shouted. "I order you to press your advantage! Use this opportunity to strike Harrsk's Star Destroyers while they are weakened. Now we can obliterate him completely."

Pellaeon frowned, thinking of fat Teradoc squatting in his bunker behind dozens of meters of the highest-quality shielding, absolutely safe from harm while the battle raged outside. Pellaeon did not think a true war commander would keep himself so isolated.

"I respectfully disagree, High Admiral. Warlord Harrsk is not my enemy. He is not the enemy of the Empire. I think we should confer with this Admiral Daala and hear what she has to say."

Teradoc's face turned from red to purple. "I don't care what you *think.* If you do not fire upon Harrsk, you're a traitor. Have you forgotten your training? Your entire life speaks of service to the Empire, of following the orders of your superior officers. You are excrement if you will not obey your rightful commander. What would Grand Admiral Thrawn think of you?''

Pellaeon frowned even more deeply as he faced the image of the fat warlord. Teradoc was correct, from a certain point of view. Pellaeon had spent many decades of his life in service to the Imperial Navy. He had commanded Star Destroyers. After the battle of Endor, he had taken over the *Chimaera* when its own commander had been killed in the hostilities. He had spent the following years trying to regain the status of the Empire through a succession of weak rulers, debilitating surrenders, and losses of territory. Pellaeon had watched his once-magnificent Empire dwindle to a mere island in what had been considered the backwater territories and formerly uninhabitable systems near the core of the galaxy.

It wasn't until Grand Admiral Thrawn had come back from the Unknown Territories that Pellaeon had finally found a true leader he could follow with a genuine chance of recapturing lost glory. When Thrawn had fallen, Pellaeon had lost his hope again, merely serving any Imperial commander he happened to find and marching in place.

Now, though, Admiral Daala's conviction and enthusiasm, and her willingness to risk all for the appropriate cause, made something stir within him again, something powerful.

Pellaeon took a deep breath and spoke to the bloated image of Teradoc. "I believe I know what he would think of me," he said bitterly, "and *you,* sir, are no Grand Admiral Thrawn."

He switched off the comm, then turned to his crew. "Prepare a shuttle and inform Admiral Daala that I am coming aboard. Time is short, and I wish to confer with her in person."

YAVIN 4

CHAPTER 11

As Artoo-Detoo trundled along in front of him, Luke Skywalker hurried out of the Great Temple to see the new visitor. Wind currents had torn the clouds to tatters in the sky above, and he blinked in the hazy sunlight of the jungle afternoon.

Most of the Jedi trainees were working inside their cool chambers or wandering out in the forest depths. Callista sat alone studying the histories that Tionne compiled for her, although over the past several days she had found nothing that would help her regain her powers.

Now Luke saw a slender woman descend from a custom-designed craft that bore the cross-hatched insignia of the Smugglers' Alliance. "Mara Jade!" he called. "What did I do to deserve the honor of your presence?"

Mara flashed a fast, sharp-edged smile at him. "You *don't* deserve it, Skywalker," she said, "but I came anyway."

He strode forward and clasped her hand. She withdrew quickly, glancing at the close-cropped weeds on the landing grid and then staring up at the dizzying height of the ancient Massassi pyramid.

"Want to come inside?" he asked.

"No, let's go for a ride in my ship," she answered. "I need to talk to you about something."

Luke nodded slowly. "I thought you might. You don't usually come here just because you're bored."

Mara shook her head, and her mane of auburn hair thrashed about like waves of exotic spice. "I'm never bored, Skywalker." She gestured to the cockpit of her ship, where the passenger seat sat empty. "It's my outlook on life."

Artoo whistled and warbled, rocking back and forth on his footpads. "You stay here, Artoo," Luke said. "If anybody asks, tell them where I've gone. We'll be back," he glanced sidelong at Mara, "before too long."

As he slid into the empty seat, finding the armrests and the protective restraints, Mara punched a button on the cockpit controls. The flip-up side door slammed down and hissed into an airtight seal. Before Luke could buckle his crash webbing, she hit the accelerators. With a blast of repulsorlifts her sleek ship rose into the air and shot off above the treetops.

Luke thought he heard the scraping of witches' fingernails as the bottom hull brushed gently against the upreaching crowns of the trees. Mara grinned as she increased speed, climbing higher. Acceleration pushed Luke back against the seat, and he decided he could either be concerned—or he could kick back and enjoy himself.

He thought of his younger days, taking a T-16 skyhopper screaming through Beggar's Canyon on Tatooine, avoiding obstacles, performing daredevil stunts. Right now Mara Jade was just showing off—and he decided to let her blow off steam. She probably wanted to rattle him, but it wouldn't work.

Below, the dense greenery looked like clouds of foliage. Mara stormed along, her eyes fixed on her piloting. The Massassi temple dropped away in the distance, but

Luke wasn't worried. Though Mara had repeatedly tried to kill him in the past, he now trusted her implicitly. Luke smiled to himself at the irony of their situation.

"So," he said, "what is it you wanted to talk about?"

"Got some information for you," she answered, flicking a glance toward him, then looking away just as quickly. "In my work with the Smugglers' Alliance I keep my eyes and ears open. Sometimes I hear things the New Republic should know about."

Luke raised his eyebrows. "Such as?"

Mara pretended to frown. "You expect me to give you important information like that for free?"

Luke stared at her in silence for a full second, then smiled. "Yes," he said. "Yes, I do."

Mara laughed. "That doesn't surprise me a bit from you, Skywalker," she said. "All right. You know the Smugglers' Alliance was specifically set up to provide a strong front against some of the more powerful crime organizations, especially the Hutts."

"Yes," Luke agreed, suspecting where this might lead.

"We keep tabs on the Hutts' comings and goings, since they're our enemies—or perhaps I should say 'competitors.' Recently they clamped down on our usual information sources. They've been building up what appears to be a respectable front—several commercial corporations, the most prominent of which is Orko SkyMine, a mineral resource development consortium."

"Shouldn't we be happy that the Hutts are trying to be 'respectable,' as Lando Calrissian would have put it?"

"We'd be happy—if we could believe them," Mara said, then concentrated on flying again as a thermal updraft buffeted them. The wind rattled the transparisteel windows of her craft, and she banked to the left around a volcanic rock outcrop. She increased altitude. "But you know as well as I do that you can never really believe what the Hutts say." She looked at Luke again. "I think they're up to something. Something big."

Luke kept his expression bland. "Even though I'm just a Jedi teacher, I have a few sources of information of my own. And I'm inclined to believe your suspicions are right, Mara Jade."

She blinked in surprise. "Ah. So my coming here was unnecessary?"

Luke shook his head. "Your coming to Yavin 4 is never unnecessary. What did you want me to do with this information?"

"I thought you might take it to your sister on Coruscant. As the Chief of State, she can probably think of something to head off trouble."

Luke tapped his fingers together, consciously relaxing in the face of Mara's breakneck piloting. "You could have just gone there yourself. Isn't Yavin 4 a bit of your way just to deliver a message?"

Mara took a deep breath. "I wanted to do this quietly. Since I'm with the Smugglers' Alliance, I need to keep things low-key. My involvement shouldn't be too obvious. Talon Karrde taught me that."

"I see," Luke said. "How is Karrde? Still retired?"

"Hah!" she said. "More than a few months of relaxation was enough to bring him to the brink of insanity and boredom. He's back at it and busier than ever, with his hands in more schemes than I can keep track of."

She pulled her nimble craft hard to starboard in a tight loop and shot over the treetops back toward the Great Temple. "The other reason I came in person," Mara continued with some uneasiness, "is that occasionally—for some unknown reason—I almost look forward to seeing you, Skywalker. Not often . . . but there are times."

"And this is one of them?" Luke asked.

"It was," she said. "I'd better be on my way before it wears off."

Luke laughed. "Why don't you stay for a few more hours at least? We'll be gathering the trainees in the mess hall for an evening meal. You need something better than stale ration bars.''

Mara acquiesced far more easily than Luke had expected. ''All right,'' she said. ''Just a quick meal, then I'm out of here.''

Callista sat alone, picking at her meal next to the empty spot where Luke normally ate—but he had gone off to set up quarters for two new potential Jedi who had arrived on a New Republic transport.

With mixed feelings of detachment and frustration, Callista stared at the other Jedi trainees in the narrow stone hall, the weakest of whom had powers greater than she could command . . . at the moment. It was painful to watch them grow in strength as they played with their Force abilities. She was denied that, though she tried and tried. She was blind and deaf to the Force.

''Hey, mind if I sit here?'' Mara Jade said, wearing her trim flight uniform and holding a tray of stew mixed with greens.

Callista barely nodded, and Mara plopped into the chair, setting her tray on the polished table. She picked up a thick bread wafer and poked around in her stew. ''Better than packaged rations, I suppose, but I can tell you don't have a gourmet droid working here.'' Mara's bright eyes flashed. ''So, you're Skywalker's new lady?'' she asked.

Callista wished she could read the emotions behind Mara Jade's visage. The other woman was good at masking her expressions, and Callista didn't know what to make of their conversation.

Though their bodies were similar in age, Callista had been born decades before Mara Jade. Her own powers were gone now, but she had been a Jedi Knight whose abilities surpassed anything that Mara could manage. She had heard of past connections between Mara Jade and Luke—and she decided it would be best if she took the initiative. "Yes I am," she answered. "And you must be Mara Jade. I've heard about you."

When Mara nodded briskly, Callista raised her eyebrows. "I also heard hints that you might have been interested in Luke yourself at one time."

Mara frowned again in distaste at her stew, but took a large mouthful. She swallowed, took a drink, and finally let loose a short laugh. "Who told you I was ever interested in Luke Skywalker? When I first met him, the thing I wanted most in the universe was to kill him. I thought that way for a long time. . . ." She shrugged. "Sometimes it still seems like a good idea to me." Mara took another bite and chewed slowly. "Not a great basis for a long-term relationship, you think?"

Callista shook her head. "No, I suppose not." Even without her Jedi powers, Callista wasn't sure she believed Mara's answer. "Aren't you with Lando Calrissian? I heard something about you two being a hot item."

"Calrissian? You've got to be kidding!" Mara actually blushed and turned away to take another drink before she could cough on her quickly swallowed mouthful. "We're still good business partners in a very profitable operation at the spice mines of Kessel right now—but I think Calrissian was more interested in *chasing* me than in *winning* me . . . which is fine as far as I'm concerned."

Mara wiped the corners of her mouth. "Well, good to meet you." She stood up, smoothing out the wrinkles in her flight suit. "Give Skywalker my regards. I've got to be heading out. Just stopped by to drop off a message."

Mara left without so much as a nod of acknowledgment to the other Jedi trainees, while Callista wondered about her mysterious message.

CORUSCANT

CHAPTER 12

Leaving the Jedi *praxeum* behind, Luke took Callista with him to Coruscant where Luke had set up a private audience with his sister. He quickly met with Leia and delivered the information Mara Jade had brought. Added to what they had already learned at the ruins of Jabba's palace, the rumors of a Hutt secret plan grew more threatening. Leia had already reinforced her network of spies, hoping to gather more hints and details.

In the ornate presidential briefing chambers, Callista sat next to Luke, her fingers resting lightly on his forearm, but he could not feel the binding of her presence around him. It was as if she did not exist in the Force.

Luke looked into his sister's large brown eyes, mapping out the faint tired lines that had begun to form around them. The weight of leadership pressed down heavily upon her. The New Republic was large and scattered, beset by hundreds of problems, brushfire squabbles, and growing threats. And Leia had three children to contend with, as well as a husband.

"Leia," Luke said, "I have a request, an important favor to ask."

She sat up straighter, looking at Callista and then at her brother. "The last time you asked for a favor was to let Kyp Durron destroy the Sun Crusher." She bit her lower lip. "But I suppose that came out all right."

Luke relaxed. "Nothing so monumental this time," he said. "Callista and I have a lot of things to work out between ourselves. We need some time alone so we can devote our attention to reawakening her Jedi powers. She could be one of our strongest Jedi, if she regains her affinity for the Force. She could teach *me* a lot. I think the only way we can crack that wall around her is if Callista and I work together. Intensely." He grasped her hand. "We need a week or so alone, to focus on salvaging her powers, not a thousand other problems. No distractions."

Leia smiled wistfully. "I know exactly how you feel. . . ." Then she became serious. "I can't order you around, Luke. There's no need for you to ask my permission."

Leia looked at Callista, and Luke could see that her face held a whirlpool of conflicting emotions: the need to see her brother happy, the desire for Callista to be his equal again, and her own need to keep Luke focused on training new Jedi Knights to strengthen and protect the New Republic.

But Leia loved her brother very much, and her choice was clear. "Take all the time you need. I wish you the greatest success." She looked up. "Or should I say, may the Force be with you?"

Later, still holding hands, Luke and Callista went to the upper westside docking platform of the former Imperial palace. The air was thin so high above ground level, and the gusting breezes were cold and cutting.

He squeezed Callista's hand, and her grip returned his twice as strong. Though Luke couldn't read anything from her with his Jedi senses, he saw her obvious eagerness mixed with reluctance. Callista shared his high hopes for their journey alone, but she was also afraid they would fail.

Leia, her robes of state whipping briskly around her, held the hands of the twins, Jacen and Jaina, as she came to see Luke off, while Han carried young Anakin propped against his hip; the dark-haired boy blinked his ice blue eyes, drinking in the sights.

Threepio and Artoo came along at their own pace, though the hairy Wookiee urged them to greater speed. "Do be patient, Chewbacca," Threepio said. "I can only move so fast. If you had replaced my leg servomotors last week—as I suggested—I'd be able to move much more efficiently." The Wookiee groaned something untranslatable back at the golden droid.

Callista stood by Luke's side at the boarding ramp to a nondescript space yacht. Luke saw her in profile—her long face and generous lips, her highlighted blond hair that had been cropped short and was still growing out from her stormtrooper cut on the *Eye of Palpatine*. Han had once called her "the blonde with the legs," and Luke couldn't argue with that description.

Callista was so beautiful to him—but that wasn't all. Many women were beautiful. With the Force, he had seen Callista *inside*. He knew her in a way it was impossible to know most women. They had fallen in love before they had even seen each other face to face, back when Callista had been no more than a wandering presence. Now she inhabited another body—a beautiful body, to be sure, but Luke would have loved her no matter what. They had treasured one another in Luke's dreams before Callista had manifested herself in the body of one of his former students.

Now, as they stood in front of the space yacht, Luke watched Callista staring wistfully at Han and Leia's children. Her lips were firm, and her eyes remained wide and clear, but he knew exactly what she was thinking.

The children. Luke and Callista had spoken of having children of their own if they were to get married. Callista insisted that Luke, being the foremost Jedi Master of the day, must have powerful children, to make the strong Jedi bloodline flourish—if one were to look at romance in such a cold and . . . *Imperial* fashion.

She was terrified that if they had children while she had no access to her powers, their descendants might suffer the same Force blindness. But Luke didn't care: he wanted Callista, though she would not listen when he tried to reassure her. Their only chance lay in severing the invisible chains around her, breaking through the maddening transparent wall.

Leia came forward to hug Luke. High above the skyline, the wind picked up, and breezes stung his blue eyes, whipping his hair in all directions. He bent down to scoop up the kids in a warm hug.

"Now do I get to hug Callista?" Han said, and came forward to give her a brief embrace as Leia laughed. Chewbacca blatted something, and Han waved him aside. "Nah, Chewie—you can hug Threepio if you want."

"Well, the very idea!" Threepio said.

Luke set foot on the boarding platform with Callista at his side. Artoo whistled mournfully, blinking his optical receptor from red to blue. "Don't worry, Artoo," Luke said. "You enjoy your time with Threepio. We need to be by ourselves for a bit."

When Artoo gave a low hoot, See-Threepio placed a golden hand on the dome of the astromech droid in indignation. "Humph! I'm sure *I* see no need for a starry-eyed couple to turn down the companionship of a faithful droid. I can't imagine why they'd need to be *completely* alone." He patted his counterpart. "Come along, Artoo. We'll find something useful to do."

As the droids hurried toward the turbolift, Luke and Callista waved farewell again and prepared for launch.

*　　*　　*

See-Threepio and Artoo-Detoo passed through nine security checkpoints as the turbolift descended deep into Coruscant's crust. "We're obviously *droids*," Threepio muttered. "I simply don't understand why they need to put us through such indignities to get down here. Virus scanning, indeed!"

Finally the doors hissed open, and they stepped into the sterile chambers of pulsating mainframe computers in the Imperial Information Center.

"Remember when you and I were here, Artoo, trying to find Jedi candidates for Master Luke?" Artoo bleeped that of course he remembered.

"This time it's nothing terribly exciting, I'm afraid, but in the process of studying backup files for Mistress Leia, I discovered some troubling computer glitches that I'm at a loss to account for. I cannot find any trace of them before the day that horrid Durga the Hutt came to visit and all chaos broke loose. At first I was concerned that our mitigation efforts might have caused some deep core damage, but standard diagnostics yielded nothing. I have been reticent to point this out to Mistress Leia because I'm sure she's still upset about that entire debacle."

Artoo trundled across the polished floor. The assassin droids trained their implanted blasters on the two newcomers, targeting systems tracking the large motions. A battery of observation cams studied them with cold objectivity from near the juncture of wall and ceiling.

"This place gives me the chills . . . rather, it *would* give me the chills, if I had the physical capability to have them," Threepio said. "As it is, my circuits are merely . . . uneasy—but if you could do anything to assist me, Artoo . . . ?"

The astromech droid was already accessing a terminal, requesting further details. Artoo's input jack locked into the main drive and spun around. Threepio paced about in stiff discomfort. The assassin droids stared at them. The slicer droids paid no attention whatsoever.

"Would you like me to tell you a story to pass the time, Artoo?" Threepio said.

Artoo blatted an emphatic NO.

"Well, really!" Threepio bent over one of the keypads and detected something most surprising. He reached down with his gold-plated fingertips and held up a small tuft of grayish fur. "Oh dear, I wonder how this got here?" he said. "This room is supposed to be kept meticulously clean."

He examined the floor and inspected the wall. His optical sensors were drawn to a small ventilation intake for the huge intake fans that circulated supercooled air to the deep levels of the Information Center. The cover plate stood ajar, but it was far too small for any intelligent creature to have come through. Could the Imperial Information Center be inhabited by some sort of large rodent?

Artoo shrilled in alarm, and Threepio strutted over to a screen where the astromech droid had begun replaying archival video records from the security monitoring cameras. Threepio saw from the date on the images that the footage had been taken while Durga's entourage met with the Chief of State in the reception halls far above. Because no security breach had been recorded down here in the Imperial Information Center, though, no one had bothered to do more than a cursory scan on them.

Artoo manipulated the images, enhancing and enlarging them, massaging out shadows by playing virtual light into the images.

"Why, I recognize those!" Threepio said. Just at the edge of the frame, motion gave away three of the furry, multiarmed Taurill scampering out of the ventilation ducts and up to the unmanned computer consoles.

"Whatever are they doing?" Threepio said. "How could they possibly have gotten down here? We rounded them all up, didn't we?"

Artoo chittered, then froze another image that showed the Taurill deliberately punching commands into a keypad.

"This is most suspicious," Threepio said.

The droids watched as the three Taurill completed their command strings and copied a file into a data cylinder, which they secreted in their own fur; then they dashed back to the ventilation shafts.

"It would appear that they've copied something from our records. What could they possibly want?" Threepio said. At Artoo's warbled reply, he added, "Of *course* I'd like you to find out! Why else would I have brought you along, you silly whistling trash can?"

Artoo replayed the images slowly, noting the Taurill command strings, then input them himself. The passworded files scrolled onto the screen, immediately recognizable. In fact, Artoo had once carried the complex blueprints inside himself.

Threepio wailed, "We must warn Mistress Leia immediately!" He ran toward the turbolift doors, shrilling an alarm. Artoo rolled after him. The assassin droids snapped to attention and trained their weapons on them.

"Summon Chief of State Organa Solo!" Threepio said. "This is an emergency. The fate of the entire galaxy is at stake."

The assassin droids were not impressed, and Threepio increased the volume in his vocal circuits. "Don't you understand? The plans to the Death Star have been stolen!"

CHAPTER 13

When Durga the Hutt returned to the asteroid belt in triumph, Bevel Lemelisk was summoned to the bottom-most deck of the Orko SkyMine ship, where Durga sat in the observation blister to stare out at the stars. Lemelisk entered the chamber accompanied by two Gamorrean guards, who shoved him into Durga's presence with a grunt, then stomped off to other duties.

Durga lay on inflated cushions. A music synthesizer warbled odd, discordant notes in a grating yet hypnotic background melody. Pink and blue smoke wafted like jagged fingers back and forth as the air exchangers alternated on either side of the room. The smoke had an acrid incense smell, a mild narcotic that affected Hutts but did nothing more than burn Lemelisk's human nostrils.

Durga's deep laugh boomed out. "Lemelisk, you're here!"

From another chair General Sulamar stood and straightened his uniform, brushing his knuckles across the jingling placards of medals on his chest. "We've been waiting for you, Lemelisk," he said.

Durga turned to glare at the Imperial. "You wait on my pleasure, General," the Hutt said. "We will start when I *wish* to start."

"Yes, Lord Durga," Sulamar said, bowing quickly and stepping back. His face became the color of soggy white cheese, and he glared at Lemelisk as if the engineer had done something wrong.

Lemelisk focused his attention on Durga, who was the most important enemy/ally at the moment. "Tell me, Lord Durga, did you get the Death Star plans?" Lemelisk felt his heart rise to his throat, and he unconsciously rubbed at the rough stubble on his cheeks and chin, scratched the shocks of white hair on his head. He had worked hard on those plans, spending so much of his life first laboring with Qwi Xux inside Maw Installation to develop the concept and the prototype, then spending months with the resources of the Empire to build the first enormous battle station.

Durga's enormous mouth bent upward like twisted rubber. With a small hand he inserted a data cylinder into a player nestled among the cushions at his side. The projector glowed, sending beams through the pink and blue smoke. A wire-frame diagram of Lemelisk's first-order blueprints appeared, rotating a three-dimensional sphere that showed layers within layers of deck plans, computer centers, defensive installations, energy storage areas—and the planet-destroying superlaser that ran through its axis.

General Sulamar rubbed his hands together, his face young and boyish again. His grin made him look like a narrow-faced rodent. "Excellent," Sulamar said. "Work must begin at once."

Durga scowled at him. "General Sulamar, *I* am in charge of this project."

"Of course, Lord Durga," Sulamar said—but his eyes remained fixed hungrily on the Death Star plans.

Bevel Lemelisk decided to use the awed moment to his advantage. "Lord Durga, if I might ask a question?

Exactly what is the Imperial general's purpose here among us?''

Sulamar straightened his shoulders like a spined puffer bird and turned to Durga. ''I bring Imperial prestige to your project. I will use my connections to obtain some of the items you need, the security codes you must possess. And when you begin your Hutt reign of terror across the galaxy''—he grinned—''think of how much more effective you will be if you're accompanied by the famed and feared General Sulamar, the Scourge of Celdaru, the man who successfully carried out the Massacre of Mendicat without losing a single stormtrooper. I held a hundred worlds in my fist—and I squeezed. The entire galaxy learned to tremble at my name.''

Lemelisk shrugged. He didn't want to press the issue, but he had never heard of Sulamar before. Of course, he had been isolated in Maw Installation for a long time. . . .

He looked again at the glowing outline of the Death Star. Though he saw only the outer layer of the projection, he knew the depth and intricacies of those plans. His heart pounded, and excitement brought a flush to his skin again. At last, a new project that he could sink his teeth into. He smiled and marveled at the design, remembering the first time he had showed it off.

''Magnificent,'' the Emperor had said, cowled in his black hood as he stared at the Death Star plans that Grand Moff Tarkin and Bevel Lemelisk presented to him.

''Yes, a technological terror,'' Tarkin said. Lean and cruel-looking, Tarkin stood at attention beside his Emperor, nodding down at the image.

Lemelisk and his naive but brilliant co-worker Qwi Xux had designed a battle station that placed fearsome power in a single commander's hands. Tarkin had been delighted with the concept and the plans and the prototype, and so he had brought Lemelisk out of Maw Installation to present the idea to the Emperor personally.

"Explain it to me," the Emperor said, extending his hands into the glowing simulation. The lines bent and buckled, curling around Palpatine's clawed fingers. Lemelisk had never seen a hologram react that way before, as if the image itself were trying to cringe from the Emperor's touch.

Lemelisk rubbed the perspiration from his palms on to his shirt as he spoke quickly, nervous in Palpatine's presence but even more excited to talk about his brainchild. "This battle station will be the size of a small moon a hundred kilometers in diameter," he said, "housing a single weapon of mass destruction. It will tax our construction skills to the limit, but I will be the chief engineer, and I'm certain I can complete the task personally."

The Emperor's reptilian eyes bored into him. Lemelisk turned back to the projected plans and brushed his hands over the surface layers.

"The Death Star will have planetary shielding, surface-to-air turbolasers, three-hundred-sixty-degree sensor capability, powerful multidirectional tractor beams, and heavy ion cannons."

"Impressive," the Emperor said in a frigid voice, "but only if our enemies fall right in our laps! How is this thing supposed to move?"

"Ah!" Lemelisk held up a finger and pointed along the equator. "The Death Star is equipped with enormous engines for propulsion in normal space as well as hyperspace. This station can go anywhere we wish." His eyes lit up, and he lowered his voice to a childlike whisper. "The superlaser is powerful enough to crack entire worlds. One blast can turn a planet into a cloud of rubble."

Grand Moff Tarkin bowed and cleared his throat. "The Death Star will be a self-contained garrison whose only purpose is to enforce your New Order. It is exactly the doomsday weapon you asked me to create, my Emperor.

"It will be crewed by close to a million officers, support personnel, and stormtroopers. It may be enormously expensive to build," Tarkin continued, "but this single Death Star alone will be worth a thousand Star Destroyers. The mere threat of this battle station will make any populace quiver in terror, for they can have no defenses against it. None."

The Emperor leaned forward to stare at the plans again. Bevel Lemelisk had never actually seen someone *gloat* before . . . but Emperor Palpatine did.

And so did Durga the Hutt and General Sulamar.

Sulamar held a personal data slate and punched up a summary, which he studied intently. "Lord Durga," he said, "I'm pleased to announce that the second pair of Automated Mineral Exploiters, models Gamma and Delta, are now functional and reprogrammed"—he shot a wicked glare at Bevel Lemelisk—"to remove the fatal flaws suffered by the original pair. The processors have begun exploiting the asteroid field and are smelting materials at this moment."

Durga nodded his large head, blinking froglike eyes. Around him small windows mounted at regular intervals around the observation blister showed streaming lights from chunks in the asteroid field as they wandered about their pell-mell courses, flashing as they rotated irregular surfaces, reflecting Hoth's distant sunlight.

"We can afford no further delays," Durga said, jabbing a stubby finger at Bevel Lemelisk. He yanked the data cylinder from the reader, and the glowing plans faded into the curling narcotic smoke. "You, Lemelisk, get to your redesign work—and take care that you don't make foolish mistakes as you did with the Mineral Exploiters." The Hutt chuckled with a chilling deadly mirth. "I'd hate to have to execute you if you disappoint me."

Lemelisk shuddered out of all proportion to the threat. He took the data cylinder from the Hutt's slimy hand and held the files close to his chest. "Yes, Lord Durga."

He bowed and scuttled backward out of Durga's private chambers. He rushed to his own quarters already grinning, eager to begin work.

CHAPTER 14

Bevel Lemelisk demanded absolute silence as he worked. He had sealed his quarters, hoping the Gamorrean guards wouldn't bumble in or pound on his door without realizing they had the wrong cabin number.

He settled into a wobbly metal seat; he had knocked it over in anger when he had been unable to complete his three-dimensional crystal puzzle. Getting the right solution meant a great deal to Bevel Lemelisk, and he disliked failure immensely . . . though it was much better to fail in private than when other people were watching.

Realizing that he hadn't eaten in nearly a day, Lemelisk had fixed himself a fast, high-protein meal and set the steaming plate of bright orange gruel beside him at the workbench. He didn't particularly like the stuff, but eating was little more than the necessary refueling of his mental machine. As he inserted the data cylinder into his terminal and began to work, though, he forgot about the meal entirely.

The image shimmered in front of him, a giant spherical battle station, detailed deck after deck, component after component. Only Lemelisk knew its true complexity.

He began to strip away the outer layers of the holo blueprint, removing extraneous levels, streamlining the construction, and tailoring it to the Hutts' needs. By eliminating the unnecessary Imperial padding, the superstructures, the personnel quarters, Lemelisk could create a weapon with far more energy devoted to sheer destruction.

The outline diagram of the main superlaser core glowed in front of him with bright lines indicating main support girders: the purity of his superlaser design, unmasked by the external shell. That was much better.

He squinted and leaned close to the projection, remembering how excited he had been to see the original construction actually taking place. . . .

Grand Moff Tarkin had arrived at the Death Star construction site in a nondescript *Lambda*-class cargo shuttle. He and Lemelisk sat in the passenger seats and discussed important matters as Tarkin's alien slave, a Calamarian named Ackbar, piloted them toward the huge mass of girders and construction machinery larger than any space station ever conceived.

Lemelisk couldn't understand why Tarkin spent so much time with the salmon-colored alien, whose fishy smell and large round eyes made Lemelisk queasy. Tarkin had crushed the world of the Mon Calamari and forced the strange creatures to serve his will. Now he made Ackbar his personal aide as another means of whipping him, tormenting him with the duties he resented so much.

Completely broken, Ackbar meekly followed Tarkin's every order. He guided the *Lambda*-class shuttle with wooden talent, chauffeuring them with as little enthusiasm as possible. Lemelisk noted that, though the alien reacted little, Ackbar seemed to hang on every word Tarkin said, as if storing information for whatever possible use a slave might make of it.

The Death Star construction hung in orbit around the penal world of Despayre in the Horuz system. The Outer Rim territories were Tarkin's personal stomping grounds—and he stomped as often and as hard as possible. The world below was a deep green, fissured with blue and brown rivers and shallow seas. Despayre looked far too calm to be a hellish prison planet, but Lemelisk knew the prehistoric jungles there writhed with vicious insects and predators, poisonous plants, and carnivorous crustaceans. The convicts huddled within the walls of their fortresses, hoping never to be exiled to the wilds.

The penal colony provided a ready pool of willing labor to build the Death Star. The volunteer lists carried five times as many names as the site could possibly support, and thus the workers in the space facility were expendable—but unfortunately they were also uneducated and surly, completely untrained for the type of sophisticated labor the project required.

Lemelisk directed the routine operations from his comfortable remote station. As chief engineer, he watched the progress reports to make sure all the components fit together properly. He didn't like to venture out into the hazardous construction area, however—he wasn't a hands-on manager.

Now, though, as Ackbar piloted the Lambda shuttle directly into the forest of girders, Lemelisk looked around, seeing bright flashes of laser welders and the glowing ends of newly smelted durasteel plates that emerged from processing plants. Curls of black smoke and the glow of waste heat spread into open space. Steam glittered in a shower of diamond-ice crystals.

When the Death Star was complete, the world of Despayre would be shrouded in an upper-orbital blanket of industrial debris as a side effect of the work. Unfortunately for the convicts, the debris would make passage to the penal colony virtually impossible. Despayre would then be off limits, and the prisoners would have to fend for them-

selves . . . until supplies ran out and the ferocious jungles came in.

"You're making good progress," Tarkin said, looking out the port.

Lemelisk cracked his knuckles. "Awe inspiring, isn't
it?" He had seen the plans so often, knew the details so
intimately—but the actual construction still took his breath
away, making him feel that all his years of exile in Maw
Installation had paid off. The small Death Star prototype
had been amazing as well, but that was merely a proof-of-
concept model. It functioned, but it wasn't the real thing.

"I will send my report to the Emperor," Tarkin said.
"Keep up the good work, Engineer Lemelisk."

The *Lambda* shuttle proceeded through the gridwork
of the Death Star and out the other side, then began a slow
orbit of the external construction. The focusing eye for the
superlaser gaped at them like a large meteorite crater. In
the piloting chair Ackbar remained silent. The alien didn't
seem terribly thrilled at the magnificence of this new
weapon.

Lemelisk smiled as the shuttle turned around and returned to the base. Everything was going so well. He felt
better than he had in years, watching his dreams come to
life.

Lemelisk presented the modified design to Durga the Hutt,
while General Sulamar brusquely inspected every step of
the process, looking over the engineer's shoulder. Lemelisk spoke as the general pressed in, squinting and scowling. He longed for an opportunity to "accidentally" jab
the general in the stomach with his elbow.

"As you know, the original design consisted of a giant sphere," Lemelisk said, "whose primary purpose was
to house the superlaser. All the framework, the decks, the
external shell also made it into a garrison for one of the
Empire's largest troop deployments."

On his floating pallet, Durga reached over to scoop a

dripping handful of some blue gelatinous substance from a bowl and slurped it up with his wide muscular lips and tongue. "Mmm hmm," he said, "we know all that."

Lemelisk said, "But *you* don't need all that wasted space. You don't require living space for a million crew members. You don't need TIE fighter hangars, support squadrons, dozens of docking ports—you just want the weapon itself."

Lemelisk's stomach growled. He wished he had eaten, though at least he had remembered to shave this time. He brushed the stubble on his chin . . . or was that yesterday? He blinked, then cleared his throat. On the holo projector, he called up his modified plans and pointed to the new shape.

"As you can see, I have scaled down the outer hull but increased power at the same time. In the original Death Star design, the superlaser formed the axis of the sphere. All the energy of the reactor core was devoted to powering each blast.

"Here, I have taken the superlaser itself"—the image projected the stalk of focusing lenses and high-energy multipliers—"and encased it in a *cylindrical* shell. Your new weapon will be the superlaser alone, surrounded by an armored hull, with appropriate navigational capabilities and a small outer ring of living quarters. Even with such reduced amenities, this vessel could hold hundreds of Hutts with their personal entourages."

"But where is the focusing eye for the laser?" Sulamar said, clasping his hands behind his back and leaning forward. Lemelisk saw an opportunity to nudge backward with his sharp elbow, but the general stepped sideways to look from a different perspective.

Lemelisk sighed and answered, "Note the end of the cylinder. I have moved the focusing eye so that the beam can come out the end directly, a straight shot through the long superlaser that allows us to achieve greater energy conversion. We can provide more power to our punch."

The plans sharpened to actual simulation of the completed weapon, a black armored cylinder rotating in space. As the animation began, the new weapon fired, and a brilliant beam shot from one end of the tube.

General Sulamar nodded. "That looks like one of those old Jedi weapons—the lightsaber," he said.

Lemelisk smiled, surprised that the pompous Imperial general had seen the connection. "Yes," he said, "now you understand why I have code named this weapon the *Darksaber Project*."

Durga chuckled with pleasure. "A good name, Engineer."

Sulamar stood stiffly, pondering the possibilities. The expression on his face tightened with anticipation. "With such a weapon we will be invincible." He smiled wolfishly at Durga. "We can collect protection money, taxes, whatever. We can hold entire systems hostage. No one will be able to stand against us."

Durga grinned with his huge lips and slurped another mouthful of the gooey blue gelatin. "We can become the overlords of the galaxy!"

Bevel Lemelisk switched off the animation and shut down the glowing plans. "Yes, Lord Durga—you probably can."

MULAKO CORPORATION PRIMORDIAL WATER QUARRY

CHAPTER 15

Hyperspace—en route to a destination Luke Skywalker fervently hoped would become a place of self-discovery, a time to recapture the inner sharing he had experienced with Callista.

He eased back in the piloting chair of the unmarked space yacht they had flown from Coruscant. He sighed with quiet contentment, happy just to be alone with Callista—no pressures, no worries, and no mission other than to find her Force ability again. He looked over at her in the seat beside him, and she gazed back with impenetrable gray eyes. Invisible doors had locked down, allowing him to see Callista only as others saw her, without the added clues and mysteries of the Force.

She smiled, and he wanted to kiss her. Her cropped blond hair showed streaks of a darker malty brown color that lent a wildness to her appearance.

"I've picked out a special place for us to go," Luke said. "A great spot. I think you'll like it."

Callista shrugged. "You're the Jedi Master. Lead me and I'll follow."

Luke raised his eyebrows. "That doesn't sound like the Callista I fell in love with."

She clasped his hand. "Then let's go find her and bring her back."

The ship flew through hyperspace on its automatic course. Luke got up from his seat and held out his hand. Callista stood beside him. She was tall, long-legged, and very attractive. Luke reached forward and tenderly cupped his palms around her cheeks, holding Callista's face in his hands as he looked deeply into her eyes.

She looked back, unblinking. "Are you trying to probe me with the Force?"

Luke shook his head slightly, not releasing her from his gaze. "No," he said. "I just wanted to look at you."

But the moment was broken. He took her hand and led her to the common area behind the pilot compartment. "Let's try a few things," he said, "some learning techniques that worked for the other Jedi trainees."

"But we've been through those already," Callista said in frustration.

"Not like this," he answered. "You're different from my other students—apart from the fact that I love you, of course," he added with a wry smile. "You've already been trained as a Jedi Knight. You know the techniques . . . you just can't use them anymore. But there is one thing you can still use."

"What?" Callista said, baffled as to what he planned.

He went to the rectangular wall compartment where he stowed his personal effects and withdrew two cylinders. He tossed one to Callista, and she deftly snatched it out of the air. "Let's try a little lightsaber fencing," he said. "It'll get you thinking and moving like a Jedi again. Maybe that'll be a start." He switched on his weapon, and the green energy blade extended.

Callista looked down at her own lightsaber, intimidated.

Luke smiled encouragingly. "Come on, I'm not asking you to deflect blaster bolts with your eyes closed.

Watch me, anticipate my moves. You don't have to use the Force—just use your eyes and your reflexes.''

Callista drew a deep breath. Her eyes flashed with determination, and she switched on her own weapon. The *snap-hiss* from both blades sizzled through the enclosed common area. Her lightsaber shone with the rich sun yellow of topaz, and she looked past her shimmering blade to Luke. ''You know this is dangerous,'' she said.

He crossed his blade with hers, testing, pressing lightsabers together with a crackle of released energy. His expression grew serious. ''I know it's dangerous, Callista—but we have to take that chance. We might stumble upon some clue to bring you back to us.''

He drew back, lifted his blade, and swung at her. She raised her lightsaber to parry, easing into the contest. ''These are deadly weapons,'' Luke said, ''but they're also fine tests of your skill.''

Callista struck back, and her face lit with an impish grin as she took the challenge. Luke had to move fast to counter her blows. He laughed and increased his offense. Callista matched him, move for move.

Fencing with Callista challenged Luke as well, because in any other foe, he could use the Force to sense emotional states, to detect subtle changes that foreshadowed impending moves, unexpected attacks, vicious tricks. But Callista was a disconcerting blank to him, an empty spot—which made her a worthy opponent. Although she could not sense his moves or his plans, he couldn't detect hers either.

They dueled, feeling their muscles sing with the effort, the unleashed energy and emotions, the joy of testing each other. Luke chuckled, and they continued, bright lights flashing, weapons hissing as he and Callista pressed each other. The mock battle went on for the better part of an hour.

Callista had an open, enthralled expression on her face, overjoyed to recapture some part of her former Jedi identity. She had not used a lightsaber since she had come back to life in this new body, and now—though Luke could sense no more of the Force touching her—she had regained an important piece of self-confidence.

Energy blades crossed, they looked into each other's eyes, pressing with all their strength, neither yielding. A complete stalemate. Sweat beaded on Luke's forehead, and he finally broke their locked gaze and stepped back, switching off his lightsaber. Callista also shut hers down.

Then, laughing, they came together and held each other for a long time.

Callista took her shift in the pilot seat as they both strapped in and watched the diagnostics. Luke kept glancing over at her. "We're about ready to leave hyperspace," he said.

She rubbed a fingertip along her chin. "I can't wait to see this mysterious place you're taking me."

The counter ran down on the navicomputer, and the swirling colors snapped into crystal focus, funneling down into bright starpoints on the black curtain of space. Nearby hung an orange sun of average size. Several bright planets cruised along their orbital paths in the gravity well.

"Over here," Luke said, pointing.

He watched Callista's expression as she noticed the swollen form of a periodic comet, its gases evaporating into space, shedding a coma and a long fuzzy tail as it approached the sun.

"A comet?" Callista said. "We're awfully close."

Luke nodded with a secretive smile. "Yes, Callista," he answered. "That's where we're going."

CHAPTER 16

As Callista watched him, her gray eyes bright with curiosity, Luke maneuvered the space yacht closer to the wandering comet. He entered the wispy coma where gas particles and ion trails scintillated against their shields, causing static over the comm system.

"This is the Mulako Corporation Primordial Water Quarry," Luke said. "A long-term periodic comet that comes back every century or so. Right now it's near its closest approach to the sun, and we're at high tourist season."

The space yacht approached the irregular lump swathed in a mane of frozen steam. Luke pointed out squarish machines crawling over the tarnished surface, strip-mining the ice. Gas geysers blasted volatiles into space where the comet's meager gravity could not hold them, trailing a tenuous tail along the comet's orbit.

"But what do they do here?" Callista asked. "I've never heard of this system."

"Hey, you've been stuck inside a computer for decades," Luke said.

"Don't remind me," Callista said.

"For much of the comet's orbit," he explained, "the mining corporation chops away water ice, storing and distilling it. They sell it at a premium to gourmets and high-class officials who like to show off that they settle for only the very best. This is absolutely pure water, formed at the creation of this solar system. Primordial ice, never before touched or recycled through organic life forms." Luke shrugged. "Of course, it's chemically identical to any other water, but they don't mention that in their advertisements."

"But why did you choose this place?" Callista said.

The Mulako Corporation Quarry sent a homing beacon, and Luke's guidance computer locked on, shepherding them toward a cavernous opening surrounded by lights—brilliant yellow alternating with deep purple, harsh red, and some that looked black—transmitted for customers whose eyes saw in different portions of the spectrum.

"Close to perihelion," Luke said, "the comet becomes one of the most exclusive resorts in this sector. The climate heats up, enough of the volatiles evaporate from the ice to form a breathable atmosphere, and people can live inside the snowball. It's very unusual. I thought you might like it—besides, no one will ever find us here."

Their yacht passed through the portal, beyond marker lights whose beams shone like lightsabers through the dense mist curling away from the comet's surface.

"The selling point of this resort is its transience. The Mulako Corporation mines it out each orbit as the comet hooks toward the sun and becomes habitable. They reinstall the facilities, open it to tourists for a few months, then close down again as the comet gets too close to the sun, where it becomes unstable with too much gas evaporating, new geysers erupting, even a small possiblity that the iceball will split apart from all the mining and tunneling. Then, when the comet races away from the sun and the gases begin to freeze out, there's another several-month period when the resort is dug out again and re-opened. When it finally becomes too cold, the quarry is closed to the public, and the mining company operates for the next hundred years out in deep space, strip-mining the newly deposited layers of ice.''

''I can't wait to see it.'' Callista reached over to clasp Luke's hand.

They landed in a warmly lit reception area. Oranges and yellows shone into the ever-present mist, and porter droids appeared to unload their luggage. Luke checked in, keying their reservations into an automated terminal, and the droids escorted them into the resort facility.

He and Callista held hands as they followed the baggage droids. Callista looked around, her cropped malt blond hair swaying slightly. She blinked at her surroundings and grinned. The Mulako Corporation's stylistic logo—the letters *MC* traced within circles with a long cometary tail shooting out—adorned most of the doors and fixtures.

The cometary resort was filled with water and amazing tropical caverns, far warmer than a ball of ice might have suggested. The frozen walls had been polymerized, showing ice locked behind a molecule-thin impenetrable layer and lit by soothing blue lights. Sections of the wall had been cleared away so that the frozen gases could drift out like humidifiers, sending trails of mist along the floor. Droplets of ultraclean water dribbled along the walls like precious springs. Waterfalls hissed from the ceilings in a diamond curtain that gurgled softly into drains in the floor.

Callista's face filled with childish wonder. ''This is beautiful, Luke. All the water. I love the water.''

''I know,'' Luke said. ''You've told me enough stories about how much you miss your home planet, Chad.''

Callista looked wistful. She had grown up on a waterworld, living with her father and stepmother on a sea ranch, destined to follow in the family business. But her Jedi calling had been stronger, and she had been forced to leave her beautiful oceans . . . though she still longed for them.

The porter droids led them down gently curving corridors, past doorways of plush suites, until they came to the set of rooms Luke had reserved. Multicolored glowlamps reflected off the polymerized ice walls, making it seem as if they walked through a rainbow caught in crystal.

Delighted, Callista stopped to kiss Luke. "This is so wonderful," she said. "I can feel the power in this place, the energy. I know we'll be able to do something here!"

Inside their spacious suite, fountains bubbled in the corners; mists drifted around the rooms, passing glowing heaters that made the multiple chambers comfortable and homey. The furniture was oddly shaped and of varying sizes, carved from rock inclusions that had been found inside the cometary ice crust, now bearing the ubiquitous company logo. The porter droids deposited their packs, and played prerecorded advertisements for the various restaurants and lounges available at the luxurious MC Quarry.

Luke hustled the droids out of the suite before they could begin a droning recitation of sightseeing opportunities. He shut the door and turned to Callista with a smile and a sigh. "We're here," he said. He slumped down onto a polished stone contour sofa. Callista joined him.

"According to the brochures, there's plenty of things to do here," Luke said. "We could explore the tunnels, or suit up and go out to the surface. The low gravity makes it fun to jump around," he said. "Or we could see one of the erupting gas geysers. Those are supposed to be quite spectacular."

She shook her head. "I just want to stay here with you, Luke. We can relax and talk . . . and just be alone for a while."

He closed his eyes and realized how wonderful that sounded. "You won't get any argument from me."

Callista stared into the foaming fountain; her eyes took on a fixed, faraway look. Luke knew she must be focusing her thoughts, though he still could not sense her, as if the Force itself didn't know she existed.

"I'm thinking of the oceans on Chad," she said, not looking at Luke but fully aware he was watching her. "Especially at night at highest tide, when all the moons are full in the sky at the same time. The wander-kelp we kept corralled in mating season would begin to shimmer with captured phosphorus, glowing like an oil slick on fire."

"What are wander-kelp?" Luke asked.

"We used to raise them at our sea ranch," Callista said. "It's sort of halfway between plant and animal—really stupid, but it moves under its own volition. A big mass of iodine-filled leaves that we could shear several times a year, distill, and sell for their medicinal content, while using the rest of the biomass as cheap protein fiber for animal feed.

"Times were tough. It's not that the market went bad, but the Emperor's crackdown fouled up the trade routes. All the tariffs and impossible regulations pushed our regular traders out of business. Sometimes we had to cook and eat the barnacles growing beneath our corral rafts. Of course, my family is all dead now . . . years ago, while I was trapped in that computer."

Her lower lip began to tremble, and she fixedly refused to look at Luke. She clamped her lips together. "Part of me feels guilty for not staying with them—but I carried that around all the years I was a Jedi. I don't have any regrets, just sadness."

Now she turned and looked at Luke. Her eyes were dry and strong. "But my Jedi Master, Djinn Altis, came and showed me the Jedi way. He arrived on his big wandering ship the *Chu'unthor,* a ship with no destination, much like your own *praxeum* on Yavin 4."

"I know," Luke said. "We found the crashed and buried *Chu'unthor* on Dathomir and brought it back."

Callista sighed soberly. "I suppose I must have known Djinn Altis was dead. Perhaps he ran afoul of the Nightsisters." Her eyebrows knitted together. "I remember once when Master Altis took me on a long, low flight above the seas of Chad. We cruised over singing schools of cyeen and the patterns of tubular eels glowing pink in the moonlight. Master Altis taught me how to sense the life forms with my new abilities. I didn't believe him at first, but when he showed me how easy it was, I knew I was a Jedi. He didn't need to convince me. It was my family that required convincing—and I don't think I quite succeeded in that.''

Luke stood up and went to a pitted black table and pulled out a small disc, a blue chit that gave them a meal discount in one of the Mulako Corporation's fine restaurants.

"Let's try something," he said. Luke let his eyes fall half closed, channeling his thoughts through the Force in a simple exercise. The small chit lifted from the palm of his hand and hung suspended in the air. "I'm going to hold this up," he said. "You try to nudge it. Bump it toward me. That should be easier than actually lifting it. Open yourself to the Force and let it flow. Just a slight push."

"I'll try," Callista said doubtfully—then caught herself as Luke replied.

"There is no try."

She answered, "I know, I know. I shouldn't have said that." Callista squeezed her eyes shut and concentrated. Her breathing grew shallow, her expression tighter, more compressed.

Luke sent out small, questing tendrils to see if he could detect her manipulating the Force. The blue disc hovered motionless in the air.

Callista's face became flushed with the effort, and finally she let out a shuddering breath and opened her eyes, her forehead creased with frustration. "I can't. There's nothing." Before Luke could speak, she held up a hand. "Please don't lecture me. Not now. You don't need to train me. I know *how* to do it—but I can't."

Luke squeezed her hand instead. "Don't lose hope, Callista," he said. "Please don't lose hope."

* * *

Later that evening, Luke sipped on a glass of primordial ice water distilled from the comet's reservoirs. Beaded droplets clustered on the outside of the glass. He looked at the mist rising along the floors and breathed the damp air, filling his lungs and savoring the sensation. "This is so different from the place I grew up."

Callista snuggled next to him in one of the oversized seats. "Tell me about it," she said. "I want to know everything about you."

Luke let bittersweet memories flow back to him. "I once said that if there was a bright center to the universe, Tatooine was the place it was farthest from." He shook his head. "A dry, hot place—a hopeless place. Anybody born there was likely to die there, going nowhere. My Uncle Owen and Aunt Beru were moisture farmers, hardworking, closed-minded people. They knew the truth about my father, told me lies, hoping against hope that I wouldn't follow in his footsteps, that I wouldn't want to pursue a dangerous and glorious life as a Jedi Knight. They wanted me to stay home where I would be safe . . . and completely uninvolved. They loved me deeply in their own way—but when you feel the calling of the Jedi, there's no denying it."

"I know," Callista murmured, resting her head against his shoulder.

"When Obi-Wan Kenobi began to train me," Luke said, "I didn't know how I was going to tell Uncle Owen and Aunt Beru." He swallowed and felt his expression harden. "I never had the chance, though. The Empire killed them and burned their farm before I could get back. They would have killed me, too, if I'd been there."

Callista brushed his arm with her fingertips, radiating a quiet warmth.

"Now Biggs is dead too," Luke said. "Biggs Darklighter, the only one of my friends who actually escaped Tatooine. He went to the Imperial academy for a while, then joined the Rebel Alliance. I met up with him again at our base on Yavin 4, though I didn't get much chance to talk with him. Biggs was my wingman when we flew against the Death Star. He saved me, but he died in the battle.''

"Was he your only friend there?" Callista said.

Luke stuck his finger into the fountain, letting the cool water trickle down his hand. "I had two other close companions, Camie and Fixer. We used to hang out at Tosche Station and talk about our dreams and how we were going to get off that dustball. Camie's family grew hydroponic gardens underground and bought water from my uncle. Uncle Owen always said we were just wasting time, but we were exercising our imagination, thinking of things we *could* do—even if we never would. It kept us from going insane on that hopeless planet."

He sighed. "I wonder if Camie and Fixer are still there. My life seemed like it was going nowhere," Luke whispered, "and now I'm a Jedi Master. I've found a twin sister I didn't know I had, and she's the Chief of State. The Empire is defeated, and I'm reestablishing the Jedi Knights." He gave a little laugh. "A lot has changed."

He smiled down at Callista and stroked her hair. She had fallen asleep in his arms.

KHOMM

CHAPTER 17

As Dorsk 81 piloted them to the main spaceport on Khomm, Kyp Durron stared out at the amazingly perfect gridwork of cities.

Dorsk 81 fidgeted at the control panel, looking anxious as he brought their craft in. A few other vessels sat parked in marked-off rectangles, out-system traders coming to the clone planet to offer their wares. The inhabitants of Khomm rarely left their world, preferring to stay at home and do what they had always done.

Dorsk 81's olive green skin flushed a deeper hue. "It feels good to be back," he said. "I was untrained when I left, but now I can trace what my senses told me as I grew up. I feel the calming influence of this place, the comfortable familiarity. After all the difficult decisions I've faced at the *praxeum,* I want to sink back into the pool of my own people, absorbing their warmth and welcome. You'll sense it too, Kyp."

Kyp nodded, masking his skepticism. "I can already feel a low-level . . . muffled sensation."

Dorsk 81 nodded his streamlined head and innocently blinked his bright eyes. "Yes, yes, that's it."

When they opened the access hatch, Kyp was amazed to see that a crowd had been shuttled in from the tall buildings. He looked at the hundreds of smooth-skinned clones gathered to welcome them. They applauded when Dorsk 81 stepped into the hazy sunlight and raised his right arm in greeting.

Kyp stood beside his friend and whispered, "Why so many? This is amazing."

Beaming, Dorsk 81 answered, "I am famous here, now that I'm a Jedi Knight." He cast a sheepish glance at Kyp. "I'm the only person in Khomm's recent memory who has done anything . . . unpredictable."

Kyp stifled a laugh, knowing that Dorsk 81 was not joking. He watched as one of the cloned aliens came forward on a levitating raft encircled by handrails. The placid-faced alien piloting it wore some sort of uniform with insignia on the shoulders.

Dorsk 81 was impressed. "That must be our city leader, Kaell 115. I've never seen him this close before. He's been our leader for decades. It's in his genetic line." But when the standing platform drifted in front of them, Kyp saw that the uniformed alien had a childlike roundness to his face that did not speak of many years wearing the burdens of leadership.

He raised his right hand in greeting, as Dorsk 81 had done. "I am Kaell 116," he said, "the new leader of this city. Welcome, Dorsk 81! We are proud to have such an impressive personage return to us." He gestured toward the open platform. "Please allow me to escort you to your domicile."

The city leader gave Kyp a stiff greeting. They climbed aboard, and the levitating platform drifted just over the heads of the crowd. The olive-skinned aliens waved in unison, giving Dorsk 81 a hero's welcome.

Kaell 116 cruised away from the spaceport toward the identical blocks of city buildings. Trees lined every street, pruned to look exactly the same. Lawns of purple and blue grass were carefully manicured in front of each building. The air held a dusty, mineral undertone that spoke of lifelessness.

The structures were squarish monstrosities made of polished green-veined rock, bordered with a rough sandstone. The outer walls bore no decorations, no sculptures or window boxes, merely a number engraved in each cornerstone at street level.

"How do you find your way around?" Kyp said. "Everything looks the same."

Kaell 116 seemed to take this as a criticism, and his face grew pinched. "We have molded our city to be the way we want it, and we've maintained it that way. Everything is numbered and cataloged, and Khomm is a stable, understandable place. Our citizens are happy and content here."

"I see," Kyp said, forcing a smile. His dark eyes flashed toward Dorsk 81, who looked so pleased to be back home.

As the standing platform drifted by, other aliens leaned out the windows to wave at them. Finally, Kaell 116 lowered them to the ground in front of one building that looked like all the others. The city leader dropped them off with a perfunctory farewell.

Dorsk 81 rushed to the building unabashedly, gazing up at the stone edifice as if he had never seen anything like it before. "This is my home!" he said. Kyp followed as the cloned alien fairly ran up three flights of stairs to his personal abode.

The well-lit corridor was lined with a dizzying succession of identical doors, like myriad images reflected from nested mirrors. One of the doors popped open as Dorsk 81 hurried toward it.

Two figures emerged, wearing grins on their smooth faces; for a moment Kyp felt as if he had seen a vortex of alternate timelines, images of an identical person at different stages of life. They both looked like Dorsk 81, one older and more weathered, one younger and slightly smaller.

All three embraced and talked quickly in low voices. Kyp stepped back, feeling as if he didn't belong there—but he didn't mind. He observed with a pang of homesickness, thinking fondly of when he and his parents and his brother, Zeth, had spent warm times together on his own world of Deyer: the floating fishing platforms, the quiet lake sunsets . . . but the Empire had crushed that place, and Kyp hadn't seen it since his childhood.

After the brief and intense welcome, Dorsk 81 gestured for Kyp to follow him inside. "This is my friend Kyp Durron, another Jedi Knight. This"—he turned to the older image of himself—"is Dorsk 80, my predecessor, and here," he clasped the shoulder of the younger clone, "is Dorsk 82, my successor."

Kyp felt disoriented by the genetically identical copies, but he had seen many strange things in the galaxy. He glanced around where the Dorsk family lived, saw adequate furnishings and all the expected rooms. "Do any of you have wives?" he asked, seeing no one else.

All three clones blinked at him, and finally Dorsk 81 gave a short laugh. The skin on his forehead wrinkled. "Kyp, no one has wives. Everyone on Khomm is genderless. That's why we use the cloning facilities. We haven't had genders on this planet for thousands of years."

Kyp chuckled in embarrassment. "Well, I just assumed . . . uh, obviously I was wrong."

"We all make mistakes," the elder Dorsk 80 said with a quick, meaningful frown in the direction of Dorsk 81. Kyp noticed, but his friend pretended not to.

Later, Dorsk 81 helped make up a bed in their small extra room, and Kyp used the moment of privacy to ask a question that had been bothering him.

"Dorsk 81," he said. "Now that I've seen how . . ." he searched for the right word, "how *stable* and unchanging your world is, I don't understand how you're going to be a Jedi watchman. What are you going to *do* here?"

Dorsk 81's yellow eyes suddenly filled with panic. "I don't know!" he whispered, his voice hoarse. "I don't know . . ." He repeated the words to himself, then he left Kyp alone, fleeing back into the outer rooms.

Kyp could not sleep for some time. He looked out the window into a night that glowed with a billion bright stars. Khomm was close to the galactic nucleus, near the dreaded Core Systems where the survivors of the Empire had gone into hiding. The stars made a blurry island in space, a lens that spilled across half the sky.

Kyp stared toward the Core Systems, fearing what they might hide, but also yearning to know.

Young Dorsk 82 spent the next morning showing off his work in the clone banks. The cloning facility was taller than the other buildings and of a different design: the only unusual structure Kyp had seen in the gridwork of the metropolis. Rather than the ubiquitous green-veined stone, the outer walls were immense rectangular sheets of transparent crystal, interlocked with chrome girders that reflected the hazy sunlight. The crystal windows were so clear that Kyp could look in from street level and see the carefully organized activity inside.

"We have maintained everything exactly as it was when you left it," Dorsk 82 said, beaming up at his "father." Inside, the air was damp and laden with a medley of chemical and organic smells that were not so much unpleasant as exotic and unusual. Dorsk 80 accompanied them like a stern schoolmaster, nodding in pride at his protégé Dorsk 82 and looking from side to side, touching controls and inspecting them as they passed.

"I didn't know this was the work you did before," Kyp said to Dorsk 81.

His friend nodded. "Yes, the computer database holds genetic blueprints of all the major family lines. When it is time to produce the next offspring, we call up the DNA strings and produce another copy of the preferred stock."

"Each clone is *usually* the same," Dorsk 80 interrupted. Kyp knew that Dorsk 81 was an anomaly, Force-sensitive against all odds, when he should have been identical to all previous incarnations of his clone pattern; but something inexplicable had changed.

Metal incubators lined row after row in banks carefully numbered and monitored where embryos were grown past the infant stage and accelerated to near adolescence, whereupon they were released and raised by their family units, trained in the duties of their genetic string.

The hissing of moving fluids, the whisper of mist generators, and the clicking of computer operators made the cloning facility a constant hive of activity, but tension grew around Dorsk 81 like a blanket of silence.

Dorsk 82 proudly led them to his own station. Flat terminal screens displayed the status of thousands of the embryo tanks. "Here is where you used to sit," Dorsk 82 said. "Everything remains fully functional, and I have followed in our family's footsteps—but now that you have returned, I gladly relinquish my position to you, so that I may continue my training and one day become your true successor."

Dorsk 81 blanched. "But that isn't why I came back. You don't understand." He looked to Kyp for support. "Continue in your duties at the cloning facility, Dorsk 82. I don't intend to take them again."

The younger clone blinked, uncomprehending. "But you must!"

Dorsk 80's face darkened. "You are my successor, Dorsk 81. You have always known your place."

Dorsk 81 whirled to look at his elder. "No. I am a Jedi Knight, and I must find my place—my *new* place."

Kyp yearned to help his friend, to support him. But this was a personal debate, and he would only hurt things if he interfered.

Dorsk 80 looked at him sternly. "You have no choice in the matter."

"Yes," Dorsk 81 said, his face filled with anguish. "Yes I *do* have a choice. That's what you don't understand." Dorsk 81's tear-filled eyes flicked back and forth to his younger and older versions. As Kyp watched, the expressions on all three faces were enough to break his heart.

Dorsk 81's family brooded for the rest of the day, shunning him. Looking wretched, the cloned alien came to Kyp, who had retreated to the guest room. He felt so sorry for his friend; he could see from the stagnant life on Khomm that the others could not comprehend who Dorsk 81 was or what he had done.

Dorsk 81 sat beside Kyp. His yellow eyes were very expressive, but it took him a long moment to gather the courage to speak. "I don't dare stay here," he said. "Even if I try to be strong, I know that if I live on this world, in this city, with my family members . . . I will eventually give in. I'll forget what it was to be a Jedi. I will fail in my vow to Master Skywalker. It'll all wash away, and my life will vanish as a minor deviation in the history of Khomm.

"What am I to do now? It all seemed so clear to me when I became a Jedi. I was going to return to Khomm and be the guardian of this system. But this system does not need—or want—a Jedi Knight to guard them. Now what mission do I have?"

Kyp gripped Dorsk 81's arm, feeling his heart pound. "You can come with me," he said. "I want you to."

Dorsk 81's smooth face became an open window through which hope streamed like sunlight.

Kyp's eyes narrowed, then he felt a glimmer of the old vendetta against the Empire. "We'll take our ship and slip in to the uncharted Core Systems," he said. "You and I together must discover what's become of the Empire."

CHAPTER 18

Daala dropped the *Firestorm*'s shields just enough to let Vice Admiral Pellaeon's shuttle approach her Star Destroyer. The self-destruct countdown continued toward zero like an avalanche of diminishing numbers.

Daala studied her bridge crew grimly. She pitied them, yet admired their stoic demeanor. She respected Pellaeon's cool, unshakable bravery—or perhaps his recklessness—for approaching a ship that would likely detonate in his face.

She turned to the comm officer. "Have you been advising Supreme Warlord Harrsk on the status of our self-destruct countdown?"

Pasty-faced, the comm officer swallowed. "Yes, Admiral, but I've received no response."

"A pity," Daala said blandly. "I hope he doesn't think I'm bluffing."

"I've assured him you're not, Admiral," the comm officer said, then looked away, his lips pushed together in a pale bloodless line.

"Time remaining?" Daala asked.

"Seven minutes."

"Vice Admiral Pellaeon has just docked in the shuttle bay," the tactical officer interrupted.

She stood firm at the control station, arms clasped behind her back. The crimson *Victory*-class warships surrounded Harrsk's fleet like a pack of hungry predators. Daala didn't quite understand what Pellaeon was doing, but the fact that so many of his battlecruisers followed his seemingly suicidal orders gave her great confidence in the vice admiral's leadership ability.

"Escort him here immediately," she said. "An honor guard of stormtroopers. Make sure he understands he's not being held captive. Treat him as a respected negotiator."

"Is there time, Admiral?" the deck chief said. "Only six minutes remaining."

"Then they'll need to run, won't they? We must be optimists," she said, her lips twisting in a bitter smile. "Though optimism is difficult in the face of juveniles like Harrsk and Teradoc."

By the time the honor guard arrived on the Star Destroyer's bridge, only one minute forty-five seconds remained on the clock.

Six stormtroopers marched in briskly, hustling a trim, mature man with a heavy mustache and neat gray hair. His eyes looked shrewd and bright, his body wiry and flexible.

"Vice Admiral Pellaeon, I presume," Daala said in a calm voice. "I'm pleased you could join me here at the moment of our death."

Pellaeon swallowed. "Admiral Daala. I've heard much about you, and I'm aware of the determination and dedication you have already demonstrated. I doubt you are bluffing. I wish Warlord Harrsk were similarly convinced, however."

"One minute, Admiral!" The officer's voice was a strangled squawk.

"Is our log pod prepared for jettison?" Daala said. "If nothing else, perhaps our desperate act will make the other warlords aware of their folly."

Before the comm officer could answer, Warlord Harrsk's grainy image appeared. "All right! Stop, stop! Cease the countdown. I order all hostilities to end immediately. Daala, damn you—stop the self-destruct!"

The deck chief froze. The bridge crew let out a collective sigh of relief. Pellaeon watched her, eyebrows raised.

Daala remained standing at the station, not moving to negate her commands, though her heart thudded with triumph. She paused just a moment longer as the countdown reached the thirty-second point. She arranged her expression into a mask of subdued disappointment, just to convince those watching that she had genuinely intended to blow up the *Firestorm*—and the *Whirlwind* with it—if her demands had not been met.

"Admiral," Pellaeon said in a careful, yet persuasive tone, "I would greatly prefer to negotiate with you . . . if you have the time." His voice was soft but intelligent.

Daala reached out casually to flick the PAUSE on the self-destruct countdown. "Very well, Vice Admiral. I prefer alternate solutions myself."

From memory, she rattled off a string of coordinates to the navigator. "We'll take the *Firestorm* to an isolated area for a private conference. However, to dispel any impression that we might be kidnapping you, Vice Admiral Pellaeon, I invite two of your *Victory*-class ships to accompany us."

She looked at him, eyebrows raised questioningly. "I think it's better to be away from any possible treachery from Teradoc or Harrsk. I don't trust either of them not to take advantage of the present situation."

"I agree, Admiral," Pellaeon said with a curt nod. The crows' feet around his eyes wrinkled, and Daala felt deep down that this man's ultimate goal for the Empire just might match her own. "If you would permit me to use your comm system, I will encode the appropriate orders to my flagship and a companion ship."

Daala turned to her helmsman. "When the navicom-

puter has calculated the best hyperspace path, drop shields
and proceed to our destination. Two *Victory*-class Star Destroyers will follow us.''

"But, Admiral—" the second in command said,
"that would leave the *Whirlwind* helpless and surrounded
by High Admiral Teradoc's warships. After your ion cannon blast—"

"I believe Teradoc will be reluctant to open fire. But
if I'm wrong . . ." She glanced down at the chronometer.
"According to my estimate, the *Whirlwind* has had sufficient time to complete repairs. In fact, Harrsk has already
had an additional six minutes. If I have misinterpreted Teradoc's actions, and if I have overestimated the crew of the
Whirlwind—then I will extend apologies later," she said,
but her grin was smug and laissez-faire.

"It's agreed, Admiral," Pellaeon said from the
comm station. "Two of my ships are ready to follow." He
bowed his head. "We're trusting that you won't lead us
into an ambush."

Daala nodded, trying to stand even more rigidly than
Pellaeon. "I understand the risk you're taking, Vice Admiral—but, believe me, I wouldn't go to such lengths just to
eliminate two small Star Destroyers. Warlord Harrsk's
fleet could have done that just as easily."

The *Firestorm*'s shields faded, leaving Harrsk's helpless Star Destroyer hanging dark in space.

Flanked by two crimson Victory ships, Daala's *Firestorm* rose up and out of the ring plane, cutting across the
debris that hung like a sparkling necklace around the lavender gas planet. The trio of ships shot into hyperspace.

Three Star Destroyers, one large and two small, hung in a
wasteland of space. The nearest star glowed dimly twelve
parsecs distant. A diffuse molecular cloud spread its cold
veil across the emptiness. Daala had discovered this stellar
desert while she and her crippled ship *Gorgon* struggled

back to the Empire after the devastating battle for Maw
Installation.

Pellaeon sat across from Daala in her private ready-
room adjoining the bridge. He sipped a cool drink, obviously trying not to succumb to comfort or social talk.
Daala appreciated that. She peeled off her black gloves,
straightened her flaming hair, and folded her hands on the
table in front of her. She leaned across so she could look
into his eyes.

"Vice Admiral Pellaeon," she said, "believe me
when I tell you, I intend no mutiny against the rightful
heirs to the Empire. I have no interest in becoming a great
leader like your Grand Admiral Thrawn. I have read of his
exploits, and I cannot replace him. I resent any attempts to
compare me with him. We are different people with different short-term goals—but I believe his long-term hopes
were the same as mine."

"And what are those hopes, Admiral?" Pellaeon
asked, as if he wanted to believe her, *needed* to believe
her—yet felt compelled to ask the question.

She nodded slowly. "I continue to bear great love for
the *ideal* of the Empire. The galaxy was so much more
orderly. Lawlessness did not run rampant. Citizens were
not confused as to their place. The Emperor gave them a
destiny. The Rebels have destroyed that and supplied nothing to fill the vacuum. They talk, they pamper, they go
through the motions, but they have yet to display any genuine leadership. Is *this* the only alternative for those of us
who served the Emperor? I don't think so.

"On the other hand, I disdain what these puffed-up,
self-appointed warlords have inflicted upon our fighting
forces. Yes, the Empire has suffered many defeats in the
past eight years, but we should not let those losses convince us that the Empire no longer has a significant fighting force. That is absurd. If we pooled all available ships,
our military would at least be comparable to the
hodgepodge fleet the Rebels have managed to assemble."

Pellaeon nodded, carefully sipping his drink again.

"But these squabbling children have caused as much damage to the Empire as the Rebel Alliance has," Daala continued. "If they would work together, decide on a leader among themselves, then we could strike back."

"I couldn't agree more, Admiral," Pellaeon said. "But how to accomplish that? Your strong-arm tactics may have caught Harrsk and Teradoc by surprise, but the others won't crumple so easily."

Daala ran her fingertip across the rim of her glass, and Pellaeon watched her. She looked out the window at the empty blackness, devoid of stars. "I don't for a moment think that Teradoc or Harrsk have surrendered. They are plotting ways to destroy me—and destroy you as well, since you have joined me for this conversation. No, they must be made to see."

Her face took on a wistful look as she turned from the window and stared at the wall and into her past. She muttered, "I was trained at the Imperial military academy on Carida. Because I was a woman, I was not allowed to advance along with my classmates, though I had the same, if not greater, capabilities.

"I excelled in the academy's exercises. I emerged at the top of my class in every case, and yet inferiors continued to be promoted above me. I was stuck in backwater assignments, forced to do menial labor. While those I had trounced in simulated combat rose up to take command of their own ships, I became a computer clerk, and then a galley overseer preparing packaged food for shipment on Star Destroyer fleets.

"I put up with all that," she said, drumming her fingertips on the table, "because I was an Imperial soldier, and we are trained to obey orders—yet I felt that I would let the Empire down if I allowed my short-sighted superiors ignore the things I could do. The Emperor's personal distaste for women and nonhuman species is one of the few things I disagree with."

"Grand Admiral Thrawn was an alien," Pellaeon said.

"Yes," Daala said, "and according to the records I've seen, the Emperor exiled him to the Unknown Territories, though Thrawn was perhaps one of the best military commanders in the fleet."

Pellaeon nodded. "I see your point. I was overjoyed when he returned and I finally found a commander I could follow with a genuine hope of victory, rather than an endless string of defeats."

Pellaeon finished his drink and set the empty glass on the table; he did not request another. "So what did you do?" he asked. "How did you gain your rank of Admiral?"

"I created a false identity for myself," Daala said. "I played simulations remotely on the Caridan computer networks. I defeated the best opponents, over and over again. Some of my tactics were true breakthroughs, variations on the zero-gravity fighting routines and space maneuvers developed by General Dodonna himself. All ships in the Imperial Navy were given copies of my battles to study. Space warfare changed because of the intuitive leaps I had made—all under a fake name, of course.

"My skills came to the attention of Moff Tarkin, who journeyed to Carida so that he could meet the mysterious individual who had developed such innovative tactics. It took him several months and two black-market slicers to dig me out of my network hiding place. Tarkin was astonished to learn I was a woman and even more astonished to see that I was a lowly corporal working in the kitchen.

"The officials on Carida were outraged, terribly embarrassed that their star tactician turned out to be someone they had buried—but when Tarkin realized that, instead of rewarding me for my exceptional intuition, the Caridan officials intended to assign me to a lonely meteorological station on the south polar ice cap, he transferred me to his own personal staff, promoted me to Admiral, and took me away from Carida."

She smiled with a memory she had not allowed for some time. "Once, he overheard a young lieutenant mutter that I had achieved my rank only because I was sleeping with Tarkin." Daala sighed. "Why is it every time a competent woman is rewarded, others assume it's only because she's having sex with a man?"

Pellaeon didn't answer her, not that she expected him to.

"Tarkin arrested the lieutenant," she said, "placed him in an environment suit with a day's worth of air in a low orbit. We both ran the calculations and estimated that he would make about twenty orbits before he dropped deep enough into the atmosphere to burn up. Neither of us knew whether his air would run out first, or if he would be incinerated. Either circumstance provided a fine punishment, a gruesome example for Moff Tarkin's crew to see. It was particularly effective that he left the lieutenant's comm system open, so that for a full day everyone aboard could hear his words over the ship's intercom, pleading, cursing, screaming. . . ."

Daala finished her own drink and placed the empty glass beside Pellaeon's. "After that time, no one ever suggested I had received my rank only because Tarkin was my lover."

Pellaeon paled, but made no comment.

"But I'm digressing," Daala said. "You and I should come to some sort of decision and get back before our respective fleets grow too impatient."

"Agreed, Admiral. What is it that you wish to accomplish?"

"I want to unify the Empire," Daala said simply. "I want someone to take the helm as leader—but I don't intend for it to be me. I have no delusions of political glory. I just want the opportunity to cause as much damage as possible to the Rebels."

"Why not call a détente council, then?" Pellaeon said. "Perhaps we could get the warlords together, make them sit down and talk. Even if they refuse to be united under a single leader, perhaps they could agree on strategy. Each could strike different targets in the New Republic, using their own tactics and their own methods to bring the Rebels to their knees. Then we can mop up the territory that's rightfully ours.'' His eyes glittered with excitement as the ideas flowed from him.

Daala nodded. ''An exceptionally good suggestion, Vice Admiral. Similar to my own ideas. You are perhaps in a better position to make those invitations, though I will do what I can. However,'' she said, going to a cyberlocked strongbox beside her personal bureau, ''if that doesn't work, I want you to take this.'' She opened the strongbox and withdrew a palm-size breathmask membrane, which she handed to Pellaeon.

''What is it for?'' Pellaeon said.

''I hope you never need to use it,'' Daala answered. ''But if all else fails, you will know.''

CHAPTER 19

Tsoss Beacon transmitted its blind signal into the fiery soup of stars and gases near the heart of the deep core. The automated station had been constructed by droids and suicide crews on a planetoid scoured clean by an endless wash of radioactive storms and solar flares that swept the region. No living thing had visited Tsoss Beacon for fifteen years, and the ionized flux had long since caused most of the maintenance droids to malfunction.

Admiral Daala considered it the perfect place to hold a meeting of Imperial warlords.

The squarish beacon station was a squat citadel with low walls more than a meter thick to block the radiation. Before sending her own Star Destroyer into the hostile region, Daala had dispatched a Gamma assault shuttle crewed by worker droids who set down and began the major overhaul chores, following programming and specifications that Daala herself had developed.

When the worker droids completed the groundwork and installed high-efficiency radiation-shield generators, Daala brought the *Firestorm* into the ravening system, where hot gas swirled around them and shockwaves from stellar storms scrambled her sensors. It reminded Daala of her hiding place in the Cauldron Nebula when she had been isolated from the Empire, with only a pitifully small fleet to attack the Rebels. If the Imperials could pool their resources now . . .

Once her ship was in place around Tsoss Beacon, Daala sent a crew of stormtroopers down to complete the preparations, accompanying them herself to oversee the efforts. She chose one of the station's main storerooms to host the détente meeting. Worker droids had already completed significant structural changes to the room, which had no windows, no exits except for the single door equipped with a thick shielded lock.

It would be perfect.

A crew of stormtroopers removed the decommissioned equipment and forgotten supplies that had been used to construct the beacon. The machinery was outdated and alive with secondary radiation. The armored troopers dumped it all out on the rocky surface.

Daala stood in her olive-gray uniform, coppery hair falling loose behind her, black-gloved hands clasped behind her back as she watched everything. She tried to appear both intimidating and compassionate—though the compassion part was difficult.

She watched Harrsk's former soldiers and saw that some remained uneasy at what they perceived to be her mutiny, though most had been converted to Daala's cause. They were Imperial soldiers trained to follow their leader; she was not surprised to discover that the *majority* of her troops had despised their service under Harrsk and secretly applauded her actions. These had all learned to respect the ideal of the Empire, and Daala offered a return to that; Harrsk promised only a continuance of civil war.

Pellaeon's *Victory*-class ships arrived a day after Daala had completed preparations. As stormtroopers ushered the Vice Admiral in to see her, she felt an icy dread in the pit of her stomach. All would be lost if he had not succeeded in his mission—but she could tell from the faint smile on his lean face and the brightness in his eyes that it hadn't been a failure after all.

"Mission accomplished, Admiral," he said, standing straight and looking directly at her. "Thirteen of the strongest Imperial warlords will arrive for these talks." His smile sagged a little, causing his mustache to droop. "It was not easy to convince them. I had to use every tactic I could think of, banking fully on your legendary reputation and my association with Grand Admiral Thrawn. This uses up all of the influence we had." He lowered his voice, aware that his words might be construed as disrespectful. "You'd better make it work, Admiral. We won't get a second chance."

Daala tugged her black gloves onto her hands. "I understand, Vice Admiral," she said. "I have no intention of failing."

Pellaeon's smile turned grim. "If I didn't believe that, I wouldn't be here with you."

The warlords arrived with their fleets bristling with weapons—and Daala knew that the slightest misstep could trigger an internecine holocaust that would wipe out the remains of the Imperial military. She shook her head in resignation, her face tight and drawn . . . then realized that if such was to be the fate of the Empire, better that it ended here, rather than through a long and dishonorable attrition.

She contacted each fleet as it came in. "Only the warlord is allowed to approach. All armed forces are denied access to this sector."

The warlords argued, insisting on their personal escorts, their guards, their protective battleships. But Daala refused each one. "No. No one will carry weapons to this meeting. No one will be allowed to position his forces for a secret attack. This is a political negotiation regarding the fate of the Empire. There is no need for demonstrations of bluster or bravado.''

The talks were delayed two days in the miserable fury around Tsoss Beacon, until finally the last of the fleets backed off. Daala was convinced they departed no farther than the edge of the system, out of range of her station's scrambled sensors—but it was good enough for her purposes. It would give her sufficient time to deal with a crisis, if one occurred.

Inside the shielded supply room, Daala waited at the head of the long table she had installed for the express purpose of the détente meeting. The table was irregularly shaped, with rounded corners and a looping perimeter intended to dismiss any subtle hierarchy in seating order. The gathered warlords were all equal as far as Daala was concerned: equally pompous fools. But she needed to foster an impression of fairness and impartiality, if they were ever to begin open negotiations.

Without windows the place seemed like a dungeon, so Daala had added electric-blue illumination crystals around the room to shed a soothing cool glow from shoulder-high metal staffs, high-tech torches reflecting off the dull gray walls. Outside the door, scarlet-robed Imperial Guards stood ominously silent, heightening the aura of command in her presence.

Daala sat back in her uncomfortable chair; she prefered rigid furniture because it kept her attention focused. She took several deep breaths, collecting her thoughts, gathering her stamina for what she knew would be a dreadfully difficult meeting. Daala despised meetings, preferring instead to make unilateral decisions and follow through on them—but that wouldn't work in this case. At least not yet. She had to give the warlords a chance.

Pellaeon stood to one side of the door as an honor guard. High Admiral Teradoc was the first to pass through the doorway, fat and sweaty-faced, staggering even in the low gravity. His beady eyes were filled with seething hatred as he flicked a venomous glance at Pellaeon. With an out-thrust lower lip, Teradoc took the nearest chair to minimize the distance he had to walk. He placed himself equally distant between Pellaeon, whom he considered a traitor, and Daala—who, as an interloper, was probably worse.

After him came Supreme Warlord Harrsk, the little man with the hideously scarred face. Then Superior General Delvardus, a tall and skeletal man with dark-brown hair and shock-white eyebrows that stood out like electrical discharges from his forehead; he had a square chin bisected by a deep cleft. Following Delvardus came an endless string of High Moffs, Honored Overlords, Supreme Leaders, and other commanders with similarly pompous yet meaningless titles.

When the last of the warlords had taken his seat, Pellaeon clicked his heels together and marched briskly to the front. Making his turns sharp and exaggerated, he came to stand at attention beside Daala. "I want to thank you all for coming here," he said. "I know this is a difficult compromise even agreeing to meet, but you must hear us out for the future of the Empire."

Daala rose slowly to her feet, moving at the exact pace she hoped would capture their attention: fast enough so as not to distract them, slow enough to give them time to dread what she might say or do. She flashed her emerald eyes. "One Empire, one fleet—only this will guarantee us victory."

From his seat obese High Admiral Teradoc made a rude sound with his lips. "Those platitudes might work with impressionable young soldiers, but not us. We're beyond all that high-sounding nonsense."

Pellaeon stiffened beside Daala, and his face blanched. She could sense the genuine anger boiling up inside him as he said, "Sir, they are not just platitudes. We're talking about the fate of the Empire."

"What Empire?" Teradoc said. "*We* are the Empire." He waved his pudgy hand to encompass the other warlords and scowled.

Daala threw her words out like a fistful of ice chips. "High Admiral Teradoc, that would be cause for immediate execution if the Emperor were here."

"Well, he's not here," Teradoc snapped back.

"And so we must function without him." Daala glared at the High Admiral for a heartbeat, then swept her gaze across the other warlords who seemed alternately amused or bored by the altercation.

"I have seen what remains of the Imperial starfleet," she said. "I've visited most of you in the past year, urging you to put aside your differences. Supreme Warlord Harrsk has a fleet of Imperial Star Destroyers. High Admiral Teradoc has a force of *Victory*-class warships. You others have blastboats, capital ships, millions upon millions of stormtroopers—unstoppable military might if we choose to use it as such!

"Grand Admiral Thrawn proved the Rebels have not yet managed to consolidate their own meager resources. Because of your rivalries, every one of your sectors has devoted vast resources to creating weaponry. It is time to use those resources against our real enemies instead of against each other."

"Fine words, Admiral Daala." Warlord Harrsk mockingly clapped his hands. "And how do you propose that we do that?"

Daala pounded her gloved fist on the table. "By forging an alliance. If the Rebels can do it, so can we."

Superior General Delvardus at a far corner of the table stood up to leave, brushing himself off. "I've heard enough. This is just a poorly disguised power grab. I've spent more funds than any of you on military buildup." His forehead wrinkled, and his bright white eyebrows crawled together. "I'm not sharing my glory."

As the skeletally thin man turned his back to Daala, she touched a hidden control panel under the table. The heavy durasteel door heaved up on hydraulic pistons and slammed into place, sealing gaskets around the edges.

Multicolored lights scrambled like outraged insects on the square panel of the operating mechanism.

"What is this!" Delvardus said, whirling.

"That is a cyberlocked door with a timing mechanism," Daala said. "Even I can't open it for the next three hours. You will sit down, Delvardus."

Several of the warlords lurched to their feet. High Admiral Teradoc attempted to rise, but his bulk dragged him back down, and he simply smacked a sweaty palm on the tabletop. The Imperial commanders shouted and bellowed and hammered their fists and lashed out at each other, but Daala stood firm, weathering their tantrums. Pellaeon remained beside her, looking decidedly uneasy.

"This is not a power grab," Daala finally said when the uproar had died down. "I know that other Imperial officers have left the fleet, throwing their lot in with criminals and lowlifes because it gives them a chance for a pathetic personal gain, but you—while I resent your destructive tactics—at least hold a shadow of allegiance to our once-great Empire.

"You have three hours to choose a nominal leader. There's nothing else you can do. We are all sealed inside this chamber—so you may as well make the best of it."

She sat down and clasped her hands, squeezing the black leather between her fingers with a soft strangling sound. And she waited.

Hour after hour the squabbling grew more strident, more childish. Rivalries erupted between competing warlords: old vengeances were redeclared, allegations of betrayals and threats of reprisals hurled in each other's faces.

For the first hour Daala was disturbed, but still held out some hope. In the second hour, though she kept her anger well hidden, she wanted to bash their skulls together. By the middle of the third hour Daala gave up any attempt to mask her contempt for the squabbling warlords.

Finally, Warlord Harrsk lost control of himself during

a shouting match with Teradoc; the little scar-faced man leaped across the table, scrambling on his knees, and launched himself at the obese High Admiral, trying to wrap his short fingers around Teradoc's fat throat. The chair tipped over, and both crashed to the floor, cursing and shouting.

The other warlords stood up, some cheering, others yelling for them to stop. Pellaeon finally stormed over to the scene, grabbed Harrsk, lifted the short man bodily in the low gravity, and cast him onto the flat table. Teradoc bellowed in rage, his face florid. His breathing rasped into his lungs like a damaged air-recirculation system.

Daala turned and ripped one of the electric-blue glowtorches from the floor behind her. "Enough!" she shouted. She raised the durasteel staff high and smashed it down upon the tabletop. The glowcrystal exploded into shards with crackling blue sparks, and transparent fragments flew in all directions. She hammered the rod down again and again, denting the table, bending the staff, and fragmenting the end. Five minutes remained on the cyberlocked door.

Her action, unexpected and violent, brought the dissenting leaders to a surprised standstill. She tossed the metal pole to the floor, where it clanged and clattered and finally lay still.

In utter disgust Daala spoke, her voice low and heavy like a blunt instrument. "I didn't *want* to rule. I had no *intention* of becoming a political leader. I wanted to crush the Rebels instead—but you give me no choice. I cannot leave the Empire in the hands of fools like you."

Daala reached into the hip pocket of her olive-gray uniform and withdrew a translucent breathmask, which she placed over her mouth and nose. She activated the mask with a fingertip, and it sealed itself to her face, grafting its edges to her skin cells. Beside her, Pellaeon suddenly looked up in dawning comprehension. He grabbed for his own mask as Daala reached under the table again and pressed a button, triggering the nerve-gas systems she had programmed the worker droids to install. The air vents made hissing sounds, like serpents expelling venomous breath into the room.

In unison, the warlords howled at the treachery; Daala noted with amused irony that at last they had found a way to do something together.

Teradoc attempted to haul his bloated form to his feet. Daala presumed he would die of a heart attack if the nerve gas didn't get him first.

Warlord Harrsk and three others didn't waste time venting their rage but rushed to the door, pounding at the cyberlock, trying to trigger its release. But the timer had four minutes yet to run, and Daala knew the gas required only seconds to complete its fatal action.

Tall, skeletal Delvardus snatched at the insignia on his chest with an intent look of concentration on his face. He managed to clip several badges and medals together. He withdrew a strut from one of his shoulderboards, and when he had finished clicking the components together, Daala saw that he had assembled a wicked-looking, if primitive, knife.

On his long, bony legs Delvardus staggered toward her, raising the blade. His face grew splotchy with rose-colored eruptions of tiny blood vessels in his cheeks and eyes. He gasped.

Daala remained standing where she was, a ready target. She stared at him with polite interest. Delvardus had accepted the fact he would die, and he meant to slash Daala before the nerve gas caused him to succumb.

The warlords were falling right and left now, slumping atop each other. Some choked, clutching their throats; others vomited. Two sprawled across the table. Most had managed to make it to the floor.

Delvardus kept coming, one plodding step at a time, as if his limbs were sheathed in rapidly hardening duracrete. His eyes were a deep red, filled with blood from the inside as he strained, lifting his knife.

Daala watched him topple at her feet. The knife clattered on the floor plates.

Pellaeon looked shocked but resigned as he watched the unexpected carnage. Fat Teradoc continued to wheeze and cough. Daala was surprised to see that the obese warlord was the last to die. . . .

A few moments later Daala and Pellaeon stood like statues, the only two survivors, surveying the massacre of Imperial military commanders. Pellaeon blinked in shock. "It's done, then," he whispered, as if he still couldn't believe what he had just witnessed.

Daala merely nodded grimly and said, "This is what had to be."

Right on time, the cyberlock clicked, and the heavy door swung open, setting Daala and Pellaeon free.

CHAPTER 20

Admiral Daala's consolidated fleet arrived in a threatening posture at the military outpost of dead Superior General Delvardus. She took an ample landing force as a show of strength when she went to parley with Cronus, Delvardus's second in command.

The skeletal Superior General had chosen a small world on the outer fringe of the habitable band from its sun, an arid place of rusty sands, barren rocks, and labyrinthine canyons left over from ancient, long-dried floods.

From her newly commandeered Star Destroyers, Daala gathered a squadron of assault shuttles that looked like deadly beetles that streaked down in an impressive phalanx through the pale green atmosphere, homing in on the secret location of Delvardus's fortress. She had taken the coordinates from highly useful spy files that Pellaeon had downloaded from the central databanks of High Admiral Teradoc's flagship.

The squadron cruised low over the broken and veined landscape, following the blistered cracks and fissures. Looming canyon walls cast thick shadows. As the ships penetrated the canyon network, the box-ended gorge stopped abruptly in an imposing facade—the personal fortress of Superior General Delvardus.

The assault shuttles landed in front of the huge stone gates, settling onto a dry wash as hard as duracrete. Daala and Pellaeon emerged, accompanied by half of her heavily armed stormtroopers. The remainder of her troops stayed inside the assault shuttles, manning the weapons. The Gamma assault shuttles hissed and ticked as their engines cooled, settling in for the siege.

She had no idea how Delvardus's second in command would react.

Two of the stormtroopers opened the back cargo compartment and withdrew Daala's most important show of force. "Vice Admiral Pellaeon and I will walk out front," she said. "Two of you will carry the trophy, and the rest follow on either side as my honor guard."

They marched up the paved wash to the towering edifice of the fortress, their boots making sounds like gunfire as they clomped across the ground. The arid wind issued a quiet moan. Daala saw no other movement.

The stormtroopers wrestled with a blocky frame on antigrav mounts, trying to keep it from jerking in the brisk breezes. Suspended in the middle of the frame, crackling and preserved in a high-powered force field, like a dead insect trapped in amber, hung the gangly, cleft-jawed body of Superior General Delvardus. His face was blotched and contorted in a grimace, his eyes squeezed shut from the effects of the nerve gas.

Daala glanced behind her, fiery hair whipping about in the cold gusts. Her lungs burned from the thin air, but she didn't want to appear weak wearing a breathmask.

Pellaeon straightened his uniform and stood with Imperial demeanor. Daala held her head up and strode toward the massive doors five times her own height—Daala suspected the grandeur was mostly for show. Despite Delvardus's proclaimed enormous military expenditures, she had seen virtually no armed presence around the entire planet, and she wondered if the second in command might be planning some sort of ambush.

Stepping apart so that all observers could witness the suspended body of Superior General Delvardus, Daala and Pellaeon stood before the towering stone doorway and waited. She spotted voice pickups cleverly concealed in crevices in the rocks.

"I have a message and a gift for Colonel Cronus," Daala said in a normal speaking voice, turning her mouth toward the voice pickups.

With a sound like a disgusted sigh, the great stone doors cracked open by two meters, revealing an armed contingent of Imperial soldiers hiding inside. Daala did not permit herself to look the least bit ruffled. "Your Superior General has acted in a heinous and traitorous manner, putting his own wishes ahead of the future of the Empire."

The guards looked as if they wanted to blast her for insulting their former master so blatantly, but they didn't dare act in front of Daala's stormtrooper escort and the heavily armed Gamma assault shuttles.

"Delvardus did not act alone, but continued a war of attrition, fighting other warlords to the detriment of us all. I present here"—she withdrew a holo cube from her pocket and set it in front of the sparkling frame that held the suspended body—"a recording of our entire détente council, so that you may see your general's actions, as well as those of the other warlords. Then you will understand why it was necessary to take such a drastic step.

"These assault shuttles are merely a fraction of our forces, but they are sufficient to cause significant damage to your fortress. The rest of our fleet waits in orbit. Look over these items and decide whether to join us as part of a reunited Imperial force—or whether to be considered renegades like your former master. You have one hour to deliberate. If we don't hear from you, we will come back and destroy you as accomplices."

She spun about. The stormtroopers set the heavy

frame down, switching off its antigrav platform before marching behind Daala and Pellaeon.

Daala did not turn to watch, but she heard the guards hustle out of the fortress and gather up their fallen leader and the message cube. They rushed back inside, and the thud of armored doors echoed in the narrow canyon.

After the hour was up, Colonel Cronus decided to join Daala's forces. Wholeheartedly.

An armored fast transport from the fortress hangars took Daala and Pellaeon, along with a contingent of their suspicious stormtrooper guards, away from the planet. Colonel Cronus himself piloted the armored transport, transmitting recognition signals into deep space. Leaving Daala's battleships behind, Cronus took them straight up out of the system, perpendicular to the ecliptic and toward the sparse cometary cloud.

Colonel Cronus was a small man but packed with power. His shoulders were broad, his chest rippled, and his swollen biceps showed that he took great care to maintain himself at peak physical form, even in the reduced gravity of the small, bleak planet. His curly black hair was seeded with silvery strands that gave him a distinguished appearance. His complexion was deeply tanned and seamed with lines that made him look weathered; his large brown eyes constantly flicked back and forth, drinking in details. He spoke sparingly, answering questions put to him with just the right amount of information.

"I need to make a brief hyperspace hop," Cronus said, "to get us far enough to the edge of the system— unless you'd rather we spent weeks at full burn of our sublight engines?"

Daala stiffened. Pellaeon frowned suspiciously, and the stormtrooper guards snapped to attention; but she decided that Cronus had little to gain here by sudden treachery—and that trusting him with a responsibility such as this could only plant the seeds of deeper loyalty. "Very well, Colonel," she said. "I'm anxious to see what Delvardus has managed to create with all the credits he's been spending."

Pellaeon looked at her as if in warning, his heavy mustache drooping; but she shook her head imperceptibly. The vice admiral sat back and forced himself to relax. Cronus accepted her orders without question and began programming the navicomputer.

Daala felt her nerves taut like high-tension wires running through her body. She kept her expression impassive, but adrenaline coursed through her as she strapped herself into her chair. Everything had gone remarkably well. The conquest had been devastating and bloody, but she had taken out selected targets—the appropriate victims—and the Empire's harvest grew stronger and richer with each weed she plucked. She felt elated when she thought of the momentum of her triumph.

Pellaeon raised his eyebrow in question, but she didn't respond. The risk had paid off for her. She would always remain on guard, but for the moment the danger was over. Now she had to work on consolidating her power.

Cronus swiveled in his pilot seat, looking at Daala with deep brown eyes that held an unexpected warmth; she wondered if he actually appreciated her takeover. She had seen him look upon the body of Superior General Delvardus with barely concealed scorn.

"Entering hyperspace, Admiral Daala," he said. "Please don't be alarmed." Around the ship, space vanished in a multicolored swirl.

Daala leaned forward to speak to the colonel. "We've researched the amount of funding Delvardus funneled into his operations, and I am not impressed with what I saw at his fortress." She narrowed her emerald eyes and continued, "I hope he hasn't been squandering the Empire's resources."

Cronus smiled and shook his head. "I assure you, Admiral, he has not. I think even you will be impressed."

Daala closed her eyes for a moment to tally her fleet in her mind, adding together the Star Destroyers she had already collected from the various warlords, all of the battleships and firepower she had to command. She vowed to put her fleet to its best use this time.

"Here we are, Admiral." Colonel Cronus flicked the hyperspace controls that dropped them back into the normal universe. Blackness washed around them, and the distant sun appeared as a bright point at the center of the system. Other than that, space was dark around the armored transport.

Then Daala noticed a blot as she stared, an enormous shadow that eclipsed the stars. It seemed to be kilometers long and grew larger as they approached.

Cronus fiddled with the comm system and transmitted a recognition code. "Power up," he said to some unknown listener. "Let's make a good display."

Daala squinted out the viewport, and suddenly she saw a whirlwind of tiny lights appear, marking deck after deck on a breathtakingly huge ship. The immense wedge-shaped shadow was a single vessel, larger than anything she had ever seen before.

"I can't believe it," Pellaeon said beside her. "Only the *Executor* was this big—and that one ship practically bankrupted the Empire."

"What is it?" Daala asked.

Cronus smiled, his expressive face showing his obvious enjoyment at her reaction—but it was Pellaeon who answered. "It's a Super Star Destroyer," he said.

Cronus nodded eagerly. "Worth twenty Imperial Star Destroyers," he said, his eyes flashing with pride. "It is eight kilometers long, can carry a crew of up to a hundred thousand—and is plated with stealth armor. That's why it appeared as only a black shadow as we approached. Though gigantic, it is virtually invisible to enemy forces."

He lowered his voice as if imparting a precious secret. "We named it the *Night Hammer*."

Daala's eyes shone with wonder, and her breath came shallow and fast as Cronus directed the armored transport to the open bay of the Super Star Destroyer. Daala could not restrain herself and stood from her seat, waiting behind the colonel. She leaned forward, unable to tear her eyes from the beauty of the black *Night Hammer*.

"*That* will be my ship," she whispered.

CORUSCANT

CHAPTER 21

Inside the cavernous Imperial palace, Leia Organa Solo and her family wore nondescript civilian clothes, stopping at a pleasant café to eat their lunch like normal citizens. It felt good to be out of uniform where Leia could pretend to be invisible—though she knew that private bodyguards, professional protectors, and crack sharpshooters followed at a comfortable distance, monitoring her every movement. Leia resented the interference—but she also knew after many attempts on her own life or on her family, she couldn't afford to grow careless. Too much was at stake.

Han carried Anakin against his side, and the young boy clasped small hands around his father's neck. "Come on, kids, there's a table over here," he said. The energetic twins raced to be the first to reach the empty seats.

Chewbacca let loose a long yowl, insisting that the kids slow down and be careful—but they ignored the big Wookiee.

"If you would simply allow me to handle this, I'm sure they would behave," Threepio said. Chewbacca flashed his fangs at the golden droid. "Really, Chewbacca! There's absolutely no call for such displays."

Artoo-Detoo whistled, but Threepio didn't bother to respond. The golden droid carried two trays of food, while Chewbacca hefted his own mounded high with dripping meat.

Their group chose a table at the edge of a towering balcony. Mists rose around it, generated from vaporizers in the synrock walls. Trickling fountains traced rivulets of water down the dozens of stories to an open plaza enclosed within the pyramidal palace.

Threepio and Chewbacca set their trays on the table, but the twins rushed to the edge barricade, standing on their tiptoes to peer far below.

"Look at the people!" Jaina said. "They're so tiny."

"Can I throw something down?" Jacen asked, looking around for any object to toss over the edge.

"No, you may not," Leia said.

"But Jaina's going to," the boy responded.

"No, she isn't," Leia repeated with a sterner tone.

"No, I'm not!" Jaina said.

"Come on, sit down," Han said, settling Anakin into a chair.

Around them the rustle of thousands of officials, bureaucrats, and aides going about their business made a drone of white noise mixed with the buzz of machinery, air exchangers, and climate-control systems. Leia felt calmer now that she could take a brief break. At least people weren't challenging every decision she made for lunch.

Leia appreciated Mon Mothma's confidence in her, when the former Chief of State had passed the torch of rulership—but Leia did not relish the work of being president, though she considered it her duty.

Jacen and Jaina sat down and began to play with their food, and she was relieved that they had chosen something that wouldn't try too hard to run away. The twins loved colored cubes of fizzing protein gelatin, though Leia couldn't stand the stuff. Han had chosen a greasy Corellian dish, while Leia contented herself with hydroponic greens sprinkled with intense flavor crystals.

She closed her eyes as she sank into her chair. "It's so nice just to be together with the family, if only for a few minutes." Chewbacca agreed with a loud rumble.

A tall, offensively efficient waitdroid came up with a gleaming empty platter affixed to one metal arm. "May I provide further assistance, honored customers?" the waitdroid said. "I am proud to offer my services while you dine in our fine establishment. May I take orders for drinks or additional items? Condiments perhaps? The pleasure of my existence is to serve you faithfully."

Threepio grew indignant at the overblown expressions of hospitality. "*I* am their personal protocol droid, you pretentious pile of scrap, and I am perfectly capable of taking care of their needs. Now if you don't mind, this is a *family* outing, and we would much prefer to be left alone. Good day."

The waitdroid sniffed, spun its torso 180 degrees, and trundled off.

Han placed his hand over Leia's and gave a crooked smile. "Bad day?"

"Exhausting," Leia answered, her eyes still shut. "Every meeting seems like I'm running uphill on a high-gravity planet. Nothing gets accomplished easily. I find myself wishing for the 'good old days' when we would just blast in, do our jobs, and leave: mission accomplished. Now I have to go through so many different steps, so many interminable committees, get agreement from an unconscionable number of opposing parties so nobody in the galaxy is offended by the smallest piece of legislation . . . it's impossible sometimes."

She opened her eyes and looked at her husband. Jacen and Jaina began throwing gelatin cubes at each other. "In a case like this, it's so perfectly plain. Why is there any discussion? We still can't come to an agreement."

"The stuff about the Hutts?" Han asked.

She bit her lower lip and nodded. "It's obvious the Hutts are pulling a fast one. We know what you and Luke found in Jabba's palace, we've got the message from Mara Jade, and we know that Durga's own Taurill stole the Death Star plans. We can't just ignore it."

She took a mouthful of leaves and crunched, thinking as she chewed. Han ate one of his grayish green sausages and smacked his lips, relishing the meal. "There are other ways to find out," he said.

Leia smiled. "I know." She felt her face grow warm, fixing her attention on the challenge. She squeezed Han's hand in both of hers. "Okay, we've had closed Senate meetings, and I've heard enough discussion to make a statue fall asleep. So what are we *really* going to do?"

Chewbacca ventured a loud opinion. "Yeah, I was thinking that, Chewie," Han said and turned to Leia. "The Hutts probably know we suspect something. We've heard news from too many different sources to hope that those slimy worms don't have an inkling yet. They'll be watching your official channels very closely. They've probably got spies scattered throughout the Imperial palace. We have to be careful."

Leia nodded. "So, since they know we're hunting for clues, let's create a diversion. We'll use a flashy show, carry a big stick in one hand and a delicate probe in the other."

Han's forehead creased as he thought. "What do you mean?"

"We'll take Durga up on his offer."

Han looked at her blankly. "What offer? You'd accept something from a Hutt?"

Leia shrugged. "He invited us to make a return visit of state. I'm sure he didn't mean it, but he can't back down now that the invitation's been made. Let's set up a diplomatic mission on the spot, head out to Nal Hutta as soon as possible. That way Durga will have no forewarning.

"And," she continued, holding up one finger, "we'll be accompanied by the New Republic fleet. Wedge and Ackbar must be itching to go on some innocent-sounding war-gaming exercises. Our ships can provide an impressive show of force. If the Hutts happen to get intimidated in the process, so much the better. Let them be nervous, wondering what we're really up to, and we'll poke around to find some answers."

Threepio piped up. "But Mistress Leia, how do you expect to learn anything if you're so obvious about it? Won't Durga the Hutt hide anything he knows?"

Leia's expression became mischievous. "If we come in with all the flash and dazzle we can muster, he may just be blinded to what else we're doing. Meanwhile, Chewbacca and Artoo can take the *Falcon* and go to Nar Shaddaa, the Smugglers' Moon. It's a seedy place where all the black-market dealings come and go. Durga will be so busy hiding his cards from us, Chewie might find something important on his own."

Artoo whistled and beeped. "And Artoo, as well," Leia added. "You two poke around. See what you can find, then we'll compare notes."

Chewbacca roared his approval, and finally Leia relaxed enough to finish her lunch.

CHAPTER 22

On the bridge of the Escort Frigate *Yavaris* General Wedge Antilles felt the old excitement of space combat. His ships charged into the Nal Hutta system under the pretense of Red Team/Blue Team simulated battles in open territory that just happened to be near the Hutt homeworld.

"Boy, are the slugs going to be surprised," Wedge said.

The lovely and ethereal scientist Qwi Xux left her station and joined him. "Much better than when we took over Maw Installation," she said. "At least we're not risking lives this time."

Wedge nodded. He wanted to hug her, but knew he shouldn't, since he was in command of the ship, and she was the science officer in training. The work was easy for Qwi, and she enjoyed being with Wedge. Since vowing never to work on developing new weapons systems again, the brilliant alien scientist hadn't yet found a new calling for her considerable mental energies.

"Check the status of our fleet," Wedge said to the tactical officer, who displayed a grid showing the components of Blue Team. Though the *Yavaris* was his flagship, it was not the largest battleship. The cornerstone of his fleet was the monstrous Assault Frigate *Dodonna,* a highly modified version of the fearsome Imperial Dreadnaughts. The *Yavaris* was smaller, but it was the ship Wedge had piloted during his successful attack on the Empire's secret laboratory, Maw Installation.

Surrounding his ships were six smaller, versatile Corellian Corvettes, whose huge banks of engines looked like rocket-launcher emplacements burning blue in the darkness of space. All his ships had strung out in a picket line, with the *Dodonna* and the *Yavaris* at the center, flanked on each side by three Corvettes. They cruised into the Nal Hutta system.

Wedge asked the comm officer, "Have we heard from Red Team yet? Has Admiral Ackbar arrived in position?"

Ackbar had taken his own complement of ships on a different approach vector: a trio of Corellian gunships, smaller than the Corvettes, and an enormous Calamarian Star Cruiser, the *Galactic Voyager,* one of the largest and most powerful ships in the New Republic fleet. Wedge knew, however, that sheer size and firepower did not guarantee a victory. Ackbar was to enter the system from the other side, and the two fleets would engage near Nal Hutta itself.

"Red Team confirms they are in position," the tactical officer said.

"General Antilles," the comm officer interrupted. "We have an urgent message from Nal Hutta demanding to know our purpose here."

Wedge tried to stifle a smug grin. "Let them know we're just engaging in peaceful combat exercises. No cause for alarm," he said, then muttered, "unless they try anything."

Admiral Ackbar waited for his helmsman to give the announcement. Finally the other Calamarian officer said, "Both teams in position, Admiral."

Ackbar nodded his huge head. "Prepare to engage," he said.

The *Galactic Voyager* was Ackbar's favorite ship in the fleet. Every one of the lumpy pod-shaped Calamarian battlecruisers followed a slightly different design devised by master shipbuilders in orbit around their world. For years the Mon Calamari had worked nonstop to replenish the losses suffered by the New Republic during fierce battles with the Empire, such as when Admiral Daala and her Star Destroyers had attacked the Calamarian shipyards and Ackbar himself had caused the destruction of the half-completed warship *Startide*.

Beside him General Crix Madine, the Supreme Allied Commander for Intelligence, said, "We need to keep the Hutts preoccupied and intimidated to accomplish our real mission here."

A bearded, middle-aged man, Madine had been in charge of the ground assault on Endor, which resulted in the destruction of the energy-shield generator, allowing the Rebel fleet to destroy the second Death Star. A long time ago, Madine had been an important officer in the Imperial military, but he had defected to the Alliance, bringing with him much valuable information. A good many Rebel victories had resulted from the secret intelligence Madine had delivered to Mon Mothma. He now kept a low profile, serving in his quiet role of necessary covert operations.

"Now that our fleet is in system," Madine said, "I doubt very much that the Hutts will dare misbehave when the Chief of State arrives on her diplomatic mission."

Ackbar nodded solemnly. "That may be your motivation, General Madine, but right now my purpose is to score a victory for Red Team."

As Ackbar began preparations for the engagement, Madine went to one of the sensor stations and relieved the lieutenant. Crix Madine was a hands-on person who liked to do his own busy work. He had no way of knowing when he might need to be proficient in every level of operations,

so he tried to have a broad background and competence in
every system on board.

Madine adjusted the *Galactic Voyager*'s long-range
scanners to zoom in on the greenish planet of Nal Hutta
and its Smugglers' Moon, Nar Shaddaa. With the arrival
of the New Republic fleet, he noted a marked increase in
traffic departing from Nar Shaddaa, no doubt small-time
criminals fleeing the intimidating military force. He resigned himself to letting so many lowlifes get away, but
right now he couldn't be interested in the dregs of society.
His real target on this mission would be much more devious.

"Blue Team has squared off in a defensive position,"
the tactical officer said.

Ackbar concentrated on his station. "Give me a display." Images of Wedge's fleet appeared in a picket line
across space. "Very well," he said, "we will be the ag-
gressor in this engagement." He stared at the arrangement
of Blue Team's ships and shook his salmon-colored head.
"I'll have to teach General Antilles a lesson in tactics and
vulnerability."

Madine returned to the admiral's side. "What do you
mean?" He had always been interested in fleet maneuvers.

Ackbar pointed a flipper-hand toward the images.
"We'll plunge through them like a dagger," he said.
"One of our gunships in front, then the *Galactic Voyager*,
then the other two gunships. We'll plow straight between
the two frigates—those are the primary targets. The lead
gunship will come in firing and pass straight through.
Then the *Galactic Voyager* will obliterate their defenses
with our superior firepower. Finally, the second and third
gunships will mop up what's left. With one pass, we'll
take out the *Yavaris* and the *Dodonna*. Blue Team's flanking Corvettes will be unable to bring their weapons to bear
because their own ships block the way."

"Sounds straightforward," Madine said.

"Just watch," Ackbar answered.

*   *   *

Wedge slumped into his command chair with a boyish grin on his square-jawed face. "He's falling for it!" He clapped his hands. "All right, Red Team just stepped across the line. We know exactly what they're going to do. Prepare for it." Wedge shook his head and looked at Qwi. "Doesn't Ackbar think I read his own tactical manuals?"

He saw Red Team coming on in a straight line, a single gunship in front, then the huge Star Cruiser, followed by two more gunships. "He's aiming between the two frigates," Wedge said. "All right, everybody, red alert! Battle stations! All weapons, low power. Just enough for them to detect all the hits we score."

"All weapons low power, sir," the gunnery sergeant reported. "Hit counters are activated."

Wedge's eyes twinkled as he watched the ships approach. He held up one hand. "Full power to lateral shields on both frigates," he said. "Drop all other shields. We know where they're going to shoot."

The gunship came right on target, streaking between the Assault Frigate and the *Yavaris,* repeatedly firing simulated shots.

"Shields holding," the defensive officer said.

Then the *Galactic Voyager* came through, its low-power weapons blazing. Wedge chopped down with his hand. "Close the net," he said.

The tactical officer shouted orders into the encrypted communication system, and the six Corellian Corvettes at the flanks—supposedly out of firing range—suddenly looped up and around, encircling the two seemingly vulnerable frigates. The Corvettes scattered like static moths, flurrying into position and firing on the Mon Calamari Star Cruiser from top and bottom.

The *Yavaris* and the *Dodonna* both fired upon the *Galactic Voyager,* catching it in the crossfire it had expected—but Ackbar had not anticipated the attack from above and below. Wedge ordered the *Yavaris* to strike Red Team's front gunship, crippling it.

The simulation computer reduced the gunship's capabilities and told its captain they were dead in space.

General Madine watched as the hit counters tallied the enormous number of strikes on Red Team's ships. Madine scratched his beard, turning to Ackbar. "He lured you, and you fell for the trap."

"Shields failing, Admiral," the helmsman said in alarm.

"Computer reports that both gunships to our rear have been removed from the game," the tactical officer said.

Admiral Ackbar flushed a blotchy reddish color. "Increase speed," he said. "Let's get away from here so we don't suffer any more hits."

"Too late, Admiral," the helmsman said. "Our shields have failed."

Madine turned to watch the hit counter's numbers spiraling upward like a cascade reaction. "Hull plates have been breached. Admiral, I'm sorry to report that the *Galactic Voyager* has been destroyed."

Ackbar's shoulders slumped. "A defeat."

The tactical officer stood up to report. "We did finally disable their Assault Frigate and one of their attacking Corvettes, but the computer lists Red Team as 'out of commission'—the *Galactic Voyager* and two gunships down, our front gunship crippled."

Ackbar sighed. "The price of overconfidence," he said. "I was not thinking. Open a channel to Blue Team." Madine watched as the Calamarian stood straight and spoke to Wedge Antilles. "This is the Red Team commander. Congratulations on your victory."

"You were too predictable, Admiral," Wedge said.

Ackbar chuckled, but it was a forced laugh. "I will

try to be more . . . *erratic* with my future commands, General Antilles.''

He checked his sensors and saw that Leia's diplomatic ship had arrived from Coruscant, exactly on time. Ackbar, as commander of the New Republic fleet, opened a channel to all ships engaged in wargaming exercises.

''Chief of State Leia Organa Solo's ship has reached the system. Have the fleet form up and escort her to Nal Hutta,'' he said. ''After that we will return for a rematch.''

Ackbar closed the channel. ''On to business. General Madine, I believe you have work to do down on the surface?''

Madine nodded and took the turbolift below decks, where he would prep his commando team for their covert mission to the Hutt planet.

CHAPTER 23

Chief of State Leia Organa Solo's diplomatic cruiser entered the Nal Hutta system, flanked by an imposing display of New Republic battleships innocently engaged in combat exercises.

Leia sat in the hammerhead-shaped command compartment of her Corellian Corvette, a diplomatic ship much like the blockade runner in which Darth Vader had captured her while searching for the stolen Death Star plans near Tatooine. See-Threepio hovered beside her, newly polished so that he gleamed under the bridge lights. Han, though dressed in less diplomatic finery than he had worn during Durga's visit, fidgeted in his clean uniform.

"They've spotted us," Han said as alarms began to go off.

"They already knew we were coming," Leia said. "We sent the Hutts full notice at least . . . half an hour ago." She chuckled. "Okay," she said more seriously to the crew, "time for our performance: I'm going to make a transmission." She stepped to the upper bridge, alone under the lights. She held the rail, primped herself for a moment, then composed a miffed expression on her face. "Please open a channel," she said.

When the Hutts responded, Leia began her tirade. "Why is there no official escort fleet? I expected Lord Durga to have taken care of that personally. What have you been doing all this time?"

The Hutt respondent was a lowly worm, thin and with a narrow head, obviously not a powerful crime lord like Jabba or Durga. His huge eyes flicked from side to side as he spoke in Basic. "Um, excuse me, Madam President, but Lord Durga is not here. We regret that we are unable to meet—"

"What do you mean, Durga isn't here?" Leia snapped. "He sent us an express invitation to visit him at our convenience. I trust you're not implying that he lied to the New Republic's Chief of State—or do you mean to suggest that he is in fact *retracting* his offer to repay our hospitality? This is an outrage! How does he expect to form some sort of treaty with the New Republic? I'd say the chances are becoming vanishingly small, in light of this snub." She crossed her arms over her chest and glared at the scrawny Hutt.

"I'm sorry, Madam President, but Lord Durga is away . . . on business." He waved his stubby hands, totally flustered. "If only you had given us some warning," the Hutt continued, "we would have prepared for your visit. But as it is, we have no facilities—"

Leia glared at him coldly. "You don't actually expect us to turn around and meekly go home after the enormous expense and trouble we went to for this highly visible expedition, do you? I hardly think Lord Durga would want to risk such a galaxy-spanning diplomatic incident. Don't be absurd."

The timid Hutt looked around, as if seeking someone else to consult, but found no one. "What do you expect me to do?" he wailed. "I don't have the authority to—"

"Nonsense," Leia said, and raised her chin haughtily. "We are coming down at Durga's personal invitation—what further authority could you need? We expect to be well treated. See to it!'' She signed off, then burst out laughing.

Han came over and hugged her. ''I think you enjoyed that,'' he accused, trying to restrain spasms of laughter. He stepped back and applauded her performance.

Threepio meanwhile was totally baffled. ''Oh dear! Perhaps we should have given the Hutts more time, Mistress Leia. At least they would have had the opportunity to prepare. I'm afraid they're so flustered now, this could put them completely off balance.''

''That's the point!'' Han and Leia said, raising their voices in unison.

Threepio staggered backward and shook his golden head. ''Well, I'm sure this sort of approach wasn't covered in any of the protocol programming *I* received. Once again, I feel I'll never understand human behavior.''

Leia sat next to Han at one of the discussion tables in her ready-room, and she reached over to clasp his hands. ''Thanks for coming with me, Han. I'm glad we're finally going somewhere together, instead of splitting up all the time.''

''Yeah, I like it too,'' he said with a lopsided grin. ''It's a nice change.''

She sighed, then her lips tightened. ''We can't cut them any slack. The Hutts are dangerous already, and they'll be unstoppable if they have their hands on a Death Star.''

Han nodded gravely, and Leia continued, as if giving an impassioned speech to the Senate. ''The first Death Star was meant to be the ultimate doomsday weapon in the hands of the Empire. Now the Hutts will become galactic bullies with a big stick—and what's to stop them from selling those plans to any other small-time dictator who wants to get his own way? We cannot let the Death Star proliferate. The galaxy will be a shambles. If anyone with enough credits can buy the plans and go around blowing up planets, then no one will be safe. We must stop this at all costs.''

One of the New Republic guards came in. ''Excuse me, Madam President,'' he said, ''but your dropshuttle is ready. We can take you down to Nal Hutta at your convenience.''

''My convenience,'' Leia said ironically. ''I'm so looking forward to this.'' She felt as if she were dropping into the open jaws of some slavering beast.

Along with Threepio and their honor guard, Leia and Han went to the Corvette's drop ship bay and climbed aboard the small diplomatic shuttle. ''You ready for this?'' Han asked.

Leia looked at him, pondering her answer. ''No,'' she said honestly. ''But we have to do it anyway. Let's go visit the Hutts.''

CHAPTER 24

Nal Hutta was a bog, flat and sunken like a sewage-recla-
mation reservoir, with standing puddles and sickly-looking
marsh grasses—a landscape the Hutts somehow found attractive. Leia realized she should have expected as much.

A Hutt sailbarge coasted toward them as the diplomatic shuttle settled on a landing pad near Durga the
Hutt's holdings. When she saw the sluggish luxury ship
cruise along, its directional sails billowing in the foul-
smelling breeze, Leia's skin crawled with the memory of
her last fateful trip with Jabba out to the Great Pit of
Carkoon.

She, Han, and Threepio stepped away from the diplomatic ship, accompanied by their New Republic escort,
and waited for the sailbarge to receive them. Above, the
sky was draped with shadowy gray clouds. As Leia and
Han stood in their formal attire, a greasy rain began pelt-
ing down, cold droplets clotted with residue from massive
strip-mining operations in industrial sectors far from the
showy palaces of the Hutt crime lords.

"This certainly is a gloomy place, isn't it?" Threepio

commented. "If we don't find shelter from this dreadful rain, I shouldn't be at all surprised if my new gold plating gets corroded." He turned his glowing yellow optical sensors toward the runnels of water trickling down his arms. "I do wish you had left me on Coruscant, Mistress Leia. I'm sure I would have done a much better job taking care of the children."

"Didn't we tell you, Threepio?" Han said mischievously. "As a matter of state necessity, we're going to present you to Durga the Hutt. He'll be your new master."

"What?" Threepio cried, raising his arms in sudden shock. "Oh, no! You must be joking. I'm doomed! Please, I urge you to reconsider this, Mistress Leia."

Leia elbowed Han in the ribs. "That's mean, Han!"

"Just kidding, Goldenrod," he said and slapped the protocol droid on one hard metal shoulder.

"Kidding?" Threepio made a flustered sound. "Why, that wasn't at all funny!"

Across from the Nal Hutta spaceport, Durga's palace rose tall. Despite the brown haze of pollution and atmospheric sludge, its walls gleamed white and clean. When Leia squinted her brown eyes, she could make out the tiny forms of slaves climbing up and down the sculptured facades in the slippery drizzle, scouring the gargoyles and crenelations.

The sailbarge hovered over them. Guards stood on deck, scowling in all directions. A thin Hutt slithered along the top deck, moving under its own power rather than on a repulsorsled; Leia recognized the narrow, emaciated face of the creature she had argued with over the comm system. He was alarmingly different from any Hutt she had seen previously—scrawny as a ribbon of mottled green leather that hung on a flexible spinal column. He did not look well.

"Greetings, Chief of State Leia Organa Solo. I welcome you in the name of His Great Obesity, the Lord Durga, who is unfortunately unable to be with us at the moment."

Leia bowed slightly. "Thank you. But I want to meet with Lord Durga. He invited us here."

"Ah, I have summoned him, Madam President. He is coming with all due haste." The scrawny Hutt envoy leaned over the barge railing.

"Good," Han muttered. "I'm not exactly crazy about the idea of staying for very long."

"I am Korrda, special envoy and slave to Lord Durga. I am not worthy, but it has fallen upon me to entertain you until he can be here in person."

"Oh, that's very nicely said," Threepio said.

Korrda seemed pleased. "I hope you find my Basic acceptable. Lord Durga insists that all his entourage learn the language so that we might better work with the New Republic. Might I offer you suitable hospitality in the meantime?"

"We can't be sure quite what a Hutt means by *hospitality,*" Han said quietly. "As I recall, I've experienced a little of it myself."

Korrda made a hissing, sizzling sound that Leia identified as a strained laugh. "Ah yes, Han Solo—I am aware of your dealings with the defeated Jabba, may his name be spoken with scorn. He is a worthless worm. No Hutt respects the memory of one whose empire has fallen. You will be pleased to note that the Hutts have lifted the bounty on both of you as an initial overture of peace."

"How very . . . heartening," Leia said with an acid-sweet smile. "Now, should we climb aboard that sailbarge, or were you planning to keep us standing here, shouting at each other in the rain all day?"

"Ah, certainly!" Korrda reared back, gesturing with his sinewy hands as a wide ramp extended to the ground.

They climbed up the ramp onto the barge. Their stoic-looking New Republic escorts remained as stony-faced as the sailbarge guards. Korrda did his best to be obsequious, and simpered as the sailbarge raised itself up, drifting away from the spaceport and across the open spaces toward the palace.

Spiders and gnats swarmed around the spiky grasses below. Roughly circular, shallow pools dotted the landscape, covered with a greenish scum. Overhead in the thin rain, flocks of large, clumsy birds squawked as they flew along, chased by rowdy henchmen on swoops who shot them with long-range blaster rifles. Smoking bird carcasses tumbled out of the sky and plopped into the bog.

Durga's palace rose taller as they approached, a nightmare of towers and crenelations with large jawed gates—plus an underground network of dungeons so vast it had achieved galactic renown.

"Ah, I don't know how long it will take for Durga to return," Korrda said as the sailbarge docked in the cavernous hangar bay, "but since I'm responsible for amusing you, would you like a tour of our dungeon levels? You'll find them most fascinating."

"No dungeons," Leia said. "Thanks anyway."

"Not interested," Han concurred. "We've seen enough dungeons to last us for the next century or so."

"Oh," Korrda said, obviously disappointed and at a loss for what to do as a backup plan.

Leia had been unable to sense anything from the opaque mind of Durga the Hutt. Korrda was much weaker, but all she could sense was flustered uncertainty and a nervous frustration, no deception. Korrda honestly didn't know what was going on, but he was afraid his neck was on the line.

Leia's Jedi powers also brought her many bad impressions from the palace itself, lingering echoes of pain and imprisonment, thoughts of murder and betrayal that seemed to ooze from the stones. It overwhelmed her, and she quickly shut her senses down again.

"Ah, perhaps we should dine instead," Korrda suggested. "We always have freshly slaughtered meats and succulent delicacies. There will be other members of Durga's family in attendance. It might be good to meet them."

"That would be acceptable," Leia said, inclining her head in a regal nod.

Han muttered, "I don't know . . . having dinner with a bunch of Hutts doesn't sound much more pleasant than touring torture chambers."

Inside the dining hall, carrion birds sat perched on stone lintels, glaring down to spot any morsel dropped to the flagstones, ready to swoop and capture any portion of the meal that attempted to escape before it could be shoveled into a cavernous Hutt mouth.

The other guests, Durga's adolescent cousins, were like wide-mouthed eels, lean and muscular, some already beginning to build up layers of flab in preparation for mid-life obesity. Their thick lips contorted and their yellow eyes darted around—but these Hutts were obviously healthy, while Korrda was emaciated by some sort of sickness. The whiplike Huttlings were boisterous and insulting, barely able to speak a coherent sentence in Basic and uninterested in the work of Durga.

Korrda played the servitor, bringing dishes of gelatinous food: stewed insects; parasites drizzled with warm honey; and roasted grain maggots, most of which lay in crispy husks on their plates, while others still squirmed about in a struggle to survive.

Leia did her best to be appreciative, though neither she nor Han found they had much of an appetite. She pushed the food around on her dish, enduring the meal as best she could. Han did the same beside her, the cords in his neck tightening as he clenched his jaw. Only Threepio was not at a loss for words, attempting to decipher the origin of the meal's components.

Korrda suffered more than Han and Leia, however. The larval Hutts proved excessively rude, slapping him whenever he came within reach. Korrda did not eat from a plate of his own, but scraped leftovers from discarded dishes into his mouth. He looked at Han and Leia with the utmost gratitude, perhaps believing they had not eaten their meals so that he could wolf down the untouched food.

"Excuse me," Leia said in a low voice when Korrda came to gather their dishes, "why don't you sit and eat with us, since you are Durga's designated assistant?"

"No, I am his lowliest servant," Korrda said. "Look at me." He gestured to his ribbon-thin body and sickly skin. "I deserve only slop. I am despised because I have a rare wasting disease. As an underweight Hutt, I am the target of all scorn. How could anyone respect such a wasted and worthless worm as I?"

"Why does Durga keep you around then?" Han asked. "You seem to be in an important position while he's gone."

"Ah, Durga detests me," Korrda said, blinking bloodshot eyes and bobbing his narrow head. "He keeps me because I am so despicable. He shames me by placing me in situations where I must appear to be important, though it is obvious to anyone with eyes that I am worthless. This makes me feel even more downtrodden—which keeps Durga happy, and therefore, I am content." Leia's mind spun with the tangled logic, but she didn't try to argue.

From their perches, the carrion birds watched Korrda himself, as if he might be their next meal. The creatures squawked as a large lumpy worrt, a long-tongued froglike creature, hopped into the dining hall from one of the outer corridors. Frills stood up around its eyes, and it bobbed obediently as it sat waiting, clasping a message placard in its wide toothless mouth.

Korrda rushed over to snatch the placard from the creature, then patted its warty head as he scanned the message on the screen. He reared up in delight, his mottled skin growing darker. "Ah, good news indeed!" he said. "My master, Lord Durga, is on his way and should be here shortly. He insists that I show you the pleasure of his private bathhouses while you wait. I'm sure you'll find them most enjoyable."

The concept of a Hutt bathhouse made Leia's stomach churn, but she forced a smile. Han raised an eyebrow skeptically, and clasped her hand under the table. "It's for the New Republic," she said in a martyred tone.

Korrda beamed with pride as he gestured at the enclosed labyrinth beneath the palace, holding acres and acres of sluggish, steaming water. The walls were covered with mold and bulbous fungus. Dim light filtered from narrow slits in the walls, giving everything a grainy, tarnished appearance.

"This bathhouse is Lord Durga's pride and joy," Korrda said.

"Doesn't surprise me a bit," Han murmured, trying to sound polite.

The maze of canals was an underground catacomb with vaulted ceilings and algae-covered support pillars dipping into the shallow water. Things splashed and swam in the twisted channels, lost in the faint mist.

"This fresh water is pumped in directly from the bogs," Korrda said, as if confiding a great trade secret. "Lumps and all."

The canals bubbled, and hairy green weed drifted along the top. Leia hugged herself in the clinging robe Korrda had provided for her. "You expect us to swim in this?" she said.

"Oh, no!" Korrda flinched backward in horror, whipping his sinuous spine back and forth. "These canals are for Lord Durga and other Hutts. We could not allow a . . . human to pollute the water."

"We certainly wouldn't want to offend Durga," Han said with relief.

"Ah, no—we have a species-segregated section for some of our honored visitors. I'm sorry we cannot be fully accommodating; this section, alas, has only pure water, with none of the special additives that give Hutt skin such a pleasurable texture." Korrda led them to a warm, crystal-clear pool with rough stone steps leading down into it so they could immerse themselves to shoulder level in the bubbling water.

"This will do just fine, thank you," Leia said, her gratitude genuine.

"As long as we've checked it for traps," Han suggested.

"Oh, indeed, sir. I have been most vigilant throughout this entire mission," Threepio said. "And I detect no treachery here. I assure you, you may bathe without fear. I'll remain on guard."

"Oh good," Han said sarcastically, "then I can relax."

Leia slowly lowered herself into the warm, fizzy water and sighed as the liquid heat swirled around her aching joints. "In spite of myself, I might enjoy this," she said.

"Please relax," Korrda said. "I must attend to my Lord Durga's arrival."

"You go right ahead," Han said, waving in dismissal. "Threepio will be here to stand guard, and our New Republic escort is just out in the corridor."

As Korrda slithered away, Han and Leia sank into the pool, listening to the simmering sounds of other creatures moving in the canals reserved for Hutt bathing. The labyrinth was so vast that they could feel alone in their little corner, although numerous Hutt visitors and the reckless Huttlings swam in other sections.

"Should we talk?" Han whispered.

Leia slipped an arm around his waist. "No," she said. "We have nothing important to discuss at the moment, and there's no telling whether Durga's listening in. Let's just enjoy a moment of relaxation—for a change."

Leia grew drowsy, though she remained on guard, half-watching the canals filled with sludgy bog water. Gradually she became aware of ripples stirring the hairy green seaweed; something large moved beneath the surface, easing toward them. She sat up straighter, stiffening.

"Oh, dear," Threepio cried. "I do believe something's approaching.'' He pointed with a golden hand just as a large bulk heaved itself out of the bog water near the canal divider opposite Han and Leia.

The sloping mound, dripping with water and seaweed, blinked two huge copper-red eyes. ''Hoo-hoo-hoo,'' a Hutt voice boomed. ''Welcome, Leia Organa Solo. I am pleased to see you again so soon.''

Leia recoiled, but managed to mask her shock. She sat back in the pool, maintaining her cool diplomatic composure as she recognized the dark birthmark on the Hutt's wet face. ''Lord Durga, welcome home.''

''Your visit comes as such a surprise,'' Durga said, heaving himself higher so that the seaweed sloughed off his sloping head and dripped back into the steaming canals. ''I did not expect you to come so soon. Does this mean you are anxious now to form an alliance with the Hutt syndicate?''

''Don't jump to conclusions,'' Han said.

''Let me handle this, Han.'' Leia squeezed his arm. ''Our visit *is* a gesture of good faith on our part, Lord Durga. I'm sure you know how quickly the New Republic can work, once it has made a decision.'' Han snorted beside her, because she had complained so often about how interminably long even simple processes took. Durga wouldn't know that, however. ''If we decide that an agreement with the Hutts is advisable, you can bet we'll move quickly,'' she said in as businesslike a tone as she could muster. ''No sense postponing profit.''

Durga, though, seemed surprised and uneasy. ''We need not rush a decision as important as this,'' he said. ''We must take great pains to ensure that all are satisfied with our alliance.''

Leia pursed her lips. ''I see,'' she said, realizing that Durga was just stalling to keep them off balance. His initial overture to her on Coruscant had merely been a ruse to gain access to the Imperial Information Center for the Death Star plans. It was clear now that he didn't want an agreement; he just wanted to keep them chasing false leads while the Hutt superweapon was under construction. Leia was determined to learn the site of the secret project and how far along they had managed to get.

"I noticed your battle fleet near our system, Madam President," Durga continued. "I can't help but express my concern—"

Leia raised her hand out of the water with a splash, and trickles ran down her wrist. "Oh, don't worry, they're just engaged in routine military exercises. They could train anywhere, I suppose, but they wanted to accompany me. You know how overprotective bodyguards can get." She sighed. "Nothing to be concerned about—we're going to be allies, remember? *If* we can work out a deal, of course. I wouldn't let a little thing like a few warships engaged in simulated combat bother you."

Durga chuckled again and raised his stubby hands out of the bog water. "Bother me? No, you misunderstand. I merely thought there must be some crucial political brushfires on recalcitrant worlds in your New Republic. I'm surprised you have excess warships that can be wasted on games."

"We haven't had any problems with the Empire at large for a couple of years," Leia said. "Even so, our fleet needs to keep in practice."

Durga widened his eyes and laughed. "Hoo, the Empire may be doing more than you think." His voice boomed in the enclosed catacombs. "To show you my good intentions, let me offer you a service, something for which the Hutts are justly famous."

"And what is that?" Leia asked, not particularly interested.

"Our network has many good sources of information—certain data that could be valuable to your New Republic. While you're here on Nal Hutta, allow me to offer you the services of one of my information brokers. I'll instruct him to check up on what the Empire has been up to recently. I think you may be surprised."

Han grew suddenly tense and alert beside Leia; under

the water his hands clenched into fists. Although she assumed the entire offer was merely another diversion, a ploy to distract them from other lines of inquiry, Leia clasped one of Han's hands and nodded. "I gratefully accept your offer, Lord Durga. The galaxy functions on the basis of accurate intelligence."

She stood up, dripping in the water. "For now, though, I think I've been in the bath too long," Leia said.

Threepio bustled off to get towels.

CHAPTER 25

As night fell outside the opulent palace of Durga the Hutt, the other inhabitants of the bog planet went about their desperate lives. Disguised in tatters, with dirt and weariness smeared across his bearded face—just like any other downtrodden victim of Nal Hutta—General Crix Madine slipped through the gathering gloom with his destination firmly in mind.

With liquid movements he had developed during years of covert operations, Madine worked his way through the dim streets between rundown prefab shacks in a squatters' village. Locked-down warehouses shone like military bunkers under the wan moonlight and harsh security beams around the heavily guarded spaceport.

Distribution centers busily processed the raw materials torn from Nal Hutta's surface and shipped the supplies to the moon Nar Shaddaa. Madine watched chains of light, the trails of regular supply ships, lifting through the cloud-strewn skies to the Smugglers' Moon and returning with cargo holds filled with black-market goods that were purchased and laundered on the moon itself.

The Hutt race had the habit of usurping a world, then using it up, squeezing it dry of resources and polluting the environment. When they eventually destroyed their stolen home planet, the Hutts would move someplace else—and their crime empire was currently in the process of digesting Nal Hutta.

Slum entertainment centers stood on rickety durasteel stilts in the glimmering wet marshland. The entertainment complex seemed like an afterthought to provide hopeless amusement for those trapped on Nal Hutta. Even from a distance Madine could hear the loud music and louder screams.

On the other side of the spaceport Durga's palace was lit up with blue-white spotlights that played across its outer walls. The structure rose like a giant ivory edifice, towering and aloof in the midst of the other inhabitants.

Carrying a partially concealed glowlantern, Madine made his way to the wire-mesh fence that blocked access to the spaceport landing field. Under the security lights Durga's private ship rested, a custom-designed hyperspace yacht, long and vermiform, its smooth iron gray hull adorned with fins and stabilizers for atmospheric travel.

As he crept to the barrier Madine saw other furtive figures huddling near the fence, staring longingly at the ships parked there, tantalizing reminders of a way to escape this world . . . but all the strangers ran away when Madine approached. He wished he could call after them, offer them some hope, promise to rescue them when all this was over—but he could not.

He reached the fence and held the thin, unbreakable wires like any other dejected dreamer. Armed Weequay guards stood in a tight perimeter around Durga's ship; their wrinkled, leathery faces were stony, and they waited like unflinching statues. Madine knew the Weequays were not terribly intelligent, but they were loyal and vicious—there would be no chance to get close to the ship. But he didn't need to.

Madine squatted at the base of the fence and pulled

the glowlantern from the billows of his ragged cloak. He found the hidden catch and opened the compartment behind the lantern. Madine reached inside and withdrew the small fluttering creature, a moon moth with powder-blue gossamer wings that beat gently as it tried to fly.

"Not yet," Madine said. "Pause."

The moth froze in midmotion. Other nocturnal insects buzzed around the brilliant security lights guarding the spaceport landing pad. This moth was a perfect replica of a common insect, crafted by Mechis III's finest droid specialists. The moth machine had limited computer memory—but it knew to follow commands, and it knew its own mission.

Madine held the moth in the palm of his hand and pointed it toward Durga's well-lit hyperspace yacht. "Acquire target," he said. The moth's antennae gyrated and its wings trembled in affirmation. Madine waited just a moment to make sure, then he commanded, "Launch!"

The powder-blue moon moth lifted into the air, spiraling on the night breezes. It flew in a careful random pattern, precisely erratic, drawing no attention whatsoever.

As Madine tilted his head up, cold pearls of rain began to drop, beading on his cheeks. He blinked, rubbed the greasy water from his face, but his beard absorbed the moisture. Staring at the moth as it approached its target, Madine's heart pounded.

This mission was simple and smooth. The moth machine fluttered down and alit on the outer hull of Durga's yacht, just behind one of the stabilizer fins.

The moth stayed on the hull for only a moment, paused to deposit its precious egg—a microscopic droplet—then it beat its wings and rose into the increasing downpour. Madine waited until the tiny droid was lost to sight up in the night blackness, flying as far from Durga's ship as the buffeting winds would allow.

He felt a twinge of sadness when he reached deep into the torn folds to his pocket for the tiny controls—and pressed the "destruct" button.

He saw a sparkle of white light, a flash of the tiny detonation. Then he turned and was already moving away from the fence, melting into the shadows around the prefab ghettos. He had plenty of time to reach the rendezvous point.

The moth's mission had been successful, and now Madine would be able to track Durga's movements, wherever the Hutt went.

DAGOBAH

CHAPTER 26

Luke woke in the middle of the night to see Callista standing over him, her slender body silhouetted against pale watery light, a backwash of reflections that penetrated the polymerized ice walls in the comet quarry.

He sat up, instantly aware. "Callista, what is it?" Warm mists curled around her like steam, and he had an eerie sense of déjà vu, a flash of memory from when he had seen her spectral image while she was trapped inside the *Eye of Palpatine*.

"Luke," she said, her voice quiet and troubled, "we shouldn't be here. . . ."

He increased the light from the glowpanels. "Why not?" He slid out of bed and stood to hold her. She felt soft and warm, fitting comfortably into his embrace. "This place is beautiful and peaceful. What better spot could there be for us to spend some time?"

Callista stared deeply at him with her gray eyes. "This is romantic and private, Luke, but . . . that's all. The comet quarry has no *focus*, no connection to anything that matters to us. It's not personal. I've got to work with something personal.'' She pressed her lips together, then continued with greater conviction, ''Oh, Luke, why not take me to where *you* learned the Force. I'll see it through my own eyes, and you can guide me.''

A silvery tinkle of water spattered from the fountains. The solidified ice walls were thick and muffling. He and Callista seemed isolated, frozen away from everyone else—as she had been frozen inside the computer banks for so many decades.

He squeezed her tightly. ''Yes,'' he said slowly. ''I can show you many places—it'll be like a pilgrimage to the worlds that influenced my life.''

She followed him as he walked out of the sleeping chamber into the common room. He whispered his request to the recessed computer terminal. As the computer search sorted public-access navigation charts, he went over to the food-prep unit and summoned two steaming cups of sweet, soothing jeru tea. He handed one to Callista, and she took it, smiling. This was her favorite beverage, and he had learned to drink it with her.

Luke sat down on the comfortable chair, and Callista took a seat beside him, running her long fingers across his shoulders, drawing a melting line of relaxation. He ran a hand through his ruffled hair to straighten it from the chaos of sleep. He took another sip of the syrupy tea and studied the navigational analysis in an outwardly spiraling list of distances.

He smiled with a wistful sigh as he found his target. ''All right,'' he said and turned to Callista. ''Looks like we'll go to Dagobah first.''

Clouds formed a thick band across the sky of Dagobah, a belt of storms that Luke Skywalker's ship plowed through. He increased the shields to prevent the lightning damage that his X-wing had sustained the first time he had come to find the Jedi Master Yoda.

Dagobah had many climatic areas, many places not

quite as teeming with life as the magnificent swamps; but Yoda had chosen to hide in the marshy areas where his presence could be masked by so many life forces.

Luke talked of Yoda as he brought their space yacht through a break in the canopy. "The first time I landed here in a bog, and my X-wing sank. I thought I'd never get out until Yoda used the Force to heave my ship out of the water. I thought it was impossible. He told me that's why I failed."

Luke risked a glance at Callista, taking his attention from the piloting. "Never believe that yourself. You will get your powers back. Don't think it's impossible."

She nodded. "I know it's not impossible, and I'm going to do it."

The ship spotlights extended brilliant cones to the wet ground below. Luke located a clearing that looked like a field of white boulders, but as he shone the light down to cut through the creeping ground fog, he saw that the white rocks were actually spherical fungi. As the beam played across them, their sensitive skins burst, showering fine spores. He could hear the faint *boom* of fungus blasts as the lumps reproduced in the sudden wash of light.

Luke set the space yacht down, keeping his fingers tense on the controls in case the ship should begin to cant or settle awkwardly. But the ground seemed stable beneath them. He switched off the engines. "Shall we go for a stroll in the swamp?" he said, offering Callista his hand.

They both wore slick, stain-impermeable jumpsuits, and they pulled on hard boots for sloshing through the brackish water. When he cracked open the hatch, the sudden buzz of millions of life forms—croaks, grunts, whistles, and death screams—assaulted his ears, a chaos of natural sounds that made the jungles of Yavin 4 seem peaceful by comparison. Minuscule gnats and biting flies thickened the air.

Luke stood stunned and a little intimidated on the boarding ramp. A mist had already begun to unfold. The snowy shower of white spores settled to the ground from the sensitive spherical fungi. He smelled the damp odor of decay and fresh life. "Yoda," he whispered, as memories fell heavy around him.

"This place is so *alive*," Callista said beside him, startling Luke from his thoughts. He still couldn't get used to the fact that he was unable to sense her with the Force, as he did everything else.

A thread of disappointment laced through her voice. "I can see it and hear it, but I can't *feel* the web of living creatures as I should."

"You will," he said, clasping her hand. "You will. Come on."

They trudged away from the ship and into the brooding swamps. Enormous gnarltrees stretched to the sky, their twisted roots like multilegged creatures balanced with bent knees. The roots were sweeping and arched, forming dark warrens for innumerable creatures. The day was gray and fog-shrouded, growing darker with each moment as sunset approached.

Luke knew that Yoda's home had long since been reclaimed by the swamp, torn to a shambles and left in far worse wreckage than Ben Kenobi's hut had been. He didn't want to return to the place where he had sat beside the alien Jedi Master's deathbed, learning the truth about his father and his sister, watching the wrinkle-faced creature fade into nothingness as his spirit left his body after nine hundred years.

He and Callista slogged through puddles, climbing over fallen trees, and scaring creatures that fled into darker hollows, splashing into the swamp. Much larger growling things moved in the distance, crashing between trees.

Luke spoke of Yoda and of his time training here: jogging through the swamp, levitating rocks and Artoo-Detoo, learning nuggets of Jedi philosophy that Yoda spouted in his convoluted language.

The ground fog thickened into white tentacles that wrapped around their lower legs. Callista's face carried an openness and a tentative wonder that Luke hadn't seen in some time. Occasionally, she gritted her teeth and seemed to be straining, trying to accomplish something. Apparently failing, she said nothing to Luke; he squeezed her hand tighter.

A knobby white spider as tall as a human heaved itself up from a pile of underbrush, its legs like twisted forerunners of the thick gnarl-tree roots. But the knobby hunter meant them no harm, and stalked off in search of smaller prey.

"We should head back to the ship," Luke said. "It's getting dark. We can start some exercises tomorrow."

They circled toward the clearing where they had landed the space yacht, then sat outside in the darkness. Callista brought out a portable glowlamp, and Luke removed a case of rations from the ship's stores. They sat on boulders surrounded by an envelope of light, and tore into their food bars. "What a place for a picnic," Callista said.

She chewed intently while Luke stared down at his tasteless rations. "Yoda didn't like this food," he said. "Couldn't understand how I managed to grow so tall if I ate food like this. He fixed me some kind of stew, and I don't think I wanted to know what was in it."

Bugs swarmed around them, attracted by the light as the night thickened. "Should we go inside the ship?" he asked. "Where it's more comfortable?"

Callista shook her head. "We were comfortable at the Mulako quarry resort. I didn't come here to be comfortable." She looked up at the impenetrable sky. "I wanted to *feel* something here . . . but it's not working." She turned sharply, flashing her slate gray eyes at Luke, and he saw devastation within them. "Why do you stay with me, Luke?" she said.

He blinked, shocked at her question.

"You are a Jedi Master," she continued, "one of the heroes of the Rebellion. You could have anyone you want."

Amazed, Luke raised his hand to cut off her comments. "I don't want just anybody, Callista—I want *you*."

She flung the rest of her ration bar angrily out into the swamp, where it splashed into a weed-covered pool. Luke heard thrashing and bubbles as underwater creatures fought for loose morsels.

Callista's expression grew stern. "Well, that's fine, Luke—but you have to think of more than your feelings. You have a responsibility to the New Republic . . . to the Jedi Knights. If I'm powerless, I'll drag you down."

Longingly, Luke caressed her arm. "No you won't, Callista. I—"

She stood, abruptly stepping away from him. "Yes! There's only one way we can be together. It's all or nothing. If I can't have my powers back, then we shouldn't stay together. You'd better start preparing yourself for that possibility. I don't want to always be in your shadow, unable to do the things you do so easily . . . taunted by the things I used to do myself. You'd be a constant reminder, opening and reopening my wounds. If I'm not your equal, I won't be part of this relationship. That's the way it has to be."

"Hey, wait a minute . . ." Luke said, trying to calm her down.

Suddenly, with a screeching subsonic cry, a swarm of nightbats crashed out of the swamp trees and swooped down. They had leathery wings and insectile bodies with six thin segmented legs bearing small, sharp claws. Attracted by the light, the nightbats came toward them. Other flying creatures flurried in front of them, confused by the high-pitched barrage of noise.

The nightbats attacked indiscriminately, scratching with their claws at Callista and Luke, slashing his jumpsuit, his neck. Luke fended them off with his hands. Two clutched Callista's malt blond hair, tugging it and fighting with each other as she thrashed to knock them away. With a hissing *thrumm* Luke drew his lightsaber, and Callista yanked hers free.

Luke used the Force to strike at his targets, but the nightbats kept coming, dozens of them. The lightsaber blades crackled and flared, topaz and yellow-green—attracting more of the creatures.

Callista hissed in anger and struck with her lightsaber, clumsily wielding it like a club that sliced through anything she encountered. Luke clipped off the wings of a nightbat, even as more swirled in, shrieking.

Callista shouted curses at them as she attacked blindly and with brute force. Her battle disturbed Luke. It was filled with a fury and a wild abandon he had never seen in her. Callista yelled at the nightbats as if they were an incarnation of her greatest enemy.

"It's not fair!" she said, targeting Luke briefly with her gaze. "I've finally found you—and now I might have to give you up." She raised her voice and chopped with the sun-yellow blade in such an explosion of fury that she sliced through three of the nightbats. "It's not fair."

And as she released her anger, Luke felt a glimmer, dark ripples that came from Callista. He caught a glimpse of her image in the Force, like the flickering afterglow of things seen under a strobelight.

"Leave us alone!" she shouted at the bats and unconsciously *pushed*. The remaining nightbats went into a confused spiral away from their campsite—buffeted by Callista's rage—and fled shrieking into the night. Stunned silence returned to the clearing.

Then Callista lowered her energy blade, slumping weakly in the aftermath of what she had done. Luke deactivated his own lightsaber and stared at her in amazement. Outside the perimeter of the glowlamp, though, Luke heard other creatures stirring, larger predators crashing through the underbrush, attracted by the commotion. Out of sight, an overhanging branch cracked and was flung to the ground as something huge lumbered forward.

Luke switched off the glowlamp, plunging the swamp into a darkness lit only by the twinkling lights of phosphorescent insects and glowing fungus. But the large, unseen predators kept coming.

Luke grabbed Callista's arm, and she stiffened, as if

he were a stranger. "Come on," he said. "We've got to get inside before they come back."

She snapped out of her funk and followed him up the boarding ramp into the space yacht. Luke activated the hatch controls and the ship sealed itself, locking down for the night.

They both collapsed on one of the passenger benches, and Callista pressed herself against him. Luke put his arms around her shoulders and squeezed. Callista was shuddering, glistening with a sheen of frightened perspiration. "I opened up for just a second," she said.

"I know," Luke answered. "I could feel it."

Then she looked up at him, her eyes very afraid. "But it was the dark side, Luke! We both recognized it."

Luke nodded, and they stared at each other with a mixture of hope and dread. "At least you've cracked through," he said. "Perhaps now you can do something."

Callista sat up straight, gathering her strength again. She spoke with absolute certainty as the muffled night sounds of Dagobah's swamp enfolded the sealed ship.

"It's not worth the cost, Luke. If I have to touch the dark side to regain my powers, then I'd rather not ever be a Jedi again."

HOTH ASTEROID BELT

CHAPTER 27

Shortly after Durga left in a huff for Nal Hutta on some unexpected diplomatic mission, Bevel Lemelisk watched Imperial General Sulamar transform into an even more pompous ass without the Hutt there to squash his dictatorial impulses.

Sulamar seemed to think he was the reincarnation of Grand Moff Tarkin, strutting about and issuing orders at his whim. But unlike Tarkin, Sulamar gave orders that had no merit, and the general had none of the personal power or iron-hard charisma Tarkin had displayed.

Lemelisk brushed him aside. He'd never had much use for military puffballs. He had work to do.

The growing magnificent construction of the Darksaber filled him with joy as he watched from the distant Orko SkyMine expeditionary ship. The main supports for the superweapon had taken shape, folding the durasteel lattice into a cylindrical tube, like a gigantic wind tunnel.

General Sulamar had supposedly used his influence to obtain surplus computer cores from old Imperial shipyards, cores powerful enough to direct the operations of the Darksaber. The Hutts had been unable to purchase appropriate computers through regular channels, but Sulamar had promised to get them, chin high with self-importance. Lemelisk would believe in the alleged computer cores when he actually saw them.

In Durga's absence, Sulamar loved to remain on the command deck, standing significantly in the space where the Hutt's levitating platform usually hung. The general wore a smug expression on his old baby face.

Lemelisk, though, preferred the private observation blister that Durga used as a relaxation lounge. Here, staring out at the orbiting battering rams of crushed rock, Lemelisk could be alone and at peace with his thoughts, letting his mind buzz as new things occurred to him, ideas he would explore at some later date. The potential for destruction made him curiously aware of the power contained within this space shrapnel. It calmed him.

Once the Automated Mineral Exploiters Gamma and Delta had gone operational—with programming altered so as to ignore each other as potential targets and resources—the construction had progressed amazingly well. Day by day, Lemelisk could see the behemoth blossoming, taking shape from a jumble of loose, drifting girders into a long and shimmering lightsaber handle whose blade would be a superlaser that could crack planets.

The Taurill workers were the key—Durga's masterstroke, and Lemelisk gave the Hutt all the credit he deserved. The multiarmed simian creatures were agile, strong, and intelligent enough en masse.

Lemelisk hadn't the slightest idea where Durga had obtained the thousands of specially made environment suits: small, airtight, heated, and with four arms and two legs to fit the Taurill. Like a pack of vermin the little creatures swarmed outside in the hard vacuum, scurrying over the construction site, working collectively.

Feeling silly at first, Lemelisk had spent hours with representatives from the Taurill, a pair of the fuzzy creatures that seemed like simpering pets. He displayed the

Darksaber plans on the holoprojector, pointing out precise construction details, tediously going over every step. It had seemed at first as if he were speaking to a nonintelligent furball that blinked stupidly at him. But he knew that those blank, half-amused stares were windows to a greater Overmind able to concentrate on the input from these two observers, absorb it, and understand it. At least Bevel Lemelisk hoped so.

These mind-linked creatures would have to work together, knowing the details of the entire design. If everything worked right, the superweapon would be built in a fraction of the time that space construction normally required.

As he looked out and saw the long, girder-sheathed tube being assembled before his eyes, Lemelisk was awed. It was so different, so fantastic to have *enthusiastic* construction workers for once. . . .

The convicts from the penal planet Despayre had proved totally inadequate for the rigors of constructing the first Death Star. They were untrained, physically challenged, mentally unstable—a lousy workforce in every sense. Finally, after their repeated and costly mistakes, Lemelisk expressed his disgust and displeasure to Grand Moff Tarkin, who took appropriate action.

After Tarkin had finished executing the entire work crew, Lemelisk and six hundred stormtroopers accompanied him on a "recruitment drive" to the planet Kashyyyk.

"The Wookiees are animals," Tarkin said, his face pinched, his eyes flinty. "They are hairy and violent, and they smell . . . but they're intelligent enough. If properly broken, they are acceptable workers, as well as expendable in the usual sense. Their planet is out of the way and barely inhabited. A few human traders visit and do a little business, but nothing that will be missed. That's why we've enslaved some of the Wookiees before."

"I know," Lemelisk said. "We used a group of the beasts to help construct Maw Installation. Didn't have much contact with them, though."

"Ah," Tarkin said, nodding, "then you know what brutes they are."

"Yes, but they're certainly strong."

While the Star Destroyers rode in high orbit, Lemelisk accompanied the Grand Moff as the assault shuttles dropped through the atmosphere, weapons blazing to get the attention of the natives. They searched for a place to land on the canopy, and Lemelisk looked out the passenger window in dismay at the leaves and branches swarming with insects and vermin. It turned his stomach to think that this world's inhabitants had done so little to improve their environment: no developments, no civilization, just primitive tree dwellings. The forest itself was unexploited—Lemelisk could barely believe it, and he lowered his expectations of Wookiee intelligence.

The stormtroopers found a crude landing pad on the canopy, supported by thousands of meter-thick branches. Though it looked rickety, the platform proved to be sturdy enough as the assault shuttles settled down with a blast of repulsorlifts.

The Wookiees they encountered had a blatting, growling language that was completely incomprehensible. Luckily, they understood blasters. A number of their leaders also understood Basic, so that when Tarkin issued his demands, the leaders translated the words into barks and snorts. When they roared in defiance, the Wookiees made it clear they understood completely.

Lemelisk sighed. Tarkin would have to do it the hard way.

So the assault shuttles circled, firing with laser cannons until sections of the towering forest gushed with flames. Pillars of smoke rose, spreading like black bloodstains on the sky. The Wookiee animals wailed in betrayal.

Lemelisk had already begun planning how best to use

the brawny brutes in the Death Star construction, calculating how many human guards would be needed per group of Wookiee workers, what the optimum size for a Wookiee labor gang would be. Such administrative and construction details always nagged Lemelisk in the middle of difficult projects.

The Wookiees were lashed with force whips, their offspring herded into hostage camps, adult males and females shoved into cargo compartments. One large bull with silver-tipped fur rebelled, knocking stormtroopers right and left. In moments the other Wookiees joined in the fight, but Tarkin didn't hesitate. He ordered his men to cut down any beast who resisted.

The silver-fringed bull went first, falling off the platform with a smoking hole in his chest. His body crashed through the canopy until it finally came to rest, caught in the thick branches far above ground. Other unruly Wookiees were shot, and the resistance ended quickly. From that point on, all the Wookiees wore binders clamped tightly to their wrists.

Lemelisk wished Tarkin would hurry back to the construction site so they could begin training the new workers. The project did have a deadline, after all, and the Emperor was counting on them. Didn't these Wookiees understand? Probably not, he thought. They were just dumb animals.

On the trip back and during the interminable days of indoctrination, the Wookiees' resistance was further broken with sonic negative-stimulation transmitters, drugs in their food, and threats against the hostages Tarkin had abandoned on Kashyyyk.

Once they got started and trained, though, Lemelisk was proud of the progress the Wookiees made. The work crews were strong and competent, so long as they were carefully watched to prevent sabotage attempts.

It was good to see the Death Star moving toward completion again. . . .

*   *   *

As far as Bevel Lemelisk could tell, the Darksaber construction was correct, but he had a bad feeling as he watched the Taurill working with such speed. He recalled the difficulties he had experienced with the unwilling Wookiee work crews, and he did a telescopic scan, comparing the lines on the holographic blueprints with what he could see of the durasteel latticework forming the large cylindrical skeleton.

The Taurill were hard workers, amazingly speedy— but their greatest flaw, Lemelisk had found, was that they were *distractible*. The hive-minded Taurill had thousands of different facets of attention, and when an asteroid soared too close to the construction site or a smuggler's ship flew within view, the Taurill focused their attention on the new sight. As the Overmind became intrigued with the novelty, more of the multiarmed components turned to look, scrambling for a better view, climbing to new positions, viewing the intriguing event from a new and well-woven perspective.

Unfortunately, this changed the positions of the Taurill bodies, and when the fuzzy creatures returned to their work, many hung at new stations, connecting different girders together, hooking the wrong circuits.

As he studied the lines, Lemelisk felt his heart sink into his paunchy stomach: a large section of the Darksaber outer framework was indeed assembled wrong, girders welded to incorrect counterparts. The computer core receptacle was connected to the waste-heat exhaust. The superlaser anchor points were offset ninety degrees from each other, as wrong as they could possibly be.

Lemelisk immediately stormed out of the peaceful womb of Durga's observation blister. He had to find one of the Taurill and shout at it, explaining where the construction had gone wrong. It didn't matter which of the creatures he talked to; they were all the same, and the Overmind would hear him—oh, yes, the Overmind *would* hear him.

He felt his stomach churning in dread that Durga would find out about the delay and order Lemelisk's execution after all. Lemelisk didn't want to be killed again.

He was relieved the Hutt crime lord was gone. Lemelisk would order the Taurill to work double time to rip apart an entire section of the Darksaber and start all over. The hive-minded creatures had to pay closer attention, though he feared that was probably impossible. But perhaps the situation could be salvaged before anything worse happened.

In all likelihood, General Sulamar wouldn't even notice the mixup.

HOTH

CHAPTER 28

The ice world of Hoth hung beneath its coterie of moons like a cracked snowball. Callista piloted their space yacht, following the coordinates Luke had given her.

He leaned forward in the passenger seat, tingling with anticipation. "Down there," he said, "that's where Obi-Wan's spirit first came to me, when I was near frozen in a blizzard. He told me to go to Dagobah, to find Yoda. Han tried to convince me it was just a hallucination."

Callista sat subdued, gripping the controls. She had been reluctant to tamper with her locked Jedi powers ever since her brush with the dark side on Dagobah. Luke was concerned that her reticence and anxiety would do more damage than any of her actual failures had, because now she was afraid to try. Somehow Luke had to dispel that fear.

Callista stared at the ice planet as they skimmed through the misty atmosphere. "I wish my master Djinn Altis would come to me in a vision," she said. "I'm sure he could offer some insight."

Luke didn't know how to respond, so he squeezed her hand.

She looked at him with a mixture of annoyance and frustration. "I'll be all right, Luke. Maybe I can't have everything I want, but I'm going to do what I can. I haven't given up."

"I'm glad to hear that," he said. "And down there is the next place to try." Luke indicated the white-pocked glacier fields beneath their soaring yacht. "This is where I really learned to fight. I had flown my X-wing against the first Death Star, but here during the battle of Hoth is where I learned to be a warrior. I left the wreckage of Echo Base to find Yoda," Luke said, smiling wistfully at the memory, "and one of the first things he told me was that wars don't make a person great."

"He was wise, your Master Yoda," Callista said. "But sometimes you have to fight. Sometimes it's all or nothing. That's the only way to win." She swallowed. "That's why I made my sacrifice in the *Eye of Palpatine*."

Luke said, "Let's hope you don't ever have to face that all-or-nothing choice again."

She forced a smile. "I'd prefer that."

Callista skimmed low under the afternoon sunlight where ice chips burned bright below the whitish sky. She darkened the viewport shields to cut down the glare.

"I don't know what shape Echo Base is going to be in," Luke said. "It suffered some pretty extensive battle damage, and it's been abandoned for years. Don't expect luxury accommodations like the Mulako quarry."

Callista looked across the frozen snowfield. "At least it won't have any bugs or bats." She sat up straight. "Hey, what's that ship?"

As they approached the line of rocky hummocks, Luke spotted a blackened hulk lying in the snow, surrounded by a starburst of greasy soot and slagged wreckage. "Can't be a leftover crash from the battle," he said. "That was nine years ago. This is something new." Luke stared at the burned debris, reaching out with his sense.

"Nothing alive there that I can tell. It's recent, but not too fresh."

Callista brought their yacht down near the wreckage, close to the hidden shield doors that sealed off Echo Base in the solid ice. She double-checked with her scanners. "Yes, the metal's all cold. Ambient temperature. It's been here a few days at least, maybe as much as a couple of weeks."

Luke opened the uniform locker and removed the two insulated jumpsuits hanging beside a pair of full environment suits. Luke and Callista pulled on the uniforms, activating the body heaters and tugging on gloves. Luke clipped his lightsaber to his belt and handed the second smooth black handle to Callista. "Here, you'd better take yours."

"I don't want to," Callista said, glancing away.

"But you should do it anyway," Luke answered. "You always have the option of not using it." White-lipped, she took it, still refusing to meet his gaze.

They climbed out of the yacht into the blinding cold of Hoth, leaving the door closed but not sealed, so they could reenter in a hurry. Callista shivered as she walked beside him. "It's chilly here," she said.

He raised his eyebrows and felt frost already collecting on the skin of his cheeks. "Chilly?" he said. "But this is the hottest part of the day."

Their boots crunched on the ice-crusted snow as they walked to the wrecked ship. "It was a single transport," Luke said, bending over a scorched hull plate. "Probably a blockade runner or a light freighter, the kind smugglers and poachers use."

Callista picked up a twisted lump of metal, turned it over in her gloved hands, then let it drop. Her breath curled in white steam from her mouth. "Do you think they crashed?" she said. "I don't see any bodies."

Luke shook his head. The icy air sliced into his nostrils like razors. "No, look at the pattern. The ship landed safely and then exploded on the ground. See, none of the snow is plowed up. There'd be a long crash furrow if it came down from orbit.''

Luke looked over at the snow-camouflaged opening of Echo Base. ''Maybe they took shelter there.'' He pointed out the blaster cannon turrets on either side of the shield door. ''Let's check this out—but be careful.''

The wind picked up, skirling around the rocks in transient whirlwinds that whipped ice crystals into the air and scoured the snowdrifts. The opening to the ice cave was flanked by rocks, though most of Echo Base had been chewed into the centuries-old packed snow and ice.

As they approached the shield doors, the pair of silent blaster-cannon emplacements standing like sentinels suddenly came to life. The turrets swiveled, the long deadly barrels seeking a target—and finding one.

''Look out!'' Callista shouted, and shoved Luke out of the way.

He dived to one side, using his Jedi powers to fling him farther. Callista rolled, hitting the ground as the first blast seared out. Steam boiled from a fresh crater in the ice.

Luke began to run back toward her, but Callista rolled aside and moved out of range. The turrets swiveled, targeting on Luke, and fired again. He leaped into the air, and the beam missed him, exploding one of the frozen rocks.

As the blaster cannon fired a third time, Luke drew his lightsaber and deflected the beam with blinding speed, countering the bolt with the energy blade. The sheer power of the blaster cannon made Luke reel, and only the strength of his synthetic hand allowed him to withstand the blast.

''Must be motion detectors, Luke. They're tracking us as we move!'' Callista shouted. ''I'm going to run and draw their fire. You use your Jedi powers to rush forward and knock out both weapons.''

''No,'' Luke shouted. ''It's too—''

But Callista was already on her way. Luke knew this

was how she did things: she made up her mind and then took action without considering the risks or even alternate ideas. For better or worse, Callista was in it now, sprinting in a zigzag pattern across the snow. Both blaster cannon emplacements swiveled, locking in on her.

Luke plunged forward until he landed in front of the cannon. Holding the lightsaber in one hand, he scrambled up the tower and slashed with the glowing blade, severing the barrel of the weapon. He threw himself onto the snow and scrambled to the second turret just as the damaged one fired. With the barrel gone and its end fused, the cannon blast blew up the entire turret.

The second weapon targeted Callista. She danced to one side, throwing herself into the snow half a second before the beam struck the glacier with an explosion sufficient to hurl Callista into the air.

Luke didn't take the time to climb the second blaster turret. He used his lightsaber to hack at the emplacement itself as if it were the trunk of a giant tree. He chopped through the armored plating, and a smoking square of durasteel tumbled to the ice. Luke stabbed inside with the yellow-green blade, slashing the power conduits and computer interlinks, slicing the heart out of the weapon. Above him the ominous barrel stuttered to one side, seeking another target, then went dead.

He looked up and noted that the weapons themselves had been jury-rigged, sensors wired in with automatic targeting systems, linked to motion detectors. He hurried over to help Callista to her feet, wondering why someone would go to all that trouble on this empty world.

"Good work," she said as they brushed each other off. "We're a team even without my Jedi powers."

With a reluctant grinding *thud,* the shield door split in the middle and began to spread apart. Icicles flaked off, and chunks of snow crashed to the ground. Figures appeared, shadowy forms standing in the crack of the partially opened door.

Luke tensed and turned around, the lightsaber

gripped in his hand. Callista held her weapon, but did not ignite it. Luke waited to see what their mysterious enemies would do.

"Don't just stand there," a gruff human voice shouted. "Get inside quick, before those creatures come back!"

A dark-eyed man wearing the shadowy stains of beard stubble and remnants of white plasteel armor stepped outside, holding a blaster rifle. Beside him came a hairy feline alien with tufts of fur sprouting from his chin and fangs protruding below narrow black lips. A Cathar, Luke recognized. The feline alien also carried a blaster rifle and sniffed the cold air, tense and ready to fight. They did not point their blasters toward Luke or Callista, though. Instead, they seemed to watch for some invisible threat from the snows.

Another human man, tall and broad shouldered, stood within the main tunnel, gesturing for them to hurry. Luke looked around at the bleak, seemingly lifeless surface of Hoth; then he felt a sudden uneasiness. He grabbed Callista's arm and rushed with her into the shelter.

Only five of them had survived.

"Seemed an easy way to make a few credits, since I was looking for a new occupation," said Burrk, a former stormtrooper who had deserted the Empire in the turmoil following the battle of Endor. Ever since that time, he had been on his own, surviving through shady dealings and illegal activities.

"I hooked up with these two Cathar, Nodon and Nonak." The two feline aliens growled and flashed their teeth, glaring through slitted eyes at Luke and Callista. They appeared identical except for slight variations in fur color.

"They're both from the same litter," Burrk continued, "and they were great hunters—at least they said they were." The two Cathar snarled, extending hooked claws from their hands. Burrk didn't even seem to notice. He rubbed the stubble on his chin. His eyes were sunken, haunted by unrelenting tension, as if someone had beaten him repeatedly and might return at any moment. Together, his group had managed to get only a dozen or so glowpanels functioning again, and none of the heater units.

"There's a huge black-market price on wampa pelts, you know," he said, and finally a spark of pride and daring appeared in his eyes. Although Luke sensed the brooding terror surrounding them in the unheated meeting room, the gaunt former stormtrooper grew more animated as he spoke.

"So, the Cathar brothers and I decided to set up big-game expeditions. For a fee, we'd take hunters here to track down and kill the 'biggest game in the galaxy'—a bit of an exaggeration, perhaps, but that didn't matter to rich Baron-Administrators, like him." Burrk gestured to the tall muscular man with chiseled features, a white smile, and hardened eyes.

"Drom Guldi," the muscular man said, introducing himself, "Baron-Administrator of the Kelrodo-Ai gelatin mines." He swelled with pride, confident that everyone had heard of him. "We're famous for our water sculptures," he said. "And this is my aide." He indicated a nervous-looking man with gray-blond hair and faint wrinkles across his skin, as if his surface layer had crumpled with a thousand pressure cracks. "Sinidic."

Burrk the stormtrooper continued with his story, giving the rich hunter a nod of grudging admiration. "We had four customers on this run, and Drom Guldi was the only one worth having."

"I bagged ten of those wampas myself when they attacked," the Baron-Administrator said, "though we couldn't go back and collect the pelts." He ground his teeth together, and a flush rose to his bronzed cheeks. "The other monsters kept coming, and we had to retreat."

"What happened?" Callista said. "How did you let yourself get so vulnerable?"

Burrk stared at his fingers, nervously twining and intertwining them. "This was our third run. The other two went smoothly. We would track the creatures, bag one or two, and then leave. By this time, the monsters had learned how to work together. We thought they were dumb brutes—all teeth and claws, and no brains—but we were wrong."

The two Cathar hissed, and their fur ruffled.

"We knew about this old abandoned base. Used it as a stopping point because there isn't much shelter on this rock," Burrk said, and he looked up at Luke. "We went out on scouting teams: me and Nodon on one ship, Nonak and the others on another. It was just a day's hunt. Sun was shining. Looked perfect." His haunted eyes stared off into the shadows of the room. "We came back, and found our pilot slaughtered—and I mean *slaughtered*. We had all those weapons. We never thought they'd attack us."

"We underestimated the problem," Sinidic said in a thin nasal voice, then ducked his head, as if realizing he shouldn't have spoken.

"When we went to investigate," Burrk continued, "the wampas must have been waiting for us. They . . . erupted out of the snow and fell upon us like a meteor strike. We couldn't see 'em. They killed one of our guides and the other three clients. Luckily we got to shelter in the base . . . we closed the shield doors behind us." He swallowed, reliving the nightmare.

Drom Guldi picked up the story, businesslike and matter-of-fact. "That's when they blew up our ship," he said. "Must have been an accident. I can't believe they knew what to do. They triggered it themselves."

"We've been here four days," Burrk said. "No supplies, and those things are out there waiting for us. We couldn't even send a distress signal."

Nodon, one of the Cathar, said, "Do you have weapons in your ship?"

Luke and Callista looked at each other. "Weapons? No," Luke admitted.

Callista said, "We didn't think we were coming into combat."

"We got the two blaster cannons working," Burrk said. "Rigged motion detectors to fire on anything approaching. But you sure took care of those." A low bubbling growl came from the Cathar throats. "Now we got no defenses other than those doors—and we can't stay here forever."

"You can't all fit in our ship, either," Callista said, anticipating their next question. "It's only a small yacht. But we can transmit a distress signal, get a rescue crew here within a day or so."

"It's getting dark," Sinidic pointed out. "Shouldn't we do something as soon as we can?" He looked up to Drom Guldi. "Why don't you order them to go back to their ship and send a signal."

"We'll *all* go to their ship," Drom Guldi said. "Otherwise, Burrk just might take them hostage and fly off and leave us here. And I don't suppose I'd blame him." The Cathar snarled, but from the way they looked at the former stormtrooper, Luke suspected they considered the possibility likely.

"We've got only a dozen charges left in our blaster rifles," Burrk said, not the least bit offended by the accusation. "We won't last long if we're under attack."

Drom Guldi squared his jaw. "We'll have to make the most of what we have. Make a stand."

Luke met Callista's gaze. Helping people was one of the primary responsibilities of a Jedi Knight, and they could not turn down even poachers and unscrupulous hunters such as these. But Luke felt his skin crawl with the memory of his own encounter with a wampa.

Coiled and tense, the two Cathar stood from the empty storage containers they had used as seats and readied their blasters. Drom Guldi slung his rifle over his shoulder. Sinidic carried no weapon, but clung close to the Baron-Administrator. Burrk wore two blaster pistols at his hips; they looked battered and well used, repaired enough times that Luke wouldn't count on them. He and Callista had their lightsabers.

"Let's do this fast," Burrk said, leading them to the outer shield doors. "We can make a dash for it . . . since we don't have to worry about the motion sensors anymore." He scowled at Luke.

"Leave the door partially open as a fallback option," Drom Guldi suggested, "in case we need to make a hasty retreat." Burrk nodded.

Luke sensed an interesting shift in command. Burrk was the nominal leader, but Drom Guldi—a hardened administrator—was equally proficient in making decisions under stress. The two men seemed to have formed a team for their own survival.

The shield door opened, and freezing air and snow gusted in. The sky had turned a hazy purple as the day drew to a close. Together, Luke and Callista led the five survivors in a sprint past the wreckage of the exploded poachers' ship to their own small space yacht.

Luke focused his senses on Burrk and the others, concerned that the desperate refugees might try to blast him and Callista in the back and take their ship—but he sensed only a gnawing fear. These people were too frightened to worry about treachery.

As Luke and Callista approached their ship sitting calmly on the snow, Luke saw that the hatch stood open, like a dark mouth. Callista said, "Hey, I didn't leave the door like that."

"I've got a bad feeling about this," Luke muttered. The Cathar looked at each other and snarled.

"Bad news," Drom Guldi said, already guessing what they would find. Luke bounded up the ramp, while Callista stayed outside to prevent the others from entering the ship.

Inside in the cockpit, Luke stared. The comm system had been torn to shreds, the panels ripped open with a silver scoring of claws. The navicomputer was gone, torn from its housing and smashed to a tangle of wires and broken chips. Severed cables dangled loose from the other controls.

It was as if the monsters knew exactly what they were doing.

A coil of fear tightened in the pit of his stomach. He turned behind him to the locker where the environment suits had hung—and found that the snow creatures had slashed both of the suits, making them unusable.

Then came a shout from outside, a panicked outcry and sudden blaster fire. Luke charged out of the cockpit, leaping down the ramp. Callista already had her lightsaber drawn, its topaz beam crackling and spitting in the cold.

Luke could barely distinguish the creatures that blended so perfectly with the snow and rock. Their white pelts made them only a blur of movement, curving horns sweeping from their heads, claws like knives extended as they boiled up, slashing and tearing and roaring.

Burrk drew both of his blaster pistols and fired, leaving a huge wampa dead in the snow with smoking holes in its fur. The two Cathar snarled, waving their blaster rifles. Burrk tried to fire again, but one of his pistols had been drained dry. The wampas bellowed, setting up an odd howl that careened across the empty steppes like a tidal wave of terror.

Drom Guldi fired carefully and precisely, taking out another wampa. The remaining monsters pushed forward. One of the two Cathar shot indiscriminately, lancing the snowy distance with blaster fire until his rifle also ran out of charge.

With an echoing roar that seemed somehow familiar, Luke turned to see a huge wampa standing on a rock outcrop, larger than the others, howling into the night as if directing the battle. Luke saw that this monster had only one arm; its other ended in a cauterized stump. It slashed its single fistful of claws through the icy air when it saw the Jedi lightsabers.

In unison, the army of wampa ice creatures surged toward their victims.

NAR SHADDAA

CHAPTER 29

The Taurill Overmind did not pause, did not rest. So many of the little interchangeable bodies swarmed over the zero-gravity construction site that work progressed at a relentless pace.

Bevel Lemelisk was ecstatic to see that in only two days the busy creatures had managed to disassemble their erroneous work, erasing the mistakes and rebuilding the entire faulty section of the Darksaber. Lemelisk watched the efforts and prayed that the Taurill did not make an even worse mistake that might somehow escape his scrutiny.

At one time during the worst setback, when much of the superstructure remained dismantled, General Sulamar had stepped up behind him on the Orko SkyMine ship with a startling click of his bootheels. The baby-faced general stared out the observation windows. "Good work, Engineer," he said grudgingly, as if Lemelisk had been waiting for such praise. "Carry on."

Lemelisk had rolled his eyes and gone to find something to eat. Somehow, he had forgotten to eat lunch again. . . .

He chose the dead hours during the designated sleep period to continue his work with the three-dimensional crystal-lattice puzzle. It amused him with a challenge that stretched him almost—but not quite—to the limit of his mental abilities. When he had reached the critical point, focusing his entire world upon the problem and adjusting the parameters ever so delicately—he was interrupted, again.

The crystal puzzle sparkled down to random shards as Lemelisk flew into a rage at the Gamorrean guard. The brute let the insults bounce off his thick greenish skin and grunted only one word: *Durga.*

Lemelisk quashed his annoyance and followed the Gamorrean down the corridor to the communications center. Durga had sent a private message to him, knowing full well that it was the middle of the sleep period—but then, the Hutt had never shown much courtesy to others.

The guard left Lemelisk alone to face the flat screen projection of Durga the Hutt. Durga could have used the holoprojector, which transmitted a small three-dimensional image—but the Hutt did not like the 3-D system, because it made his enormous body look diminutive. He wanted the flatscreen, which projected his sloping, birthmarked face as a large and dominating visage. The speakers amplified his voice to a thunderous bellow.

"Lemelisk," Durga said. "I know Sulamar is on his rest period, so I can speak to you without his interference. Those computer cores he obtained have arrived on Nar Shaddaa. I want you to come to the Smugglers' Moon personally and check them out. No telling what sort of garbage he's found for us. You must inspect them."

"But—I can't leave the construction site, not now!" Lemelisk said.

"Why?" Durga demanded. "Have there been problems?"

"No, no," Lemelisk answered, holding his hands up. He hoped Durga couldn't see the sudden film of cold sweat that sprang out on his skin. "Uh, everything's going smoothly. The Taurill are hard workers, and very fast."

"Good. I'm sending a ship to get you. You will make no contact with me. Just come to Nar Shaddaa and do your work. I am still trapped in an unpleasant diplomatic matter here."

"When—" Lemelisk swallowed, his mind whirling, "um, when will you return to the asteroid belt, Lord Durga?"

"Soon," the Hutt answered. "This visit of the Chief of State is tedious, but necessary. She has brought a fleet of warships, supposedly engaged in battle exercises, but I am no fool: she means to flaunt her power. That is throwing a bent hydrospanner into our talks, though I don't believe the New Republic suspects anything."

Durga suddenly growled and snapped back to the matter at hand. "Enough pleasantries! Get to the Smugglers' Moon as soon as possible. Once my Darksaber is finished, I won't need to be so disgustingly nice to these disgusting humans anymore."

Lemelisk didn't know the type of ship he boarded. It was a battered old craft that seemed heavily (and ineffectively) modified. It had been through numerous battles, judging from the blaster scars on its outer hull plates, and the swollen engines looked sufficient to power a craft ten times the size. It bore no registry markings.

The Twi'lek pilot said little, even to the human co-pilot. One of the alien's head-tails was scarred and shriveled, as if it had been burned or partially shot off. Two Gamorrean guards accompanied Lemelisk onto the ship, saying little, throwing supplies on board, and grumbling during takeoff.

The Twi'lek pilot launched them from the expeditionary vessel, away from the Darksaber site, and out of the asteroid field before Lemelisk managed to strap his crash webbing into place. He craned his neck and tried to look out the rear viewports toward the dwindling construction lights.

Lemelisk hated to leave, especially at a time like this. He never knew what was liable to happen if he was not there to supervise personally. . . .

Darth Vader had come aboard the first Death Star while it was still under construction. "I'm here to supervise personally," he said, his deep voice echoing through his impenetrable black mask. His breath, drawn through pumps on his chest, sounded like a hissing serpent.

Lemelisk stared in awe at the Emperor's greatest warrior, the black-caped Dark Lord of the Sith, who already had the blood of billions on his gloved hands, and still had a long career ahead of him.

Grand Moff Tarkin had insisted that a small section of the Death Star's living quarters be completed posthaste so he could move his offices aboard the battle station. He had set up a large armed reception for Vader's arrival, with an honor guard of stormtroopers, waves of warriors ready to die at the Emperor's command.

Lemelisk had forgotten to shave, and was afraid his personal appearance might be less than adequate as Vader towered over him. The Dark Lord stared through impenetrable eye goggles and hissed through the respirator. "I am here to . . . motivate your workers," he said, looking from Tarkin to Lemelisk.

Lemelisk rubbed his pudgy hands together, smearing grease stains into the cracks on his knuckles. He wiped his hands on his thighs. "Good, Lord Vader! They need some motivation. The Wookiee work crews are strong and competent, but they take every opportunity to stall progress." Tarkin looked at Lemelisk, astonished, and the engineer wondered if he had said something he shouldn't have.

"Then perhaps the construction foremen need to exercise a tighter grip," Vader said. "Or perhaps I need to demonstrate the limits of discipline."

Lemelisk found Vader terrifying. Yes, a pep talk from the Emperor's right-hand man would make even the most recalcitrant Wookiees work harder and faster.

But Vader did not have a pep talk in mind. Looming over terminals, he scanned through the computer records and work activity reports and selected the Imperial crew bosses who supervised the construction teams with the poorest performance.

Grand Moff Tarkin summoned all supervisors to sit around a big table in the largest briefing room in the completed portion of the Death Star.

"I am most displeased with your progress," Vader said after he had singled out the two least effective construction foremen. As the others watched, trembling with terror around the table, Vader raised his black leather glove. No one could read any expression through his skull-like plasteel helmet.

The two unfortunate foremen gasped and choked, clawing as if an invisible, iron-hard fist had wrapped itself around their windpipes. They kicked and thrashed, spasming, choking. Drool ran from their mouths—then there came a *crunching* sound, and the spittle ran a thick red. Their eyes nearly popped out of their sockets like spoiled fruit.

Then Vader lowered his arm, and the two dead bosses crumpled across the table. Vader looked at the sweating construction foremen who remained at the table. "I expect the rest of you to do better from now on," he said.

Vader ordered Tarkin's stormtroopers to take the pair of dead bodies out to the space construction site, where they wired the vacuum-frozen corpses to crossbeams on the outer shell of the half-finished Death Star.

Lemelisk was surprised and appalled at Vader's tactics, but he changed his mind when he noticed that the crews did redouble their efforts. Tarkin was also very pleased. His own future seemed bright indeed.

*   *   *

Now, Lemelisk didn't know how he had gotten into such a mess. He rode in a surly silence with the other pilots of the smugglers' ship approaching Nar Shaddaa. Space traffic around the Smugglers' Moon was subdued, illegal ship activity hampered by the presence of the nearby New Republic fleet.

As Lemelisk watched Nar Shaddaa, anxiety gnawed at the pit of his stomach. He didn't want to go there, didn't want to be around so many people, didn't want to walk willingly into that nest of vermin. The crew accompanying him was unpleasant enough—and they were on *his* side. Lemelisk had no way of knowing what sort of scum he would encounter in the rundown streets of Nar Shaddaa.

He hoped to be in and out as soon as possible, and he hoped—though he didn't expect it—that General Sulamar had actually obtained acceptable computer components for the Darksaber.

Already, Lemelisk found himself longing to be alone with his plans and his dreams. But to make his brainchild a reality, he had to make certain sacrifices.

As always, Bevel Lemelisk would do his duty, even if it cost him his life . . . again.

CHAPTER 30

The New Republic fleet engaged in out-system/in-system speed trials and maneuverability runs. Ackbar's ships leap-frogged Wedge's squadrons as they pushed their piloting skills to the limits, always remaining on call should trouble arise for the Chief of State.

Fortunately, everything had been quiet for several days, and it did not appear that the Hutts were going to be a problem. Leia sent word that she believed her mission would be over in a day or two, so General Wedge Antilles, taking the opportunity to apply for some rest and recreation, accompanied Qwi Xux down to the Smugglers' Moon.

"You always take me to such interesting places, Wedge," Qwi told him, staring around at the seedy sections of Nar Shaddaa, her indigo eyes filled with amazement, and drinking in details.

Wedge laughed. "Well, this isn't exactly one of the more . . . romantic places I've shown you."

Qwi shrugged and tossed her head. Her hair was like a mass of spun crystal fragments, pearly white strands made of fine feathers that sparkled around her head. "No, but it's still fascinating," she said. She had an elfin appearance with a faint blue tinge to her skin that gave her an exotic charm—yet she looked and acted completely human.

Qwi Xux had been brainwashed as a child to become a weapons designer for the Empire. In Maw Installation she had helped design the original Death Star with Bevel Lemelisk, and she had developed the Sun Crusher by herself. She remembered little of that, however, because young Kyp Durron, flooded with dark side powers, had erased much of her memory in a disastrous attempt to make it impossible for anyone to re-create such weapons. Despite her many ordeals, Qwi retained a childlike sense of wonder at discovering new things. Wedge found it endearing, and he loved her more with each day he spent at her side.

They left their small shuttle at the Port Authority and paid a fee to guarantee its protection—an exorbitant enough price that Wedge was reasonably sure they would have no troubles. He wore no uniform, only a nondescript jumpsuit in the pockets of which he had stashed an assortment of weapons, communicators, and locator beacons. They should be fine.

Nar Shaddaa was a nightmare of decrepit buildings, empty warehouses, and closed doors marked "Keep Out" in numerous languages. Low-level fliers cruised across the sky, belching smoke from poorly tuned engines. Industrial processing centers spewed toxic wastes into the air and down drainage pipes.

The atmosphere itself was murky and oily, laden with vapors that made visibility equivalent to looking through a glass of dirty water. The planet Nal Hutta filled much of the stained sky, a bruised green, blue, and brown sphere, rising halfway over the horizon like a heavy-lidded eye.

Wedge and Qwi strolled along the stuttering glidewalk, looking at flashing signs that advertised bizarre services. Giant, open repair bays yawned wide, full of dismantled parts stolen from ships that hadn't paid exorbitant protection money, as Wedge had done. The Smugglers' Moon seemed like a world-size mechanics' shop, dingy and grease-stained, filled with discarded components that might eventually find some use, or just as likely might remain forgotten in a corner until the end of the universe.

Vendors wedged their carts into alleys under waterproof canopies that deflected the droplets drizzling from overhead gutters. A plantlike alien sold sizzling hunks of bluish meat on a stick; beside it, a fanged carnivore sold sliced vegetables. The two glared at each other with animosity.

They passed gambling establishments and card-reading cubicles, where fortunes were told, or made, or lost. Qwi blinked as she watched a random game of blinking lights and metal spheres hurled by the players. If the players managed to strike one of the lights while it was illuminated, they won some sort of prize, usually a coupon to play another round of the game.

Wedge found the nuances incomprehensible, but as Qwi absorbed them she slowly shook her head. "The probabilities make this game extraordinarily difficult to win," she said.

Wedge smiled. "*Now* you're starting to understand."

A pair of rickety old starships roared overhead, and the sounds of explosions made Wedge glance up. The two ships fired upon each other, and the pursuing ship exploded into a cloud of shrapnel that rained down on the buildings. Across a yawning open space, Wedge watched patrons seated on an outdoor balcony run for their lives as smoldering chunks of metal pelted the building. The victorious ship continued to limp away, its damaged engines faltering; then, with a hollow-sounding *boom,* the engines gave out, and the ship spiraled down into the distance, where it crashed.

In a parking area for maintenance vehicles, Qwi stopped to inspect a vendor's table of trinkets and exotica, including boots made from rancor leather and glistening claws that he claimed came from wampa ice creatures.

"How do we know these are real?" Qwi asked the vendor, a reptilian creature with a long tapering forehead and three eyes across his brow ridge.

"You have my word on it," the vendor said.

"No thanks," Wedge said, and took Qwi by the elbow, leading her to a small self-serve café under the fluttering awnings of an open-air bazaar. Wedge ordered samples from the few recognizable items on the menu, carrying a tray laden with fizzing colorful drinks and glossy dessert pastries.

"This place is different from Coruscant," Qwi said, summarizing her feelings. "Much more . . . lived in, less polished."

Wedge raised his eyebrows, "You can say that again."

Qwi blinked at him. "Why should I?"

"Never mind," he said, smiling indulgently.

They selected a table far from where two enormous, gray-skinned brutes were bellowing at each other in what seemed to be either a blood feud or an argument; the longer Wedge watched, however, the more he realized that this was merely their method of conversation.

The torn umbrella over their heads leaked some of the residue drizzling from above, so Wedge and Qwi moved to the opposite side where the table was relatively clean. They stared out across the crowded streets and saw a long wall of identical-looking warehouses, some guarded, some merely locked.

Qwi sipped her drink and sat up, startled, as the fizz bubbled around in her mouth. She swallowed, drew several quick breaths, and gasped, "That's very good, but I shall have to restrain myself!"

"Just take a sip at a time," Wedge said, "and you'll enjoy it."

Qwi looked at her dessert pastry and spoke distractedly. "You've shown me so many places, Wedge.

Maw Installation is still a blur, though I can remember what it was like . . . at least since you took me back there. It was much smaller than this place, not so many people. Quiet and private and clean. Everything in its place, regimented, easy to find.''

"But without much freedom," Wedge pointed out.

"I believe you're right," Qwi answered. "Of course, I didn't know that at the time. I didn't know much of anything. You've already given me far more worthwhile memories than I lost," she said. "There are times when I think Kyp Durron simply removed the bad parts from my brain, leaving room for you to show me more wonders."

"So you don't think your past will ever come back?" he said.

"The pieces that are missing are gone," Qwi said, "but those that remain are vivid images, bright pieces that I'm able to connect in my mind. I can string them together, so that it *seems* like I remember, even though much of it is just my imagination." Qwi stared across at the warehouses, intent on something.

Wedge watched her. He liked looking at her face, liked seeing her reactions to new things, and it made him see old familiar places with a new eye. He found it refreshing.

Suddenly Qwi's body went rigid, and she gave an absurd high-pitched whistle as she sucked in a little gasp of air. Qwi stood up too quickly and bumped her drink, spilling the foaming liquid across the tabletop.

"What is it?" Wedge grabbed for her thin wrist.

Qwi pointed across at the warehouses. "I just saw him—there! I recognized him."

"Who?" Wedge said, seeing nothing out of the ordinary.

Qwi had better eyesight than he did—he knew that from long experience—but none of the figures moving toward the warehouses seemed distinctive: an assortment of surly-looking humanoids, a few hardbitten aliens, and a paunchy man, all of whom disappeared into the murky building.

"I know him," Qwi insisted. "I worked with him. Bevel Lemelisk. We designed the Death Star together. He's here. Why is he here? How could he be here?"

Wedge held her, and her entire body was trembling. "Come on, Qwi—that couldn't possibly be him." He lowered his voice. "You can't see anything clear enough from here. We were just talking about your old memories. It must have sparked something in you. Don't let your imagination run away with you."

"But I'm sure it was him," Qwi said.

"Maybe it was," Wedge answered doubtfully, "but if so, what does it matter? Maw Installation is no longer a threat. The Empire is gone. Maybe he's fallen in with some smugglers."

Qwi sat down, still troubled. "I don't want to stay here anymore," she said.

Wedge handed her his drink. "We can share mine. Drink up," he said. "We'll go back to our ship"—then he added with a wry smile—"unless you want to go find one of those Hutt bathhouses I've heard so much about?"

"No thanks," Qwi said.

Bevel Lemelisk went with his entourage through the back streets of Nar Shaddaa until they reached the warehouse sector. Lemelisk kept pausing to rub his feet on cleaner patches of the pavement, trying to remove the sticky residue and slime he stepped in every time he averted his eyes from the path.

The Twi'lek captain drew his blaster and stomped toward an old, ugly warehouse. The towering, corroded door stood locked; giant letters painted across its riveted surface proclaimed RESTRICTED and TRESPASSERS WILL BE DISINTEGRATED—but then, Lemelisk realized that *everything* on Nar Shaddaa was restricted, so the warning hardly mattered.

As they waited for the Twi'lek to access the heavy door, Lemelisk looked around at the brooding, shadowy city. His skin prickled with the creepy feeling that someone was watching him. He turned and looked, but noted nothing out of the ordinary. When the Twi'lek opened the door into the cool and musty-smelling warehouse, Lemelisk ducked down to be the first inside.

The Twi'lek switched on a bank of glowpanels. One flickered and died, but the remaining four cast their dirty light into the crate-filled warehouse. Cargo containers stood high against the far wall, stenciled with an indecipherable language; many of their sides were cracked and oozed a noxious-looking substance.

The human copilot gestured to Lemelisk and grunted, taking him to a pair of crates in the center of the room. From the footprints on the dusty floor Lemelisk could tell that the crates had been placed there recently. The wording on their sides marked them as "Sewage Inspection Systems—Quality Control Samples."

The Gamorrean guards tore open the crates, spilling out the self-digesting packing material and exposing a pair of large computer cores, antique cybernetic systems, slow and long obsolete.

Lemelisk stifled a laugh. *This* was the best Sulamar could do with his great Imperial connections? He went forward and brushed at the ID plates, scanning for their numbers. These things had been old when Maw Installation was built—but if he had no other choice for the Darksaber . . . Lemelisk began to consider the possibilities. It was a challenge, and he liked challenges.

The computer cores would need extensive modifications and upgrading, but Lemelisk was up to the task. The Darksaber had only a thousandth of the systems the original Death Star had required, without surface defenses or living quarters for a million personnel. The Darksaber only needed to move itself and to fire its weapon—that was all. Even those two tasks might prove daunting for such prehistoric computer cores, but perhaps Lemelisk could make it work.

As he studied the equipment, the lowlifes behind him suddenly stood at attention. The Gamorrean guards grunted and turned around.

"Hoo-hoo, will they function, Engineer Lemelisk?" Durga the Hutt asked, emerging from the shadows on his repulsorsled.

Startled, Lemelisk brushed packing material off of himself and tried to compose his response. "Lord Durga, this is a surprise! I didn't know you'd be here personally."

"Will they work?" Durga repeated.

Lemelisk answered cautiously. "They can be *made* to work. I don't know what Sulamar told you, but these are bottom-of-the-line junk. I believe they can be sufficiently upgraded, though. I'll give it my highest priority."

"Good," Durga said. "I have made my excuses to the New Republic's Chief of State and called our diplomatic meeting to an end. I'm anxious to get back and see what progress you have made on my superweapon."

"I think you'll be pleased, Lord Durga," Lemelisk said.

"I had better be," Durga answered. "We will take my own ship back to the asteroid belt," he said. "I want to be where I can watch my Darksaber."

Lemelisk nodded in full agreement. "I'll be happy to get away from Nar Shaddaa," he said, leaning over and whispering conspiratorially to the bloated Hutt. "There are too many unsavory types here!"

CHAPTER 31

Piloting the *Millennium Falcon* with only the assistance of Artoo-Detoo, Chewbacca brought the modified light freighter out of hyperspace as close to the Nal Hutta System as he dared. With the bank of sublight engines flaring white behind them, Chewbacca cruised toward the Smugglers' Moon.

He had no trouble flying the ship by himself. He had logged enough hours on the *Falcon* to make most space pilots envious of his experience. But he still felt alone without Han Solo. Long ago Chewbacca had sworn a life debt to the human, and though his obligations had certainly been discharged by now, the Wookiee still considered Han's life to be in his care.

He had visited Nar Shaddaa with Han more than once, and they had nearly lost their lives. Right now Han was in the Hutt System as well, engaged in one of the inexplicable diplomatic rituals that Leia performed, so Chewbacca had accepted his assignment with good grace, eager to poke around and learn what he could about Durga's underhanded activities.

As Artoo kept track of the in-system traffic, Chewbacca slipped into the flow of other unmarked vessels approaching Nar Shaddaa. The New Republic wargaming fleet showed up conspicuously on the sensors: large battleships engaged in mock attacks, shooting low-powered turbolasers at fake targets. Chewbacca watched the blips on the screen. Han was either aboard one of those warships, or down on the big, bruised-looking planet below.

Artoo warbled in alarm, and Chewbacca snapped his attention back to the piloting controls, avoiding a collision with a large ore freighter that had lumbered into the system.

Chewbacca couldn't risk contacting Han to inform him that they had arrived. He and Artoo had to remain completely invisible, slipping in as just another anonymous visitor to Nar Shaddaa. They had to find out the real story of the Hutt secret weapon—not the diplomatic lie Durga would likely tell Leia.

Chewbacca landed the *Falcon* in one of the astronomically priced docking bays in the grimy heavy-traffic sectors. As Artoo trundled down the boarding ramp, Chewbacca took out decoy beacons, warning lights that signified the *Falcon* was poison-encased in a deadly protection field. The beacons were fake, of course, but they looked real and eliminated the need to pay the exorbitant protection surcharges many of the docking barons charged, which foolish and unprepared visitors were forced to pay.

Chewbacca snuffled with his damp nose, detecting the acrid odors of engine coolant, fumes from propellant systems, decaying engines in need of repair, and the bodies of a thousand species mingled with the exotic spiced substances they consumed for nourishment.

He and Artoo moved purposefully away from the *Falcon,* plunging into the grease-encrusted, machine-humming metropolis. They had credits to spend and information to buy—and Nar Shaddaa was the place to be.

*   *   *

Artoo jacked into the nearest "tourist information ki-
osk"—a thinly disguised directory of available black-market services and vendors. The smugglers didn't even try to
hide their real activities, though some of the cryptic descriptions seemed ominous indeed.

Artoo chugged through the electronic listings, searching for anyone willing to provide detailed information
about the Hutts—but because Nar Shaddaa was a Hutt-
controlled world, those willing to offer such dangerous
assistance were extremely few; only one of the information centers listed Durga specifically as a resource.

Chewbacca attempted to decipher a grid map of the
upper levels of the city. He and Artoo spent the better part
of an hour tracking down the center connected with Durga
and were disappointed to discover in the end that the office
was merely a public relations front for the Orko SkyMine
Corporation.

They endured a holographic propaganda presentation
about the wonders that Orko SkyMine would bring to the
galaxy. When Chewbacca began to ask the toadlike bu-
reaucratic representative about Durga, the assistant flailed
his long-fingered hands and curved his fat lips into a
smile.

"You must understand, my Wookiee friend, that all
information about Lord Durga's activities is strictly confi-
dential, to protect the identity of Orko SkyMine's largest
investors." He blinked his lantern eyes and gave a thick-
lipped smile again. "However, if you wish to donate a
million credits, you could become one such investor and
gain access to all of our files." His leathery skin furrowed
on his forehead in falsified hope.

The Wookiee and the little droid left indignantly.

Chewbacca decided to forgo the black-market services directory and began asking likely-looking vendors
on the streets. He went through a hundred credits, bounced
from one scrap of information to another—until in a nar-

row, dim alley he and Artoo finally found a decrepit old slicer whose face was a mass of oozing blemishes and flaking skin. The slicer carried his own portable terminal and a laser welder that he used to cut into the power sources and splice his input cables into computer systems, through which he would scrounge for information, undetected for a few hours or a day; then he would slip off to find another place to work.

The slicer took their credits and didn't seem to care why they wanted information about the Hutts: he merely verified that the money was good and began tapping into the Nar Shaddaa computer systems.

"No listings," the slicer said. "Nothing for Durga."

Chewbacca growled a question.

"I didn't mean there aren't any," the slicer said, speaking through swollen lips and scowling at his keyboard. "I just can't find the files. They must be coded or passworded. No way I could get at them, unless I knew exactly what they were."

Artoo gave a disappointed whistle.

"Wait a minute—let's stand this on its head," the slicer said, rubbing a finger along his lower lip, causing even more skin to fall off. He squinted his beady eyes in the dimness. "I was looking for files *about* Durga, but let's do a broader-based search, track down anybody who's selling things *to* Durga." His fingers, though scabbed with sores and armored with calluses, flew over the keypad. A blur of numbers scrolled up, and the slicer began cackling. He held out his hands for more credits. Chewbacca growled, but willingly paid, hoping the information would be good.

"I've found a major customer for Durga," the slicer said, then lowered his voice. His words came out in a whisper. "An Imperial customer."

Before Chewbacca could growl a new query, another bulky creature strode into the mouth of the alley: a large cylindrical torso surrounded by waving tentacles and eye stalks protruding from the top. A gurgling alien voice came from the creature's mouth orifice.

"I'm busy," the slicer said. "Can't you see I got a customer? Come back later, and I'll be happy to run a search."

But the tentacled creature insisted on its answers *now* and lunged forward, flailing its tentacles threateningly, as if it wanted to lash the slicer into submission.

Chewbacca roared and stood up tall, his tan fur bristling. He grappled with the alien creature and, after a short brawl, managed to tie five of its tentacles into knots. With a grunt, the Wookiee sent the moaning, impatient creature on its way down the street, where it stumbled along burbling for assistance in untying its tentacles.

Chewbacca squatted next to the slicer and motioned for him to continue. "Yes, an Imperial customer, somebody selling to Durga," the slicer said. "It's a major expenditure: computer cores, powerful ones. I can't imagine what a Hutt would need them for. Especially such old models."

Chewbacca, feeling exhilarated after the scuffle, listened intently.

"The man's name is a General Sulamar, apparently working with the Hutts. He is somehow connected with Imperial deserters, people who left the service of the Empire and went into business for themselves. According to these files," the slicer continued, tapping the screen, "this Imperial General Sulamar is the big boss in charge of everything the Hutts do around here.

"If that's true, they've kept it a secret from me," the slicer said, raising his eyebrows. More dead skin flaked off and fell to the ground. "Durga is supposedly just a minor partner in the operation," he cackled.

Artoo whistled a question, and Chewbacca reinforced it.

"Who is this Sulamar?" the slicer asked. "Is that what you want to know? He doesn't hide his credentials. In fact, he types them all in capital letters, claims to be an

Imperial military genius. Takes all responsibility for the Massacre of Mendicat. Calls himself the Scourge of Celdaru.''

Chewbacca groaned. He paid the slicer again, then stood up, gesturing for the droid to follow him. He strode along on long, hairy legs as Artoo hurried to keep up. The little droid whistled anxiously, squealing his alarm. They had to get back to the *Falcon* where they could pass their news to Coruscant. They had learned more than they had ever expected to.

Chewbacca felt a bestial rage rising within him as he considered the ominous possibilities. If the Empire and the Hutts had indeed teamed up, they would make a formidable enemy.

This threat was far worse than they had feared.

CHAPTER 32

Standing on the auxiliary command deck of the *Galactic Voyager,* General Crix Madine, Supreme Allied Commander for Special Forces, studied the screen that showed the bright green tracer he had planted on Durga's private ship. He scratched his brown beard and watched his best female commando, Trandia, double-check the readings.

"Still hasn't moved, sir," Trandia said. She had long strawberry blond hair knitted into a complex braid that hung neatly at her back, pretty but serviceable—Madine suspected she let it hang loose while she was off duty. Her face was scrubbed clean and flushed with concentration as her blue eyes stayed riveted on the computer.

"He departed from Nal Hutta several hours ago, sir, and landed on the Smugglers' Moon. No word since. We could contact the *Yavaris,"* Trandia suggested. "General Antilles has taken some time off to visit the moon. Perhaps he could keep an eye out."

Madine shook his head. "Too dangerous. We have the tracer planted, and Durga suspects nothing. Let's just see where he goes. The Chief of State says he ended their meeting rather abruptly, so he must be on his way back to his hiding place. We'll find it. Be patient.''

Madine wandered across the auxiliary command chamber. There were no windows to stare through, only status screens. The secondary bridge was designed to function as an alternate bridge if the Star Cruiser's main forward compartments were somehow put out of commission.

Madine paced restlessly, anxious to do something. A driven man, he had given his utmost strength and imagination to the New Republic for the past nine years, ever since he had defected from the Imperial military. He felt good to be working with the Rebel Alliance, a cause he could believe in—and the more he devoted himself to serving the New Republic, the more Madine could distract himself from the lingering guilt that still had not gone away.

Long ago he had given an oath to uphold Palpatine's New Order and to serve the Emperor, and he had meant it. Crix Madine did not give oaths lightly, nor had he ever broken one before his defection. He hoped he never had to make such a conscience-rending decision again.

At one time his future had seemed golden with the Empire. His rank increased on a fast track, indicating important things to come. Madine had been given heavy responsibilities, remarkable accolades, medals, and citations. The Emperor himself had commented upon his brilliance and impeccable service.

He had been deeply in love with the daughter of an important ambassador; they were going to be married. His fiancée, Karreio, was devoted to the New Order, spouting propaganda about the frailties of the Old Republic, but blind to the excesses of the Empire. In his military service Madine had seen and done much that would have revolted her—such as using his elite storm commandos to plant the seeds of Candorian Plague on the uncooperative world of Dentaal.

That last horrendous mission had nearly twisted and pulled free the underpinnings of Madine's moral character, and he had chosen to sacrifice everything rather than give up his own beliefs. Such vicious retaliation was *wrong*. He had discarded his bright, guaranteed future. He had tossed aside his own rank, telling Karreio nothing of his plans, because that would have made her an accomplice to his treachery, and she would have been forced either to report him or to suffer a traitor's fate.

During wilderness exercises on Dentaal, leading his team of storm commandos, Madine had just . . . *vanished* into a series of caves. Later, after a week of hard survival in the jungle, he had made it back to the temporary Imperial base and commandeered a shuttle, stealing archives filled with Imperial encryption schemes, classified data, secret plans.

He had fled into the starry sky of the Mid-Rim without the least idea of where he was going. He simply hoped that he could track down a representative of the Rebel Alliance before the Imperial headhunters found him.

In all the time since, he had never dared to send a message back to Karreio, never attempted to see her again. He hoped that she had survived without him . . . hoped that she believed the stories branding him a betrayer of the Empire—and that she had found someone else to love.

When the Rebels did indeed recapture Coruscant after a long and bloody battle, Madine had haunted the personnel archives, searching the records to find Karreio, to make certain that she was safe. Instead, he learned that she had died in the attack, an unnoticed name on a long list paired with ID numbers and casualty descriptions. So many civilians had been killed in the battle that only the letter *D* for "deceased" burned beside Karreio's name.

Crix Madine had much to feel guilty for. One of his first missions after defecting to the Rebel Alliance had been to plan the successful commando raid on Endor that took out the shield generator and allowed the Rebel fleet to destroy the second Death Star. Thus Madine's own actions had resulted in the death of Emperor Palpatine, the man who had once issued him a citation for his exemplary service and commendable loyalty.

For Madine the time for second thoughts was long past. The decision had been made. He had not had any doubts, regardless of the consequences. Threats continued to harry the New Republic, and Madine could not rest until his chosen government was safe.

He feared that meant he would never rest.

The motion of the green blip on the diagram of Nar Shaddaa startled him out of his reverie. Trandia sat up straighter. "Sir, the target ship is departing. Tracking now."

"So, he's on his way," Madine said, and laced his fingers together in anticipation. He took a deep breath before snapping into motion. "All right, we're ready to pursue. Trandia, I'd like you on my team—and Korenn," Madine said, thinking of the enthusiasm and unquestionable talent of the sandy-haired boy who looked far younger than his experience and skill suggested. "Let's get prepped. Ackbar has given us three scout A-wings. We'll streak in and see what Durga is up to.

"But," Madine said, extending a finger, "we'll also implant emergency transmitters, because we may be pressed for time. Wherever this hidden weapon is, if we see a chance to sabotage it, we must take it. We can't afford to let the Hutts complete their own Death Star."

Madine stood in the launching bay, admiring the three trim A-wing fighters. Trandia came up to him, moving with the lithe grace that had convinced him she would be good in covert operations. She wore a flightsuit now, her braid tucked beneath the collar. She carried a helmet in the crook of her arm. "Ready to depart, sir," she said, "as soon as you give the order."

A moment later Korenn, the other young member of the team stepped up. His eyes sparkled with excitement, and his sandy hair was spiky and unruly. Korenn popped a helmet on his head.

"Do we have our destination yet?" Madine said.

Trandia flashed a faint smile. "The Hoth Asteroid Belt, sir. That's where Durga's gone to hide."

Madine raised his eyebrows. "Interesting. Asteroids will call for some tricky flying." He fixed his gaze on Korenn and Trandia. "How's your piloting?"

"Excellent, sir," they responded in unison.

"Good," Madine said. "Let's go then."

HOTH

CHAPTER 33

The ice creatures lunged in a mass of white fur, spread claws, and flying blood.

"Watch your back, Callista!" Luke yelled, slashing as a white-furred monster bore down on her. His lightsaber opened a sizzling, blackened gash through its rib cage, and the wampa fell to the snow, gurgling hot bile.

Callista lunged, decapitating another creature as it leaped toward Luke, its fanged mouth open and ready to tear flesh. "I'll watch my back if you watch yours," she said, raising a challenging eyebrow.

Burrk, the former stormtrooper, fired until he emptied his second blaster pistol. His face held a haggard hopelessness, yet a foolish determination. Luke knew he would keep fighting until the wampas took him down.

"You—Jedi!" Burrk shouted, "we've got to get back to the base. Can you clear us a path with your lightsabers?"

Luke and Callista both nodded curtly. The heavy shield door under the icy overhang was their only sanctuary. Luke felt a sudden relief that they had left the shield door partially open so they could dash back inside.

One of the Cathars, Nodon, fired the last trickle of charge from his blaster rifle, just as a huge wampa rose before him, muscular arms dangling to its knees and curved claws extending a dozen centimeters beyond. Nodon yowled and spat a primal feline sound and thrust the blaster rifle toward it like a blunt spear, punching the attacking monster below the sternum. The creature roared in pain and lashed out to knock Nodon to the snow, his shoulder ripped in a sequence of parallel furrows, spraying red.

The Cathar's brother hissed in fury and leaped to Nodon's aid. Nonak sprang onto the back of the attacking wampa and slashed with his own claws, tearing into the wampa's neck with sharp fangs. The monster forgot about the wounded Cathar and bellowed, reaching behind him to pluck away the vicious feline alien. Nodon, wounded, backed away, trying to scramble to his feet as his blood stained the snow.

From the rocky outcrop where he directed the battle, the one-armed brute roared something incomprehensible. Other wampas turned on Nonak, who still fought with the wampa who had injured his brother. The wampas came in, focused on a single target.

They tore Nonak apart.

"Follow me!" Drom Guldi bellowed without the slightest trace of terror or even tension in his voice. Sinidic, his aide, huddled under the protection of his muscular master's rifle, a high-powered brand-new hunting weapon. Drom Guldi still had charges left, and he fired with slow precision: no random spraying of high-energy bolts, but surgical shots that killed or injured an ice creature every time he pressed the firing stud.

The big Baron-Administrator trudged toward the base doors, not hurrying, making sure the others followed. Nodon got to his feet and wailed at seeing the bloody remnants of his brother. Burrk grabbed him by the fur on his neck and yanked Nodon around. "Come on!" he shouted.

Luke and Callista flanked Drom Guldi as they fought their way back to Echo Base. With their lightsabers they each killed another creature. The base doors seemed immeasurably far away, but Luke and Callista pushed forward.

Drom Guldi blasted three more wampas that blocked the open shield door. As they kept moving, his aide Sinidic seemed paralyzed, stumbling along because his master told him to. Sinidic tripped over the smoldering body of an ice creature. Without pause, Drom Guldi grabbed his aide's collar and yanked him to his feet as if he were no more than a rag. The Baron-Administrator reached the shield door and shoved Sinidic into the waiting darkness.

Burrk helped Nodon inside Echo Base, pushing the wounded Cathar ahead of him, though the feline obviously wanted to throw himself back upon the monsters in a frenzy and die ripping them to shreds.

Luke and Callista waited in the cold outside the door, driving back the last of the wampas.

"Get in here, Jedi!" Burrk said. "Now!"

Luke and Callista jumped into the waiting darkness. Burrk hit the shield door controls, and the heavy door ground shut. At the last instant, the wampas pushed forward, grabbing at the durasteel door with their claws, but the relentless pistons were too powerful even for these creatures.

In the sparse light of the few functioning glowpanels, Luke, Callista, and the four survivors slumped against the hard-packed snow walls as the sudden loss of adrenaline hit them, leaving only exhaustion. Everyone trembled in silence for several moments, shielded at last in the temporary safety of walls.

Then came a scratching sound, muffled howls, and a repeated pounding from outside. Burrk turned bloodshot eyes toward the sealed door. Sinidic glanced up in terror, and then looked to Drom Guldi for comfort.

"They can knock, but they can't come in," Drom Guldi said.

Callista got up and went to the picked-over supplies, finding discarded Rebel uniforms she could tear into bandages to tend Nodon's wounds; but the Cathar's healing abilities had already stopped the blood flow. As he sat in silence, staring with slitted eyes toward the blank white wall of packed snow, Nodon's feline claws repeatedly extended and sheathed themselves as he wrestled with inner anger.

Outside, the monsters kept pounding, foolishly trying to find a way in, though the base was impenetrable. Night was falling on Hoth, and the temperature would soon plummet. All living creatures should be taking shelter until the meager warmth of sunlight returned—but the wampas were relentless. They had their quarry cornered.

Drom Guldi's tanned, sculpture-beautiful face wore a contemplative look. "Think of all those prize pelts out there," he said, shaking his head. "What a waste."

A loud *clang* reverberated against the thick door. The wampas had picked up a rock chunk . . . but they could batter uselessly for years without breaking through the durasteel.

Burrk's gaunt face was filled with exhausted resignation. "Now would have been a perfect time to use those perimeter guns," he said, looking pointedly at Luke and Callista.

"Let's move away from the door," Luke said. "That pounding will only wear us down."

Weakly, they shuffled into the dim briefing room where Burrk had told his terrifying story. The former stormtrooper took a quick inventory. "My blaster pistols are out of charge. Nodon's rifle is drained. Drom Guldi, what have you got left?"

The big-game hunter inspected his weapon. "Ten shots," he said, as if that was all they could possibly need.

"And we've got your two lightsabers," Burrk said to Luke and Callista.

Luke pursed his lips. "Given time, we could work out some way to recharge the blasters. There must be a way to jury-rig a thermal unit or a light source to dump power into the blaster charge packs."

Burrk shrugged. "If you've got the time and the resources and the inspiration . . ."

Luke rummaged around in the scrap equipment. Burrk squatted and took a more primitive approach; pulling out pipes and rods, he used instant-set epoxy to fasten on knife blades fashioned from metal shards. He made four crude spears. They were hopeless weapons against an onslaught from the ice creatures, but the former stormtrooper had no intention of giving up.

Drom Guldi cleaned and polished his blaster rifle. Sinidic sat listless beside him, fidgeting with his hands. The Baron-Administrator elbowed his aide. "We need a morale booster. Sinidic, see if you can't find us some rations. Maybe something hot to eat and drink. There isn't much, but we need to keep our strength up."

"Me?" Sinidic said, blinking stupidly.

"You're sitting there paralyzed—you need something to do. Keep yourself busy. First order of business."

Sinidic got up, swallowed, and nodded. His grayish skin grew more flushed. He looked at Drom Guldi for confirmation of the orders, then trotted off to one of the storerooms to do his master's bidding.

Luke and Callista sat together, holding each other for comfort. "This isn't quite the vacation I planned," Luke said.

Callista leaned her head against his. "Remind me never to listen to your fancy talk again."

Burrk stood up, grasped one of his new spears, and tossed it across the room. The sharp tip plunged into the packed snow walls, and the spear hung there, quivering. "I think that'll do," he said.

A loud shriek erupted from the darkened storeroom,

followed by a wet ripping sound and then a gurgling gasp. The five survivors in the room lunged to their feet, Drom Guldi the first among them. They had taken no more than a few steps down the ice-walled corridor before a bloodied wampa lumbered out of the storeroom, his claws dripping, his white fur drenched with fresh gore.

Drom Guldi faltered for just an instant, then he brought up his blaster rifle, firing three times in rapid succession. He hit precisely each time—the wampa's stomach, the center of its chest, and its hideous head. With no more than a hollow cough, the monster fell to the packed floor with the sound of a crashing cargo hauler.

"Must have slipped in the open door while we were fighting outside!" Burrk said.

Drom Guldi looked toward the supply room where he had sent his aide. He didn't bother to go inside. Instead, the Baron-Administrator reached toward Burrk and grabbed one of the stormtrooper's newly fashioned spears. With the metal blade, Drom Guldi hacked down, chopping off one of the wampa's curved tusks. The big-game hunter held the dripping prize in his hand and inspected it critically. "This one," he said coldly. "This is the one I'll take for my trophy. And for Sinidic." He threw a second glance at the darkened storeroom, and his face grew stony. "These monsters are persistent."

From outside, the dull echoing thuds continued as the ice creatures attempted to pummel their way inside.

Then, to make things worse, all the lights went out.

"They trashed the generator," Burrk said, his voice coming from the emptiness of darkness.

Luke pulled out his lightsaber and pressed the power stud. The green beam crackled out with an eerie glow that illuminated the walls of ice and snow. Callista drew her blade, and the two stood side by side.

Luke tensed. He heard something . . . a scratching, digging sound. He wondered if other wampas lay hidden in the darkened rooms. The pounding outside the shield door redoubled, and everyone turned, though they knew the wampas could not get through.

Just then the walls crumbled on all sides, blocks of hard-packed snow showered down as more of the creatures plowed their way directly through the ice.

Luke realized that the futile pounding and scratching on the outer shield door had been a distraction, something to preoccupy the victims, while the wampas dug through the snow, burrowing their way into Echo Base. With bellows of triumph and anticipation, an army of ghostly white monsters surged into the corridors.

Nodon, finally unrestrained, yowled and threw himself upon the nearest wampa, but the others turned and fell upon him. The Cathar went down fighting, a blurry mass of fur and claws and biting teeth—and sudden, spraying blood.

Burrk backed against a rough rock that protruded from the carved snow. In each hand he held one of his metal spears, thrusting and jabbing, trying to intimidate the ice creatures—but though the blades were sharp and the points long, the spears were pitiful against the blood-thirsty monsters. He stabbed and lunged, making no outcry. He wore a grim, defeated look as he fought—until the mass of attacking snow monsters swallowed him up. Finally, in the last instant, he screamed.

Luke and Callista remained back-to-back, slashing with lightsabers and slaughtering the monsters that came too close, but there were too many. "Get back to the shield door!" Callista said. "We have to run to our ship. Try to fix it. That's our only chance."

Luke said, "I don't have a better idea," then swung his lightsaber. With a sizzle he sliced a towering creature in two. Luke recognized dimly that the monsters had stopped pounding outside. They must have flocked to the new openings that allowed them access into the base. The front might be clear.

Drom Guldi used his seven remaining shots, killing a wampa each time he pressed the firing button; but that drained the weapon. He tossed the blaster rifle to the ground, tucked the wampa tusk into his utility belt, as if it remained important to him, then gripped the metal spear he had taken from Burrk, sweeping it from side to side. He laughed, his eyes bright, his tanned face flushed. The wampas surrounded him, and he grinned. "Come on!" Drom Guldi said. "Get what's coming to you!"

The wampas came.

Trying to drown out the last gurgled screams of Drom Guldi, Callista and Luke fought their way down the corridor toward the shield door. They mowed down the ice creatures who threw themselves recklessly at the glowing blades. Though Callista was unable to use the Force in her fighting, the wampas were not difficult targets, huge hulks of white fur and taut muscles. But it would take the slip of only an instant for a raking claw to slice open either Luke or Callista.

As they passed beyond where the wampas had tunneled through, the attacking monsters grew sparse, and Luke and Callista were able to run at full speed. The shield door reflected the light of their weapons, and Callista ran for the controls.

"We'll seal ourselves in the ship and hope that within just a few minutes we can rig it to blast off," Luke said. "Those things could rip open the hull in no time."

The shield door heaved open. Callista turned to defend their backs as Luke made ready to run out into the night. The dark chill struck him like a sledgehammer, knocking the wind out of him with an intense freezing blast, colder than anything Luke could remember.

Directly outside, under the wan light of multiple moons, stood the one-armed wampa ice creature, the tallest of them all, blocking their escape from Echo Base.

The monster roared into the ice-bright night and raised his one enormous hand, spreading the claws. Luke felt a momentary flash of remembered fear that made him falter. He stood gripping the lightsaber. Finding no danger behind them, Callista turned back to see what the problem was.

And, with its eyes fixed on Luke, its nemesis . . . the one-armed monster lunged for Callista, instead.

She couldn't react fast enough. Seeing the down-sweeping arc of the sharp claws and the blinding speed with which the wampa charged, Luke yelled, ''No!'' and cut sideways with his lightsaber.

Putting all the Force behind his swing, Luke cleaved the one-armed snow creature in half.

The dead monster continued to growl and gurgle as it lay smoking on the threshold of the shield door. ''I thought I had done that a long time ago,'' Luke whispered.

More wampas surged from the tunnels below. Outside in the night snow creatures stood up from the outcrops, no longer bothering to hide.

''Don't just stand there,'' Callista said, shoving Luke as he stared at the dead one-armed creature. ''Run!''

The two sprinted across the hard-packed snow. The cold slashed like razors at their lungs as they gasped for breath, already exhausted from the battle.

The wreckage of the poachers' ship looked ominous in the watery light, but their own space yacht shone like their only hope. As the wampas pursued, leaping across the snow-swept rocks, Luke and Callista ran with their last surge of strength.

Reaching the ship, Luke hammered at the door controls. Callista stood behind him, her lightsaber glowing. The door slid open, and Luke pulled her inside, then sealed the door again.

He ran to the pilot compartment and stared at the controls, stifling the sickening despair that swept over him. The controls were smashed. The navicomputer gone. The comm system ripped out. The wampas hadn't ruined the engines, though the cables for thrust control had been torn free.

He and Callista set to work, removing dented or

slashed panels and trying to cross-wire anything, just to get them lifted off.

Outside, the wampas began to batter the hull of the space yacht with sharp rocks. If they breached the hull, Luke knew he and Callista could never leave the atmosphere of Hoth. Callista hunched beside him, working on a different panel. She sorted wires, traced connections, moving with a frantic, efficient energy that wasted not a second. "Try this," she said, and pulled out an alternative power source, which he jacked into the thruster control.

"We can ignite the engines, lift up out of here," Luke said.

Callista agreed. "We'll never be able to restart the engines if we land again. We have to move now, and we have to get *off* this planet."

Luke triggered the firing button, and the space yacht's engines roared to life at full power. They had no directional control. The ship lurched up off the ground—and the last thing they heard from the wampas was a long, shrieking scrape of claws against the metal hull as the ship tore away, plunging upward into the night. The icy cracked surface dwindled below them with dizzying speed. They had no maneuverability, just a blind ballistic takeoff that hurled them into the atmosphere.

Callista worked at the other controls. Luke already knew what damage the wampas had done, but her voice faltered as she gave her own assessment.

"No comm system, no navicomputer, only five percent life support." She sighed. "Who knows where we'll end up? We might have been better off staying down there."

NAL HUTTA

CHAPTER 34

Though See-Threepio was miffed that Durga the Hutt had cut short the diplomatic visit so suddenly (after offering a wealth of excuses and apologies), Leia felt an oppressive weight leave her shoulders as soon as the fat slug was off the planet.

It had become clear that Durga either had no overall authority from the Hutts or no inclination to enter into a bargain with the New Republic—as Leia had suspected. Their negotiations had gone exactly nowhere, and Durga feigned ignorance every time Leia mentioned the subject of secret weapons.

"We are businessmen, not warriors," Durga had said. "Our battles consist of under-the-table negotiations, not blasters and detonators."

Although Han glanced at Leia with an I-told-you-so expression, she could tell that she had managed to shake Durga. The birthmarked Hutt had hoped to stall longer, and he seemed decidedly uncomfortable throughout their "diplomatic" visit—but Leia had not given him any easy opportunity to get rid of them.

Han and Leia were both surprised, however, when even after his speedy departure, Durga did provide access to one of his private information brokers—true to his word. Before Leia and Han departed in their diplomatic ship, Korrda the emaciated Hutt ordered one of the brokers brought in to "service" them.

Gamorrean guards dragged a cart with creaking wheels into the dining hall. The carrion birds still perched on their ledges, waiting for dropped food or for a guest to stop moving long enough that they could pounce.

The cart was old and stained with clumps of decomposing refuse, as if someone had mistaken it for a garbage receptacle. A huge, spiral-shaped mollusk shell filled the cart, its ridges worn and covered with algae. The opening to the corkscrew shell was black and foul-smelling. Leia wasn't sure she wanted to know what lurked within.

Korrda slithered forward to rap briskly on the shell with a thin stick. With a sound like a long stream of sand poured into thin mud, a fleshy appendage nudged out of the open hole in the corkscrew shell, protruding like a long tongue. The creature emerged like a worm from a piece of rotten fruit, sickly tan-gray with a cluster of five milky white eyes on its smooth rounded head. "What do you want?" the creature said in a surly voice.

Korrda reared up to glare at the shell creature. "Lord Durga commands that you provide information to these guests. They need to know about Imperial activities." Korrda finally seemed filled with self-confidence, now that he spoke to a creature even lower in the pecking order than he was.

The information broker grumbled. "Information on Imperial activities, eh? Couldn't narrow it down a little, I suppose? Noooo, that's too much to hope for, isn't it? We could at least limit ourselves to *current* Imperial activities, couldn't we?"

"Yes," Leia said. "We want to know what the remnants of the Empire are up to right now."

"Oh, good—that's *much* easier, isn't it?" the shell

creature said sarcastically. "I suppose you require a specific listing of every individual's activities—I have records of five billion or so, and that's without even looking hard—or would generalizations be good enough, hmmm?"

"Generalizations would be sufficient," Leia answered tightly.

Without a word, the smooth head slipped back into the dark opening with a wet *pop*.

Leia heard muffled rummaging sounds as the creature stirred about, as if it were searching through a labyrinth inside the enormous shell. She wondered what the creature could be doing in there; then the damp head popped up again and turned its eye cluster toward Leia.

"You're in luck, aren't you?—plenty of schemes afoot. Imperial forces have been unified, squabbling warlords executed. Starship construction increased tenfold, new soldiers appearing by the tens of thousands—that the sort of thing you're looking for? Imperial military forces have clustered around a single commander, and it would appear that even women and aliens are allowed to serve to the extent of their abilities—a vast change from the Emperor's way of thinking, wouldn't you say? Charming to see an enlightened Imperial commander, isn't it?"

Han looked over at her, and Leia sat up straight. The alien information broker had piqued her interest, despite her initial resistance. Could it actually be telling the truth? Leia suspected this entire charade was still part of Durga's scheme, a distraction to keep them concerned about one threat while the Hutts completed another one. But even Durga's ulterior motives did not preclude an actual Imperial plot.

Leia said, "Do you know what their plans are? Has the Empire formed some sort of strategy?"

The information broker wavered in the air. "Scattered Imperial fleets have come together with such a buildup of weapons they are almost certainly planning a major assault against the New Republic, wouldn't you think? Specific target unknown, so it's no use asking, is it?''

The information broker swiveled its eye cluster toward Korrda. ''May I go now? I have a lot of work to do—you *can* see how busy I am, can't you?''

''Wait,'' Han interrupted. ''Who is this new Imperial commander? I need to know.''

The information broker rumbled deep inside its body. ''Oh, *that's* all you want, is it? Why not ask for the number of sand grains on the beaches of Pil-Diller, or ask me to count the leaves in the forests of Ithor, eh?''

Korrda rapped the shell with his gnarled stick again: ''Shut up and answer the question.''

''All right, all right, I was just getting to that, wasn't I?'' the information broker said, and slithered back into the shell, where it rummaged around for an interminable time before it finally popped out again. ''Daala,'' the creature said. ''The admiral in charge of the Imperial forces is named *Daala,* you see? But that's all—I've scraped the walls, haven't I? Since I have no more information, good night!''

With that, the fleshy head popped back into the shell, leaving Leia and Han to gape at each other in amazement. Leia had expected nothing like this.

Han looked sickened. He blinked his eyes uncomprehendingly. ''But how could it be Daala?'' he mumbled. ''She's . . . dead.''

Leia met his eyes and decided she didn't want or need an explanation right now. ''Apparently not,'' she said. ''This puts a whole new spin on things—doesn't it?''

CORE SYSTEMS

CHAPTER 35

In Admiral Daala's hands, the remnants of the Empire became a machine, a massive cohesive engine being tuned to peak performance.

Cogs spun. Components fit together. Armament factories processed resources into additional weapons: TIE fighters, blastboats, AT-STs, and structural components of new Star Destroyers. Hyperdrives were mass-produced and installed in ship after ship. Weapons' cores were charged with tibanna gas. Formerly downtrodden workers—even aliens and females—were given responsibilities and put to work for the glory of the Empire.

Daala reveled in the progress reports she received. Now aboard her great black ship, the *Night Hammer,* she progressed from system to system, knitting together once-scattered allegiances, cementing loyalties, and squeezing more work out of subjects who had been lax for too long, drawing tight the Imperial net.

Accompanied by awesome red Imperial Guards, she spoke at armaments factories and shipyards, raising her voice and building morale, making herself visible so that all could see a charismatic leader who was there to *do* something against the enemy, fostering hope in the future once more.

She paced around the *Night Hammer*'s ready-room, a private strategy chamber that was itself as big as the entire command deck on a *Victory*-class Star Destroyer. Daala stared out the viewing window, drinking in the brilliant spatter of stars at the heart of the galaxy. Nebular material streamed in ribbons across star clusters.

The huge ready-room seemed extravagant, almost intimidating. She would have preferred a more confined place to gather her thoughts, but in her position she could not take command of any ship other than the Super Star Destroyer. The ready-room had its own sleeping quarters, food-processing stations, even access to command-level escape pods, should disaster befall the warship. Though it was immense, the *Night Hammer* functioned with a relatively small crew, relying on massively redundant automated command systems.

Vice Admiral Pellaeon cleared his throat and waited for her attention. Daala knew the older officer had arrived, but she let her thoughts wander a while longer. "Our fleet is growing strong," she finally said out loud. "I can feel it."

Pellaeon waited for her. "Yes, Admiral."

"I don't want to strike before we are ready . . . but I'm anxious to go to battle again." She sighed and turned to Pellaeon, who stood holding a datapad with the latest fleet statistics. She frowned wearily and sank into one of her chairs. "I *do* grow tired of administrative details, though," she groaned. After only a moment she stood up again and began to pace around the ready-room, a blur of nervous energy.

"These details are necessary," Pellaeon said. "Without sufficient attention to detail, all your work will fall apart. You must understand that, if you intend to run the Empire."

Daala fixed him with a sharp stare. "But I have no

designs on running the Empire. That's not what I'm after.
Surely you understand that by now? Once the battle is
won, I intend to relinquish command with great pleasure—to you or whomever else is most suited to the damn
job.''

Pellaeon's head snapped back and his watery eyes
widened. ''*Me,* Admiral? I am no emperor!''

She let loose a laugh. ''Neither am I, Vice Admiral—
but let's not worry about that until the war is over. Give
me a rundown. Where do we stand?''

With obvious relief at the change of subject, Pellaeon
sat down at the table while Daala continued to pace. He
called up numbers on his datapad. ''We now have one
hundred twelve fully functional *Victory*-class Star Destroyers. I've placed them under the command of Colonel Cronus, as we discussed at our last meeting.''

''Yes,'' Daala said, ''a good choice. He seems a competent commander.''

''We also have forty-five Imperial Star Destroyers—
and of course we have the *Night Hammer*.'' He slid the
datapad across the table. ''There's a full listing of our TIE
fighters, interceptors, and bombers as well as a tally of
Gamma assault shuttles, *Lambda*-class shuttles, AT-ST
walkers, scout transports, and blastboats. The next entry
summarizes our entire complement of personnel and their
areas of expertise.''

Daala glanced at the numbers but felt her green eyes
glaze over. This was not her strength. ''I'll study these
later,'' she said. ''Right now my mind is occupied with
other concerns.'' She drew a deep breath. ''We are getting
close, very close. You and I must discuss the strategy for
our first attack. I prefer not to make this decision alone.
You have decades of experience and a wealth of knowledge. We are here with the door sealed and no one watching—I want your honest opinion.'' She lowered her voice.
''I will not make the same mistakes again.''

Pellaeon swallowed slightly. ''I appreciate your faith

in me, Admiral, but surely you recognize that this time you have a genuine fleet at your disposal.''

Daala slapped the palm of her hand down on the table, her eyes blazing. ''And I will not waste it!''

Pellaeon stood up. ''Shall I get us a drink, Admiral?''

She nodded and turned her eyes to stare out at the stars. She didn't speak until he had returned with a tall, cool glass of stim tea.

''As I see it, Admiral,'' Pellaeon said slowly, ''we have two obvious primary targets. The first is Coruscant, the capital—the most heavily populated and fortified world in the New Republic. If we destroy that planet, it would turn the Rebels into a scattered flock of whipped animals, fleeing for sanctuary to a hundred separate bases all over again.''

''I agree,'' Daala said. ''However, the battle for Coruscant will be long and difficult. And bloody. We will lose a large portion of our new fleet if we choose that as our first target.''

Pellaeon nodded, tugging at his gray mustache. ''I'm forced to concur, and I must also confess to a certain reluctance to devastate the former Imperial planet.''

Daala's lips drew together in a pinched expression. ''What I'm looking for, Pellaeon, is a decisive victory, an important Rebel target that we can utterly squash with minimal loss to our forces. We need a morale-building strike that will set the Rebels reeling and buoy our own troops up in an ecstasy of renewed patriotism. At that point we can come back with twice our strength and hammer Coruscant to rubble. I have such a target in mind,'' she said. ''Are we thinking of the same one?''

Pellaeon took a sip of his cool tea. She watched him. He paused a moment, then answered without hesitation. ''Yavin 4.'' He raised his eyebrows. ''Where the new Jedi training center is located.''

''Yes,'' Daala said. Her smile congratulated him. ''The Jedi Knights are powerful symbols to the Rebels— and they will be powerful enemies if we let them proliferate, as the enemy seems to intend. If we strike now and uproot this weed before it goes to seed, we can strike a mortal blow to these Rebels.''

Daala recalled her iron-willed mentor Tarkin, who had taught her everything about tactics, strength of character, and love for the Empire. Tarkin had died while attacking the Rebel base on Yavin 4—and she thought it would be a fitting target in her new campaign.

''Excuse me, Admiral?'' Pellaeon said, startling her out of her thoughts.

She glanced at him and realized he had just said something. ''I'm sorry,'' she said. ''I didn't hear you.''

''I suggested that we diversify our strike. Allow Colonel Cronus to take his Victory fleet and strike at dozens of minor targets, so that the Rebels believe they're under attack at all points. This will cause damage far beyond the risk incurred, and it will add to the turmoil and confusion surrounding our own surprise attack.''

Daala smiled. ''Excellent idea, Vice Admiral. Colonel Cronus will launch his strikes. You will take a fleet of Imperial Star Destroyers directly to begin the obliteration of the small jungle moon. And I will follow in the *Night Hammer* to ensure that we retain possession of this worthless system.''

She gulped down the last of her cold stim tea, and it felt like a thick rivulet of ice crawling down her throat and spreading through her body.

''We'll begin at once,'' Daala said.

CHAPTER 36

Kyp Durron hunched forward in front of the control panel. His dark eyes narrowed as he scanned the enemy forces arrayed around them.

Dorsk 81 piloted their stolen Imperial ship into the massed battle fleet. His slender, olive-green hands danced nervously on the controls; his yellow eyes widened in astonishment, as if he were still unable to believe what Kyp had talked him into doing.

"I'll bet this is the biggest gathering of the fleet since the battle of Endor," Kyp said, "or at least since Thrawn's last attack."

Dorsk 81 licked his thin lips and nodded, keeping his eyes on the frenzy of ship activity, like flotsam tossed about in a hurricane. "There certainly are a lot of ships," he said. "We'll be blown out of space the moment they suspect us."

Kyp waved his hand dismissively and leaned forward to squint out the front viewport. "They won't suspect anything. This ship has all the right markings. Don't let it get to you," he said, then turned his attention to running a full analysis of forces on the computer.

Over the past few days Kyp and Dorsk 81 had penetrated deeper and deeper into the Core Systems. Kyp had watched with growing horror as he realized just how far along the Empire's plans had already progressed. They had seen weapons depots, giant factories that spewed out TIE fighters by the hundreds, construction yards with skeletal frames of Imperial Star Destroyers in progress. They had witnessed a massive migration of people, soldiers gearing up for a deadly conflict, and dozens of overloaded supply trains hauling resources deeper into the Core.

Kyp had convinced Dorsk 81 to tag along just at the fringe of sensor range behind one of the convoys. When they arrived at the massing point of the new Imperial fleet, though, Dorsk 81 had been terrified.

"I still think we should get out of here," the clone Jedi said. "We need to bring this information back to the New Republic. They don't even know about the Imperial buildup."

Kyp shook his head. "We've got to find out more, see exactly what they're up to. We won't get a second chance like this."

"But if they capture us, then everything—" Dorsk 81 began.

Kyp held up his hand and watched Dorsk 81 stop and swallow hard. In the past, the cloned alien had struggled with a lack of self-confidence, and he had overcome it. Kyp did not see him as a coward—only as someone who did not push his bravery to its limits.

Kyp pointed at him, wearing a serious expression. "You are a Jedi Knight, Dorsk 81," he said. "A Jedi does not take the easiest choice. We will do what we have to." Dorsk 81 slowly nodded in firm acceptance.

The comm system crackled, startling both Kyp and Dorsk 81.

"Shuttle pilot," a stern voice snapped—a *female* voice, which in itself was unusual since most Imperial soldiers were male. The woman said, "You're behind schedule to attend the rally. Hurry up. Follow this vector—and move it! The admiral would be most displeased if late arrivals disturbed the speeches."

Dorsk 81 stared blankly at the speaker, but Kyp instantly responded. "On our way. Apologies for the inconvenience." He snapped off the comm system. "They're going to let us in," he said. Already his mind was churning, wondering who "the admiral" could be.

Ships large and small clustered around a staggeringly immense grid of landing platforms and docking bays, a huge nexus built of metal and glittering with panes of transparisteel. It hid in the dark void of space between star systems and would not be easy to locate unless one already knew where to look. The complex was studded with antennas and trackers, perimeter defense satellites, and automated droid ships that monitored the dizzying flow of ship activity. The coordinate vectors took them to a central platform where thousands of ships had already gathered.

Dorsk 81 stiffened in his seat. "Easy," Kyp said. "We have to do this." The alien gave a jerky nod and brought the shuttle in to land among all the other ships.

Figures streamed toward the open mall area of the nexus station, a room large enough for an audience of tens of thousands. Stormtroopers marched about, ushering spectators to acceptable standing places for the rally.

"I can't go out there," Dorsk 81 said. "The Empire doesn't allow nonhuman soldiers."

"They seem to have changed their rules," Kyp answered, indicating some of the uniformed personnel, an array of exotic humanoids and strange flying creatures. "Here." Kyp rummaged in the shuttle's uniform bin. He pulled out two sets of overalls with the insignia of the repair team assigned to the outer depot where Kyp and Dorsk 81 had stolen the shuttle. "We'll wear these, and nobody will know the difference."

Dorsk 81 looked at the outfit dubiously, but adrenaline sang through Kyp, whispering in his ears. "Look," he said in a reassuring voice, "this rally should give us all the information we need. We'll find out what the Empire is up to—and then we can go back and make our report." He grasped the cloned alien's arm. "Just be brave for me a little while longer, Dorsk 81."

They stepped down the landing ramp, and the current of the crowd swept them into the open mall area of the nexus station. The sounds and smells assaulted Kyp, an exotic mélange of the familiar and the fantastic. The main language was proper Imperial Basic, though a few muttered comments came in a variety of languages Kyp did not recognize. Dorsk 81 followed closely, still looking stiff and nervous.

In the distant center of the open space, a speaking deck had been raised to enclose a stage, tall amplifiers, and a turbolift that could bring guests onto the stage without forcing them to pass through packed crowds. Scarlet-cloaked Imperial Guards stood on all corners of the stage. High-resolution screens towered over the audience like video billboards projecting an image of the speaker at the podium; the effect was to turn the distant figure into a titan looming over those gathered for the rally.

A gaunt, trim old man was speaking in a precise voice that held little charisma. His eyes were pale and narrow, his forehead creased as if with heavy thoughts. A bushy pale mustache covered his lip.

"He looks familiar," Kyp said. "I've seen his image before."

Stormtrooper guards appeared out of nowhere, their white armor clacking, voices snapping gruffly through their helmets. "Silence while Vice Admiral Pellaeon is speaking."

Kyp held back a retort, though excitement kept him on edge, making self-control difficult. With an effort, he nodded meekly, turning back to look at the towering visage of the Imperial commander. Was this the man leading the new troops? Kyp recognized his name. From what he had heard, Pellaeon had had something to do with Grand

Admiral Thrawn, though Kyp himself had been deep in the
spice mines of Kessel during Thrawn's rampages.

The vice admiral had apparently been speaking for
some time. He and Dorsk 81 were indeed late for the rally,
and Kyp wondered how much valuable information he had
already missed.

"The main phase of our assault," Pellaeon continued, "will be a decisive attack on the new training facility
where the Rebels are attempting to create a commando
force of their own Jedi sorcerers. Our fleet will strike their
training center and destroy it before the Rebels even know
that we are on the march. Without their Jedi Knights, the
Rebel Alliance will be a weak assemblage of inept ideal-
ists."

The audience cheered, and Kyp felt compelled to ap-
plaud as well, so as not to draw further attention to himself. Dorsk 81 looked ill, and Kyp knew what the cloned
alien was thinking—that they needed to leave immediately, warn the New Republic, gather defenses around
Yavin 4.

But to move now would focus the attention of the
entire Imperial fleet on them. They had to wait.

Pellaeon droned on, and Kyp felt himself growing
tenser. The audience seemed to be keyed up and enthusiastic. Along the walls holographic images of Emperor Palpatine played, animated murals of how the New Order had
supposedly brought a too-brief golden age to the galaxy.

"Our preparations are nearly complete," Pellaeon
said. "Your superior officers will give you full details of
troop movements and how you will best serve in this sudden and decisive attack. But first, allow me to present the
one person responsible for bringing us all together."

He gestured toward the turbolift as it opened on the
stage behind him. The towering videoscreens showed a
figure emerging, slim and tall with a mane of hair that
looked like copper fire. "Admiral Daala!" Pellaeon said,
and stepped aside.

Kyp felt a bomb with a rapidly burning fuse drop

down into his guts, as he stared in disbelief and horror.
The Imperial admiral stepped up to speak, her face narrowed and sharpened by failure; its once hard beauty was
now even more angular . . . more evil.

Daala had captured Han Solo and Kyp after they escaped from the spice mines of Kessel, and because she
deemed Kyp a worthless prisoner, she had ordered his execution. Kyp had thought to destroy her in the Cauldron
Nebula, using the Sun Crusher to ignite a cluster of hot
blue suns. Somehow, she had miraculously escaped to attack the Maw Installation again—but she had died there.
Kyp was sure of it. She could not be here! She *could not*
be in charge of the new Imperial fleet!

All of this passed through his mind in a fraction of a
second, and Dorsk 81 sensed through the Force the volcano waiting to erupt within Kyp. The cloned alien placed
his olive hands on his shoulder to hold him back—but the
sudden grip startled Kyp into losing control.

He shouted, "No!" tearing himself away from Dorsk
81's grasp. "She's dead! Daala has to be dead."

While others in the audience cheered, those nearest to
him turned at the disturbance. Kyp brought himself under
control, furious at his own lack of restraint.

The stormtroopers appeared again, efficient and fast
moving. "Stop this outburst immediately!" they said,
blasters already drawn. "This is your second warning.
Show me your work assignment and papers." Two others
came up, pointing weapons at Kyp and Dorsk 81.

"Yes, yes—sure," Kyp said, patting his pocket. His
mind whirled. Dorsk 81 looked as if he were about to
faint, though the alien stood up straight, tense, ready to
fight if necessary. Kyp knew they had no other choice. He
slid a hand into the pocket of his overalls, ostensibly to
remove his work assignment card—and wrapped his fingers around his lightsaber handle.

The stormtroopers were more annoyed than uneasy.
Kyp would take them totally by surprise.

Admiral Daala's voice boomed out from the amplification systems like a horrible echo from Kyp's past. "You can all be proud of what you are about to do," she said.

Yes, Kyp thought in a flash, *yes I am.* He snatched out the lightsaber, and with a *snap-hiss* the energy blade sprang out. In a single sweeping arc he slashed off the stormtrooper's armored hand at the wrist, taking the blaster pistol with it, then followed through to strike down the second trooper in line. Dorsk 81 moved like a flicked whip. His own lightsaber came out ablaze as he struck down a third stormtrooper.

The audience around them recoiled in surprise and confusion. The lightsabers were unmistakable weapons of the hated Jedi Knights. The uproar spread like the shockwave from an exploding star. Spies had appeared in the rally, and the mob of dedicated Imperial defenders would demand blood.

"We've got to get out of here," Kyp shouted, hacking right and left with his lightsaber. People and alien workers spread apart like ripe grain in a strong wind, though more fled in panic than were actually cut down by the blazing lightsabers. Kyp and Dorsk 81 fought shoulder to shoulder.

"Jedi Knights!" Admiral Daala shouted from the podium. Even from her distance she could recognize the unmistakable glare of lightsabers—and now her face, dozens of meters tall and reflected over and over again on the immense videoscreens, seemed like an outraged deity demanding justice. "Kill the Jedi Knights!"

Stormtroopers clustered around them, firing blaster rifles. Dorsk 81's lightsaber deflected the first bolt high into the ceiling of the mall, while the second shot burned through the back of a fleeing Imperial lieutenant.

"Don't fight unless you have to," Kyp said. "It'll only slow us down. Run." He knew now that his partner had been right in wanting to leave earlier. They needed to get their information back to the New Republic, and if they let the Empire capture them, billions would die unwarned.

The size of the crowd worked in their favor, and as ripples of mob panic ricocheted from the walls, mass confusion swallowed all details of where and what exactly the disturbance was.

Kyp and Dorsk 81 sprinted back to where they had landed their stolen shuttle. Blaster bolts followed them down the corridors of the nexus station, spanging off wallplates, but the shots were poorly aimed.

When Kyp and Dorsk 81 reached their ship, they rocketed off the landing pad with repulsorlifts and sublight engines at full power in a pinwheeling escape. As Dorsk 81 worked the stabilizers to straighten them, their tumbling course aided in their escape because the droid perimeter ships, attempting to lock onto them, shot repeatedly but missed.

"Launch into hyperspace fast," Kyp said.

Dorsk 81's long fingers scrambled over the navicomputer board. "There's no time to calculate a long path," he said.

"Then make a short jump! Just get us out of here."

"The coordinates for Khomm are programmed," Dorsk 81 said briskly, punching up a readout. "I, uh, did that earlier. That's just beyond the outer core. We can send an alarm from my homeworld."

"Fine! Fine!" Kyp said.

Just then, one of the droid ships struck, singeing their sublight engines. They nearly stalled, coasting along with only their considerable momentum.

"The damage is bad," Kyp reported as Dorsk 81 flared up the main lightspeed engines, coaxing them to readiness, "but it's only the sublight engines, not our hyperdrive. We need to *go.*"

Behind them on the nexus station hundreds of ships had already begun lifting off.

"Engaging hyperdrive," Dorsk 81 finally said.

Droid perimeter defenses closed in on their drifting ship. More crippling turbolaser bolts spat past them, barely missing. An ion cannon blast rippled by, brushing against their shields and causing minimal damage.

"If an ion blast hits us, we're dead in space," Kyp said. "We have to go *now*."

"Got it!" Dorsk 81 said. "Hang on."

They vanished into starlines as the Empire scrambled after them.

CHAPTER 37

Three acceleration-enhanced A-wing fighters streaked off, separating from the cluster of ships around Admiral Ackbar's *Galactic Voyager* and vanishing into hyperspace with a silent bang of light.

General Crix Madine stared down at his cockpit controls through the smooth curve of his helmet faceplate. Powerful engines roared around him, making the A-wing throb. Madine had flown many ships before: fast ships and cargo haulers, interceptors and scouts. He had participated in raids for the Rebel Alliance, and earlier for the Imperials. But since the battle of Endor, he had spent most of his effort behind the scenes, setting up covert missions that younger recruits carried out.

But not this time.

The eerie flickering glow of hyperspace roared around him as the A-wings tunneled through the walls of space-time, crossing the galaxy faster than the speed of light. Before launch, Madine's team had sent no message to Ackbar, no comm signal whatsoever. The Hutts must not know of their departure.

Their navicomputer had plotted the shortest path to the coordinates provided by the tracer on Durga's personal craft. On either side of Madine flew Korenn and Trandia, in communications silence, intent on their mission. He smiled grimly, acknowledging the caliber of his companions. The Rebels had always been astute at getting top-flight volunteers.

In the muffled boredom of hyperspace, during the programmed hours of their journey, Madine let his thoughts wander. He had been one of those Rebel recruits, too, convinced to defect from the Empire by a few of his companions, friends from early days before the New Order had broken the backbone of the Old Republic—friends such as Carlist Rieekan, who had risen to the rank of general in the Rebel Alliance and had commanded Echo Base on Hoth.

Shortly after joining the Rebellion, Madine had begun working closely with Mon Mothma, who had taken him in as a trusted adviser even while others were not so certain about this new defector. Ackbar himself had been a good friend, after his own rescue from the Empire. Gruff and courageous, the Calamarian knew how to administer the Rebel fleet.

But Crix Madine had always been different in his priorities and the lengths to which he was willing to go to accomplish his objectives. Mon Mothma valued his opinions because he gave a fresh perspective. Madine himself had fought against the Rebels on the side of the Empire. He knew the tactics that were effective and those that had failed utterly.

Madine also knew his place: he was necessary, though covert tactics weren't always pretty. Before the battle of Endor, while planning strategy and deciphering the precious data that trickled in from a fragile network of Bothan spies, Mon Mothma's original plan had been simply to destroy the second Death Star while it was still under construction. When the Rebels learned, however, that Emperor Palpatine himself would inspect the battle station, Crix Madine had rejoiced at the opportunity.

Mon Mothma, though, appeared sickened. "The assassination of political leaders is not the sort of tactic the Rebel Alliance will condone," she said in a closed-room session with Madine and Ackbar. "Even if they are our enemies."

"Then we will lose," Madine said. "The Empire has no such reluctance. Do you think they would hesitate to assassinate you in an instant, Mon Mothma, if they were given the chance?"

Mon Mothma stood, her face flushed, her voice rising uncharacteristically and hammered her fists on the table-top. "I will not allow my government to become as warped and as evil as the Empire."

"Mon Mothma," Ackbar said, "we have risked too much to put this operation together. Our fleet is ready to depart for Endor. Our decoy mission has already begun at Sullust. We cannot scrap our plans just because the Emperor will be on the Death Star."

"We will save millions of innocent lives," Madine said. "There is a cost to ourselves, but the payback is potentially much greater. If we allow that Death Star to be completed, Alderaan will be only the first in a long chain of planets turned to rubble at the Emperor's whim."

And so Mon Mothma had eventually agreed that the Emperor was to be a target as well. Once the decision was made, she gave it her full enthusiasm, issuing orders with firm determination.

Thus the Death Star had been destroyed, the Empire overthrown, and the New Republic established . . . though peace and harmony had not come about as quickly as they might have hoped.

Now, Madine found himself streaking through hyperspace in an A-wing scout vessel toward another superweapon being built by another tyrant hoping to rule the galaxy.

Sometimes he felt it would never end.

*   *   *

The A-wings emerged from hyperspace on the fringes of the asteroid belt, and suddenly it seemed that a giant invisible fist had hurled a handful of crushed rocks at him. The tracker on Durga's ship had given them the exact location deep in the heart of the rubble-strewn danger zone, but it offered no safe path to follow.

Madine risked a burst of comm traffic tightly focused to the two craft paralleling him. "Trandia," he said, "take the lead. Thread the needle. Find a way through these rocks so we can get to the construction site and see what's going on there."

"Yes, sir," Trandia said, her voice bubbling with exuberance at being selected. He would let Korenn lead the flight back out.

Trandia's A-wing shot through the clusters of asteroids, arcing in tight curves and accelerating through openings created by stony bodies drifting apart. Her rear engines glowed blue-white as she increased speed. Madine and Korenn kept pace with her, locked on and following her tortuous route.

Madine admired Trandia's flying as her A-wing battered its way through the space-borne pebbles. Her forward shields glowed faintly as she increased power. Madine hated to break comm silence again, but he opened another channel. "Trandia, no need to impress me. Be careful."

"Don't worry, sir," she said.

Before Madine could say anything else, though, Korenn suddenly jerked his A-wing and dropped back. "Sir," his voice crackled with static, "I've been hit by a small piece of debris that penetrated my rear shields."

"Trandia," Madine snapped, "throttle down. Korenn, give me a status report. How much damage?"

"Partial engine loss," the young pilot said, and as Madine looked through the cockpit window he saw sizzles of blue lightning around the engine banks of

Korenn's A-wing. More than minor damage: the core was
breached.

"Korenn, listen to me—" Madine said, his heart
pounding. The crippled A-wing slung to one side out of
control and spun as the asteroids continued to hammer
around them like a giant grinding machine.

"Loss of altitude control," Korenn said in a rising
voice. "I can't stabilize!"

"Korenn!" Trandia shouted. Her A-wing swung
around.

"Pull up, pull up!" Madine shouted.

Trandia zoomed toward her companion. Madine
didn't know what she expected to do, but before she could
reach him, Korenn's A-wing slammed into a jagged shard
of rock. His engine core buckled. The ship erupted in an
aftershower of fire.

Trandia cruised low over the still-smoldering wreckage on the surface of the large asteroid; the detonation had
flung hull plating and slagged components into orbit.

"Checking for survivors, sir," Trandia said, her
voice strained close to the breaking point.

Though Madine knew it was hopeless, he allowed her
a few moments to cruise over the spinning rock until she
brought her ship close to his again.

"Nothing to report, sir," she said. Her voice was
bleak.

"I know," Madine said. "But we have to proceed."

"It's my fault, sir," Trandia said. She sounded as if
she were begging.

"And it's my fault for ordering you to take the lead,"
Madine said. "And the Chief of State's fault for ordering
the mission in the first place, and the Hutts' fault for
building the weapon at all—and so on, and so on. We
could spend a great deal of time assigning an endless
chain of blame—but I'd rather accomplish our mission.
Wouldn't you?"

Trandia took a long moment to respond. "Yes, sir,"
she said finally.

They continued slowly, nearing the heart of the asteroid belt. Edging forward with low engine power, their running lamps off, they came at last upon the spangle of
lights at the construction site.

Madine set his course and transmitted a comparable
trajectory to Trandia's A-wing. Once locked into the appropriate path, they shut down their engines and drifted
along, just like other hunks of space wreckage.

With dry eyes and an intent stare, Madine watched
the construction site approach with infinite slowness. He
drank in the details: a huge cylindrical fortress, a gleaming
metal structure almost completed, like a giant tunnel in
space. Along its axis, this battle station appeared to con-
tain one of the planet-cracking superlasers.

The Hutts had extensively modified the Death Star
plans. That could only mean they had impressive engineering expertise available to them.

He and Trandia landed their A-wings on a large asteroid at the outskirts of the construction site. The newly
built battle station rode high against the black star-strewn
sky. Madine sent a narrow-burst communication again.

"We'll stay on this asteroid to do our reconnais-
sance," he said, "then we'll suit up and attempt to infil-
trate."

CHAPTER 38

As their damaged ship limped away from Hoth, Callista worked side by side with Luke Skywalker. They desperately cross-wired systems, bypassed ruined components, and fastened vital equipment back into place, trying to repair each failure before another one occurred.

The wampa ice creatures had not actually breached the yacht's outer hull, but they had caused a wealth of damage. The craft's sublight engines, operating at barely half power, had lurched away from the frozen planet, reluctantly heaving them into orbit. The engines attempted to fail several times, but somehow struggled on.

Their ship's hyperdrive was gone, their navicomputer beyond repair. They plunged headlong into the broken asteroid field at the fringes of the Hoth system with only minimal shields and virtually no control over their course. The asteroids began to grow thicker around them, battering at the tiny ship. Callista did not voice her growing dread.

Luke looked up at her with red, bleary eyes and a haggard face. Callista knew she probably looked just as bad with her malt blond hair mussed and her gray eyes bloodshot, but Luke's pallid skin had begun to flush again with hope. "I might be able to use the Force to navigate us," he said. "At least enough to keep us from a major collision—but I don't know where we're going to go."

"I wish I could help you," Callista said. "But I can't. I can't, and I'm afraid to try."

"You fought well with the lightsaber against the snow creatures," Luke answered reassuringly, "and I didn't feel any glimmer from the dark side as I did on Dagobah."

"No," Callista said. Her words were a whisper. "I didn't let it out." She knew, though, that the dark side had been there like black wings hovering at the edge of her consciousness, demanding to be set free. She had refused—but, oh, the temptation had been great. . . .

In a shower of sparks and burned circuits, the life-support systems gasped and died. Luke and Callista pulled components from nonessential computers trying to get the systems functioning again. "It's only at about ten percent," Luke said. "That's not going to help us much."

Callista shivered. The temperature had already begun to drop in the cabin. "We're not going to get out of this, are we?" she said with quiet, brutal honesty.

Luke stared at her for a long moment, then his face forced a smile. "Not in any obvious way," he finally said with a sigh. "That just means we have to look for a solution that isn't obvious."

Luke and Callista studied the torn environment suits the wampas had shredded. Somehow, using several repair kits and other patches they found in forgotten packages left by some unknown station mechanic on Coruscant, they managed to piece together one of the suits. But only one.

Within the hour, the atmosphere began to thin noticeably, and their body heat did little to warm the cabin as the cold of space leached it away.

Luke ran his fingers along the crude, lumpy patches

in the suit, and he took Callista's hand. "You have to wear it, Callista."

"I won't let you sacrifice yourself," she said. "You wouldn't let me do it on the *Eye of Palpatine*."

Luke raised her hand to his cheek. "I have no intention of sacrificing myself. I can go deep into a Jedi trance and slow down my metabolism, put myself practically in suspended animation. Then we wait, and hope."

Callista eyed the repaired suit, still reluctant, then she gazed into Luke's clear blue eyes, wishing she could read his thoughts and his emotions.

"Maybe I can use the Force to contact someone," he said, "send out a message with my thoughts. I doubt anybody'll be able to read it, but we have to try."

Callista slowly pulled the thick fabric of the environment suit over her long legs. "Yes," she said, defeated, "we have to try." Before she clamped her helmet in place, she kissed Luke. "Will you be all right?" she said.

He smiled wanly at her. "As long as you're here to watch over me."

Luke's blue eyes fell closed and rolled upward slightly as he sank into himself, using his Jedi techniques to enter a deep trance that walled him off from the rest of the universe.

Callista longed to join him, but her grasp on the Force had become so slippery she could not touch her abilities. She was unable even to begin the deep Jedi trance that Luke brought upon himself.

She watched him, feeling her heart ache with love as she struggled with the silence of the Force in her mind. Once again, she saw the dark shadows of possibilities in her mind, luring her with an easy way to use the Force again—

Join the dark side!

—even if it meant she had to succumb to evil influences.

"No," she whispered to herself, though she knew she could not disturb Luke now. She fled from the dark alternative, and it frightened her that the persistent shadows had come more easily this time.

The silent cabin grew colder and colder. The environment suit crinkled around her as she curled up next to Luke, conserving energy and wanting to be next to him.

He appeared to be a statue. Frost formed on his cheeks from the faint exhalations of his breath. She desperately wished she could touch his thoughts, share in his efforts to send out a plea for help—but Luke's mind remained closed to her.

The crippled ship drifted through the outer fringes of the asteroid belt with minimal shields and failing life support, while Callista sat alone in the darkness.

Inside the featureless Force shell he had wrapped around himself and his mind, Luke Skywalker centered his thoughts into a single projectile, a tangible shout across space and time. In his mind his words thrummed along the lines of Force that connected everything in the cosmos.

He recalled hanging on Cloud City's lower antennas, dangling above the clouds as he held on for dear life. He had issued a similar call then, before he had known the truth about his sister . . . before he had realized there was a connection between them. Luke had still known whom to ask for assistance.

"Leia!" he called from the far fringes of the asteroid belt, flinging his thoughts undirected across space. "Leia . . . Leia . . ."

CHAPTER 39

Exhausted from the fraying effects of constant tension during the diplomatic mission to Durga's fortress—compounded by the startling knowledge that Admiral Daala was still alive and gearing up for another assault against the New Republic—Leia sat in her comfortable seat in the diplomatic shuttle. Han piloted it away from Nal Hutta, avoiding the Smugglers' Moon entirely and arrowing out to open space where Ackbar's fleet waited.

Relieved that he no longer required stuffy diplomatic finery, Han wore his familiar old clothes again: black vest, white shirt, and dark pants that had seen better days. Leia wished she had brought along comfortable clothes herself, but she had forgotten to pack them while preparing for her surprise performance on the Hutt homeworld.

Beside her, Threepio helpfully chattered his list of all the duties waiting for her upon returning to Coruscant. His thin voice rattled off one obligation after another; some she had forgotten, some she had ignored, and some she just didn't want to remember. As Threepio continued with unbridled enthusiasm for the safe trivialities of a governmental life, Leia found herself lulled into an uneasy doze. The smooth vibrations of the diplomatic ship hummed into her bones like an electronic massage. Her thoughts drifted. Her breathing became more regular. . . .

And suddenly a spear of thought lanced through her. Leia sat bolt upright as a convulsive shudder made her skin crawl. She blinked her large brown eyes and gasped. The thought came again like a bullet of ice shooting through her mind.

Leia. . .

Leia!

"Luke?" she whispered.

Threepio, still reciting his list, finally noticed that something was wrong. "Mistress Leia, are you all right?"

Han turned from the pilot's seat, an expression of concern on his face. "Hey, Leia—what is it?"

Leia shivered and squeezed her eyes shut. She ran her fingertips across her forehead . . . and the voice continued to echo through her skull, a distant pleading call with no details, just the repeated summons.

Leia!

"It's Luke," she said. "He's in trouble."

"Do you know where he is?" Han said, his face filled with questions he did not ask. In their years together, Han had learned not to inquire about certain details of the Jedi, because he would never understand anyway. He no longer considered it a "hokey religion," but he still didn't comprehend it.

"No," she said. Luke's ethereal voice faded to the back of her mind where it remained, its insistent summons growing no worse but issuing a continuous call. "I think I can find him if I concentrate hard enough, though. We have to—"

"Hey, look!" Han pointed out the cockpit as they approached the New Republic fleet. Wedge's escort frigate *Yavaris* hung in front of them like a jagged monstrosity. Connected to one of the docking ports was the familiar battered shape of the *Millennium Falcon*. "Chewie must be back with Artoo." Han spun in his chair and looked at Leia. "When we get to the fleet, we'll give them our news about the Hutts. Then we can take all these warships with us to rescue Luke—or we can just go in the *Falcon*."

"All right." Leia bit her lower lip. "I don't think the whole fleet would help, though. We've got to go *soon*." She swallowed, trying to ease her dry throat. "We'll have to brief Ackbar on what we learned about Imperial activities. He'll need time to plan strategy."

When the diplomatic shuttle pulled into the receiving bay of the *Yavaris,* they sprang out of their ship with the New Republic armed escort. Before Han could get his bearings, the towering lanky form of a bellowing Wookiee rushed to greet him. Chewbacca embraced Han so hard that Leia thought she could hear bones crack.

Wedge Antilles came running up breathless. "Han, Leia! Glad you're back. Chewie and Artoo found out something on Nar Shaddaa, but once they heard you were on your way, they insisted on waiting."

Chewbacca barked a rapid story that Leia could not understand. Artoo also wheeled up whistling and chittering. "Wait a minute, you two," Leia said, raising her voice.

Han held out both hands, palm outward. "Chewie," he said, "hey, buddy—talk slower! I can't understand you."

It took several minutes for Han to extricate the message about Imperial General Sulamar linking up with the Hutts to build their superweapon. This—tied with the information that Admiral Daala had unified the remaining Imperial forces and was planning her assault—made the galaxy a dangerous place indeed.

Leia listened, sick with anxiety for Luke, yet knowing she had to give instructions, issue standing orders for her fleet before she went rushing off.

"General Antilles," Leia said, "let's go to the war room and link up with Admiral Ackbar. We've got to discuss strategy, but Han and I have to leave with all possible speed—my brother, Luke, is in trouble. Everything's happening at once.''

"Luke's in trouble?" Wedge asked. "Let's go!"

They rushed to the sealed war room, and a coded transmission brought a holographic simulacrum of Admiral Ackbar into the room with them. Leia drummed her fingertips on the table, looking around, feeling the prodding of Luke's mental call that hadn't lessened.

Luke needed her. He was trapped somehow. She had to leave. She *had to leave.*

"The Hutts are building their own superweapon with Imperial assistance," Leia began. "And our old friend Admiral Daala is unifying a new fleet to strike against the New Republic. All this is happening right under our noses."

She glanced from Wedge's square-jawed face to Ackbar's glassy, unreadable Calamarian eyes. "I want all of our teams on yellow alert from this moment on. Make sure everyone is ready for immediate deployment to battle, wherever the Imperials may strike." She turned toward Wedge. "But, we mustn't tip our hand. The only advantage we have is that they don't *know* we know what they're up to. They probably realize we suspect something because we're here snooping around . . . but they won't think we've found anything. You will continue your maneuvers, as before.

"Right now Han, Chewie, and I will take the *Falcon* and go rescue Luke. We can't let the Hutts think anything has changed. Wait for your report from General Madine's mission and act accordingly if I haven't returned—I trust you all."

Leia stood with a determined look on her face. "Now I have to go save my brother." Han took her hand as they ran to the *Falcon.*

Leia sat strapped into her seat, still concentrating, following Luke's gradually fading request for assistance. Her

Force abilities had been sharpened through Luke's training, and though she couldn't give Han any direct coordinates for his navicomputer, she could take him in the right general direction; as they approached closer, she narrowed down Luke's location.

The battered space yacht looked like a derelict careening in a random path along the fringes of the asteroid belt. Artoo-Detoo squealed as he detected the ship on the sensors, and Chewbacca triangulated on its position as he steered the *Falcon* to the rescue.

With the *Falcon*'s tractor beam, they took the ruined yacht in tow and brought their airlocks together, sealing them so that Han, Leia, and Chewie could open the outer hatch and enter the darkened wreck. Leia had noted disturbing marks on the outer hull, not simply dents and scars from meteor impacts—but long scratches that looked as if they had been made with impossibly sharp claws.

She couldn't understand what he had been doing out in the Hoth system. When he and Callista departed from Coruscant, Luke had intended to go with her to the exclusive and romantic cometary resort of the Mulako Primordial Water Quarry—but something must have changed.

Panting, Han dropped down into the empty hold of Luke's ship with a thud, and called up for breathmasks. "Almost no air left in here," he gasped, "and it's freezing cold. Reminds me of Kessel."

Chewbacca tossed a clatter of glowlights and breathmasks down before lowering his hairy body into the dim chamber. Han and Leia placed the masks over their faces, and each took a light, which they shone into the dim chambers. Chewbacca shivered and rubbed his fur-covered arms.

"They're completely out of power," Leia said. "Life-support systems are practically dead."

"Doesn't seem to be any engine control, either," Han said.

Leia shook her head. "I can sense Luke, though. It's just a whisper now, but he's here."

They found the two motionless bodies in the back chamber, the small sleeping area: Luke lay on the floor like a statue, and Callista clung to him in a tattered and failing life-support suit. Luke looked frozen solid. A rime of frost covered his eyebrows, his eyelashes, and his upper lip. His skin appeared colorless and flat, like wax.

Callista gave a rattling groan, shifting in her slick suit. Powdery frost crumbled from the joints in her arms.

"Her suit's almost gone. Let's get them into the *Falcon*," Han said. "Chewie, carry Luke. Leia and I will get Callista."

They carried the sagging Jedi back into the warmth and the air of the *Falcon,* then disconnected from the ruined space yacht, letting the hulk drift into the asteroid field like discarded rubbish, where it would soon become crushed in the relentless chaos of the meteor storm.

Callista revived first. With a change into warm clothing and generous cups of stim tea, she recovered enough to insist on helping tend Luke Skywalker as they nursed him back to health. In his deep trance he had depleted his reserves, keeping himself at the ghost edge of death when the life support had ceased to function. Only his will to survive had kept his heart beating and oxygen molecules moving through his lungs. In another few hours he would have succumbed.

Callista's gray eyes were red-rimmed as she took a poly sponge soaked in warm water and bathed Luke's face, his forehead, his neck. She whispered to Leia, "I had to watch him as my own supplies dwindled. As he dwindled." She shuddered. "I held him, but I couldn't touch him. I told him so many things. . . ." She reached out with her fingertip, gently caressing Luke's cheek.

Suddenly his blue eyes snapped open, and he took a deep breath. He blinked, and color flooded back into his cheeks. Drawing several more slow breaths, he revived like a time-lapse exposure of a blossom unfolding. "We're safe?'' he said. His voice was a hoarse croak, but it was alive—*he* was alive!

Callista hugged him, and Han and Chewie and Leia gathered around, barely restraining themselves from smothering him again with their delight.

"Yes, Luke, you're safe now," Leia said, "and we're on our way. We'll take you back to the Jedi academy, where you can relax and recover."

CHAPTER 40

From his personal offices on the nearly completed Dark-saber battle station, Bevel Lemelisk gazed out the array of latticed windows, studying the final steps in the mammoth construction project.

His office was unabashedly austere, with cold metal walls, little furniture, and no decoration whatsoever. He didn't waste time on frivolities like artwork or comfort. The thing that concerned him most was ensuring that he had the right equipment—and plenty of it. He was only truly happy when surrounded with technological toys.

As Lemelisk watched the continually shifting chaos of the asteroid belt—random patterns of motion from the drifting rocks tugged by their own minimal gravities into complex fifth-order permutations—he noted the distant light reflected off the hull of some other ship in the asteroid belt. He squinted. Yes, it was definitely a vessel, not another asteroid.

"Spies?" he wondered with a thrill of adrenaline; he doubted it. This huge weapon was doing nothing to conceal itself. More likely it was a group of smugglers who thought they were safe in an uncharted area of space.

Most bothersome, though, in Lemelisk's opinion, was the fact that the Taurill had once again been thrown into a frenzy of distraction by unexpected movement. He couldn't imagine how the busy little creatures in their tiny, custom-made spacesuits could notice something so faint and far away, but the Taurill Overmind had thousands of eyes—and it took only one to notice.

The tiny Taurill construction workers jockeyed around for better views of the moving reflected lights, leaving their positions so they could stare upward and point with multiple arms.

Lemelisk scowled. Now he would have to go on another plate-by-plate inspection outside the Darksaber just to make sure they didn't mess up again. He had successfully managed to conceal the first debacle from Durga the Hutt, but he wasn't confident he could continue to trick the crime lord.

He waddled down the hall, taking a turbolift to the construction access bay, and climbed inside a smelly old inspection scooter, a tiny spherical craft that held one person—and that just barely.

Lemelisk tucked his paunch behind the crude controls and sealed himself in. The laboring air-recirculation systems did little to dampen the odor of decaying upholstery that continued to outgas even so many years after the scooter had been put into operation.

Lemelisk raised the small vehicle off the floor and passed through the magnetic atmosphere field, then puttered along the cylindrical hull of black anodized plates.

He remembered the time he had taken a similar inspection tour of the original Death Star with Grand Moff Tarkin . . . and he hoped *this* time it wouldn't turn out to be such a disaster.

*   *   *

He and Grand Moff Tarkin had departed from the Governor's palace on Eriadu, an important trading and governmental hub on the Outer Rim, where Tarkin had established his primary base of operations when he became the regional governor of the fringe worlds. With the Death Star completed, Tarkin had summoned Bevel Lemelisk back from one of his new weapons-building assignments to Eriadu so they could perform the first test flight of the battle station together.

Tarkin took his pet Calamarian, Ackbar, to pilot them in an unmarked *Lambda*-class shuttle away toward the Horuz System where the Death Star hung in orbit over the penal colony of Despayre.

Tarkin preferred to travel without a full complement of guards because it allowed him to move unhindered, to slip in where he might hear traitorous words and then crack down accordingly. He also didn't want to draw attention to the superweapon's location now that it was so nearly finished.

"What are you waiting for, Ackbar?" Tarkin snapped from the passenger seat beside Lemelisk. "Let us go see this weapon that will crush all resistance to the Emperor's New Order."

The Calamarian hunched over his controls and made no response, taking the *Lambda* shuttle away from Eriadu toward the jump point where they would enter hyperspace.

Tarkin took every opportunity to taunt and harass the quiet, unflappable Calamarian slave. Ackbar was supposedly intelligent, according to Tarkin, and Lemelisk knew that the Grand Moff spent merciless time showing Ackbar the tactics he would use to defeat the Rebels, the secret plans, the tricks and feints designed to evoke despair from those who resisted Imperial rule. Ackbar seemed suitably downcast, all spark of resistance crushed . . . or at least well buried.

"Preparing to enter hyperspace," Ackbar said with a complete lack of enthusiasm, his words devoid of inflection. "Destination—Despayre in the Horuz System."

Without warning, three Rebel Y-wings appeared out of nowhere, bearing down on Tarkin's shuttle and firing their laser cannons.

"It's a Rebel attack!" Tarkin said. "Ackbar, take evasive action."

The Calamarian moved with sudden efficiency—but instead of launching them immediately into hyperspace, Ackbar shut down the shields.

"You fool!" Tarkin shouted.

"Er, what do you think we should do now?" Lemelisk asked.

The Rebel Y-wings came around again, firing precision shots. Explosions erupted from the rear of the *Lambda*-class shuttle. The craft rocked back and forth. Flames and smoke poured from the rear compartment, and the ship reeled out of control.

"You will die for this, Ackbar," Tarkin said.

Then the Rebels hit again, sending the crippled shuttle spinning. Tarkin had just climbed to his feet, and the new jolt hurled him against the far wall. He tumbled over Lemelisk, still strapped into his seat.

"Shields are down, our engines crippled," Ackbar said. "And now they are coming in for the kill." He looked up at the front viewport. "I just wanted you to understand that *I* have brought this upon you, Grand Moff Tarkin, in exchange for all the pain you have inflicted upon me and others like me."

Lemelisk saw the Rebel ships approaching again, deadly weapons already glowing in preparation for firing. Tarkin scrambled to his feet and grabbed Lemelisk by the collar, ripping him out of his chair.

"The escape pod," Tarkin said. "We'll leave this traitor to the fate he's earned for himself."

Together Tarkin and Lemelisk dived into the small escape pod intended for the comfort of only one person. Lemelisk stumbled and fell flat against the bulkhead and felt something crack in his face; blood poured out of his nose. Tarkin did not pause, but punched the automated launch button. The rear hatch of the lifepod sealed, and with an explosion seemingly greater than anything the Rebel Y-wings had inflicted upon them, the lifepod soared away from the shuttle as the Y-wings came in for their final attack.

The universe reeled, spinning in confusion as Lemelisk tried to stanch the flow of blood from his nose. He saw the Rebel ships circle the crippled shuttle, but instead of immediately detonating it, they clustered around, connecting hatches.

"They'll be after us in a moment," Tarkin said as he triggered the distress signal built into the escape pod. Lemelisk saw that the Grand Moff had also been injured, burned by the hot bulkhead.

Suddenly, with a miracle of good luck, space around the Eriadu System rippled and an Imperial Star Destroyer stabbed out of hyperspace. He learned later that it was Admiral Motti's flagship; Motti had come to escort Tarkin, though the Grand Moff had not asked for it.

The Star Destroyer locked onto the distress signal and came toward the would-be Rebel assassins, its turbolasers ripping through the darkness with spears of disintegrating light.

Lemelisk looked up and saw the three attacking Y-wings fire again at the *Lambda* shuttle, this time destroying it utterly. As it exploded, the Y-wings split off in three different directions and vanished into the cloaking distance of space. . . .

As they spun around, dizzy inside the careening lifepod, Lemelisk felt as if he were about to be spacesick. The engineer's part of his mind wondered distantly just how much of a mess he would make if he vomited into the confined atmosphere of the craft as it whirled around like a child's toy.

"Very strange," Lemelisk commented. "It appeared as if those Rebel ships wanted to rescue your Calamarian slave."

Tarkin was incredulous. "Rescue Ackbar? Why should they bother with an animal?"

Lemelisk shrugged as Admiral Motti's Star Destroyer followed the distress beacon and approached them for rescue. "I've never understood the Rebel mind," he said. . . .

Later, they recovered in the Death Star's infirmary rooms. Lemelisk nursed a broken nose, and Tarkin lay bandaged from sprains and superficial burns. They received the grim news that the assassination attempt on Tarkin had been only part of the Rebel treachery. A group of commandos had succeeded in stealing a copied set of the full Death Star blueprints, the technical readouts that specified every system, each component, all the weaponry capabilities of the great battle station, and smuggled them to the Toprawa Relay Station, from which point they had vanished.

A young corporal with spit-polished boots, clean uniform, and neatly trimmed hair stood nervously as he delivered his message, afraid that Tarkin might fly into a rage and order the young man's execution. "Darth Vader is even now tracking down the Toprawan Rebels, sir. He anticipates capturing them before they can deliver their stolen plans."

Lemelisk watched Tarkin and was amazed by the Grand Moff's seeming lack of concern. He gave a mysterious thin smile while his hard eyes flashed. "Seeing the full details may even increase their fear of this battle station," Tarkin said. "They won't find a flaw." He looked over at Lemelisk, who felt foolish with the cumbersome bandage across his nose. "My Death Star is invincible."

Lemelisk leaned back on the infirmary bed and hoped Tarkin was right.

Now, as he cruised in the inspection scooter over the outer hull of the Darksaber, Lemelisk didn't have such confidence in the new Hutt superweapon. He would have to chastise the Taurill for their shoddy work once again, and the little creatures would scramble to perform the necessary reparations . . . until the next screwup.

But the Taurill weren't the only problem.

Sulamar's antique computer cores kept crashing, no matter how carefully Lemelisk reprogrammed them and backed them up. The devices must have been defective from the time of manufacture, and now they were so outdated few people remembered how to fix them.

Some of the thick metal sheeting purchased from low-bid contractors was found to have millions of micro holes—bad enough for structural material, but this had been intended for the *engine shielding*! This entire Darksaber project was one misery after another.

The front-end girders of the kilometers-long cylinder didn't exactly match up with the aft girders in the final assembly, and if the superlaser was not perfectly aligned when Durga fired the weapon, the deadly beam could vaporize the Darksaber rather than its intended target.

And there was more. . . .

His groan echoed inside the inspection scooter. He had overseen repairs to each of these problems, but finding so many instances of ineptitude made him wonder about the many problems he had not yet found.

CHAPTER 41

Crix Madine and Trandia locked down their A-wing fighters in the dense shadows of rocky outcrop bristling from the rugged surface of a small asteroid.

"All systems on standby and powered up," Madine said. "Even if everything goes as planned, we need to be ready to leave here fast."

Trandia responded with the grim fatalism she had shown since the death of Korenn, the third member of their team. "Are we going to return from this mission, sir?" she said.

Madine thought of responding with a reassuring answer, then decided she deserved something more honest. "We must remain optimists," he said. "There's a chance we'll get back home eventually."

Trandia said, "Good enough for me, sir."

Madine and Trandia wore heavily padded, single-mission spacesuits, walking outfits of armor like self-contained mobile ships. They stood on the crumbly surface of the asteroid, checking their complement of detonators, life-support packs, and surveillance systems.

"Ready to go, sir," Trandia said.

Madine stood beside her, bulky in the hardened survival suit. They looked out at the enormous structure taking shape as it hung at a stable point in the asteroid belt. "Launch," Madine said.

He and Trandia leaped upward, tearing themselves free of the asteroid's negligible gravity. Momentum carried them across the gulf of space toward the superweapon under construction. As he and Trandia drifted like tiny pieces of rubble toward the giant cylindrical assembly, Madine had a good deal of time to stare at the Hutt project through his faceplate.

The design concerned him. He was aware that the Hutts had copied the Death Star plans from the Imperial Information Center—but this was no Death Star. It appeared instead to be no more than the superlaser, a straight cylinder that would serve as a destructive offensive weapon. If this weapon were completed, the Hutts would show little reluctance to use it against any system that failed to pay them for protection.

And the construction seemed nearly finished.

The two suited figures floated in, specks against the kilometers-long assembly. Madine spoke in a focused line-of-sight beam at Trandia. "We may be able to cripple the weapon if we can get inside and place our detonators in appropriate spots."

"From the looks of it, we'd better not wait too long, sir," Trandia said. "Seems like the Hutts are ready to go."

At last, their magnetic boots made contact with the armor plates, black metal that reflected little starlight. Using his adhesive gloves, Madine clambered like an insect along the hull. The Hutt weapon was so vast that the curvature of the cylinder was unnoticeable beneath him.

He and Trandia worked their way along the metal plates, and Madine was surprised to see that many of the hull segments were mismatched and loose, welded together but leaving gaps and uneven seams. Such a construction couldn't possibly hold an atmosphere. He was appalled by the reprehensible workmanship.

At least it would be easy to get inside.

They came upon one particularly loose plate, and Madine removed a crude crowbar from the tool compartment of his bulky suit. With it he was able to peel free some of the crumbling welds. The sheet of metal drifted away, tumbling end over end. The missing plate left an opening large enough for Trandia and Madine to crawl through even in their cumbersome suits.

They entered a darkened, half-completed corridor, little more than an access space between the shoddy outer hull and a not-much-better inner wall. Bright beams from their helmets lit the way as they pulled themselves along. Finally they reached a bulkhead door that allowed them to pass deeper inside the construction and work their way toward the aft interior chambers. They cycled one at a time through a cramped airlock.

Clomping in his heavy boots, Madine entered another dimly lit passageway and stood waiting for Trandia. When she joined him, Madine removed his helmet. "There's atmosphere here. Let's take off our suits," he said. "We'll need the freedom of movement. We might have to hide on a moment's notice, and I can hardly move inside this contraption."

Trandia disassembled the heavy components, piling her armor beside his in an unused storage alcove. The empty suits looked like enough metal to be the shrapnel from an Imperial scout walker. Trandia's braid had come loose, and strands of hair swam around her face. Perspiration dampened her neck, and her skin was flushed—but her eyes were flinty.

Madine and Trandia removed the tools and the detonators from their packs. He scratched his beard and held a clenched fist in the air. "To the success of our mission."

Trandia matched his upraised fist. "We will succeed," she answered.

Ducking low and moving quietly, they sprinted along

the corridors, heading toward where the propulsion systems would be. Some of these decks were already inhabited by a skeleton crew, and they hesitated at corners, crept
past droning voices of guards and crew members who
lurked in open rooms.

As they hurried, though, Madine noted many darkened glowpanels, wires dangling from ceiling plates but
connected to nothing, and dead blank computer terminals
that seemed as if they had never functioned. Madine muttered to Trandia, "Maybe we don't need to sabotage the
weapon after all. This whole thing is a disaster waiting to
happen."

The engine sections were a great pulsing dungeon
filled with smells of oil and coolant, hissing steam that
might have been intentionally vented or just leaking from
reactor cores. The storm of noise and flashing lights
throbbed around them, drowning their surreptitious sounds
as they crept into the tangle of engines.

More guards patrolled the catwalks above—stupid-
looking Gamorreans and a hodgepodge of unsavory alien
creatures: Weequays, Niktus, and walrus-faced Aqualish.
Madine checked the blaster pistol and the four detonators
he carried, then gestured that he and Trandia would split
up.

The Darksaber's guidance computers were giant
banks of circuit boards fenced off by a transparent mesh
that steamed with supercooled air blown through the hot
circuitry.

The enormous engines themselves thrummed behind
a thick shielding wall. If they could plant remote detonators in various spots around the compartment, the two of
them unaided could cripple this great weapon, leaving it
dead in space until New Republic forces could finish the
job.

He and Trandia moved apart into the deeper shadows
and the loud, unmuffled machinery. Trandia held her precious store of detonators as she slithered through the

murk, darting from cover to scant cover, working her way over to the shielding wall that blocked the engines.

Alone, Madine moved to the mesh surrounding the propulsion computers. He bent down and removed a cutting tool from his equipment pouch, intending to slice through the protective fence. A detonator or two could completely kill the computers that drove the superweapon. He switched on the small vibroblade and felt the high-pitched hum through its handle. He hacked at the thin flexible mesh—but as soon as he severed the crystalline cords, a squawking alarm burst from the top of the computer.

Madine deactivated the vibroblade with a curse, grabbing for his blaster pistol. The guards in the engine compartment hurried to discover the nature of the disturbance, though they seemed somewhat apathetic. Madine wondered how often they responded to false alarms resulting from the inept construction work.

Madine decided not to fire just yet and slid back into shadows as the alien guards lumbered toward him, their own weapons drawn. If he could just be silent, they might miss him and go about their business. His heart pounded. The guards came closer.

Suddenly Trandia stood up from her hiding place near the wall of the engine compartment. She waved her arms and yelled to draw attention to herself. As the guards turned in astonishment, she fired her blaster at them, hitting a leathery-faced Niku, who hissed as he fell to the floor.

The other guards spun about and launched a volley of blaster bolts in Trandia's direction. She ducked, but one bolt burned through her arm. She cried out and slumped behind one of the consoles for cover. The guards converged on her hiding place, completely forgetting Madine.

"Run!" she shouted at him. Her voice was high with pain. "Run."

Madine cursed again under his breath, wishing Trandia hadn't been so impulsive. He began to crawl away from the propulsion computers, pulled his blaster, and looked for a chance to draw the guards away from her. The vicious aliens pushed toward her position—and just as they reached her, Trandia triggered every one of the detonators she carried.

The resulting explosion drowned out even the cacophony of engine sounds. A wall of flame gushed outward in a blazing ring. The explosion took out the entire complement of guards as well as Trandia herself, though it barely damaged the engines' containment wall. Lights flickered and went out.

The shockwave knocked Madine flat, turning his consciousness into a static of black insects before his eyes. He shook his head, gasping for breath, and struggled back to his feet. The enemy was alerted, the infiltration ruined. It would do no good to stay.

Madine stumbled as he ran. He couldn't think straight, stunned as much by the loss of Trandia as by the explosion. Then a deeper core of Madine's personality asserted itself, reinforced by the years of training he had undergone, the lessons he himself had taught his commando team members.

The mission was paramount.

They had to succeed.

The mission.

Madine hauled himself to his feet and found that his back was bleeding, nicked by several chunks of shrapnel unleashed by the explosion. Alarms continued to whoop and screech, demanding attention. Madine somehow reached the doorway, though he was disoriented and couldn't recall how to find his way back to their armored mission suits.

He lurched through the open door, staggered down the dimly lit corridor—and stumbled right into another group of alien guards rushing to see what the commotion was all about.

Madine's heart sank. Trandia had given her life hoping to cause irreparable damage, hoping to let her commander escape—but she had accomplished neither.

Gamorreans clasped stubby fingers around his arms, throwing Madine to the deck and piling on top of him as if they meant to keep him from moving.

"Saboteur!" one of the Weequays snarled down at him.

They hauled Madine to his feet. Five separate guards clutched him, as if in a contest to see how many could actually claim credit for his capture. Madine struggled, but said nothing.

The guards hauled him off alone, a trophy to be brought before Durga the Hutt.

CHAPTER 42

Up on the Darksaber's supposedly functional control deck, Bevel Lemelisk watched the childish glee evident on the faces of both General Sulamar and Durga the Hutt. The two normally surly partners sat enthralled with the controls in their grasp as they itched to begin their grand plan of conquest.

Despite the difficulties Lemelisk had experienced with the Taurill and any number of other convoluted problems encountered during construction of the massive superweapon, the Darksaber project had somehow bumbled along, adhering to its schedule more through mutual annihilation of errors than actual efficiency.

Per Durga's demand, the Darksaber was now technically complete, constructed according to Lemelisk's modified plans and completed in conjunction with the work and inspection crews—though Lemelisk did not want to guarantee the quality of any portion of the project. In fact, he felt great anxiety when he began to think Durga might actually wish to use the weapon anytime soon.

"Observe," Durga said, summoning a holographic

map of the galaxy centered on the Nal Hutta system and extending outward in the intended path of the Hutts' "outreach program," using the Darksaber to hold rich and vulnerable planets ransom.

Sulamar gave far too much unwanted advice, and Durga refused to listen any longer, gloating over the holo map, his rubbery lips forming a leer that pushed the discolored birthmark up the side of his face.

On the control deck Durga's other crew members sat strapped into their chairs, secured with lock restraints because Durga did not want them to leap from their booby-trapped seats if he grew displeased with them.

Lemelisk rubbed the scratchy stubble on his chin, as Durga peered into the map of the galaxy, which would soon be under his entire control.

Without warning, the alarms went off, whooping from the security stations. Klaxons echoed through the empty corridors of the Darksaber. Startled, many of the crew members on the command deck tried to flee, but the locked webbing held them in place.

Durga bellowed, "I demand to know the meaning of this racket."

"That's the security alarm, sir," Bevel Lemelisk said. "I selected its sound to be particularly unpleasant and attention grabbing."

Sulamar sneered. "You did your job well, engineer."

Durga was not satisfied. "And why did this alarm go off?"

Lemelisk shrugged. "Because of a security breach, perhaps?" he suggested.

"You mean sabotage?" the Hutt said.

Before Lemelisk could answer, the echoing thump of a distant explosion vibrated through the walls. "I think that would be a safe bet, Lord Durga," he said.

"Damage report, sir," said one of the Devaronian crew members. "An explosion has occurred in the engine levels. A saboteur planted a bomb."

"Extent of damage?" Lemelisk asked.

"Unknown at this time," the Devaronian said.

Durga howled in outrage. "Sabotage! This will put us behind schedule. How did anyone penetrate our defenses?" His lanternlike Hutt eyes scoured across the members of his command crew. "I demand to know who is in charge of security!" He reared up on his levitating platform. "Who?"

Everyone on the bridge deck huddled down and cowered until one pasty-faced Twi'lek finally raised a clawed hand. The wormlike head-tails dangling from the back of his skull quivered with fear. "I . . . I am in charge, Lord Durga. We did not anticipate—"

Durga roared and reached for his small control pad, punching a fat greenish finger against one of the buttons. The Twi'lek let out a little yip of anticipatory terror—but instead a hapless Weequay at another station yowled and began to jitter as arcs of blue electrical fire curled up from the base of his booby-trapped seat. The discharge crisped his flesh, electrocuting him in an instant. The Weequay's smoldering corpse slumped against his navigational station.

Durga frowned and glanced down at his control pad. "Oh," he said. "Sorry, wrong button." The smell of disintegrated flesh wafted through the bridge deck in greasy, sooty wisps from the collapsed body.

"Well, let that be a lesson to you, then," Durga said, glowering at his intended victim.

The demon-faced Devaronian interrupted, consulting his communications panel. Everyone on the bridge deck trembled in fear. "I, uh, I have something more to report, sir," he said. "Security has announced the capture of one terrorist. One other was killed."

Durga growled, looking at the Weequay corpse slumped at its stations. "There will be more executions when we get to the bottom of this."

Hearing this, Bevel Lemelisk shuddered and tried to remain inconspicuous. Simply hearing the word *execution* brought back to his mind the full horrors of the Emperor's executions, the excruciating deaths Palpatine had inflicted upon Lemelisk each time he made an error. . . .

The deaths remained in Lemelisk's mind, ever-present shadowy nightmares—seven executions in all. Once, Palpatine had launched him out an airlock; the pain had been excruciating, though the death was mercifully swift as the sudden drop of pressure and the freezing cold destroyed his internal organs.

He also remembered being slowly lowered into a vat of molten copper, watching his body burn away inch by inch. (Why molten *copper*? Lemelisk had wondered. Finally one day, more than a month later, he asked the Emperor. Palpatine's answer had proved surprising in its utter mundanity. "It's what the smelter used that day.")

Lemelisk had also been trapped in a vault filled with thickening acid mist so that his lungs dissolved and he coughed blood, and the acid continued to eat him from the inside out. The other deaths had been as imaginative and just as painful.

He was certainly glad the Emperor had been killed in the destruction of the second Death Star. Otherwise Lemelisk would *really* have been in trouble!

Now, on the Darksaber's control deck, while Durga reeled in shock at the news of the captured saboteur, General Sulamar saw an opportunity. He became even more overbearing, swelling his chest so that the medals jangled. As if trying to outdo Durga's obvious annoyance, Sulamar glared accusingly at Lemelisk.

"How could this happen?" Sulamar sniffed, as though Lemelisk had caused the problem by failing to plan for terrorists and sabotage in his original holographic blueprints. "In all my years serving the Empire, with thousands and thousands of people under my command, we performed the dirtiest, most difficult deeds. But I *never* had such a disastrous act of sabotage occur. Not while I was in charge."

Lemelisk averted his gaze and muttered under his breath. "Well, there's a first time for everything."

*   *   *

Durga's guards were angry and brutal. They beat Crix Madine every time he faltered, which made him stumble again . . . which allowed them to beat him again. . . .

He was bruised and bloodied by the time they shoved him into the turbolift on the way to the command deck. He felt none of the pain, focusing his thoughts, still in angry shock over Trandia's death . . . but he accepted his capture and the consequences. This possibility had always been a shadow over every mission he led.

Madine kneaded his hands together, though they were bound behind his back. He was satisfied and confident—he had triggered the transmitter implanted in his palm. Even now the high-powered, specific-frequency message would be beaming across space, summoning assistance. The coded signal would be transmitted instantly through a security channel in the Galactic Holonet directly to Ackbar's fleet.

It was just a matter of time . . . if only Madine could hold on.

The Gamorrean guards shoved him forward just as the turbolift doors opened, and he blinked in the command deck's flood of light. His vision swam in and out of focus. He wondered if he had received a concussion from one of the vicious backhands the guards had dealt him.

Madine moved with a numb resignation. He had lost his team: Korenn dead in the asteroid belt, Trandia blowing herself up to save him and damage the Hutt battle station. In his youth Crix Madine had served the Empire faithfully for years. After defecting to the Rebellion, he had always suspected that this day would come, that he would continue to volunteer for more and more difficult covert operations—as if he wanted to be caught. Somehow he had known he would be captured and brought in chains to the enemy.

The guards dragged him into the presence of Durga the Hutt. Madine tried to sneer, but his face produced little more than a grimace and a wince of pain. Blood from a cut near his eye dribbled down his cheek into his beard.

The bloated Hutt lounged on his repulsor platform, the discolored blotch on his face like dye that someone had thrown across it. Madine swiveled his throbbing head and noticed a swaggering man in an Imperial general's uniform. The general marched across the metal deck, striding toward him in polished black boots.

Madine looked up at the close-set eyes, the boyish face, the weak chin—and from the depths of his past a geyser of recollection erupted. He reacted with astonishment, drawing himself up as he stumbled against the guards holding him. Madine saw a flash of horrified recognition also wash across the face of the general.

At the moment their eyes met, they yelled in unison, "You!"

KHOMM

CHAPTER 43

Through hyperspace, the escape to Khomm lasted only an hour. Dorsk 81 shot their stolen shuttle toward his homeworld, frantic to deliver his warning to the cloned aliens and the New Republic. He was dismayed to see that traffic control accepted him as yet another incoming ship, not at all alarmed by an unscheduled Imperial craft charging in at top speed.

"This is Dorsk 81," he said, "issuing an emergency call. We must use your long-range comm systems immediately. Prepare for an Imperial attack. Announce a red alert."

The traffic controller responded, "Message received, Dorsk 81. We will arrange a meeting with you and City Leader Kaell 116 as soon as possible upon your arrival."

"You don't understand," Dorsk 81 said. His olive skin flushed a darker green, and his hands trembled. He looked wildly at Kyp Durron, who wore an expression of disgust.

"Don't worry about it now. It's a waste of breath arguing," he said, then took over the comm system. "This is Jedi Knight Kyp Durron. I'll require full use of your spaceport communication systems.'' The anger behind Kyp's eyes seemed barely restrained by his Jedi calm.

''That can be arranged,'' the controller said with maddening calmness.

When they landed on the empty spaceport grid, Kyp leaped through the access hatch with Dorsk 81 close behind him. ''I'll go transmit the wide-band alert to the New Republic,'' Kyp said. ''You warn your people. Admiral Daala is going to launch in only a couple of days. We have that long to mobilize the fleet.'' His face was drawn and grave as he ran to the tall transmitting tower.

Dorsk 81 hurried to meet the cloned aliens who approached him. They were flustered and uneasy—not because of the dire warning, he knew, but because of the unexpectedness of the situation. ''We must hurry,'' he said to the stony-faced driver of the floating platform. ''We have little time. Kyp and I have to go help defend the Jedi academy.''

The driver nodded calmly, but did not increase the speed of the vehicle. The floating platform took Dorsk 81 away from the landing grid, and he looked back at the transmitting tower, hoping Kyp would get the message out.

They reached the opulent political headquarters where a quick meeting had been rammed through the schedule of the generational politician Kaell 116. Dorsk 81, still wearing the clinging work overalls he had taken from the garment locker in the Imperial shuttle, brushed his slender hands down the fabric, trying to make himself more presentable. He smelled of smoke and blood and violence.

Kaell 116 already stood in the large, white meeting room. The walls were made of curved arches that glittered in the light as if molded from solidified salt. Dorsk 81 had never been in such important chambers, and he doubted anyone in his genetic line had either.

The city leader stood dressed in full diplomatic finery; his expression held a mixture of annoyance at this unsettling break from routine and continuing admiration for Khomm's galactic celebrity.

"Dorsk 81," he said, "for a person of your importance, we can shuffle our schedule to allow a brief audience, but no more than fifteen minutes. I suggest that our primary goal will be to work out a better time for a full conference of appropriate duration and with an official agenda."

"No," Dorsk 81 said, pounding his fist on the table and astonishing everyone there. "Fifteen minutes will be enough—if you *listen* to me."

Kaell 116 sniffed. "Of course we will listen. We always listen."

Dorsk 81 leaned over the table and fixed his yellow eyes on the politician. "But this time you must *hear*. You must understand this, because the fate of our world and of the galaxy may be at stake."

Kaell 116 squirmed uncomfortably and then sat down. "Yes, yes, of course. We'll take detailed notes."

Before Dorsk 81 could speak, the door opened again, and a flood of outside light shone into the white chambers, sparkling off the crystal-embedded walls. Dorsk 81 turned to see the older and younger copies of himself, his predecessor and his successor at the cloning facilities. Both wore the uniforms of their profession and appeared confused at being summoned away from their daily tasks.

The older Dorsk 80 saw him and snorted. "I might have known."

The younger version looked first at the elder clone, then at Dorsk 81. "Why have you come back?" Dorsk 82 said.

Kaell 116 motioned for them to sit down. During the interruption, an assistant came in bearing cool beverages. The others gratefully took theirs and sipped, nodding their thanks. Dorsk 81 ignored the sweating glass in front of him. "Kyp Durron and I just returned from the Core Systems," he said, speaking slowly and carefully.

"You should not go there," Dorsk 80 said.

Dorsk 81 looked at his predecessor and jabbed a finger at him. "Be silent and listen. This is important." Offended, the elder clone glowered.

"Kyp and I found a full Imperial fleet massed and ready to launch. We infiltrated one of their rallies and learned their plans. The Empire is back under the command of Admiral Daala. They will attack the New Republic within a matter of days. Until now, no one has suspected, and Khomm"—Dorsk 81 spread his arms to indicate the world—"is right on the fringe of the Core Systems. The Empire could strike here. You must prepare. Engage your defenses. Establish emergency plans."

Kaell 116 leaned across the table, putting his elbows on the salted surface. "Khomm has always remained neutral in these galactic conflicts, and we've never had problems before. I don't see why this should be any different."

"You don't have to see why," Dorsk 81 said. "Listen to me. Admiral Daala intends to attack where she is least expected. She *knows* Kyp and I heard her plans. This entire world is in great danger."

"Yes . . . well." Kaell 116 stood up with a vague smile of dismissal. "We'll see what we can do, then. Thank you for bringing this to our attention."

"You can't risk this continued complacency," Dorsk 81 said, growing impatient. "I have done and seen things you cannot imagine. Trust me in this: there is great danger."

Dorsk 80 stood to rebuke him. "You left us. Ages ago our predecessors determined that our society was the perfect model, but you felt *you* knew more than our forefathers. You've forsaken our ways for your own independence. Why should we listen to you? You have not listened to us. In all your escapades, where is the voice of wisdom? You'll never accomplish anything more important than what you could have done here."

Dorsk 81 turned to him. It was obvious that his elder presumed the vindictive words would destroy the younger clone's composure—but Dorsk 81 felt nothing but a sad pity at the narrowness of his elder's viewpoint.

"You're wrong," he said coldly to his predecessor, "and you will never see how wrong you are, because you are blind."

Dorsk 82 came over to him, and it appeared that the younger clone might actually believe part of Dorsk 81's warning. "We don't know how to make defenses," the younger clone said. "But you've had that experience, you've had the training." Dorsk 82's yellow eyes flashed. "Perhaps you could stay here and help us establish our defenses? Then you would be here to defend us if you are indeed correct. If you're wrong, you could still stay and perform your old duties in the cloning facility . . . until the threat has passed."

The younger clone's face held an ocean of hope. Dorsk 81 heard the plea and thought of his beautiful, peaceful homeworld, of the years he had spent as part of an enormous machine working smoothly, without worries, without threat. How could he abandon this place to its fate? But what if Dorsk 82's words were just a ploy, a desperate trick to get him to stay on Khomm so that all could be normal again?

"No," Dorsk 81 said, and stood up. He touched the cylindrical shape of his lightsaber inside the pocket of his work overall. "I am a Jedi Knight, and I have important work to do."

"And *we* must get back to the cloning facility," Dorsk 80 said sourly. "We know our place—and we have important work to do as well."

Dorsk 81 did not respond, but instead returned to their ship to meet Kyp Durron. As they departed in their shuttle, he looked across the misty vistas of Khomm with vague apprehension, a premonition that he would not see his familiar homeworld ever again. . . .

During the brawl and confusion at the Imperial rally, Admiral Daala and Vice Admiral Pellaeon ducked into the nexus station's turbolift and plunged away from the frenzied mob. Daala breathed rapidly, cold air whistling through her clenched teeth. She couldn't believe it. "Jedi spies! Right in our midst. They heard everything."

Pellaeon nodded. "We'll have to reevaluate our security."

Daala shook her head, and flaming copper hair swirled around her. "Later. For now we must reconsider our plans." Then a grin cracked through her outrage as a new tactic occurred to her.

The turbolift stopped at a lower level, and Colonel Cronus strode up to them, looking harried. "They've escaped, Admiral," he said. "The perimeter defense droids fired on them and caused minor damage, but their ship still managed the jump into hyperspace."

Daala nodded at the short and compact colonel. Cronus appeared surprised that she hadn't ordered his immediate execution. "Have you tracked them?" she asked.

"Not completely, Admiral, but we did match their vector, and we believe there's only one place in the vicinity they would likely have gone: a planet called Khomm at the edge of the Core Systems."

Daala ran a fingertip along her lips. "Is it inhabited?"

"Yes," Cronus said, "though unremarkable. Its people were neutral during our previous conflict with the Rebels. However, we did match the physical appearance of the alien Jedi spy with the natives. Khomm must be more than just a neutral world if Jedi have come from there." Cronus's muscular chest and upper arms pressed against the seams of his tight uniform.

Daala strode down the corridor with Pellaeon and Cronus flanking her. She remained silent as the possibilities flickered through her mind. "I have learned that my strategy must be flexible," she said. "I failed before, but now I will adapt our plans quickly. Our fleet is ready to launch, is it not?" She glanced from Cronus to Pellaeon.

"Yes, Admiral," Pelleaon said, "for the most part.

What remained for the next few days is personnel reassignment, inventory, supplies, and—''

Daala cut him off with a sideways swipe of her hand. ''Those Jedi spies heard that we were planning to launch in the next few days. Instead we shall launch immediately. Colonel Cronus,'' she said, ''you have the list of preferred targets for your *Victory*-class fleet?''

''Yes, Admiral.''

''Add the planet Khomm to the top of the list. Gather your forces and go at once.''

Cronus shot a grin at her. ''Yes, Admiral.''

''Remember,'' she added sternly, ''your orders are to strike fast and frequently in many different systems. Cause as much damage as possible, but your main goal is to create confusion, not to conquer. The Rebels will disperse their fleet to find you—while we approach the main target.''

She turned. ''Vice Admiral Pellaeon.''

''Yes, Admiral?''

''You will take your fleet of Imperial Star Destroyers directly to Yavin 4 and proceed with its complete destruction. I will follow in the *Night Hammer* with sufficient force to occupy the Rebel base permanently.'' Her green eyes flashed at her two commanders. ''I want the fleet launched within the hour.''

Pellaeon and Cronus dashed off to their respective commands. At two minutes short of an hour, Daala's Imperial fleet was spurred into motion like a great slavering monster suddenly unleashed on the New Republic.

Like crimson projectiles the *Victory*-class ships scattered across the orbital lanes of Khomm, their full turbolaser batteries directed at the cities below.

Colonel Cronus sat in the command chair of Vice Admiral Pellaeon's former ship, the 13X, issuing orders to the gunners in his fleet. ''Target the communication and observation satellites first.''

The words were barely out of his mouth before a cleansing fire of turbolaser bolts scoured the blackness of space, obliterating silver dots of orbiting satellites and leaving behind spangles of debris.

"Now they're blind," he said, "before they even know what's going on." He sat back and pressed his hands together, pushing, performing his endless ritual of isometric exercises that pitted one muscle against the other to strengthen him, even as he sat and watched the massacre of Khomm.

He spoke through the comm channel to all ships. "Target weapons indiscriminately on the metropolis below. This is our first target, so let's make it memorable. Launch TIE bomber squadrons, and let's get busy."

He watched the hail of laser fire rain down through the atmosphere, and clouds of small fighters spewed from the hangar decks. Cronus observed the flurry of destruction. According to old intelligence reports, Khomm barely had token defenses. He doubted the inhabitants even remembered how to use them. They would wish differently after his fleet had finished.

"Quick and easy," he muttered. His arm muscles tingled with weariness from his exercises, but he pushed harder, making them ache.

After watching the battle for half an hour, Cronus signaled the other ships. "Hurry up," he said. "We have a lot of other targets on the list."

An uneasy Dorsk 82 left the cloning facility at the end of his afternoon shift, as he always did, while Dorsk 80 remained behind to put in an extra hour of work, making up for the loss of Dorsk 81—as *he* always did. Predictability was comfort. On Khomm people lived by those words.

But the younger clone kept hearing the statement of Dorsk 81 echo in his mind. Changing possibilities opened up ideas he had never considered. What if, against all previous history, the Empire did decide to attack their peaceful world? *But why?* he wanted to ask. What would it gain them?

He knew that question would be carefully considered and settled by Kaell 116 and the political leaders. It was their job. They had no other task but to make such decisions. Young Dorsk 82 was confident in the Khomm system. It had worked perfectly for centuries. He had no cause to doubt it now.

A moment later, rivers of fire spat down from the hazy white sky, setting the identical buildings ablaze and drawing destructive fingers across the perfect gridwork of the organized city. TIE bombers roared overhead at a pitch that struck terror into the cloned pedestrians. The ships dropped proton explosives that flattened entire blocks at a time. Flames scorched skyward as fuel tanks and kindling from the ancient constructions were set ablaze.

TIE fighters screamed down from the sky, firing laser cannons and strafing the terrified aliens who poured from their buildings but knew not where to go.

Dorsk 82 fled into a narrow alley between two tall buildings. An unwise move, he supposed, with the imposing structures collapsing all around him. His mind was ablaze with shock and horror. Dorsk 81 had been right! Khomm had no plans, no defenses—and no chance.

A proton bomb exploded above the buildings like a huge slapping hand that knocked walls down. Dorsk 82 crouched near the ground, expecting the avalanche to crush him in an instant—but the flat wall slabs toppled against each other, forming a miraculous tent above him. Rock dust and fractured stones bit into his smooth skin. He supposed a bone or two was broken—a new experience for him in his gentle and predictable life—but he huddled in the unexpected darkness and waited as the screaming chaos continued around him for what seemed like an age, though he knew it must have been less than an hour.

The physical pain came to him as he tried to dig himself out from under the fallen slabs of rock. He was

aching and sore, bruised and cut . . . but he was *alive*.
He moved the rubble away and emerged blinking into an
early afternoon dusk caused by black smoke and orange
flames.

He stood completely numb. He saw but could not
comprehend the magnitude of the devastation around him.
The shining cloning facilities were entirely gone, turned
into a jumbled mass of molten girders and shattered crystalline dust—all that remained of the broad sheetcrystal
windows that had once shone so brightly in the sun.
Greasy smoke drifted to the sky like an accusing finger
pointing at the Imperial fleet high in orbit.

Old Dorsk 80 had been inside the cloning facility,
and the younger clone stumbled with sick apathy into the
rubble, looking without hope for some sign that his predecessor had survived.

This shock competed with the overwhelming consequences in his mind. The devastation of his entire world,
the wreck of the cloning facilities—how were they to proceed now? How could his civilization continue after such a
mortal wound? The survivors of Khomm—who even now
moaned from the pain of their injuries or wailed from their
grief as they staggered across the ruined metropolis—
would have to change.

And that frightened him as well.

Colonel Cronus watched the remaining fighters return to
their ships. The burning world of Khomm lay beneath him
like a festering sore.

He glanced impatiently at the time record and at the
damage assessment for his fleet. Two fighters lost. Judging
from Khomm's lack of defenses, Cronus assumed that the
two downed TIE ships had been destroyed through accident, malfunction, or inadvertent friendly fire.

He shook his head at the appalling weakness of the
clone world.

On his command station computer he punched up the coordinates of Admiral Daala's designated targets. He hoped all the raids would be as successful as this.

"Next system," he said. "Let's be on our way. We've got a schedule to keep."

CHAPTER 44

In the middle of the night shift on the Escort Frigate *Yavaris,* General Wedge Antilles sat quietly in the command chair, relaxed but alert. Despite the yellow alert, the *Yavaris* seemed deceptively calm; the soldiers moved about their routines with calm efficiency. The glowpanels were dimmed, the sounds of movement hushed and muffled. The tension was thick, though invisible.

The alert status had been uninterrupted for a day. They had heard nothing, no word of an Imperial strike, no report from Crix Madine—and it was beginning to wear on them.

Qwi Xux crept up behind him on the bridge and squeezed his shoulders with her long, pale blue fingers. He flinched, startled, then reached up to clasp her hand against his shoulder. He turned to look into her deep indigo eyes. "Couldn't sleep either?" he asked.

She shook her head, and her feathery, pearlescent hair flickered. "The waiting is so hard," she said.

Wedge nodded. "Much as I hate war, at times like this I almost wish something would just happen."

And it did.

All at once.

Crix Madine's silent distress signal came in at emergency priority, tunneling through space, its specific frequency targeting the New Republic fleet. Signals went off at the communications console, which triggered automatic red alerts throughout the *Yavaris*. Madine's implanted transmitter could give no details; it simply sent a distress.

Wedge knew that General Madine, the Supreme Allied Commander for Intelligence, would have used it in only the most extreme circumstances.

He said, "We've got to go pull him out."

Qwi stood suddenly tense, blinking her large eyes. Her fingers tightened on his shoulders. "That means he's found the site of the Hutt superweapon. We have to destroy it before the thing becomes operational. We can't let the Hutts or the Empire or anyone else have another weapon like the ones I used to design."

"You're right about that," Wedge said.

A viewscreen message instantly came from Admiral Ackbar on the Mon Calamari Star Cruiser. "This may be the beginning of the overall attack," Ackbar said, dressed in his fine white uniform and holding his flipper-hands out in a gesture of tension.

"Yes, Admiral. Shall we deploy the fleet? We can home in on Madine's distress and get there at top speed. We don't know what sort of situation he's gotten himself into—"

Before Wedge could finish, though, another broad-spectrum message swept across the communications systems, a second emergency signal, preempting all other transmissions across the New Republic Holonet. "This is Kyp Durron with an urgent message to the New Republic military!"

Wedge flinched, setting his teeth on edge. Beside him Qwi held her composure, but he noticed her stiffen. Kyp had returned from the dark side in service of the Jedi way, and Qwi claimed to have forgiven him—but still the over-eager Jedi Knight unnerved both of them.

Nevertheless, Kyp broadcast his message to anyone who would listen, raising the alarm. "My fellow Jedi Knight Dorsk 81 and I have penetrated the Core Systems. We've discovered a massive Imperial strike force ready to launch in the next day or so. Admiral Daala is command-ing this fleet. I repeat: Admiral Daala is not dead as we had expected.

"Their main target is said to be Yavin 4. Daala means to destroy all of the new Jedi Knights. Dorsk 81 and I are on our way to the Jedi academy at this moment to help with the fight. We request any assistance possible."

"So it's a two-pronged attack," Ackbar said. "The Hoth Asteroid Belt and Yavin 4. They must be confident in their ability to surprise us."

"We know about their plans now," Wedge said. "Should we split up?"

Ackbar rumbled. "That message was sent to the full New Republic fleet. We can perhaps hope for reinforce-ments—yet I believe we should divide our forces now. I doubt either of these attacks is a feint. I will take the *Galactic Voyager* and head to Yavin 4. You go and rescue General Madine. We cannot ignore the threat from the Hutts."

"Understood, Admiral," Wedge said.

Ackbar's image nodded deeply. "I must bring the remainder of the fleet up to full combat status. This is just the beginning."

"Don't worry—we'll get Madine and his team out of there," Wedge said. "And we'll try to wreck that Hutt superweapon while we're at it."

All personnel were summoned from their sleep peri-ods. Lights increased on every deck of the *Yavaris*. Troops ran up and down the corridors, mustering.

All during the war-gaming exercises, the fleet had re-mained coy, hiding their real purpose and readiness. Now, though, the ships dropped all pretense and ignored the

Hutts who were undoubtedly watching from the greenish planet below.

The New Republic war-gaming fleet split into two separate prongs and established their course vectors, drifting away.

Ackbar and his ships funneled down to starpoints, plunging into hyperspace, while Wedge ordered the *Yavaris* to proceed at full speed toward the Hoth Asteroid Belt and Madine's distress signal—hoping they would get there in time.

CHAPTER 45

The seventeen Star Destroyers under the command of Vice Admiral Pellaeon sliced out of hyperspace in a well-ordered fleet. Their perfect formation demonstrated the precision and unrelenting dedication of the new Imperial forces Daala had forged.

Standing on the bridge of the *Firestorm*—the Star Destroyer that Admiral Daala herself had commanded during her double cross of the war criminal Harrsk—Pellaeon watched the green jewel of the jungle moon approaching, a living emerald sphere dwarfed by the enormous gas giant Yavin, whose gravity tugged at his attacking fleet of ships.

He stared with narrowed eyes out the viewports of the bridge tower. He had trimmed his gray mustache, made certain that his hair lay neatly beneath his vice admiral's cap. He brushed down his uniform to present a more imposing image, a leader for his fleet on their victorious mission. It invigorated him to be in command of a worthy ship again, not the small *Victory*-class Star Destroyer . . . though even now Colonel Cronus would be using the fleet of crimson ships to cause significant destruction throughout the Rebel-aligned worlds.

Pellaeon thought of his days in command of the *Chimaera* serving Grand Admiral Thrawn and how close they had come to defeating the Rebellion once and for all. Now, with Admiral Daala they had that chance again—and Pellaeon would not waste it.

"Orbital insertion successful, sir," the navigator said from her station.

Pellaeon continued to marvel at the new women officers in Daala's fleet; they seemed to serve with even more dedication than the other soldiers. "Any sign of defenses?" he asked. The jungle moon seemed too quiet, too vulnerable. He was astounded that such an important site to the Rebellion would have no apparent defenses whatsoever.

"None detected, Vice Admiral," the tactical chief said dubiously. Apparently the man felt the same concerns.

"All right," Pellaeon said, moving to the next phase. "Deploy the jamming net. We need to get in place and be operational before the Jedi sorcerers can send a detailed signal to their military."

The seventeen Star Destroyers shot out clusters of small satellite transmitters that jockeyed into position around the green moon, forming an interlinked electromagnetic web that disrupted any messages the Jedi trainees might send. The jamming satellites took only moments to lock themselves into position, transmitting an all-clear signal back to the *Firestorm*.

Pellaeon spoke into the ship-to-ship comm unit, and his voice rang through his fleet. "Strike teams prepare," he said. "We launch in five minutes. All Terrain Scout Transports and jungle assault vehicles will be the first wave. TIE fighters will provide air cover.

"This is a relatively unpopulated world, and it shouldn't take us long to finish here. Our victory on Yavin

4 today will be the first large step in the rebirth of a new and even stronger Empire.''

Pellaeon signed off and stood against the bridge railing. He was pleased to be in command of an operation sure to succeed, rather than another doomed last-gasp attempt at Imperial supremacy. Outwardly calm but thrumming with energy inside, Pellaeon pondered the immense Imperial strength Admiral Daala had placed under his control.

He didn't expect much resistance from a few untested Jedi trainees.

Back at the nexus mustering station in deep space, the Super Star Destroyer *Night Hammer* prepared for launch. Admiral Daala spent the last frantic moments ensuring that everything had been placed in perfect order for her own decisive assault.

By now Vice Admiral Pellaeon's fleet should already be attacking the Jedi moon, and she longed to be there with him, taking personal satisfaction with each slaughtered Jedi, each destroyed Rebel building, each burning tree—but she would not alter her plans now. She knew this was the way to strike the greatest psychological blow to the Rebels. Her initial assault had to be an absolutely crushing defeat of the Rebel target.

Right now, simultaneous with this major assault, Colonel Cronus was causing a wealth of damage with surgical hit-and-run strikes at various spots in the galaxy. His swarm of crimson *Victory*-class ships would roar in with lightning speed, blow up the most convenient targets, then flee into hyperspace again . . . leaving destruction, confusion, and panic in their wake.

The jungle moon of Yavin with its Jedi training center would be the true symbolic victory, though. Daala smiled, and her green eyes took on a faraway look as she imagined the unskilled wizards under attack by Pellaeon's hopelessly overwhelming forces; she then imagined the despair they would feel on seeing her enormous ship arrive—like a second mortal blow. Not a rescue, not reinforcements, but a black Super Star Destroyer. Their hopelessness would increase tenfold.

After today, when Daala departed in triumph, the jungle moon of Yavin 4 must be no more than a cinder. Every last Jedi student had to be killed, their bodies strewn about the burning jungle as an unmistakable message to those who would still dare resist the Empire.

As her last order before launching, Daala took the time to rechristen her dark ship, adding a letter to call the Super Star Destroyer the *Knight Hammer,* just to prove that she did indeed have a sense of humor . . . so long as it involved the ultimate defeat of the Rebel Alliance.

CHAPTER 46

Dorsk 81 and Kyp Durron arrived back at Yavin 4, broadcasting their constant alarm. They landed their Imperial shuttle near the Great Temple and called the remaining Jedi trainees to arms—barely an hour before Pellaeon's forces arrived.

Dorsk 81's stomach had been a hard knot since their embattled escape from Admiral Daala's staging area; he had felt even worse upon seeing the apathetic refusal of his homeworld to accept the possibility of an impending threat. The censure of Dorsk 80 and Dorsk 82 had struck to his core, affecting him even more than his choice to become a Jedi. But he *was* a Jedi. He could not change that, and he vowed to be the best his potential would allow, as Master Skywalker had taught him.

Dorsk 81 and Kyp stepped out of the stolen Imperial shuttle to total silence. The humid jungles seemed smothered with a blanket of tension and anticipation.

"Where is everyone?" Kyp said. "We've got to find Master Skywalker."

Dorsk 81 looked up at the enormous stepped pyramid

where the Jedi *praxeum* had been established. His face
grew calm, and he closed his yellow eyes, reaching out
with the Force until he sensed the group of Jedi trainees
across a narrow tributary of the river at one of the other
temple ruins.

"Over there," he said. "At the Temple of the
Blueleaf Cluster."

Kyp nodded, his dark eyes flashing. "We have to
warn them and begin preparations."

They rushed through narrow jungle paths, crossing
the river to the tall Massassi ruin, a cylindrical tower made
of crumbling stones, much in need of repair. Dorsk 81 saw
the Jedi trainees working together, nearly thirty in all.

He recognized Kirana Ti, the warrior woman from
Dathomir and the older, somewhat-confused hermit from
Bespin, Streen, working to haul fallen rocks from a collapsed portion of the temple. They used Jedi powers to lift
broken slabs out of the way, and to keep themselves safe
from the pebbles that continued to shower down as they
removed debris. Kam Solusar, the hard-bitten Jedi veteran,
sternly watched the activities, directing the work of the
lesser-trained Jedi students who had arrived at the *praxeum* in the last year.

The silvery-haired Jedi scholar, Tionne, spotted them
first. "Kyp," she called. "Dorsk 81. You're back! Good,
we could use some help." Tionne smiled, and her mother-
of-pearl eyes lit up. She explained breathlessly, gesturing
with small, quick movements of her delicate hands. "With
all the new students arriving, we had to find additional
living quarters. This old temple is—" Then she finally
registered the alarm and emotional turmoil emanating
from them.

"What is it?" Kam Solusar said, breaking through
the conversation. Kirana Ti stepped beside him, tall and
imposing in her reptilian armor.

"Where's Master Skywalker?" Kyp said. His voice
cracked, and the words came out in a cold, strained tone.

"He and Callista left more than a week ago," Tionne

said. "It's only us here. I'm directing a few training sessions while he's gone but—"

"The Jedi academy is in great danger!" Dorsk 81 blurted. "Admiral Daala has assembled a new Imperial fleet, and Yavin 4 is their target this time. The Star Destroyers could be here any moment."

"No," Streen said, shaking his frizzy gray head and blinking red-rimmed eyes as he gazed up into the pale blue sky. "No. They're already here."

As the old hermit said this, Dorsk 81 also felt a brooding oppressiveness far overhead, like a stain of starless darkness across the canvas of space.

"Look," one of the new trainees said, extending a clawed finger as her bright bluish frill rose up in alarm. A snakelike hiss came from her wide, scaly mouth.

A shower of bright streaks danced through the upper atmosphere toward the jungles—lines traced in fire by sharp fingernails made of lava.

"Landers and ground assault vehicles," Kam Solusar said.

"We must prepare to fight them," Kirana Ti insisted.

"But Master Skywalker isn't here!" cried one of the new trainees.

Kyp Durron drew himself up, though he was smaller in stature than many of those gathered at the ruined temple. "Master Skywalker will not always be here to help whenever we are in trouble. Dorsk 81 and I have already sounded the alarm, and New Republic forces should be on their way. For now, though, we must defend the academy ourselves."

"But there are so few of us," a birdlike trainee squawked, his hard beak gaping open, then clacking together.

"Yes," Kyp said, "so they won't expect much resistance. We'll have to prove them wrong."

Dorsk 81 stood beside his friend. "We are Jedi Knights. Remember what Master Skywalker has taught you: *There is no try.*"

The Imperial landers crunched into the jungle not far away, then deployed giant vehicles from drop shells.

"Here comes the air strike," Kyp said, just as a flurry of black dots in the air screamed closer with a roar of twin ion engines, a full wing of TIE fighters plus a strong complement of TIE bombers.

"Take cover," Kirana Ti shouted. With a forceful motion she pushed Streen toward two mammoth blocks of stone that had toppled from the front of the ancient temple.

The TIE fighters swooped overhead as the Jedi trainees scrambled for shelter. Laser cannons shot from the Imperial ships, setting tall trees alight and blasting rubble from the old temple. The TIE fighters fanned out, uncertain of their target as they searched for the Jedi Knights hiding in the jungle.

TIE bombers cruised low, dropping concussion missiles that exploded into pillars of fire and smoke above the thick jungle canopy, splintering Massassi trees that had lived for a thousand years. But once the first wave of TIE fighters spotted the trainees at the Temple of the Blueleaf Cluster, the forces concentrated their firepower on the far side of the river.

"We don't have any weapons," Streen said as he covered his head.

"We have the Force," Dorsk 81 replied.

Three TIE fighters roared in, laser cannons shooting continuously as they approached in a triangular formation. The warrior woman Kirana Ti stood out in the open near the piles of rubble the Jedi trainees had so meticulously removed from the ruins. The TIE fighters saw her and fired. Ignoring her own danger, she gestured with her hand and, using the Force as a sling, she snatched one of the squarish boulders cut by Massassi slaves thousands of years before—and hurled it with all her Jedi strength.

The stone flew through the air and smashed one of the TIE fighter's flat power arrays. It careened to one side, and the pilot could not regain control. The ship exploded in the trees on the far side of the temple.

Kam Solusar stood on the other side of the clearing and, using the Force, he, too, began hurling rocks at the remaining two TIE fighters. The boulders battered the Imperial ships, smashing through the cockpits. All the Jedi trainees had the idea now, and a blast of sharp rock shards hammered the two fleeing ships out of the sky. Both exploded in midflight to the cheers of the embattled Jedi students.

The second wave of four TIE fighters came immediately after. Streen, however, did not pick up rocks or other weapons with the Force. He used the air itself, moving molecules in the atmosphere to summon storm currents and scramble the air attack line with a wall of wind that achieved hurricane strength. The gusting currents buffeted the TIE fighters right and left, forcing the pilots to concentrate on simply flying and not allowing them to fire a single shot.

Streen looked up into the sky, his eyes wide and bloodshot, his hair wafting about his head. He held his trembling fingers outstretched and then brought his hands together symbolically, slamming his hands of wind so that the heavy crosscurrents smashed the four TIE fighters together. They crashed into a single knot of molten wreckage that tumbled out of the air.

A pair of TIE bombers came in low from behind, barely visible over the treetops but moving at full speed. Kyp shouted a warning. The first TIE bomber cruised over the temple and let three concussion missiles fall out of its bombing bay—but Kyp reached out, staring at the ship, and holding his palm flat and upright. He pushed upward with the Force, visualizing the three dropped concussion missiles, and nudged the explosives back up into the bomber's bay . . . where they detonated.

The second TIE bomber dropped a single missile and then, seeing the fate of his partner, shot off at top speed. Dorsk 81 used the Force to pick up a boulder, which he hurled with all his might. The flying rock closed the distance to the bomber, striking the second cockpit and damaging its altitude control. The TIE bomber spun through the air and landed roughly in the jungle underbrush on the far side of the river. Its lone concussion missile struck the ground nearby and detonated, sending a rumble through the jungle that shook the Temple of the Blueleaf Cluster. Loose stone blocks slid down the walls in a shower of dust, crashing around the Jedi trainees.

"This old structure won't last much longer," Kyp shouted. "We've got to get back to the Great Temple. That's more defensible."

Another wave of TIE fighters soared in with twice the numbers of the previous strike, and the Jedi trainees gave no argument as they sprinted away from the smaller temple and headed into the underbrush.

Overhead, more lines of fire appeared as Pellaeon's seventeen Star Destroyers launched another wave of ground assault machinery to finish mopping up.

As they reached the giant pyramid that had once been fortified as a Rebel base, Dorsk 81 saw that the trainees' desperate defense at the crumbling temple had served a secondary purpose he had not expected—a diversion, a decoy for the Imperial forces who now thought the Temple of the Blueleaf Cluster was the Jedi stronghold. The TIE fighters and bombers concentrated their forces there.

Despite the fear that rattled through him, Dorsk 81 felt an exhilaration and a camaraderie with the other Jedi. He was fighting for something meaningful. All his life, as yet another duplicate on a world of clones, he had never felt he had a choice in his destiny. Everything had been preset for him until he climbed out of the rut that had been dug in the Dorsk bloodline. Now he was a Jedi Knight—his own choice. And he had just proved he could be good at it.

The long horizontal door in front of the hangar levels

of the Great Temple hung halfway open, a dark mouth
with thin cool air breathing out from the shaded interior.
The Jedi trainees ducked down and rushed inside, hoping
that the millennia-old walls would shelter them from the
brunt of the Imperial attack.

Tionne rushed past Kyp Durron, who grabbed her
arm and shouted, "Go to the communications center!
Contact the New Republic and let them know we're already under attack. The Imperials struck faster than we
expected." Tionne nodded, her pale porcelain face so brittle that it looked as if it might shatter.

Across the river TIE fighters circled over the Temple
of the Blueleaf Cluster, firing repeatedly with laser cannons. Black smoke etched the air.

Kyp looked toward their stolen Imperial shuttle still
on the grassy landing grid. He gestured toward it as Dorsk
81 headed for the relative safety of the deep hangar levels.
"I'm going back to the ship," he said. "We've got some
weapons there. It's all we have."

Dorsk 81 hesitated, then followed as Kyp sprinted
across the clearing without looking behind him. Dorsk 81
paused when a clanking noise crashed through the outer
rim of trees, and the trapezoidal head of an Imperial AT-
ST scout walker shoved its way out of the forest. It thundered twice with its mechanical legs, finding support on
the rough ground. The head swiveled, its laser cannons
targeted, aiming at Kyp as he ran.

Dorsk 81 froze for just an instant. He saw what was
going to happen—but he couldn't allow it. In an instinc-
tive gesture, he released the Force; he did not restrain himself, did not channel or direct the flow, merely releasing
his fear and his wish to get the scout walker *away* from his
friend.

A wall of invisible force slammed into the AT-ST,
flattening its cockpit and crushing the walker backward
into a tree.

Kyp whirled to gawk at the smashed scout walker.

Everything had happened in only a second. "Thanks," he said.

Dorsk 81 found himself trembling. "It just came automatically," he said. "I didn't even think about it."

"Then you're a true Jedi," Kyp said with gentle admiration, but wasted no more time as he ducked into the shuttle and emerged with a pitifully small assortment: five blaster pistols and one laser cutter. "Better than nothing," he said.

Dorsk 81 looked at them. "Not by much."

They glanced up at the continuing thunderous sound from the sky as wave after wave of ground assault landers spewed from the fleet of Star Destroyers in orbit. . . .

Inside, deep in the war room on the second level of the pyramid, the Jedi Knights gathered, unable to shut out the echoing thumps of the constant attack.

Tionne shook her silvery head. "The Imperials have a jamming net in place," she said. "No communications can go out. We have to hope the New Republic heard your original warning, Kyp."

"They'll be here," Kirana Ti said with grim confidence. She held the deactivated lightsaber in her grip. This was the weapon that had been built by one of the other Jedi trainees, Gantoris, a year earlier . . . back when the trainees had encountered the dark spirit of Exar Kun. In fact, in this very war room the Jedi trainees—again without Luke Skywalker—had met to plan the defeat of Kun and free their Jedi Master.

"But will the reinforcements be here soon enough?" Kam Solusar said skeptically.

Kyp Durron paced the enclosed room. "The Star Destroyers in orbit are the primary threat," he said, gesturing upward. "Though we're being attacked by TIE fighters and ground assault machinery, we're seeing only a fraction of the complement those Star Destroyers carry.

Tionne, were you able to determine how many ships there are in orbit?''

She looked at him with her quicksilver eyes. ''Seventeen, I believe. *Imperial*-class.''

Some of the newer trainees gasped, but Kyp stood straighter. He placed his hands on the tabletop, pressing down with his fingernails until his knuckles turned white. ''Right now we feel strong because of all those ships we smashed over at the other temple—but no matter how good we are, no matter how many of their ground forces we successfully take out, those Star Destroyers will keep sending ship after ship. We can't succeed if we fight them on such a limited scale.''

''But how else can we fight a Star Destroyer from here?'' Kirana Ti said.

Kyp looked around hopefully. ''I don't suppose anybody has an idea?''

Dorsk 81 sat in turmoil, rigid, his hands clasped on the table as thoughts whirled around him. He remembered how easy it had been to smash the AT-ST walker, how he had used the Force to shove it away. If only . . .

''I have a suggestion,'' Dorsk 81 said. His lips were a thin line; his olive green face was blotched as his emotions roiled beneath his skin.

Kyp looked at his friend, and Dorsk 81 could feel the sudden upsurge of anticipation from the gathered students. He had to give them something to cling to. He swallowed. ''We cannot succeed if we fight small battles individually,'' Dorsk 81 said. ''But together we are more powerful than the sum of our parts. We can join our abilities.''

Kirana Ti and Kam Solusar looked at him, musing. He leaned over the table and gestured to the other trainees. ''Some of you were there when we finally defeated Exar Kun. We pooled our strengths, we joined as one, as champions of the Force—and, united, we unlocked a greater reservoir of strength than any of us could have imagined.''

''But what can we do?'' the young reptilian trainee

said, her voice thin and hissing from the back of her throat, her blue frill still raised.

Dorsk 81 hesitated for a moment. The suggestion was preposterous . . . but right now the situation was so grim they would take even an impossible idea seriously. He kept his voice flat. "We can use the Force to . . . *move* the Star Destroyers away."

The collective gasp among the trainees was a mixture of disbelief and delight. "It's too much," Kam Solusar said. "There are too many. Seventeen *Imperial*-class Star Destroyers!"

Dorsk 81 was not flustered. "Size matters not," he said. "How many times has Master Skywalker told us that? At first many of us didn't believe we could lift a pebble or a leaf. A little while ago we hurled giant boulders at ships flying high above our heads. Streen just knocked four TIE fighters together with nothing more than wind. All this was without planning, without preparation, and without help.

"The Force is in all things," Dorsk 81 continued. "There is no fundamental difference between a pebble and a Star Destroyer. Besides, the ships have no way to prepare against an attack such as this."

As others began to mutter, Kyp hammered his fist down. "Hey! Haven't you listened to Master Skywalker's teachings?" he said. "If it doesn't work, we'll have to find something else—but I think we should do this."

That stopped further discussion. Dorsk 81 rose to his feet. "These temples were built long ago by the Massassi. We have learned," he nodded to Tionne, "that their original purpose was to serve as a focus for the energies that the Dark Lords of the Sith manipulated. We can use these temples for a similar purpose—but to serve the light side, to protect ourselves.

"I will go to the top of this temple and be the focal point for all of your energies. We will join together, some thirty of us bound by the Force."

Dorsk 81 raised his voice. Inner power grew in him

as he spoke. He had never before desired leadership of any kind, but now he no longer felt like a follower. He felt strong and driven.

"Pool your resources, and I will draw from you, channel it through myself, and *push out* just as I did with that scout walker. I'll shove them away, tumble them end over end, knock the Star Destroyers far from here."

He trembled as he said this, and Kyp stood beside him, clasping the cloned alien's thin shoulder. "And after we get the battlecruisers away," Kyp said, "then we can mop up the remnants of the attackers down here." He smiled. "It might be all finished by the time the New Republic gets here."

"We must not wait," Dorsk 81 said. "We are all together now, but the attack is intensifying. Even this Great Temple won't be stable for long, unless we do something."

At the apex of the pyramid, Dorsk 81 stood barefoot on the sun-warmed flagstones that had been locked together to form an observation deck. The Jedi trainees frequently came up here to watch the rainbow-filled sunrise at the limb of the gas giant overhead.

Tall fires in the jungles surrounding the temple complex crackled and rose into the sky. Below, squadrons of mechanical scout walkers and ground-chewing siege machinery worked their way toward the Jedi stronghold.

The Imperials had figured out that the Jedi Knights were no longer at the Temple of the Blueleaf Cluster; now that the trainees had gathered in the tallest temple, Pellaeon's attackers would soon direct their strike at the ziggurat.

Dorsk 81 tilted his smooth face up to the sky and held his hands at his sides, fingers spread. The stone felt strong beneath the soles of his feet, and he calmed himself, reaching within him for threads that he could spin together with the others.

Kyp and Kirana Ti, Kam Solusar, and all the other Jedi trainees—some he knew well, others he had barely met—also focused their abilities. Dorsk 81 recalled how they had banded together to fight Exar Kun, and now he felt the same invisible whirlwind surrounding him.

The new Jedi Knights joined together with invisible cords of light. The bonds were strong, reinforcing their skills from person to person. Dorsk 81 stood in the middle, the eye of the storm, where he could draw upon the Force, magnify it with a strength greater than he had ever conceived.

In his mind an evil shadow of doubt flickered. He suddenly wondered if it wasn't indeed impossible to move such a huge fleet. His doubt began to grow and he recalled again the face of his elder clone, Dorsk 80, scowling at him—*You'll never accomplish anything more important than what you could have done on Khomm.*

Why don't you stay with us? the younger Dorsk 82 had pleaded. *Everything will be fine, just the way it always was.*

But Dorsk 81 wanted more. His life had a greater purpose. He had sensed that from early on, but had ignored it for so long. Now he was a Jedi Knight. A Jedi Knight.

His determination formed a crushing vise in his mind that obliterated the doubt—and before he could be distracted by other thoughts, Dorsk 81 reached out and grasped the threads of Force the other trainees offered to him. He felt as if he had tapped into a huge power source, an overload of energy that he channeled through himself without hesitation.

He reached upward with his hands, picturing the Star Destroyers in orbit: seventeen wedge-shaped engines of death bristling with weapons, loaded with more TIE fighters and assault troops. His thoughts soared outward, leaving the emerald jungle moon behind, and trailing behind his presence came a battering ram of invisible, irresistible Force that would be undetectable on any Imperial scanners. The Star Destroyers waited, overconfident, power-ful—unsuspecting.

He found them. Touched them with his mind. They were huge, greater in mass than he had imagined; even so, he used the Force to *push*.

Dorsk 81 strained, touching the cluster of ships . . . but they proved immovable, too large. The Force held them, yet it could not do what he needed it to do. He tried harder.

He drew more energy from the others. He could feel the determination and controlled anger of Kyp Durron, the clean fighting prowess of Kirana Ti, the powerful deep knowledge of Tionne, the grim pain of Kam Solusar, the childlike wonder of Streen—and more . . . *more*. He took all of the Jedi trainees within himself, braiding the threads together, becoming a vast and complex set of memories, strengths, and skills. He reached deeper and deeper.

The Force seemed to be a bottomless well, offering more than he had thought possible—but as Dorsk 81 pulled it inside himself, he also felt the danger, the de-structive potential: too much of this strength could be his downfall.

He pushed again, straining harder, abandoning all caution.

The Star Destroyers moved slightly in space, bucking and resisting—but it was still not enough. In his mind Dorsk 81 saw yet another wing of TIE fighters launched with orders to finish the destruction of the Jedi Knights.

That must never happen.

Dorsk 81 exerted his mind to the breaking point. His body trembled. His yellow eyes saw nothing around him now, because every thought was focused out into space where Pellaeon's Star Destroyers waited.

You are a Jedi Knight, Kyp had told him, *and some-times that means we must make difficult decisions.*

Dorsk 81 knew this, knew it in his heart—and he didn't allow fear. The Force was with him. Perhaps more

Force than he could handle . . . but he still had a mission
to perform. No matter what it might take.

All the other Jedi Knights depended on him alone,
and he knew that this was what he had to accomplish. *This*
was the deed that his predecessor Dorsk 80 would never be
able to comprehend.

Without a second thought, without hesitation, Dorsk
81 reached all the way down, drawing from the deep wells
of Force that the thirty gathered Jedi Knights had opened
for him. He took more and more without restraint, hoard-
ing it within himself, letting it build as he absorbed the
full searing power amplified through the Great Temple,
focused it through his body and launched it at the fleet of
Star Destroyers.

"Move!" he shouted.

The words themselves were like power incarnate,
white-hot energy flaming out of his mouth, from his fingertips, surging through his body and burning, *burning*.

The inside of his head went bright like a star going
supernova behind his skull, and his consciousness rode
along with the tidal wave of Force. He felt it strike the
seventeen Star Destroyers, and they slammed backward
like twigs in a typhoon. The shockwave flung the entire
fleet far out, cast them helplessly beyond the fringes of the
Yavin System, their computers fried, their propulsion systems wrecked, still accelerating from the storm of the
Force.

Pellaeon's fleet of Star Destroyers went . . . *away*.

Dorsk 81 also rode the storm—to its ultimate, unknown destination.

The Force dropped Kyp like a severed rope. All the Jedi
trainees tumbled weakly to their knees. When he could see
again, blinking through colored spangles in front of his
eyes, he saw Dorsk 81—or what remained of him—still
tottering at the center of the observation platform.

Though his own legs wanted to collapse, Kyp struggled forward to grab his friend. Dorsk 81 collapsed and fell against him. The two of them slid to the sun-warmed flagstones.

"Dorsk 81," Kyp said, looking down in horror as the cloned alien's skin sizzled from within, as if the tissues had been brought to a boil. Dorsk 81's wide yellow eyes were now only smoldering sockets. Steam rose from his body.

A breath of words curled out of his gaping, blackened mouth. "They're gone, my friend," he said.

"Wait!" Kyp said. "Wait, we'll find a healer. We'll get Cilghal back. We'll find—"

But Dorsk 81 was already dead in his arms.

CHAPTER 47

Admiral Daala's black *Knight Hammer* arrived, the second wave of the assault on the Jedi stronghold. The ship hung as an opaque wedge eight kilometers long, silhouetted like a knife blade against the pale orange sphere of Yavin.

Daala's troops were on full alert, and her weapons systems had been powered to maximum levels. She stood on the bridge deck looking out over the sweeping metal plain that formed the *Knight Hammer*'s upper hull.

By the time she reached the system, she had expected to find Pellaeon virtually finished with his attack, so she could enjoy the final destruction of the Jedi Knights. But as the *Knight Hammer* sliced through space, Daala felt her enthusiasm crumble into astonishment. She saw no sign of Pellaeon's fleet in orbit around Yavin 4.

The bone-white Imperial Star Destroyers were simply not there. Space around the green jungle moon was empty.

"Where is he?" Daala demanded. "Open a channel. Find Pellaeon."

"Scanning the area, Admiral," the sensor chief said. "No sign of Star Destroyers in the Yavin System."

Daala glowered down at the jungle moon, appalled and speechless.

"He was here, sir," the tactical officer said. "The jammer satellite net is in place. The Jedi Knights have not sent any signals, as far as we can tell, and I do detect some ground activity. Heavy weapons fire in the jungles. Ground assault troops have been deployed—but the Star Destroyers are no longer here."

Daala ran a gloved finger along her chin. She scowled. "Something has gone terribly wrong." She turned back to the sensor chief. "Expand your scan," she said. "Look across the entire planetary system, not just near the gas giant. Did Pellaeon retreat? He knew I was coming."

The sensor chief checked and rechecked her readings, shaking her head. She looked up at Daala. "There's no sign, sir. I've run a sweep all the way to the outer planets and I find no ships. No wreckage either. Vice Admiral Pellaeon *was* here at the jungle moon—but now he's gone."

Daala felt cold needles of sweat prickle her scalp as anger raised her body temperature. She looked down at the jungle moon and thought of the Jedi Knights down there, fledgling sorcerers wielding a Force she did not understand. They should have been such an easy target. . . . Daala knew where to channel her anger.

For most of her professional life, Daala had restrained a wealth of spite and venom, barely controlled fury that would have eaten its way out of her if she had not found a way to express it.

Life had been peaceful for her once, long ago, when she had been young and in love—but that was before the Carida military academy, before Tarkin (whom she admired more than loved). Now she was left with only anger.

Luckily for the Empire, her methods of releasing that inner pressure had often resulted in devastation to the enemy. She could keep herself psychologically strong only if she had a target—and now she decided that target must be the Jedi Knights on Yavin 4. They had ruined her straightforward total victory.

The *Knight Hammer*'s launching bays were packed with thousands of TIE fighters and TIE bombers, fully loaded and ready to be deployed, but Daala decided against it. Pellaeon would have taken that tack, and if the Jedi Knights somehow had a secret defense against individual fighters such as those, she must adapt—and use a different strategy.

"Order all TIE pilots to stand down for the moment," she said. "Have them return to their crew quarters and remain on full alert. I won't be launching their ships just yet." She wanted to waste no time.

"Do we have plans for an attack, Admiral?" the weapons chief said from his station, looking disappointed as he assessed his array of weaponry.

"Yes," Daala said. "We strike from orbit. All turbolaser batteries, full strength. Fire at will, targeting any structures in the jungle."

"Yes, Admiral!" the weapons chief said with obvious enthusiasm.

Lances of brilliant energy shot down to the placid surface of the small moon below. The gas giant Yavin seemed unperturbed by the holocaust occurring on its tiny sibling.

The *Knight Hammer*'s weapons chief fired another volley of deadly turbolasers, and another, and another. Daala stared fixated at the target. She slammed her gloved fist into the bridge rail with each shot, as if she could add to the destructive potential of the blast.

She stood and waited, feeling her anger smoldering with a barely expressed satisfaction. Her appetite for destruction had merely been whetted. Even from her place in the *Knight Hammer,* high above Yavin 4, she could already see the forests starting to burn.

CHAPTER 48

Like armored birds of prey, the *Victory*-class Star Destroyers struck target after target, leaving a swath of flames and destruction in their wake.

Colonel Cronus sat back in the uncomfortable command chair of the 13X and scrutinized his dwindling list of targets compiled by Admiral Daala. He clasped his hands together, squeezing, flexing his arm muscles. His entire body felt tense, coiled with fierce pride. His mind was ablaze with success after success—but he did not allow himself to grow giddy with satisfaction, because then he might let his guard down and perform less than perfectly. He couldn't afford that, not after such a glowing record.

He sat back, strapped himself in, and prepared for another battle. "Shields up," he said.

"Acknowledged," the tactical officer said.

"Prepare to engage." One by one, the other Victory ships checked in automatically as their computers sent coded responses. Cronus leaned forward, squeezing the arms of his command chair so tightly that his fingertips left indentations. "Full forward," he said.

The fleet of crimson ships plunged through the Chardaan Shipyards, a Rebel space facility that produced a variety of starfighters—from the old-model X-wings and Y-wings to the newer A-, B-, and E-wing fighters. After this assault, Cronus thought, the facility wouldn't produce much of anything at all.

The shipyard's zero-g pressurized hangars were silvery spheres, clusters that provided a shirtsleeve working environment for the mechanics who assembled components to form the sleek ships. As Cronus's fleet roared past their targets, the hangars exploded with satisfying eruptions of burning air and outflying metal. Significant enemy casualties. No Imperial losses.

A boxy ore hauler lumbered away. The huge corroded vehicle had seen better days and was now manned by only a skeleton crew that tried to lurch their ancient vessel out of danger.

Cronus took pleasure in targeting the ore-hauler's rear engines, knocking the behemoth out of control. It trailed flames as it crashed into an outer docking ring filled with the personal quarters of engineers.

Cronus did not slow down. He led the fleet through the thick of the construction area, firing indiscriminately.

The Rebel forces mobilized with remarkable speed. Starfighters, old and new, streaked toward the Victory ships, piloted by construction workers and off-duty fighters.

"Hit everything you can, but do not engage the Rebel defenses," Cronus ordered. "It's not worth our bother. We'll cruise through at top speed and leave them trembling as we depart."

He could tell by the rapidity with which the Rebels mustered their forces that they must have been put on alert. Somehow they had been forewarned of Daala's planned attacks. He flexed his arm muscles again.

The small Rebel ships concentrated their firepower on

two of the crimson battlecruisers, and Cronus admired
their strategy. The fighters were too small and too few to
cause significant damage across Cronus's fleet . . . but if
they picked a single target at a time, they just might—

One of the Victory ships exploded, blowing shrapnel
in all directions and taking out a dozen of the harrying
Rebel X-wings.

Cronus felt annoyance as much as disappointment.
"Increase speed," he shouted. "Let's get out of here."

The second *Victory*-class ship blew up, but this time
the ship's commander didn't have the foresight to use the
destruction of his Star Destroyer for a final advantage, and
the resulting detonation caused no collateral damage.

Cronus no longer had a perfect record, and he was
upset.

As they passed through an exploding fuel-supply station and a hazardous forest of loose, drifting girders, Cronus ordered his Star Destroyers to deploy their timed
seeker-detonators with chaff and debris clouds. The small,
powerful mines would hunt out innocuous-looking targets,
where they would be triggered later—a surprise for the
Rebels to find during cleanup operations. Cronus took a
great deal of satisfaction in knowing he could continue the
destruction even after he departed.

"Rebel defenses are aligned, sir," the sensor chief
said, "and gathering force."

Cronus nodded and leaned forward. "Time to go.
We've caused all the devastation we can here."

The fleet of *Victory*-class ships escaped cleanly into
hyperspace as the Rebel forces came gunning after them.

The sweeping cultural museums on Porus Vida were renowned throughout the galaxy, centuries old—and aston-
ishingly undefended against attack. Colonel Cronus didn't
consider them military targets . . . but Admiral Daala
had included them as a psychological strike, and Cronus
followed orders.

It was a simple act for his ships to sweep by with turbolasers blazing to set the art and document storehouses aflame. His remote sensors transmitted images of sculpture gardens melting under waves of heat, graceful figures with arms upswept in aesthetic expressions of joy, buckling in agony as they melted into lava.

The green grasses of manicured gardens were crisped brown at the moment of flashpoint. Reflection pools and fish ponds boiled into steam, and screaming patrons stumbled and fell in their tracks. The museums burned, their treasure houses annihilated.

Colonel Cronus tapped his fingers together and pursed his lips. Who cared about cultural records anyway? He was in the process of destroying their history, and making history of his own.

The Imperial fleet stumbled upon the diplomatic convoy through sheer serendipity, but Cronus took advantage of the surprise.

The convoy consisted of nine rounded cylinders strung with gossamer solar sails, which made them look like flower petals spinning through space, augmented by sublight engines as they came toward a refueling station. Beautiful to behold, Cronus thought, but sluggish, poorly maneuverable, and slow to respond to an overt attack.

When the desperate alien transmissions came to him, he saw the aliens were a species of fragile-looking insectoid creatures with sweeping butterfly wings—and very little weaponry. When his *Victory*-class fleet charged among the ships, turning their solar sails to cinders, he received an immediate and unconditional surrender.

Colonel Cronus was not interested in surrender.

He checked their identification and stated mission, filing away the data in case Daala might need it. Then he ordered their complete annihilation.

"These are allies of our enemy, bringing gifts and swearing allegiance to Coruscant," Cronus said. "They chose the wrong side in this galactic conflict, and now they will pay for it.''

He fired upon the lead ambassadorial ship, using turbolasers like hot razors to rip open the ship's metal belly, so that atmosphere and passengers spewed into space like spurting blood.

His ships continued the bombardment until the aliens' reserve fuel tanks detonated. Cronus opened the comm channel again to his fleet. ''Since this convoy is unarmed, we may as well take the time to finish the job.''

The *Victory*-class ships and their pilots, still angered by losing two ships at the Chardaan Depot, took great relish in slicing apart every last one of the butterfly ships. . . .

They drifted for a moment surrounded by total wreckage. Cronus caught his breath from the excitement and ordered the fleet to proceed. ''A job well done,'' he said over the comm system. ''Now it's time to rejoin Admiral Daala at Yavin 4.''

He closed his eyes and relaxed for a moment as his fleet of Star Destroyers soared onward, unchallenged.

CHAPTER 49

In the hushed mechanical silence of the Darksaber's control deck, General Crix Madine, the Supreme Allied Commander for Intelligence, glared accusingly at Sulamar.

The Imperial officer stood stiff with self-importance, but his expression was wild and panicked. His cheeks flushed scarlet, and his close-set eyes flicked back and forth. The other guards grasped Madine's arms, squeezing hard enough to bruise.

Durga the Hutt leaned forward and smacked his huge lips together, the distorted birthmark across his face rippling like spilled ink. "General Sulamar—you know this saboteur?"

Madine laughed, making sure he spoke loudly enough for all to hear. "Did you call him a *general*?" he said. "That buffoon's no general."

Sulamar waved his hands in a frenzy, as if he could wipe out Madine's existence with a gesture. He blinked his eyes like the fluttering wings of a night insect drawn against its will to a bright hot light. "Don't listen to this man, Lord Durga! He's a traitor to the Empire—"

Madine snorted. "And you're a good-for-nothing junior technician, third grade—transferred from assignment to assignment because you kept screwing up your duties!" He made a rude noise.

Sulamar stormed forward, but stopped, his fists clenching and unclenching. He looked about to choke on thick, syrupy anger. He whirled to face the Hutt. "Lord Durga, you've seen my command abilities—don't let this traitorous spy lie to you."

Durga jiggled as he laughed. "Hoo, hoo, hoo! I *have* seen your so-called command abilities, Sulamar . . . and I'm inclined to believe this man."

Sulamar gasped and stammered as if seeking just the right words, but his tongue kept getting in the way. The motley assortment of armed guards looked uneasily from Madine—their known enemy—to Sulamar, perhaps another target in their midst.

"Sulamar," Durga said, his voice low and rumbling. Madine noted with a satisfied leap of his heart that the Hutt had intentionally left off the title of general. "We will take care of this prisoner. You need not fear. Please surrender your blaster pistol to me." Reclined on his repulsor platform, the Hutt extended a stubby-fingered gray-green hand.

Sulamar stood rigid. Beads of sweat appeared on his high forehead. His Imperial general's uniform—no more than a costume, Madine knew—appeared immaculately cared for: all the seams neat, all corners pressed with sharp edges, all the command insignia polished until it gleamed.

"But . . . Lord Durga," Sulamar said. "Perhaps I should be the one to—"

Durga bellowed with all the threatening volume he could generate from his vast trembling belly. "Do you question my orders, Sulamar?"

The Imperial impostor leaped to obey. He snatched his blaster pistol from the holster on his hip and extended it barrel forward, pointed at Durga; then he realized his mistake and quickly fumbled to turn the weapon around, handing the butt end to the crime lord.

"Good," Durga said, holding the weapon but keeping its energy barrel aimed at Sulamar. "Next, you will seat yourself there in the Darksaber's pilot chair." Durga gestured with the blaster to an empty station surrounded by command terminals and a navigational array.

Madine could see that the chair was rigged with some sort of booby-trap system, power cables running up the stem of the seat, electrodes spaced across metal contact points in the chair.

Sulamar looked at the pilot seat and paled. "There, Lord Durga? But I can serve you so much better if I—"

"There!" Durga said.

Sulamar seemed absolutely terrified—much more so than simply having his lie exposed should warrant. But he moved like a droid under incontrovertible programming, resigned as he shuffled toward the empty seat. Strapping himself in at the Darksaber's piloting station, he slumped, seemingly more resigned to his fate than Madine, who was already marked for death.

Crix Madine stood battered and sore and utterly exhausted. He clenched his hands, waiting and waiting. Eyes closed, he sensed the silent invisible signal pounding out from the implanted transmitter, summoning help, pleading for a rescue party *now*. Now! What was taking so long?

He ground his jaws together and urged the ships to hurry.

Empty space rushed by until it began to be cluttered with debris. On the command deck of the *Yavaris,* General Wedge Antilles leaned forward to peer out the front ports. "Come on," he muttered. "Come on!"

Beside him, Qwi Xux clamped her lips together, picking up on Wedge's anxiety.

"Are we still at maximum speed?" Wedge called to the helmsman.

"Best we can manage, sir," the young officer responded. "Hazardous conditions up ahead, though—General Madine's signal is leading us directly into the Hoth Asteroid Belt."

Accompanied by the Assault Frigate *Dodonna* from his arm of the fleet, Wedge rode the *Yavaris* into the asteroid belt. "Shields on full," he said.

"Agreed, sir," the helmsman answered. "But I'm reluctant to proceed at high speed into such a navigational hazard."

Wedge shook his head. Somehow he knew they had to hurry. *Hurry!* "Just stay on your toes, Lieutenant," Wedge said. "And keep moving with all possible haste."

The asteroids flew around them like a cannon blast of fragmented rubble, but Wedge's fleet continued undaunted, homing in on Madine's signal, hoping to rescue him in time.

Strapped in to the pilot's chair, barely able to move, Sulamar was livid. He spun around, still sputtering and trying to justify his existence.

Durga the Hutt growled, looking down at him from the height of his repulsor platform. "Why don't you tell us again about this Massacre of Mendicat you kept bragging about, Sulamar?"

Madine rolled his eyes and snorted. One of the Weequay guards jabbed him in the kidneys; he gasped in pain, but recovered quickly. "Mendicat?" he said with a sneer, knowing that if he could provoke these people, keep them bickering among themselves . . . then he had a chance. A slim one.

"Mendicat was a scrap mining and recycling station." Madine glared toward Sulamar. "Because of *his* error in programming the orbital computers, the station went off course and fell into the sun. He barely rescued himself, and now I see that was a wasted effort."

Durga chuckled, deep hollow belly laughs that resonated through his Hutt bulk. "After my days of working with the great crime lord Xizor, I should have learned to double-check pretentious stories from my underlings."

Madine answered the Hutt, as if speaking to an equal. "I've come to the conclusion that those people who truly do great deeds don't feel the need to talk about them all the time."

"You must stop listening to him, Lord Durga," Sulamar squeaked, struggling against the pilot chair restraints he had strapped across his own chest. "Lord Durga, we must execute this man!" His words became sweeter, more insidious. "Imagine the possibilities. We could use a laser cutter to dice him into pieces, or we could chain him to the reactor core of the Darksaber as we power it up so that he cooks against its shell."

Bevel Lemelisk, the pot-bellied, grizzled old engineer, who appeared to watch the entire proceedings with a combination of amusement and distaste, made a comment seemingly to himself but loud enough that everyone heard. "The Emperor could have imagined more . . . entertaining executions." The old man visibly restrained a shudder.

Durga grumbled, still waving Sulamar's blaster pistol around. "I don't see any need to draw this out. After all, we have better things to do. A galaxy to conquer, and so forth."

Madine stood bravely, clapping his heels together and staring into the large coppery eyes of Durga the Hutt. He said nothing for a moment as he thought back on his years of service to the New Republic.

He had had a good run, had helped the New Republic grow strong. And now he had followed his duty to the end. He didn't regret defecting from the Empire many years ago, though he did wish he could have seen his fiancée Karreio one more time—but it was too late for those regrets now. He saw her image in front of his eyes. She had died in the battle for Coruscant, and he had never been able to explain anything to her. Madine just hoped that if she did love him, she must have understood in the end

. . . and if she didn't understand, then she hadn't really known Crix Madine at all.

He fixed his eyes forward, watching the streaming white lights of the asteroid field clustered around the construction site, hoping against hope that at this last minute he would spot an oncoming fleet of rescue ships. But he saw only the rocky ruins of a planet that had broken apart millennia ago. He decided not to give Durga the satisfaction of begging for his life.

The Hutt pointed the blaster pistol at Madine and fiddled with the controls until he finally figured out how to set the weapon to KILL.

"Any last words?" Durga said.

Madine lifted his bearded chin. "Not to you." Out of the corner of his eyes he saw the brief, white-light flicker of approaching ships. His heart swelled. They were coming to rescue him!

Durga's fleshy, smooth shoulders rippled in a shrug. "All right."

Guards scattered out of the way.

Durga fired the blaster pistol, letting loose a long blast of deadly energy.

Madine was thrown backward into the metal wall as the killing beam burned through to his heart. His entire life evaporated in a brief flash of pain.

And then blackness.

CHAPTER 50

Heading back toward Yavin 4 aboard the *Millennium Falcon,* Luke Skywalker and Callista recovered rapidly from their ordeal in space. They looked forward to a long and well-deserved rest at the Jedi academy.

Han, Leia, and Chewbacca tried to cheer them up, but Luke and Callista both felt a brooding sense of failure and frustration. Threepio's pestering ministrations failed to help, though the golden protocol droid meant well. Artoo-Detoo hovered protectively beside Luke, whistling and guarding his master like a faithful pet.

When they were alone together, Luke looked into Callista's open gray eyes; even without Jedi powers they could share some thoughts.

"It isn't going to work, is it, Luke?" Callista asked him. "I'm never going to get my Jedi powers back."

"There's always a chance—" he said.

"Don't coddle me," she snapped, then flicked her gaze away, though the muscles beneath her cheeks flinched as if she wanted—*longed*—to look back at him, but didn't dare risk it.

"We've tried everything," Callista said. "We've worked all this time, but accomplished nothing. The Force has abandoned me. Its currents are diverted around me, so that I can't touch them."

"But you *did* touch them," Luke said. "On Dagobah. I felt it."

"That was the dark side," Callista said.

"But it might be the key to regaining your powers," Luke insisted, unwilling to give up all hope.

"The dark side is never the key to the light," Callista said. "You would never teach that to your students at the *praxeum,* so don't give it to me now as a platitude."

"What are we going to do, then?" Luke said. "Just give up?"

"I can't give up. I love you too much. But I have to make my own decisions," Callista said.

Luke leaned forward, took her hands, and held them until she finally looked at him. "You can," he said softly. "But I'd like to be part of them."

Her expression softened, and she lowered her voice. "You will be, Luke—if I can find any way to make it so."

They held each other tightly for a brief moment until Threepio bustled in to the common room. "Master Luke! Master Luke!" he said. "We've almost reached the Yavin system, and Captain Solo thought you might wish to join us in the cockpit."

Luke and Callista continued to hold each other, and the protocol droid suddenly stammered and stepped back. "Oh dear, have I intruded at an inconvenient time again? I do beg your pardon. I'm afraid I'm dreadful at that sort of thing."

"No, Threepio," Luke said, standing up and holding out his hand to help Callista climb to her feet. "We were finished talking."

Arm in arm, Luke and Callista followed Threepio along the corridor to the *Falcon*'s glassed-in cockpit where Leia sat just behind Han, leaning over and watching as Chewbacca worked the controls.

"Glad you could join us, kid," Han said. "Time to get back to work."

Artoo warbled at the navigation console, and Han yanked back on the controls to slow them to sublight speed. "Welcome to Yavin 4," Han said, gesturing with his hand. "The Jedi vacation resort."

The *Millennium Falcon* shot out of hyperspace, broadcasting an announcement that Luke Skywalker had returned. They plunged toward the jewel-green moon around the orange gas planet . . . and nearly rammed into the Super Star Destroyer *Knight Hammer*.

"Whoa!" Han cried.

Chewbacca roared and grabbed the controls, sending the *Falcon* whizzing up and around, past the kilometers-long Super Star Destroyer.

"What the—" Han said. "It's not my fault!"

The *Knight Hammer* continued to fire upon the jungle moon, but as soon as Han arrived, a few stray turbolaser blasts sliced across space toward them. "Chewie, take evasive!" Han said, but the Wookiee copilot was already one step ahead of him.

"Han," Leia snapped, "stop transmitting your identification signals. You're drawing their attention."

"Uh, right," Han said with a sheepish look, and slapped at the comm system, switching off the beacon.

A transmission burst across their speakers, crackling at a high volume because of the power behind the Super Star Destroyer. "This is Admiral Daala, commander of the *Knight Hammer*. You will surrender immediately or be destroyed."

Han groaned. Chewbacca roared. Artoo squealed a shrill note of alarm. "Admiral Daala! Oh, my!" Threepio said.

Han toggled the communication system. "Daala, you are such a pain," he said, then snapped it off, dodging another burst of turbolaser bolts by flying in a figure eight past the Star Destroyer's targeting locks.

"Han, stop showing off," Leia said.

A cloud of TIE fighters spilled out of the fore hangar decks of the Super Star Destroyer, swirling toward the *Falcon*. "Shields up!" Han said, and Chewbacca grunted in acknowledgment. Han turned back to Luke. "Sheesh, you go away for a few days, and the whole place falls apart."

Chewbacca roared.

"Uh, Han," Leia said, pointing. "Han!"

Two TIE fighters screamed toward them, their laser cannon shots ricocheting off the full-power shields in front of the *Falcon*. Han punched his own laser cannons, clipped one of the TIE fighters and sent it reeling out of control. The other screamed by without damage.

"Can we transmit a signal to the New Republic? Sound the alarm?" Leia shouted. "We've got to get the whole fleet here."

Chewbacca flicked the comm system and groaned. Han looked over at the panels. "She's doing what? That takes a lot of power."

Threepio said, "I believe Admiral Daala is successfully jamming all distress signals."

"Terrific," Leia said.

"Go to the gunwale," Han said.

"I'll take it," Luke responded.

"I'll get in the other one," Leia said.

"You?" Luke asked.

She shrugged. "I've been practicing." She ran.

Luke climbed into the gunner's seat and shouted to Han. "Daala's got more ships than we can possibly handle. Don't stick around to fight them. Just get down to the moon." Luke fired the laser cannons, and from below Leia shot and hit another TIE fighter.

"You sure we wouldn't be better off just hopping back into hyperspace?" Han said in a low voice.

Callista stood behind him, gripping the back of Han's chair. "The Jedi academy is under attack," she said, knowing exactly the turmoil going through Luke's mind. "We have to help. We need to do whatever we can."

"All right," Han said. "Chewie, full forward shields. Punch it. We're gonna make a straight line."

The *Millennium Falcon* soared beneath the immense *Knight Hammer*. A flurry of TIE fighters blocked their way, flying in a tight formation as they shot a constant pattern of blasts. Han streaked toward them at full speed. Chewbacca roared in alarm.

"Oh, but, sir—" Threepio cried.

"I see 'em," Han said. "They'll move."

The TIE fighters held their position, still firing. The *Falcon*'s forward shields began to weaken, but Han plunged onward, right down their throats. Luke and Leia in their respective gunwales continued shooting, taking out TIE fighters.

"Ummm, please get out of the way?" Han muttered.

At the last possible moment the TIE fighters scrambled aside in such a pell-mell frenzy that two crashed into each other while others spun out of control. The *Falcon* shot through the defensive formation and grazed the atmosphere of the jungle moon, diving toward the treetops.

They cruised over the jungle. Billowing black smoke rose from scattered forest fires. Strips of the jungle were ripped up and incinerated where the powerful turbolasers had sliced down from orbit.

Callista grabbed Luke's arm as he climbed out of the *Falcon*'s gunwale, wearing a boyish grin. "It's been a long time since I've done that." But then his smile faded again. "The Jedi academy must be under attack. We have to get to them."

"I know," Callista said. "I've already told Han."

Han called, "Hey, I'm flying as fast as I can." Leia came up to join him. "Great shooting, Leia," he said.

"Plenty of incentive when the Imperials are using us for target practice," she answered.

Two TIE fighters soared over the treetops, firing at the *Falcon* from the sides.

"These guys just don't give up, do they?" Han muttered. He launched one of his concussion missiles directly at one TIE fighter, which was obviously expecting a laser-cannon retaliation. The TIE fighter tried to veer away, but the sensor on the tip of the concussion missile homed in on the flat panel and detonated, sending Imperial wreckage tumbling out of the sky.

The second TIE fighter zoomed upward out of range, apparently not wishing to continue the engagement. Below the *Falcon,* ground assault machinery moved about, mechanical scout walkers and bulky flying fortresses combing the jungle and heading toward the Great Temple.

"We've got to see if the trainees are okay," Luke said.

Han looked around. "Well, maybe we could get them all aboard the *Falcon,* take them to safety."

Luke flashed Han a grim expression. "I don't think we'll be leaving Yavin 4," he said.

"But that's crazy, Luke!" Han said.

"Look," Luke said, "if it's only a matter of survival, my Jedi trainees would probably do better split up and alone in the jungles than all aboard the *Falcon.* No insult to your piloting skills, Han, but if we evacuated the Jedi trainees on the *Falcon,* one lucky strike from Admiral Daala's Star Destroyer would take out nearly every Jedi Knight in the New Republic. I can't risk that. We'll fight here. You can take off. Go back and get help, or stay and fight in some of the ground battles. But the Jedi aren't leaving here."

"Okay, okay," Han said. "Let's see what the situation is first."

"Well, if you ask me, I believe I should prefer to attempt an escape," Threepio said.

"Shut up, Threepio," Leia said.

"Why is it that nobody ever listens to my opinion?" the golden droid said.

Han set the *Falcon* down beside a landed Imperial shuttle in front of the Great Temple. A battered AT-ST walker lay ruined at the edge of the jungle. Forest fires raged nearby; even the great Massassi temple appeared changed, blackened from air strikes, but it seemed structurally intact.

Luke hoped the Jedi trainees had either taken shelter inside the pyramid or had gone out to hide in the jungles.

The *Falcon*'s ramp extended, and Luke and Callista were the first to dash out, followed quickly by Han, Leia, and Chewie. Artoo rolled down the ramp, chittering agitated electronic sounds. Threepio hovered at the top. "Perhaps we should stay here, Artoo—to guard the ship," he said. But the little astromech droid gave him an electronic raspberry.

Luke and Callista hurried toward the temple. The heavy horizontal hangar door ground upward a fraction and a figure appeared as the thunder of battle continued around them.

Kyp Durron plodded out into the sunlight, bearing in his arms the limp, blackened body of Dorsk 81. Callista winced, and Luke gasped.

Kyp's voice was hoarse and strained as the other Jedi trainees flowed out behind him. "There were seventeen other Star Destroyers," he said. "We worked together, linked our abilities with the Force. Dorsk 81 guided us. He took the power upon himself. He got rid of the other Star Destroyers—but it cost us his life."

With a clanking sound and a crashing of trees, another Imperial scout walker emerged into the clearing, its blaster cannons leveled at the gathered Jedi, but before it could fire a shot, a fiery bolt roared out from one of the *Falcon*'s gunwales, blowing up the scout walker. Its trapezoidal metal head smoldered from a gaping crater where the pilot had sat.

A moment later a flustered See-Threepio scrambled out onto the boarding ramp. "I did it! Oh dear, did you see that? I said I would guard the ship. Oh my, I shot an Imperial walker! I'm sure I had no intention—" Artoo squealed in triumph.

Callista turned to Kyp. "We have no time to grieve now," she said.

"He was a Jedi," Kyp said. "A Jedi Knight."

"You all are," Luke said. "Come on—we've got to defend the academy."

In the jungle they heard more explosions, crashing noises, humming machinery as ground assault vehicles converged on their main target.

Han gestured to Leia and Chewbacca. "Come on, back to the *Falcon*. We'll break out our weapons."

Luke and Callista moved toward the Jedi trainees, ready to join the fray.

CHAPTER 51

"We can spread out and strike the Imperials," Luke said to the Jedi trainees gathered in front of the Great Temple.

The mechanized assault troops crashed forward through the jungle, firing at imagined targets. Artoo-Detoo trundled toward the open door of the Great Temple, vanishing into the shelter of the hangar bay's heavy shadows.

"They'll be here in a moment," Luke said. "If we Jedi can spread out in the jungle, we can hit them with surprise attacks."

Tionne was concerned. "They're much bigger than we are," she said, "with a lot more firepower."

"Yes," Kirana Ti said with a stern expression, "but we can hide better than they can."

"And," Kam Solusar added, "we're *Jedi Knights*. They're just Imperials."

Luke smiled at their confidence. "Callista," he said, "maybe you should go with Han and Leia on the *Falcon* where you'll be safer."

She shook her head vigorously, the short malt blond

hair waving in the humid air. "Not on your life. I'm staying here with you."

He smiled gently at her. "All right, I'll protect you with my Jedi powers. Just stay close."

She scowled, suddenly reminded of her inability to use the Force, but her face flushed with a fiery determination. Callista had her lightsaber, and Luke switched on his own green-yellow energy blade. Kirana Ti held Gantoris's old weapon with the harsh amethyst-white glow. Kyp drew his weapon. Some of the newer Jedi trainees took hold of the few blasters Kyp had retrieved from the stolen Imperial shuttle.

Luke held his lightsaber high. "Jedi Knights," he called, "may the Force be with you!"

The trainees split up and disappeared into the jungle thickets.

As damp vines and tangled undergrowth wrapped around her, Kirana Ti stuck close to Streen. They made an odd pair, but the addled Bespin hermit was her good friend. Kirana Ti was strong and muscular, tall, a warrior even without the Force. Streen, on the other hand, was self-absorbed and distracted, wanting primarily to be left alone. Kirana Ti accepted him as he was. She knew he held great power within him when confidence let him tap into his full potential. Together, they formed a solid team.

Imperial siege machines crashed toward them, another troop of gawky scout walkers clomping through the underbrush. They blasted trees out of their way, knocked down heavy branches, and ripped up vines that tangled around their cumbersome, jointed legs.

"They're not trying very hard to be quiet," Kirana Ti said. "Bad tactics. Shows overconfidence."

"What's their plan?" Streen said, twisting from side to side. "What's our plan? Does anyone have a plan? We should plan."

She took cover in the shadow of a thicket and yanked

him after her, squinting toward the approaching AT-STs. Sweat beaded on her brow, and she brushed it away. Kirana Ti gripped the smooth handle of her lightsaber. "The Imperials didn't expect much resistance from a handful of trainees, so they're not organized. It's just a mad scramble with plenty of weapons and no plan."

"No plan," Streen agreed, nodding vigorously.

A pair of AT-ST walkers stomped into the clearing. Before she could stop him, Streen popped to his feet and chattered, "I'll take care of these!" He rushed out to stand in plain sight of the two square-headed scout machines.

"Streen!" she yelled. Both walkers swiveled their boxy heads and trained weapons on the old hermit, but Streen raised his fists in the air and let out a loud yell as he swept his arms forward, using the Force to propel a battering ram of wind.

Kirana Ti was amazed at the speed with which he focused his mind on the Force, channeled his thoughts into exactly what he wanted to do, and then unleashed his powers. Or perhaps Streen didn't concentrate at all . . . and therein lay his unusual strength.

The two scout transports toppled backward as if they had been slapped by a giant hand, tumbled end over end until they slammed into the bole of an ancient Massassi tree, flattened by the Force.

Streen rubbed his hands together. "There," he said, then flashed a lopsided grin at Kirana Ti.

A third scout walker clomped out of the jungle, and Kirana Ti reacted swiftly this time, igniting her lightsaber and leaping toward the two-legged armored transport. She slashed sideways with the glowing purple-white blade and severed a mechanical leg at its knee. The scout walker toppled sideways and Kirana Ti jumped out of the way.

The pilot fired his laser cannons as the machine fell, but the bolts went wide, incinerating heavy branches from the trees. Hidden animals crouching in the underbrush burst into flight, squawking and shrieking as they scrambled through the forest debris.

Kirana Ti lopped open the armored hatch of the scout walker. The Imperial soldier inside scrambled to free himself from the crash netting, reaching for his blaster pistol—but Kirana Ti skewered him with the blazing lightsaber. He gave a short cry, and then a crackling hole in his chest prevented him from uttering another sound.

Kirana Ti climbed to the top of the smoldering hulk of the AT-ST like a warrior who had just vanquished a monster. Streen stood looking at the two vehicles he had crushed. Kirana Ti shouted to him. "Three down!" she said.

"Are there many more left?" he asked, sounding concerned.

"Plenty," she said.

Still wearing his perpetual frown, Kam Solusar met the Juggernaut alone. It was an ancient, cumbersome ground assault vehicle, obsolete throughout most of the Empire, though many old hulks could still be found in the Outer Rim Territories. Solusar remembered these massive "rolling slabs" that had been used to strike fear in Imperial opponents because of their mammoth size, though certainly not their efficiency or flexibility.

The Juggernaut was a huge tank bristling with three heavy-laser cannons, a pair of concussion-grenade launchers, and one medium-blaster cannon. Its five sets of wheels moved on independent axles, allowing it to roll through difficult terrain. The front and back ends each held a cockpit for pilots to drive the clumsy vehicle in either direction, since it was nearly impossible to turn the monstrosity around.

A lookout tower rose in a narrow unprotected stem above the front cockpit where the lowest-ranking stormtrooper had the unenviable assignment of spotting targets—while becoming the most obvious target himself. Because the Juggernaut was one of the least sophisticated heavy assault vehicles the Empire had designed, Kam Solusar assumed that its crew was not the best Admiral Daala's fleet had to offer.

Alone, he had no obvious weapons: he had not yet built a new lightsaber, in part out of reluctance to wield such power again; he had done plenty of damage before he had temporarily given up his Jedi heritage. But he considered it a greater irony if he could convince the Imperials to destroy *themselves* using their own weapons. He couldn't imagine a more delightful outcome.

Reaching out with the Force, the hard-bitten warrior sensed the crew of eight through the thick durasteel armor. He found no powerful or charismatic officer inside, just a group of weak-minded fools . . . exactly as he had expected.

Kam Solusar didn't even bother showing himself. He remained hidden behind an ancient tree as he closed his eyes and concentrated. This would need to be quick.

He used the Force to wrench the barrels of the Juggernaut's heavy laser cannons, punching the guns around to point down at the body of the vehicle itself. Welds shivered and metal strained as he ground the barrels into firing positions they had never been designed to use.

Then he sent out a spike of thought, an urgent message to the weakest mind he found, a simple Imperial gunner who had no idea where he was or why he was fighting.

Shoot the enemy! Kam Solusar commanded.

Reflexively, the gunner followed the order. He fired both heavy laser cannons at full power. The Imperial Juggernaut exploded under its own fire.

Kam Solusar ducked, but the trunk of the Massassi tree shielded him from the flying shrapnel. He shook his head in disgust. "Stupid idiots," he thought, then slipped off to seek another target.

The horizontal hangar door beneath the Great Temple stood wide open, a gaping vulnerability into the pyramid stronghold of the Jedi academy.

A single AT-ST clanked forward past the abandoned Imperial shuttle Dorsk 81 had landed on the jungle moon. The scout walker fired several times, blackening parts of the temple rock. Then, unchallenged, it strode across the landing grid toward the open and waiting hangar.

The walker hesitated outside, then brilliant white spotlights stabbed into the cavernous darkness of the hangar bay. Nothing moved in the empty hangar, only shadows thick and motionless. A few lizard-rodents scurried to avoid the light.

The AT-ST commander, still apparently nervous, fired twice into the empty chamber. The bolts of his laser cannons ricocheted off the inner walls and flashed, causing minor damage spots on the stone. Receiving no retaliatory fire, the AT-ST lumbered forward. Its commander no doubt thought he could take over the Jedi stronghold and prevent any long siege.

As the scout walker stepped under the heavy upraised door, though, Artoo-Detoo, hiding in the shadows, chittered and came forward to activate the release controls. The heavy armored slab, thick enough to seal off the temple from heavy blaster fire, came crashing down.

Propelled by hydraulic pistons, the door squashed the scout walker in an instant, hammering it into the stone floor. Fuel tanks erupted, coolants spilled, and smoke poured into the air. The body casing of the AT-ST lay unrecognizable, like hammered-flat pieces of scrap metal.

Artoo whistled and hooted in triumph, then he worked the door controls again, raising up the stone slab and falling silent. The temple grew dark and sat waiting again, vulnerable.

Artoo watched the sunlit jungle outside, hoping to lure a new target.

As Kyp Durron ran to join Han Solo in the *Millennium Falcon,* Callista followed Luke and Tionne as they slipped behind the Great Temple into the thicker jungle where more Imperials were massing.

Callista felt anger and helplessness crippling her again. Luke had meant well, and had spoken only out of concern for her—but unconsciously he had flaunted the fact that *he* had Jedi powers and implied that she was helpless without them.

I'll protect you, he had said.

That was the wrong thing to say to Callista. She didn't want him to protect her. She wanted to do her own part. She had to find some way that she could strike as many blows to defend the Jedi academy as Luke did. She needed to prove that they could exist on equal terms. Otherwise their relationship had no future, as far as she was concerned.

She sensed the scratching hum of dark side shadows in the back of her mind, tempting her, luring her to dip into their evil powers for just a few moments, and then she would be able to use the light side.

But she knew that was a lie. Callista held her lightsaber and sprinted beside Luke as they dove through a tangle of vines and lacy purple ferns.

A huge piece of heavy assault machinery plowed its way through the jungle toward the temple. Luke gestured for them to follow, but Callista hung behind. He and Tionne would work together, linking Jedi powers in a way that she could no longer share.

Callista came to a dreaded realization that perhaps she had been unable to attempt new techniques to regain her powers because she was *too close to Luke.* He intimidated her with his own abilities, unconsciously emphasizing the fact that she had so little left. Perhaps she needed time by herself, to operate on her own terms, with no expectations, no need to perform for Luke Skywalker, to meet his level of ability. She and Luke were bonded, joined heart and spirit—but perhaps she needed to find her own strength again so that she could join his.

Now, in the midst of the jungle battles, she felt help-

less and alone, tagging along like a burden rather than a
companion. She didn't need to prove anything to Luke—
but she did need to prove it to herself.

"Here it comes," Luke said, but his attention was
focused on Tionne as the two Jedi Knights prepared to
meet the Imperial battle machine. With their attention diverted, Callista formed her own plan.

The Imperial Flying Fortress approached them about four
meters off the ground, hovering over an ancient deadfall
where several giant Massassi trees had toppled in ancient
storms.

Luke recognized the immense vehicle. Tactically, it
was like a huge Imperial AT-AT walker but without the
legs, merely the armored body loaded with heavy weaponry. It was rectangular with rounded corners and two
heavy blaster cannons on a hemispherical turret on the top.
A target identification network operated from sensors
mounted around its outer hull. The machine hummed as it
cruised forward, nosing its way through the thick
branches, snapping them off when they refused to yield.

Its outer armor plates were already scarred from
weapons fire, scraped from hard branches, and splotched
with sticky smears of spilled sap. It cruised forward, heavy
blaster cannons moving like rigid tentacles. Receiving signals from the target identification network, they fired
deadly bursts upon any hapless forest creatures that happened to flee at the wrong time.

Luke concentrated on the armored monstrosity cruising toward them. He whispered to Tionne. "Together," he
said. "See that sharp tree stump? When the Fortress flies
over . . ."

Tionne nodded, and they waited as the low hum of
repulsor lifts drove the Flying Fortress over the ancient
deadfall.

Luke focused his blue eyes on the sharpened trunk.
"Now!" he cried. Luke and Tionne used the Force to-

gether, heaving the stump upward like a wooden stake through the lower hull of the Flying Fortress. The impaled siege vehicle spun about roaring with a burst of engine power. Its blaster cannons fired in all directions, setting trees aflame—but it couldn't move.

"That tree." Luke nodded toward another ancient trunk half-collapsed but held up by a net of vines. He and Tionne tugged on the dead tree with the Force, snapping the coiled vines and heaving the massive trunk down like an ax blade, many tons of solid wood slamming the Flying Fortress down into the deadfall, crushing it into an unrecognizable mass of smoldering armor plate.

Luke and Tionne leaped from their hiding place in triumph. They clasped each other's hands in a celebratory grip.

"See, Callista!" Luke called. "We'll take care of them, one by one!"

But when he turned to look behind him, he saw no sign of her. "Callista?" he called, glancing around in alarm.

Tionne also looked, but they saw no motion, received no answer in the thick jungle. Callista was completely masked from the Force, and therefore invisible even to their Jedi powers. Luke could not sense her, no matter how hard he tried.

"Callista!" he called again.

But she had vanished by herself into the thick jungle.

CHAPTER 52

Qwi Xux leaned forward and pointed just as Wedge began to discern the organized cluster of lights ahead of them. Her indigo eyes were better than his, and she could make out details he hadn't yet been able to imagine.

"Okay, increase magnification," he said.

In the viewscreen they saw the long cylindrical construction amid islands of hardened slag and discarded spare components. The Hutt weapon appeared to be complete and ready to move.

"They actually built it," Qwi whispered. "I hope we're not too late."

"So it was all true," Wedge mumbled. "And the Hutts got this far without us detecting them." He nodded grimly to the helmsman. "But they won't get any further." Trailed by their three Corellian Corvettes, the *Yavaris* and the *Dodonna* approached the enormous Darksaber.

Without ceremony, Durga's guards dragged the dead body of Crix Madine off the Darksaber's command deck.

Bevel Lemelisk watched the fallen Rebel saboteur with mixed feelings, pursing his lips and scowling with a thousand conflicting thoughts. The expression on Madine's face—fixed there forever so that Lemelisk would never forget it—was one of secret triumph, as if Madine knew something that the Hutts and the Imperials would never understand. Lemelisk saw the body with a certain amount of envy as well, knowing that at least Madine would stay dead and not have to worry about being brought back again and again and again to be tormented.

Several Taurill scurried across the bridge, watching the entire execution ceremony with intense curiosity. Lemelisk shooed them away, and the multiarmed creatures scrambled to the inner decks where the rest of the hive mind now rested with the completion of their labor.

Sitting imperiously on his levitating platform, Durga the Hutt issued commands to the impostor Sulamar. "Power up our engines. You will pilot us out of here. Now. I'm anxious to get under way."

Sulamar stammered, "But Lord Durga, I can't—"

"I have confidence in your abilities, Sulamar." He rubbed his green finger lightly over one of the booby-trap buttons. "Or would you prefer that I dispose of you and choose someone else?"

"No need for that, Lord Durga!" Sulamar said and focused his attention on the controls. "I appreciate your faith in my skills. I won't let you down."

"I'll make sure of that," Durga said. "My Darksaber is finished. I've had enough waiting around here. Let us begin our sweep across the galaxy and begin collecting our due."

Upon hearing Durga's words, Bevel Lemelisk snapped out of his reverie and gaped in disbelief. "You— you're not actually going to *use* this weapon, are you?" he said. "It's not yet tested." He stumbled over his words. "Lord Durga . . . we need to verify all the subsystems and—"

Durga made a loud, impolite noise and dismissed

Lemelisk's comments. "Nonsense, chief engineer. Your job is nearly finished. Don't try to prolong your usefulness. My Taurill workers followed your own plans exactly. What could go wrong?" He gestured to Sulamar. "Go, I told you. Move out."

Lemelisk nervously twiddled his fingers and scanned the other crew members at their stations, all strapped to booby-trapped chairs. He didn't speak his concerns out loud, but he had a bad feeling about the overall workmanship of the superweapon. Too often he had encountered gaffes such as the ancient and incompatible computer cores, the below-par materials. Too many miscommunications. Too many malfunctions.

Lemelisk knew the Hutts were obsessive about getting the best bargain for their money, but Durga had accepted the low bid far more frequently than quality control should have allowed; and the Hutts, being such fearsome crime lords, had somehow missed a basic commercial axiom—you get what you pay for, and nothing more.

Lemelisk gradually backed toward the turbolift door as the bridge crew busied themselves, preparing the superweapon for its maiden flight.

"Ah, excuse me, Lord Durga," Lemelisk said. "I believe my place should be down by the superlaser, monitoring it to make sure everything functions properly."

Durga, too intent on the excitement of finally getting into motion, dismissed Lemelisk distractedly. Lemelisk slipped into the turbolift, and his stomach lurched as the elevator platform dropped rapidly down. He patted his stomach, feeling a growl of hunger. He wondered if he might have time to grab something to eat . . . but decided he shouldn't risk delaying. He would be in a great deal of trouble if the Darksaber failed to fire as Durga expected, and Bevel Lemelisk had no intention of being around when that happened.

He exercised the better part of valor and went not to the superlaser control systems, but off to his private launching bay, where he dashed over to the small inspection scooter he had used to watch the final construction of the great weapon.

Everyone on board the Darksaber had been called to their stations, so the bay stood empty and dim with only standby systems lighting his way. Lemelisk strutted over to the single scooter and climbed into the hatch, working his stiff knees and weak arms until he settled into the seat. The cramped cockpit still smelled awful, and he wished he had thought to order the Taurill to clean the upholstery— but it was too late now.

He strapped in and powered up the inspection scooter, drifted through the atmosphere-containment field and away from the enormous weapon.

Bevel Lemelisk would take his chances out in open space.

CHAPTER 53

"Battle stations!" Wedge Antilles cried.

"The Hutt weapon is moving out," the tactical officer said, stating the obvious as the cylindrical behemoth powered up its rear engines like a star exploding.

"It's huge," Qwi whispered. "I understand it now, what they've done—they got rid of the extraneous superstructure and channeled all of the power directly into the superlaser. This weapon should be more maneuverable than the Death Star, more easily recharged, able to fire more frequently."

"We won't let it escape," Wedge said.

"Bad news, sir," the sensor chief said, a lieutenant with close-set blue eyes and a pointed nose. He turned away before he continued. "We've . . . sir, we've lost the signal from General Madine's transmitter."

The news struck Wedge like a blow to the stomach. He slumped in his seat. "Oh no."

Qwi didn't understand. "But we've found the weapon," she said. "We don't need the transmitter anymore, do we?"

Wedge's voice was hoarse. He intended to speak only to her, but the bridge fell quiet enough that everyone heard his words. "That transmitter is keyed to Madine's life monitor. If the transmitter has stopped, that means—"

He sat up straight and gestured violently forward. "All weapons on full. We must not let them get away. The *Yavaris* and the *Dodonna* will dive in directly. Corellian Corvettes will target the main engines to slow it down." He clenched his teeth. "This time, the Hutts picked the wrong people to tangle with."

On the Darksaber's command deck, the Devaronian sensor chief squawked in alarm. He jerked his horned head up. "Lord Durga, Rebel fleet approaching! They're powering up weapons."

"What?" Durga recoiled, blinking his lanternlike eyes. "How did they find us?" Then he turned to Sulamar. "It's time to test your piloting skills."

The engines fired again, and the Darksaber heaved into motion, picking up speed. The thrum vibrated through the hull with barely contained power. The Darksaber built up momentum. Durga laughed with delight at the performance of his superweapon.

Deep down within the core, a loud groaning sound came from the engines, followed by a clunk and a thud.

Durga looked around in concern. Sulamar concentrated on the piloting controls, biting his lips and pretending to hear nothing out of the ordinary. Sweat streamed from his temples. The strange sound faded away, and Durga ignored it.

"Power up the superlaser," the Hutt crime lord said. "We must be ready to fire a shot when the time is right. We'll blast the Rebel fleet into space dust."

The New Republic warships streaked after the Darksaber as it plowed through the flying rubble of the asteroid belt.

The shields sent out bright flashes as they disintegrated small rocks that crossed their path. Several large chunks broke through, though, pounding the hull of the *Yavaris*.

"That Hutt weapon is like a battering ram, breaking up the rubble," Wedge said.

One of the Corellian Corvettes was struck broadside by a large spinning meteoroid and fell behind in the pursuit. The captain transmitted to Wedge that his engines had been severely damaged, but that containment fields and bulkhead doors had trapped the escaping air from small hull breaches. "No crew loss," the captain said, "but we'll be undergoing repairs for a while. Go get the Hutts for us, sir."

Wedge nodded. "We'll do our best."

"He's going into the densest part of the asteroid field, General Antilles," the navigator said, her face pasty white with tension.

"Then we're going in after him," Wedge said.

The Assault Frigate fired its turbolasers and splintered a jagged asteroid careening toward them. The *Yavaris* flew through the debris cloud, sustaining little damage. "Thanks, *Dodonna*," Wedge said.

When they got close enough to the Hutt superweapon, he ordered all ships to open fire.

Asteroids whirled around them, as the field became denser and denser, and Sulamar worked frantically to keep the Darksaber moving forward and in line. It was an impossible task, and Durga spent altogether too much time with his stubby finger poised over the "execution" button linked to Sulamar's chair.

"I won't be able to navigate much longer, Lord Durga," Sulamar said. "This is the most deadly part of the asteroid belt. None of our scout ships even dare to enter here."

"Then the Rebels will be too frightened to follow us," Durga said.

"Just *look* out there, Durga!" Sulamar cried, pointing toward the moon-size rocks grinding together like the molars of a beast as large as a planet.

"Do I need to choose another pilot?" Durga said.

"No, Lord Durga," Sulamar mumbled in exasperation.

The Hutt nodded. "Our superlaser is powered up. We have nothing to worry about."

Sulamar swallowed—he could think of plenty to worry about.

The Rebel fleet came in, firing with their full complement of weapons. Each blast was insignificant in itself, but hundreds of turbolaser bolts struck home, peeling loose plates from the Darksaber's hull, rattling components loose. The unnerving noises grew louder deep within the engine core.

The Darksaber had no outer hull defenses, no turbolaser turrets of its own, and no squadrons of TIE fighters to drive off Rebel pests. Several of the larger asteroids plunged in from the side, denting and battering the weapon's hull—but Sulamar continued flying with grave trepidation. Durga would severely punish any mistakes . . . if they managed to survive.

The impostor general looked along their flight path and saw a nightmare. The Darksaber plunged along much too fast to maneuver effectively. Deep inside, the vessel groaned again, startling him.

Up ahead a pair of the largest rocks he had yet seen spun about, grinding together, like granite jaws waiting for new prey. Sulamar knew they could never avoid the hurtling planetoids at the velocity they were cruising. He squeezed his eyes shut.

Durga raised his hand in defiance. "Get those asteroids out of our way," he said arrogantly. "Fire the superlaser!"

Sulamar's finger trembled on the FIRE button, but he could not hesitate. They hurtled toward the asteroids. He punched down and covered his eyes to block the blinding glare of the deadly energy beam. "Firing now, sir!"

But instead of a scream of destruction and a pulse of power through the superweapon, Sulamar heard only a loud *pfffffit!* A fizzle of sparks splattered out the front end of the Darksaber, but nothing more.

"Oh no," Sulamar cried. He punched the button again and again—but the Darksaber refused to fire.

The two broken planetoids smashed together with the Hutt superweapon between them. The Darksaber was crushed in an instant, becoming yet another hunk of space debris that would float forever in the Hoth Asteroid Field.

YAVIN 4

CHAPTER 54

Luke Skywalker's voice echoed through the thick jungle and the sounds of battle. Callista froze when she heard him calling her name, and her resolve began to melt. She shouldn't be leaving him—but she had to. There was only one way . . . if Callista had the courage to follow through.

"Callista!" Luke called again, but she plunged on through the underbrush, not looking back.

From above, bludgeons of turbolaser fire slashed through the atmosphere, leaving screeching ionization trails as Admiral Daala's *Knight Hammer* pounded Yavin 4. Callista looked up and saw another blast come down. With a single strike, the Super Star Destroyer obliterated an acre of ages-old growth. One lucky shot could level the Great Temple.

According to Kyp Durron, Dorsk 81 had flung away an entire Imperial fleet, seventeen Star Destroyers hurled beyond the range of battle. The Jedi trainees would have been safe right now had it not been for the appearance of the Super Star Destroyer. The real enemy remained in orbit, out of range.

Callista pushed thorny twigs away from her face, searching for an opportunity. Up ahead in a flattened section of trees, broken branches, and plowed-up dirt, she spotted a crashed TIE bomber, a ship with angled power plates and a double cockpit, one for the pilot/bomber and a second to hold concussion missiles. The ship had been damaged, part of its rear engine exhausts crimped as if from a thrown boulder.

The TIE pilot wore an opaque black helmet and padded black flightsuit that seemed uncomfortable and cumbersome; he worked frantically and alone. He had straightened the exhaust crimp, with a toolkit from the cockpit, and test-fired the engines.

Callista seized the opportunity, plotting an unexpected way to strike at Daala. She didn't have Jedi powers, and she was armed with only a lightsaber—but Callista *knew* she had the power to take out the Super Star Destroyer. She alone held that responsibility, and she had no choice but to follow it.

Moving silently with a smoothness born not from the Force but through her own training, Callista eased herself out of the thorny undergrowth and sprinted toward the TIE pilot as he moved toward the access hatch, ready to climb into his bomber again.

The pilot must have seen some flicker of motion through his helmet visor, though, some telltale signal that gave away Callista's stealthy approach. He turned, and she found herself facing her dull reflection in the black plasteel of the facemask.

He reacted with blinding speed, snatching a blaster from the holster at his side. Callista kept moving, picking up momentum, her arm sweeping in an arc as she punched the lightsaber's power button. With a *snap-hiss,* the topaz beam speared out, dazzling the TIE pilot.

In a smooth stroke she lopped off his black-gloved hand. Before he could cry out in pain, holding up his smoldering stump, Callista struck sideways across his chest.

Deactivating the lightsaber, she didn't slow as she kicked his steaming body away from the repaired TIE bomber. Callista hauled herself up to the hatch and dropped into the cramped cockpit.

Like a ghost, Luke's voice echoed thinly through the trees, calling her name. But she forced herself not to hear it. She had seen her personal weakness, watching the other Jedi Knights fighting together—she wasn't part of their brotherhood anymore. Callista would fight in a different way, her own way—and together they would all succeed.

She sealed the hatch overhead. The cockpit was cramped and smelled of old lubricants and stale flightsuits. The pilot would normally be wearing a breathmask and helmet, so he wouldn't notice the recirculated air. Callista didn't care.

She easily deciphered the controls. The Empire did not waste time or energy modifying their flight systems, and a TIE bomber still functioned the same way Imperial fighters had worked decades earlier, when Callista had first begun the fight.

The dark ship rose slowly from the crash scar as its engines warmed up. Climbing into the air above the tangled treetops, she could see the burn path where the damaged craft had plunged through the canopy.

Then the twin ion engines kicked in with a bone-chilling roar, and the TIE bomber angled up to where the atmosphere thinned—toward the *Knight Hammer*.

"I'm sorry, Luke," Callista whispered, and continued on course.

The nightmare ship hovered overhead, eclipse-black and so large that Callista could barely grasp its size. She knew little of its internal configuration, though she had once studied sketches of Darth Vader's flagship *Executor*. She knew, though, that the Super Star Destroyer—fabulously expensive and cumbersome despite the benefits it gave in sheer magnitude of weaponry—had very few vulnerabilities.

She had to get on board somehow and work from within.

The bomber's engines didn't respond at maximum capacity, but Callista headed toward the *Knight Hammer* with all the speed she could manage. Her mind spun as she tried to concoct a sufficiently audacious bluff that would allow her to land inside the bays: doubly difficult because she was a woman and could not immediately pass for a TIE bomber pilot; she would have to speak gruffly and muffle her words over the comm system.

Other TIE fighters spun about through space. Admiral Daala's superiority over Yavin 4 seemed complete, and she could safely sit back and launch deadly volleys against the entire moon without risking herself.

Callista was surprised to hear a female voice over the comm channel, a battle director requesting her identification and status. *A woman!* Callista had never heard of the Empire placing female officers and bridge crew aboard their ships; Admiral Daala herself must have changed things. Callista swallowed and leaned forward to respond. She intentionally tuned the comm system slightly off-frequency.

"This is TIE bomber number—" she adjusted the knob to give a burst of static to obliterate her number, then switched back to a clear signal again, "—sustained heavy damage. All of our Star Destroyers are gone. The Jedi Knights did something, and the entire fleet . . . wiped out. No sign of them."

"TIE bomber," the female battle director transmitted back, "please repeat, with augmented details. Give a full summary of the battle below."

"Most ground forces are destroyed," Callista said. "The Jedi Knights have put up an incredible resistance, far more than we expected. Our losses are heavy. I've managed to escape, but my engines are damaged. I need a place to land *right now.*" Callista twisted the knob, adding a few extra bursts of static for good measure.

"State the extent of your damage," the battle director said.

"Engines failing," Callista answered. "My solar panel has been damaged. I think I'm leaking coolant or radiation . . . can't be sure. Suggest you find an isolated bay where I can land. Evacuate it and seal down just in case something goes wrong. I'll check the leakage and report."

"Acknowledged, TIE bomber," the battle director said. "We are eager to debrief you about the battle for Yavin 4."

Callista smiled but made her voice sound ragged. "Understood." She drifted toward the Super Star Destroyer until finally the battle director gave her instructions on where to land.

The rear bomber bay was cavernous, though the entrance seemed no more than a tiny blemish on the hull of the *Knight Hammer.* Callista guided her stolen ship inside and was immensely pleased to see that she had reached a hangar that held an entire squadron of TIE bombers. Apparently Admiral Daala was not planning to use this particular squadron, content to blast with her turbolasers. All personnel were evacuated from the bay because of possible hazardous leakage from Callista's bomber.

As she landed, she found herself inside a vast unoccupied chamber filled with row upon row of TIE bombers each fully loaded with a complement of concussion missiles.

Callista's lips curved in a hard smile. She couldn't have hoped for better than this.

CHAPTER 55

The *Falcon*'s engines roared as Chewbacca sat in the co-pilot's seat, grabbing the controls for liftoff. Leia strapped in, while Han Solo stood on the boarding ramp gesturing toward Kyp Durron. "If you're coming with us, Kyp—get moving! In the *Falcon* at least we can provide air cover."

Han's heart wrenched as he watched the young Jedi who had already been through so much, who had been helpless while his companion Dorsk 81 perished from his overloaded contact with the Force. With brittle movements and a hard expression, Kyp took one last glance around the jungle and the temples, then ran to the *Falcon*.

"Take us up, Chewie," Han called.

Threepio stood behind them flustered. "Oh, dear! You're not going to ask me to operate the gunwale again, are you, sir?"

Han dropped into the pilot seat and strapped in. "I don't know, Goldenrod. We might make a commando out of you yet."

"Thank you, sir, but that's not in my programming."

Han ignored the droid and punched the accelerators. "Let's go. We've got some loose ends to take care of."

"I'll take one of the gunwales," Kyp said.

Han gave a nod of encouragement. "Be my guest." Then he turned to his wife. "Feel like showing off again, Leia?"

She smiled. "As Chief of State I don't often get the opportunity to take any direct action. If the Council were here, we'd still be having a meeting about which button to push to fire the guns."

The *Falcon* roared away from the Great Temple, its white-hot sublight engines rippling thunder across the misty sky. Han followed the lines of fire through the tree canopy below and saw armored machinery moving, scout walkers plodding through the thick trees, rolling ground-assault vehicles, Juggernauts, and Flying Fortresses.

In the gunwales Kyp and Leia shot repeatedly, but they had a difficult time targeting through the tangled mesh of tree branches.

"Chewie," Han said, pointing through the cockpit window, "see that Flying Fortress down there, just barely between the branches?" Chewbacca grunted. "Let's drop a concussion missile on its head."

Chewbacca launched one of the *Falcon*'s missiles, which burned through the treetops and exploded below. Through the dense knot of trees, Han saw only wreckage where the Flying Fortress had been a moment before. Chewbacca made a chuffing sound of Wookiee laughter.

"Company from above," Leia shouted, her voice hollow and tinny through the gunwale corridor.

"I see 'em," Kyp said, then both gunwales began firing. A squadron of TIE fighters soared overhead, either the remnants of Pellaeon's forces or a new wing deployed by Daala's *Knight Hammer*.

"These are targets more to my liking," Han said, and took the initiative, charging straight at the oncoming fleet.

Chewbacca groaned in distress, and Threepio covered his optical sensors with his golden hands. But again the bluffing trick worked, and the TIE fighters scrambled out of the way, firing crazily as they split apart.

Han was disappointed to see that their usual clumsiness had improved so that the TIE fighters' stray bolts did not destroy any of their own ships. Kyp and Leia concentrated their firepower on the lead ship; both of them cried out in excitement as it exploded on its hectic flight to escape.

Taking advantage of his new tactic, Han streaked forward with the *Falcon,* chasing after the fleeing TIE squadron. He wondered how long it would take them to realize he was only one opponent and they had many more laser cannons to turn against him.

Then an indiscriminate river of fire seared through the atmosphere, ripping the air apart in a screaming ionization path. A massive turbolaser bolt from orbit struck one of the TIE fighters and disintegrated it in a puff of released energy. The shockwave buffeted the *Falcon,* making Han and Chewbacca scramble to regain control of the ship. Han pulled the *Falcon* away, did a backward loop through the air, and rocketed off in the opposite direction. The remaining TIE fighters spun about, spiraling out of control. They lost their formation and whipped about in a flurry of confusion.

Another turbolaser bolt came down in the distance, igniting a portion of the jungle kilometers away.

"That's Daala," Han said, shaking his head in disgust. "She doesn't even know what she's firing at."

Kyp climbed out of the gunwale, and the look of twisted determination on his face made Han shudder. "Admiral Daala owes both of us big time, Han." Kyp looked away with his sharp, dark eyes. "Dorsk 81 sacrificed himself to get rid of the first Imperial fleet. We would all be safe now if it weren't for Daala. She's the target I want to go after."

Threepio stood up, indignant. "But sir, that would be a highly irrational course of action. The *Millennium Fal-*

con is no conceivable match for the likes of that Super Star Destroyer."

"You're crazy, kid," Han said uncertainly.

Kyp shrugged. "Just determined—and it's worked to my advantage before."

Chewbacca growled his reservations, but Kyp squatted beside Han. "Before I came to Yavin 4, Dorsk 81 and I sent an alarm to the New Republic fleet. Reinforcements should be on their way. I don't know how long they'll take, but we can't let Daala destroy everything before they get here."

Han thought again of how Admiral Daala had strapped him in the torture chair of her Star Destroyer *Gorgon*. "Whatever you say, kid," he answered slowly. "It's like a big sabacc game, so let's throw all our cards on the table and hope Daala doesn't see that we're bluffing."

The *Falcon* peeled through the outer skin of atmosphere and headed into the blackness of space where the immense planet Yavin filled most of the vicinity like a giant eye watching the battle. The *Knight Hammer* lorded over the tiny jungle moon, a dark city in space loaded with deadly weapons.

"Punch it, Chewie," Han said. The *Falcon* soared forward, picking up speed directly toward the *Knight Hammer*.

Leia came down and stood beside Kyp next to Han. "I don't know what you're doing, but I hope you have a plan," she said.

"A plan?" Han answered, raising his eyebrows. "I'm just trying to get Daala's attention."

TIE fighters swirled about the front of the Super Star Destroyer, but the *Falcon* came in so fast they didn't have time to scramble and acquire the new target. Han punched the comm system.

"Hello, Admiral Daala! Han Solo here, with my friend Kyp Durron. Maybe you remember us?"

Within seconds the *Knight Hammer* had stopped

blasting the jungle moon below and targeted the *Falcon* instead.

"Let's get out of here, Chewie," Han yelled, slammed back into his seat as acceleration hurled them away from the *Knight Hammer.*

"That was real smart," Leia said.

"At least we got her attention," Han said. "Not to mention that she stopped shooting down at the Jedi academy for a few minutes."

The forward bay doors opened on the Super Star Destroyer, and four squadrons of TIE fighters launched after the *Millennium Falcon.*

"I hope our shields are strong enough," Leia said.

Daala's TIE fighters closed in, firing repeatedly. The *Falcon* rocked and lurched from endless blows hammering its shields. Han uneasily looked at their power levels, and though the *Falcon* fled at top speed, their shields were drastically weakening—and the TIE fighters kept coming.

"Sir," Threepio said, "by my estimate there are two hundred and eighteen TIE fighters after us, each firing with two laser cannons. That provides an anticipated shot number totaling—"

"I don't want to know, Threepio. We're doing our best."

"But what I meant to say," Threepio continued, "is that statistically we can't possibly hope to—"

"Threepio!" Leia said, "I think we've figured that out for ourselves."

Then an unexpected volley of fire came from the side, blasting through the swarm of TIE fighters and sending them into absolute confusion.

"What was that?" Han said.

Chewbacca yowled, and Kyp smiled. "It's our reinforcements," he said.

Admiral Ackbar's *Galactic Voyager* dove into the system, flanked by four Corellian gunships. The Calamarian Star Cruiser stabbed through the clustered TIE fighters, wiping out half of them in its first pass. The

Corellian gunships, more specifically designed to take out attacking starfighters, enclosed themselves in a cocoon of blaster fire as the ranks of independent gunners took on the mass of enemy ships, while a few desperate stragglers fled back toward the *Knight Hammer,* their twin ion engines coaxed to maximum power.

Ackbar's voice came over the comm system. "General Solo, is that you? You look as if you could use a bit of help."

"Admiral, are we glad to see you!" Han said.

"I suggest you come to safety aboard the *Galactic Voyager,*" Ackbar said.

"Oh, I think that's a splendid idea," Threepio said.

"We'll do that, Admiral," Han answered, but Leia grabbed the comm system.

"Admiral Ackbar, I'm sure you can see what's going on down at the Jedi academy. Luke and his trainees need our help, but I don't know if you can take on Daala's Super Star Destroyer."

Ackbar made an indecipherable angry sound. "I will never forgive Admiral Daala for the damage she caused my beautiful home planet."

Kyp shook his head with an ironic smile. "Daala's not very good at making friends, is she?"

The *Falcon* was welcomed into the protected landing bay of Ackbar's Star Cruiser just as Daala opened fire on the Calamarian battleship. The four Corellian gunships continued to sweep space clean of TIE fighters, but the *Knight Hammer* still out-gunned their combined force. . . .

"The remainder of the New Republic fleet is coming to join us," Ackbar said as Han, Leia, Chewbacca, and Kyp came to the bridge of the *Galactic Voyager.* Threepio found another protocol droid and was soon busily regaling him with tales of their adventures so far.

"The Empire has launched a concerted attack on all parts of the New Republic," Ackbar continued. "General Antilles has taken his arm of the fleet to answer a desperate signal from General Madine. We believe Madine has tracked down the Hutt secret weapon—and we've been receiving reports of destructive Imperial attacks at strategic targets across the New Republic.''

"We have to stop them here and now," Kyp said.

"We will," Leia said, and looked up at Han and Ackbar. "That Super Star Destroyer is a much bigger target than we can handle, but we have enough firepower to hold our own, delay Daala's attack until reinforcements get here. It shouldn't be long."

As if hearing them, Daala launched a powerful salvo of turbolaser bolts.

"Shields on full," Ackbar said. "Drop back."

As the *Galactic Voyager* and the four Corellian gunships wheeled about, increasing their distance from the *Knight Hammer,* an invincible wall of turbolaser fire appeared off to starboard, without warning. Ackbar's shields were damaged, and one of the four Corellian gunships, taken completely by surprise, split apart and exploded beneath the *Galactic Voyager.*

Ackbar wheeled on the bridge, rocking back in dismay and confusion to see that space had filled with ships. Imperial ships.

The reinforcements had indeed arrived.

Admiral Daala's reinforcements.

Colonel Cronus returned to Yavin 4 with twenty of his crimson Star Destroyers. The remainder of his fleet had been sent off to continue harassing the secondary list of targets, but Cronus had accomplished his primary mission.

When the *Victory*-class ships arrived, though, Cronus was forced to reassess the situation. Vice Admiral Pellaeon's seventeen Star Destroyers were nowhere to be seen. Admiral Daala's *Knight Hammer* hung in orbit, and she fired upon a group of Rebel battleships that should not have been in the system at all, a giant organic-looking Mon Calamari Star Cruiser and four Corellian gunships: a significant fighting force, though nothing comparable to the Super Star Destroyer alone.

Colonel Cronus smiled. With the addition of his twenty smaller Star Destroyers, they would make short work of the Rebels and leave only a few burned hulks cooling in space, where the heavy gravity of the planet Yavin would suck them down inside its swirling gas clouds.

He went through his entire chain of contemplation in only a second and immediately broadcast orders to his fleet. "All ships engage," he said. "Let's get rid of some more targets."

The *Victory*-class battleships attacked with no forewarning and with full deadly force. They took out one of the Corellian gunships on their first pass and caused significant damage to the Calamarian Star Cruiser's shields. But the Rebel battleship rapidly came out of its stunned hesitation, and its powerful weapons began lancing out across the *Victory*-class Star Destroyers.

Cronus wished he had brought his entire fleet with him, though he was certain twenty of his ships would be sufficient. He flexed his arm muscles and leaned forward.

"Attrition," he said. "Take out the other Corellian gunships first." He designated five of his *Victory*-class Star Destroyers to concentrate firepower on the remaining three smaller ships, while Cronus took the 13X and fourteen warships against the Calamarian Star Cruiser.

Daala's *Knight Hammer* continued spewing turbolaser bolts through the frenzy, damaging one of Cronus's own ships. He hissed in anger, but didn't dare open a channel to criticize her. The Calamarian cruiser fired a storm of retaliatory bolts, while the remaining Corellian gunships spread out, launching themselves into the fray . . . where they were doomed.

Cronus's head spun in the free-for-all, and he forced himself to concentrate on his primary target, while his other Star Destroyers fought their designated ships. Turbolaser fire shot fast and loose around them in space. He received a message from one of his squadrons. "A second Corellian gunship destroyed, Colonel," the voice said. "Another crippled close to you."

Cronus double-checked the location of the crippled gunship and recoiled in sudden alarm. The cylindrical armored craft oozed flames from a dozen fatal wounds, but its engines still blazed at full power. A few of the gunwales continued to launch bolts of energy in all directions, but the gunship itself—though only a quarter the size of the 13X—lurched forward in a last-ditch effort. It was doomed, its hull rupturing, its life-support spilling into space, its engines aflame from within . . . but somehow, the captain drove forward to ram Colonel Cronus's flagship.

"Evasive action!" Cronus called. The 13X spun about its central axis and veered to the left, but the wounded Corellian gunship had already picked up speed, moving much faster than Cronus could get out of the way.

"Increase—" he shouted, and then squeezed his eyes shut in a wordless scream as the gunship rammed the 13X from behind, crashing into the Victory's bank of engine exhaust ports and then exploding in a fireball that turned the bridge compartment around him into a searing white void.

"Keep firing," Ackbar shouted. "Status report."

One of the Calamarian tactical officers reported. "Three Victory-class ships destroyed, Admiral, but only one of our Corellian gunships remains."

The *Victory*-class fleet fired and fired on the *Galactic Voyager,* and Admiral Daala's *Knight Hammer* shot at them with even greater power from the opposite side.

On the bridge, Han gripped Leia's hand. They looked into each other's eyes and then stared out at the overwhelming tide of battle.

Ackbar continued to hold his command together,

while Kyp Durron leaned forward, his face hopeless except for a flickering core of unfocused determination.

"Shields failing, Admiral," the Calamarian officer said. "Approximately ten seconds remaining."

The *Victory*-class Star Destroyers and the *Knight Hammer* closed in from both sides, unrelenting in their attack.

Admiral Ackbar's ship sat practically defenseless, without shields, in the midst of the deadly enemy fleet.

CHAPTER 56

Vice Admiral Pellaeon had no idea what had happened to him.

One moment he and his seventeen Star Destroyers were in orbit around the fourth moon of Yavin, engaged in their assault. They had encountered resistance, but nothing they couldn't obliterate with another sortie or two.

And then they found themselves hurled across space as if a giant hand had slapped them aside.

Pellaeon had been thrown over the bridge railing to sprawl on his back atop a command station, extremely lucky that he hadn't snapped his spine.

His crew had been tossed about like debris in a storm system. Several uniformed soldiers lay unconscious, possibly dead. Others sat blinking and bloodied. The shocked crew picked themselves up as ripples of astonishment echoed in whispered conversations, rising to a gabble of confusion and embarrassing fear.

Automatic alarms roiled through the *Firestorm*. The communications channels buzzed with activity as the other sixteen Star Destroyers demanded to know what had occurred—but Pellaeon could give them no answers.

He climbed back to his feet, smoothed his vice admiral's uniform, and staggered as his vision became blurred with black specks, like static from a jammed transmission. "Status report," he called.

Pellaeon coughed and wiped blood from the corner of his mouth. His crew grumbled and glanced at each other in confusion and dizzy perplexity.

"To your posts," Pellaeon said, raising his voice. More blood came from his lips, but his commanding tone snapped the personnel out of their torpor. "I said I want a status report! What happened to us? Tell me where we are."

"Stabilizing, sir," the navigator said.

The stars outside the viewports of the *Firestorm*'s bridge tower spun around like a whirlpool. Pellaeon, already disoriented, found the effect nauseating, but gradually the Star Destroyer regained its firm position.

He clutched the bridge rail for support. Ahead of him the brightest star was a brilliant yellow dot, far away. He had the sinking premonition that this distant star might be the sun of the Yavin system.

"Sir," the navigator said, "I've managed to cross-check our position. We've been thrown far outside the solar system in a matter of seconds."

"Our hyperdrive is also damaged," the helmsman added. "We can effect repairs in a few hours, but we can't make any jumps—especially not in-system—because the navicomputer has been wiped."

Pellaeon gripped the bridge rail, forcing himself not to slump with dismay. "Check the status of all our remaining Star Destroyers," Pellaeon said. "I want full repairs on our hyperdrives as soon as possible. For now, proceed back to the Yavin system at full sublight power."

"But sir, that'll take weeks!" the helmsman said.

Pellaeon looked at him, cold and calm. "In the meantime," he said, "we'll calculate micro jumps—by hand if necessary, even without the navicomputer. We must get back to Yavin 4!''

His crew heard the determination in the vice admiral's voice and snapped to their duties. They tried to regain their composure and bring the Imperial Star Destroyers back to peak performance.

The fleet began to move, lumbering across the impossible gulf of space. He couldn't imagine what Admiral Daala would think when she arrived in the system and found that his entire fleet had vanished. He trembled, already imagining her fury, disheartened by his own incompetence . . . though when Jedi Knights were involved, logical prediction was often irrelevant.

He gazed out the bridge window again, fixating upon the suddenly distant yellow sun of the Yavin system. He kneaded his hands together in anxiety and frustration. His eyes burned with shame.

No doubt the battle would be completely over by the time his fleet finally returned.

CHAPTER 57

The *Knight Hammer*'s fully loaded TIE bomber bay was like a trap waiting to be sprung—and as Callista landed her hijacked, damaged ship among the other deadly bombers, she vowed to trigger the destructive energy just waiting here for her.

All the pilots had been evacuated because of Callista's warning of a leaking engine core, but investigators would come soon. She had to hurry.

Squadrons of unmanned TIE fighters and bombers sat in rows on the gleaming metal deck. The ships had been powered up and ready to launch, but for some reason Daala must have decided to keep them aboard the Super Star Destroyer. Callista guessed that the Admiral had opted to continue the battle from a safe distance rather than unnecessarily risking her bombers. Daala was convinced she would win anyway, and she could just as easily continue the onslaught from orbit.

Just as Callista settled in and the bay doors closed, she heard additional alarms pounding through the *Knight Hammer*—announcements that a new Rebel fleet had arrived, and that the Super Star Destroyer was engaging in space combat. *Good,* she thought. That might delay the Imperials from interfering here for a few more minutes.

Callista's injured bomber sat in a cleared area recently used for repair and maintenance of ships. The damaged bomber had flown well enough: the TIE pilot she'd killed had completed field repairs admirably.

She dropped lightly to the deck, crouching low and scanning around to make sure no one had waited to see her, no "helpful" rescue party or medics—but the bay was empty.

Breathing fast and hard, Callista set to work. She heard the *thrum* of battle echo through the hull of the *Knight Hammer.* She hesitated a moment, telling herself she didn't care—but she had to find out what was going on.

She raced over to a wallscreen and requested a current battle display, surprised to see the *Millennium Falcon* disappearing into Admiral Ackbar's flagship, the *Galactic Voyager.* The stakes were now raised. Ackbar's Calamarian Star Cruiser bore heavy weaponry, but not even the combined New Republic ships could stand against a Super Star Destroyer.

Admiral Daala fired, pummeling Ackbar's shields, and the Star Cruiser backed off. Callista knew she had to hurry, but just before she turned away, she saw another fleet of *Victory*-class Star Destroyers appear out of hyperspace and join the trouncing of Ackbar's fleet. The New Republic rescuers would be cut to ribbons in no time—if Callista didn't move soon.

She code-locked the bay's access door from the outer corridors to ensure her privacy. The protection wouldn't last long if an Imperial slicer tried to break in, but she just needed to hinder any interference.

Callista sprinted back to her damaged TIE bomber and opened the armament reserves, where she assessed the cargo of concussion missiles behind their launcher systems.

Rushing back to the wall, she studied the simple schematic of the *Knight Hammer*. It wasn't very detailed, designed mainly to aid new recruits lost aboard so vast a vessel—but Callista recognized that her greatest hopes had been fulfilled. The TIE bomber bays were far to the rear of the *Knight Hammer,* separated by thick bulkheads from the immense engine and propulsion systems.

Callista fixed her gray eyes on the armored wall at the far end of the bay and pointed the leftover missiles from the TIE bomber directly toward it. She set their timers for automatic launch. It should be enough for a breach. And that would be just the beginning.

Then she raced to the next TIE bomber and opened up its launcher, fiddling with the full rack of concussion missiles. Her breath came fast, her thoughts pounded loud and heavy in her head. *So many explosives, and so little time!* she thought with a smirk.

Long ago, she had attempted a similar thing to stop the Emperor's automated death machine, the *Eye of Palpatine,* from destroying former Jedi colonies. Her spirit had been trapped inside a computer, where she had hung in limbo for decades. Her sacrifice had indeed diverted and delayed the Dreadnaught in its mission, until Luke Skywalker had finished the job and rescued her at the same time.

Luke. She forced the thought away, concentrating on her mission.

Right now Callista was all alone—and she liked it better that way, because then she needed to worry about no one but herself. She didn't have to argue with Luke about the best way to salvage a mission. The risks and the costs were hers alone.

She wished desperately that she had found her Force powers again, that she and Luke could have made a life together as two powerful Jedi. She loved him very much . . . but this was more important right now. All the new Jedi Knights would be killed if Daala's *Knight Hammer* was not stopped. And she would stop it herself.

Callista had a second chance. She had tried to save the children of the Jedi so many years before, and now that the new Jedi were so desperately few, she had to make a terrible choice. A personal choice. But since she had none of her powers anyway, the loss of Callista would not be such a terrible wound to the New Republic.

Would it?

She could strike a great blow against the Empire. Nothing else mattered.

Callista raced from bomber to bomber setting each store of missiles on target, diverting a few to strike the fuel tanks of other bombers in the bay so that the explosion would be perpetuated, a chain reaction, building and building.

The *Knight Hammer* would fall.

With all the charges set, Callista locked the access door behind her and raced along the harshly lit corridor, finding an empty transport tube that shot her along the inner hull, racing away from where the deadly explosions would occur.

The *Knight Hammer* and the *Victory*-class Star Destroyers closed in on Ackbar's flagship. The Calamarian Star Cruiser's defenses were failing, and its destruction was imminent.

Callista prayed that she had set the timers to go off soon enough.

The *Knight Hammer* veered away from the jungle moon and lumbered out into space, pursuing Ackbar's retreating ship toward the gas giant Yavin, but the huge planet offered no safety whatsoever.

Callista knew she had no hope for her own escape. She accepted that. If her plan succeeded, the *Knight Hammer* would be destroyed—and if her attempt failed, she would stay and fight to the death, making another attempt and another, doing everything she could to stop the brutal Imperials.

In either case, she vowed to make her way to the bridge deck of the Super Star Destroyer. At the last, she wanted to face Admiral Daala, look the destructive renegade in her emerald eyes, and strike the admiral down with her own two hands.

Callista gripped her lightsaber as the transport tube shot her kilometer after kilometer along the length of the black warship. She'd just begun rising toward the bridge tower when all the charges blew—

Missile after missile shot into the armored retaining wall behind the *Knight Hammer*'s powerful bank of engines. As the first wave of explosions breached the containment wall, other timers went off and more missiles flew, erupting through the blast craters or streaking sideways to detonate the fuel tanks of other TIE bombers . . . which in turn blew up in an increasing concussion front that doubled and redoubled its destructive power.

Eight kilometers long and heavily armored, the *Knight Hammer* was far too immense to be destroyed by even such a spectacular explosion—but Callista's intent had been to rip out the core of the engines, to hobble the Super Star Destroyer and leave it hanging dead in space.

Lights went black around Callista. The transport tube lurched to a halt, and alarms began shrieking at bone-jarring volume. Callista laughed with the ecstasy of adrenaline, then popped the evacuation hatch. Breathing hard, she hauled herself out into the dark access tunnel.

Callista flicked on her lightsaber, and by the topaz glow of its blade she found an emergency exit port that took her out into the chaotic corridors of the giant ship. In a defensive crouch, Callista flung sweat from her close-cropped blond hair, and with the greatest possible speed she made her way to the bridge decks.

She had an appointment with Daala.

The *Knight Hammer* began to drift, dead in space.

CHAPTER 58

Admiral Daala watched the last of the battle unfold toward its inevitable conclusion, and she stood back and smiled with thin, pale lips.

Seeing themselves hopelessly outgunned, the meager Rebel fleet attempted to escape—but the *Knight Hammer* and the *Victory*-class Star Destroyers flew after it toward the huge orange ball of Yavin, pummeling the Calamarian Star Cruiser's shields. According to her readings, the Rebel defenses had practically been exhausted. It would be only moments until the battlecruiser was crushed between Imperial jaws of steel.

A dark-haired young lieutenant rushed up to her. His face had been scrubbed so clean that a flush of pink still stood out, enhanced by his excitement. His words came in a breathless rush. "Admiral, good news from the sensor station!"

She allowed a smile, reveling in the continued satisfaction. "I'm always willing to accept good news. What is it, Lieutenant?"

The lieutenant beamed. "We've located Vice Admiral Pellaeon's fleet."

She whirled, suddenly focusing her attention. "Where?"

"They're on the edge of the Yavin system, Admiral, making their way here as fast as they can. We've established communication."

"What happened to them?" she said. "Did they suffer engine problems? All at once?"

The lieutenant shook his head. "No, Admiral—it is very strange." He looked away as if embarrassed. "The Jedi Knights physically hurled them out of the system with their sorcery. The vice admiral is unable to increase his speed, and it may be days before they can reach the battle."

Daala clasped her leather-gloved hands in front of her and nodded. "Very well," she said. "By that time we'll be finished here—but it's good to know all those ships weren't destroyed." She forced herself not to show her immense relief at avoiding yet another disastrous failure. It felt so good to be victorious at last!

Daala leaned closer to the bridge window and slapped one fist into her open palm. "So let's redouble our efforts and be celebrating our victory by the time the vice admiral gets here!" She drew a deep breath, swelling with pride and satisfaction. At last, Grand Moff Tarkin would have been pleased with how she had redeemed herself. She had done everything right this time, and the Rebels would pay in blood.

At that moment, the rear portion of the Super Star Destroyer exploded, tearing out all the *Knight Hammer*'s engine systems.

It took seconds for the shockwave to travel through the kilometers of armored metal and sealed bulkheads. The bridge tower shuddered with the blow. Power went out, leaving the command station bathed in red emergency lights. Daala was thrown to the floor.

The *Victory*-class Star Destroyers continued to pursue

the Rebel Star Cruiser. The bolts of their turbolaser fire showered fireworks across the *Knight Hammer*'s bow. For a moment they didn't realize what had happened—and neither did Daala.

"What was that?" she shouted. "Status report. I want power back on—*now*!"

Several members of her bridge crew lay stunned or unconscious from the explosion, and one had been crushed to death under a toppled tactical station. Alarms continued pounding.

The fresh-faced lieutenant hauled himself up to a station that was not his own and valiantly punched up a summary in the bloody glow of emergency lights. His face looked stricken with horror.

"Admiral, there have been numerous massive explosions in the engine compartments! Source—rear TIE bomber bays 14 and 17. The inner engine walls have been breached, and all our propulsion chambers are wrecked. We're on fire. The rearmost third of the *Knight Hammer* has been sealed off by automatic emergency systems. Life support . . . has failed."

He paused, taking a deep breath, but he had not finished his litany. "Outer hull breaches reported in decks 293, 181, and 75. Massive loss of containment. Toxic and radioactive wastes pouring into the habitable decks. Our rear bomber bays are all ruined."

Each phrase seemed like a slap to Daala. "How could this happen?" she demanded.

The lieutenant stared at her, mouth open, eyes glassy. "Unknown, Admiral. It seems impossible."

But Daala knew the only answer—direct sabotage. Such widespread destruction could not have been accidental.

Several of the *Victory*-class Star Destroyers broke off their pursuit of Ackbar's ship. The comm system squawked. *"Knight Hammer, Knight Hammer*—please respond!" She recognized the voice of one of the Victory commanders, though she couldn't place his name in her sudden shock. "Admiral Daala, your ship is in flames. From out here it's—it looks hopeless, Admiral."

She lurched to the communication station. "Where is Colonel Cronus?" she said. "We need him to double his efforts. We may require rescue assistance."

The commander's voice cracked. "Colonel Cronus's flagship was destroyed in the Rebel attack, Admiral. I believe—I'm not certain who is now in command—"

"*I* am in command!" Daala snapped, but then she slumped backward as if the wind had been knocked out of her. Pellaeon wouldn't be here for days. Cronus was dead. The *Knight Hammer* had been severely damaged.

Everything had changed in a matter of minutes.

She whirled, shouting to anyone on the bridge. "How long until repairs? When can we get our engines up and running again?"

One of the engineers gaped at her, appalled. Blood dripped down his cheek from a small cut near his temple. "Admiral, you don't understand! Our engines are *gone*. It will take months to refit. We have no hope of repair. None. Everything is on fire."

"We have no propulsion?" Daala said.

"None whatsoever. We're drifting out of control, and there's nothing we can do about it. Nothing!"

Daala raged, turning from side to side. She held her gloved fists at her hips but could find no outlet for her fury. "We can't navigate? We can't move?" she shouted, and then turned slowly to her viewscreen as the immense gas giant filled their full view, growing larger every second. The *Knight Hammer* drifted along on a tidal wave of momentum, following its last course . . . but it began to turn, tugged by the unbreakable chains of gravity from enormous Yavin.

Her green eyes seemed to fill with steam from within. "Check our course," she whispered. "Tell me I'm wrong."

The navigator stared out the window as if he had seen

and understood the same horrible fate that Daala imagined.

She shouted to snap him out of his daze. "Check our course, I said!"

He jerked, startled, then scrambled to call up the screens he needed. "Computers are down, Admiral. Let me double-check." He punched up a different suite of sensors, and his face sagged. "We're heading directly into the planet, Admiral—a straight nosedive. Unless we get full power back soon, there is no way in the universe we can save this ship."

Daala glared at the fleeing Rebel Star Cruiser, wanting nothing more than to see it explode so that she might be vindicated that much at least.

As five of the Victory Star Destroyers continued to pursue the Rebels, firing recklessly, the rest of the New Republic fleet suddenly appeared in front of them. Scores and scores of reinforcements, Assault Frigates, Corellian Corvettes, five more Mon Calamari Star Cruisers, Loronar Strike Cruisers, *Carrack*-class gunships—an overwhelming force.

Daala wanted to cry out in outrage and despair—but she bottled it within herself and the anger flowed like lava, compressing into a diamond of desperate resolve within her. She thought fast. She had to be realistic, not allow her fury and outrage to stain her rational thought like last time. She had to think of the future of the Empire, not her personal vendetta.

Revenge would come later. There would be time.

She still had Pellaeon's fleet. She still had numerous *Victory*-class ships. More and more great battlecruisers were being built in the Imperial shipyards. This was merely a setback. She had to rethink her strategy again— or perhaps her disgrace was so great that she should never attempt to guide the Imperial fleet again.

Right now, though, the *Knight Hammer* was doomed, and there was nothing she could do. Nothing. She felt stripped of options. Her only chance was to escape and reach Pellaeon's fleet.

Because the *Knight Hammer* was exceedingly automated, it carried a relatively small crew. They could all fit in the hundreds and hundreds of evacuation pods if they *moved*. Her crew of loyal soldiers could escape to fight again.

She sounded her own alarm. Her voice bellowed through the intercom systems. "This is Admiral Daala. I am ordering an immediate evacuation of this Super Star Destroyer. All personnel, abandon ship! Reach the nearest evacuation pods and launch into space. There are *Victory*-class Star Destroyers here to pick us up, and Vice Admiral Pellaeon's fleet is on its way. But this ship is going down."

She switched off and stood looking at the red-washed bridge deck. Overhead white lights flickered but failed to come on. Her bridge crew gazed at her, astonished that she had ordered a retreat.

"Go!" she shouted at them. "That's an order. Get to the escape pods."

"But, Admiral, what about you?" said the fresh-faced young lieutenant. Tears streamed from his eyes. Smoke hovered in the air, but Daala could tell that he wept not because of chemical irritation but out of despair for the lost glory of the Empire.

"I gave you orders to evacuate, Lieutenant," she said, and turned her back to him, refusing to move.

The crew gave one last look to their commander and then fled down the corridors to the evacuation pods.

Daala stood alone at her command station as the universe crumbled around her. She stared out the viewport wordlessly, her face white, her lips pressed together.

The *Knight Hammer* hurtled toward its doom, its rear sections molten and spewing radioactive fire. But she remained unmoving, like a captain dutifully about to go down with her ship.

CHAPTER 59

But Daala had no intention of letting it end there.

When the bridge personnel evacuated, leaving her to stand alone at the helm as the ship crashed toward its inevitable destruction, she knew the image would burn itself in the minds of her crew. She could rest assured her legend would live on if any of them survived in the escape pods.

However, Daala herself intended to survive, though it never hurt to make contingency plans. She had more battles to fight for the Empire, more ways to strike against the Rebel Alliance.

This time she had caused the enemy pain at least. Her victory was not total—but neither was her defeat.

Daala went to the wall by the command station, where she gained access to her spacious ready-room and its private compartments that held escape pods keyed to command-level personnel only. Before, she had thought the huge room with its amenities and backup systems to be extravagant, but now she blessed the designer who had thought of every contingency.

Another wave of explosions thrummed through the

hull of the *Knight Hammer,* throwing the ship from side to side. With one last glance out the bridge windowports, Daala saw the giant gravity well of Yavin looming larger by the minute, hungry and waiting to devour her ship. She had to make good her escape—now. The Super Star Destroyer would be crushed within moments, its outer hull already burning as it screamed into the upper atmosphere.

She stumbled as another explosion rocked the black ship. The lights flickered in her ready-room, then the red emergency glow came on again. She searched for the rear alcove that contained the escape pods—and stopped when she saw a lone person waiting for her.

A woman.

A Jedi Knight holding up a sun-yellow lightsaber blade. Its topaz beam crackled in the red-washed dimness of the doomed ship.

"I've been waiting for you, Admiral Daala," Callista said.

She stood face-to-face with her Imperial nemesis.

Callista drew a quick breath, giddy with anticipation and exhilaration. Gratifyingly loud explosions continued to ripple through the Super Star Destroyer, chain reactions building up as the destruction tunneled deeper into the *Knight Hammer.*

Daala, the iron-willed and unpredictable Imperial admiral about whom Callista had heard so many legends, now looked harried and cadaverous in the emergency lighting of the command ready-room.

Daala froze upon seeing her, her face contorted in fury. "I don't believe this. Jedi vermin, everywhere I turn!" She spat out the words and stalked forward. "You can't stop me."

Callista stood her ground in front of the access hatches to the escape pods. "I only need to delay you, Daala," she said. "That'll be enough." Her lightsaber thrummed in her hand. "And I have the means to do that."

Callista felt the deep-seated anger boiling through her. Admiral Daala was the target for her rage—and this close to the climactic end of her life, just as had happened on the *Eye of Palpatine,* Callista found herself filled with a sudden freedom. She wanted to touch the Force again one more time, and it didn't matter now whether she allowed herself to be tainted by the dark side, if that was the only way—and it was. The ship would be engulfed in moments anyway.

All that mattered was that she stopped Daala from escaping and wreaking more destruction upon the New Republic. If she confronted the shadowy temptation, Callista could use the Force again. The dark side of it. The easy abilities. The strength that grew stronger because of itself, not because of any innate qualities its wielder possessed.

The possibilities danced before her gray eyes like smoke, tantalizing her, luring Callista to reach out and grasp them, though she might be unable to let go again—

Seeing her instant of hesitation, Admiral Daala whipped out a blaster pistol from its holster at her hip. With a flick of her finger, she switched the power to a KILL setting and blasted at Callista.

Callista couldn't avoid the deadly bolt, but she could use the Force to snatch heightened abilities. With no choice, she let herself go in a fraction of a second.

Using the lightsaber as an extension of herself, Callista struck defensively. Her Jedi weapon knew where it was going, following the inexorable path of the Force so that the topaz blade struck each blaster bolt as Daala fired again and again. The deadly fire reflected from her lightsaber and splashed blackened stains against the ready-room's metal walls.

Daala shot four times, but in each instance, Callista let the Force flow through her, allowing the dark side to guide her actions. Flaring with anger, she struck right and left, deflecting Daala's beams.

"The Force is more powerful than you are, Daala," Callista said through gritted teeth. She felt the frightening strength surging within her, as her anger fed upon itself, growing more and more powerful. She could feel the Force again! She tried to back away from the dark side, concentrated on throttling back her efforts, to free herself before its grip became too strong.

Daala ceased firing—but only for an instant as she switched the setting to STUN. Before Callista could react, Daala shot again. This time, the beam was not a discrete bolt of power, but outspreading arcs of tenuous blue energy.

She raised the lightsaber to deflect the stun blast, but the paralyzing energy rippled around her from all sides and hammered Callista to the floor. Her lightsaber short-circuited, flashed out—and Callista crumpled into blackness. . . .

Daala stood over the fallen Jedi woman. With her polished black boot she kicked the dead lightsaber away.

Outside, the atmosphere of Yavin scraped against the hull of the *Knight Hammer* with a wailing of lost spirits. The winds tore at the helpless ship as it careened into the crushing depths of the gravity well.

Daala glared at the stunned Jedi woman, annoyed that even the brief battle might have been too much of a delay, that she could no longer escape. "I told you you couldn't stop me," she said, and stepped over Callista's body on her way to the escape pod.

CHAPTER 60

The jungle battles continued to rage, but the Imperial ground assault vehicles began to lose their momentum as the Jedi Knights mounted a brutal guerrilla defense, destroying scout walkers, Juggernauts, and Flying Fortresses. The remaining TIE fighters and bombers circled overhead, but most had already been knocked out of the sky by Force-hurled projectiles.

Luke Skywalker fought hard, the lightsaber throbbing in his hand—but his attention was focused on his desperate mental search for Callista.

Overhead, through the tattered jungle canopy, he could see the swollen planet Yavin filling much of the sky. The black sliver of the *Knight Hammer* stood out plainly, creating a triangular eclipse against the gas giant.

Brilliant streams of turbolaser fire danced across space, a flickering light show . . . and Luke remembered a time long, long ago when he had been no more than the adopted nephew of a moisture farmer, a wide-eyed enthusiastic kid who had stared up into the bleached skies of Tatooine to see the distant space battle above his world. He had never dreamed that Darth Vader's capture of Princess Leia's ship would have so changed his life—and the future of the galaxy.

Back then, Luke had heard only rumors of the Jedi Knights, had no idea who his father was, and couldn't imagine the possibilities of the Force—and now Callista was just as helpless as he had been then . . . but she *knew* what she no longer had.

Luke charged through the underbrush shouting her name over and over. Because she had been walled away from the Force, he could not sense her, had no idea where she was.

"Callista!" he called again, drawing fire from a hidden scout walker in the jungle. Laser cannon blasts erupted on either side of him, but he dodged out of the way, still partially distracted by his search. With a rapid sweep of his lightsaber, he felled a tall Massassi tree and used the Force to nudge it, toppling it on to the AT-ST in a shower of sparks and flames.

He had to find Callista. His Jedi Knights had fought remarkably well, a small band of Force-talented soldiers battling independently and wreaking great destruction on far-superior Imperial technology.

Not long ago Luke Skywalker had been one of the only remaining Jedi Knights—but now he had created the core of a new order of valiant fighters loyal to the New Republic, trained in using the Force. The Jedi Knights would rise again—of that, he had no doubt.

As he thought of Tionne, Streen, Kirana Ti, Kyp Durron, Kam Solusar, Cilghal, and all the others he had worked with, he pondered again Callista's stated objections: that she could not be with him because she had not yet regained her Jedi talent . . . that if they married and had children, she was afraid that their sons and daughters would not be able to use the Force, would be isolated from it as she was.

But what did it matter? He loved Callista, whether or not she had Jedi powers. He had already created a fine

league of defenders for the New Republic, and he would
continue to train Jedi on Yavin 4. It didn't matter if their
children might not have the full potential for the Force. It
didn't matter if Callista could use her Jedi abilities. It
didn't matter!

He wanted her, and no one else. He had to make that
clear to her when he finally found her. He had already
brought back the Jedi Knights. Luke had searched all of
his life for Callista, and he could not allow himself to lose
her, not now.

He made his way back to the Great Temple to the
clearing where some of his other Jedi trainees had gathered to form a combined force against the rag-tag leftovers
from Vice Admiral Pellaeon's ground assault troops. His
heart sank when he failed to see Callista among them.

Where had she gone? Why had he let her out of his
sight? He had so much to tell her. So much to promise her.

But she wasn't there.

"Callista," he whispered longingly, knowing she
could not hear him. But then he looked up into the misty
white sky, and suddenly he *felt* her through the Force. It
was like a door opening to let in a ray of light.

His gaze snapped over and fixed on the black silhouette of the doomed Super Star Destroyer. It was in flames,
plunging into the gas giant. A few straggler lifepods
sprayed out in all directions as the crew evacuated—and
Luke knew with a clawing dread that Callista somehow
had gone up there.

He groaned to himself, recognizing exactly what she
must have done. Feeling helpless without Jedi powers, Callista had taken the problem head-on, charging in with focused attention and a rigid adherence to the lone solution
she thought would work. She would consider no other possibilities, only her single-minded way.

"No, Callista," he said. "No!" He got only a flicker
of sensation from her, a dark glare through the Force that
felt like a shudder down his spine. She had opened herself
up to her powers again, but she was using only the dark

side. Callista had been tempted and let herself slip, but at least now Luke could sense her through the tangled skein of the Force.

And then the flicker went away, the door had slammed shut again, as if Callista had lost her powers—or as if something had happened to her.

With stinging eyes he stared up at the dwindling, sharp-edged silhouette of the *Knight Hammer,* trying to focus his Jedi senses to enhance his sight. But he could detect nothing from her anymore. The door into the Force had slammed shut and locked, blocking him away from any ability to detect her—but he knew she was up there on that dying ship.

Luke saw the Super Star Destroyer plunge like a knife blade into the atmosphere of Yavin, its black-armored hull glowing cherry red with friction against the atmospheric gases and the buffeting storms.

With a final series of explosions that ignited scarlet and yellow glows in the upper clouds, the *Knight Hammer* vanished into Yavin, swallowed up forever—and taking Callista with it.

CHAPTER 61

The *Yavaris* and the Assault Frigate *Dodonna* swerved aside as they escaped the treacherous core of the Hoth Asteroid Field, leaving the wreckage of the Darksaber behind.

"Saves us the trouble," Wedge said, shaking his head. "But Madine is gone. I wish we had some way of knowing what really happened there."

Qwi stared behind her with wide indigo eyes. "At least the weapon was destroyed without its ever firing a shot," she said, then heaved a long sigh. "I wish people would stop trying to build bigger and better means of destruction."

"I couldn't agree more," Wedge said, hugging her. "I wouldn't mind in the least if I found myself looking for a new line of work."

"General Antilles," the sensor chief said, "we're picking up one small craft registering a single life form aboard. It's too small to be much of a ship."

Wedge frowned. He felt a surge of hope for just a

moment—perhaps Madine had escaped!—but he knew that couldn't be true, because the life monitor wouldn't lie.

"Maybe it's somebody who jumped ship," he said. "Activate tractor beams. Grab it and bring it aboard."

He left the *Yavaris*'s command station, gesturing to Qwi. "Let's go meet it." He flicked on the intercom. "I want a full security detail to meet me in the forward docking bay. Bring your weapons. We might have some trouble."

Wedge and Qwi waited inside the bay. Around them a squad of armed guards held blaster rifles at their shoulders, fidgeting nervously and still keyed up from the days-long alert status they had just experienced, as well as the week of space battle simulation in the Nal Hutta system.

Wedge watched through the transparent atmosphere field as a bright dot came closer, a metallic hull of a spherical ship reflecting light from the distant sun. He realized with a strange shift in perspective how tiny this craft was, that it already hovered just outside the containment field. A round construction pod no more than four meters in diameter, a single-person inspection scooter.

"Where was he expecting to go in that?" Wedge said.

"Sometimes you take advantage of the only thing you have," Qwi said. "In desperation you have few choices."

Wedge looked at her, surprised at the insight. Qwi had always struck him as sweet but naive. However, she had learned much since her rescue from Maw Installation.

The battered inspection scooter drifted in and thumped to the deck plates, guided by the grip of the *Yavaris*'s tractor beams. The New Republic guards pointed their rifles, standing ready.

The hatch hissed as it unsealed, then popped open. Wedge tensed, then blinked in surprise as a paunchy old man hauled himself out. His face was grizzled, his white hair stood up in unruly shocks. He took deep breaths, scowling in disgust at the interior of his scooter.

The guards rushed forward to take the man prisoner. He didn't resist, looking about him in confusion.

"Bevel Lemelisk!" Qwi said, her eyes filled with anger and surprise.

"You know this man?" Wedge asked.

Qwi nodded. Her glittery hair tinkled around her. "He helped me design the Death Star," she said. "Grand Moff Tarkin removed him from Maw Installation to be the chief engineer on the project in the Horuz system. I thought I saw him on Nar Shaddaa, remember?"

He raised his eyebrows. "Maybe you weren't seeing things after all."

The guards ushered Lemelisk forward. The old engineer looked at Wedge, then blinked his rheumy eyes in amazement at seeing Qwi. "Ah, Qwi Xux—fancy meeting you here! Are you working for these people now? What a coincidence!"

Her pale blue skin flushed darker. Wedge had never seen Qwi exhibit such anger and agitation before. He realized that the sight of her former engineering partner must be gurgling up old memories that had been sealed away during her forced amnesia.

"You deceived me, Lemelisk," she said, her voice high and sharp. "You lied to me! While we were working in Maw Installation you never told me our weapons would be used for such death and destruction. You claimed they all had legitimate, peaceful purposes."

Lemelisk blinked at her again and frowned in disbelief. "Qwi, you were always so brilliant—but in other ways you managed to be incredibly dense."

She looked as if she had just been slapped, and Wedge grew angry. "You were aboard that Hutt superweapon?"

"Aboard the Darksaber?" Lemelisk said. "I helped them build the thing! I designed it. Oh, did they get away after all?" he asked, raising his eyebrows.

"No, the weapon was destroyed in the asteroid field."

"Ah," Lemelisk said. "A pity. Not that I'm surprised, though. I doubted it would work."

"What about our New Republic commando team?" Wedge asked. "Did you see them?"

Lemelisk nodded. "Ah yes, the Rebel saboteur. We killed one of their team when they tried to sabotage our engine systems. The other—I believe his name was Madine—was brought before Lord Durga and summarily executed. He died bravely, of course."

Wedge felt anger simmering around him, and he gestured to the armed guards. "Take the prisoner and lock him up. We'll bring him back to Coruscant and put him on trial." He lowered his voice in a threat. "But I have no doubt we've got sufficient evidence to order your execution as a threat to galactic peace."

"Ah, well." Surprisingly, Bevel Lemelisk reacted with resignation instead of fear. "If you're going to execute me," he said, "just make sure you do it right this time."

CHAPTER 62

Seventeen Imperial Star Destroyers hovered near the edge of the Yavin system, ordered not to go deeper inside or to engage the overwhelming Rebel forces that had converged to defend the Jedi academy, battleship after battleship. All had been confusion for more than a day, but the Rebels seemed to be reestablishing order.

Shortly after the destruction of the *Knight Hammer,* most of the *Victory*-class Star Destroyers had already fled back to their rendezvous in the Core Systems. Pellaeon's fleet waited, a distant threat, but able to do nothing.

"We've detected one more escape pod, Vice Admiral," the sensor chief said.

Pellaeon tapped his fingers on the command railing and ran his right hand over his mustache. "Very well, lock on the coordinates," he said. "Let's pick it up. I believe most of them have been accounted for now."

"This one's slightly different, sir," the sensor chief said. "It's broadcasting a command frequency. It's been out there for quite a while."

Pellaeon felt his heart leap. "A command pod? Haul it into our forward bay. I'm going down to meet it."

He strode briskly to the turbolift and rode the platform down, feeling very old. The Imperial fleet was in a shambles. The battle on Yavin 4 had been a complete rout. The *Knight Hammer* had gone down in flames: the most powerful warship in Daala's newly unified fleet, as well as a symbol of Imperial power—trounced by Rebel blind luck and reckless determination.

He stepped into the forward landing bay just as the space-scarred escape pod penetrated the atmosphere-containment fields. He felt a surge of hope upon seeing it, another module launched from the *Knight Hammer,* this one with heavier armor and no external identification. A command-level pod, obviously. Frost began to dust the outer layers.

Pellaeon didn't know what to think, what the Empire should do next, how they could salvage this utter defeat. The loss of morale would be devastating. He stepped forward. Stormtrooper guards along the walls stood with weapons ready, just in case the pod happened to be booby-trapped.

Before Pellaeon could open the hatch, though, it popped open of its own accord, released by an internal access panel. As soon as the stale atmosphere hissed out to mix with the oily, metallic smell of the *Firestorm*'s enclosed bay, Admiral Daala climbed out.

Soot smeared her face. Her olive-gray uniform, usually neat, was torn and stained. Blood smeared one cheek, but Pellaeon couldn't tell if it was Daala's own blood or someone else's.

Pellaeon's knees grew watery with relief upon seeing her. Daala would know what to do. She could give orders to straighten out the Imperial fleet.

She stood up slowly, locked her gaze with his, and brushed off her uniform. "Vice Admiral Pellaeon," she said in a dull, lifeless voice, as if forcing the words through her teeth. "In light of this disaster, I—I hereby resign my rank . . . and hand over command of all Imperial forces to you.''

The instant of silence sounded like an avalanche. She continued, ''I will be happy to follow your orders and assist with rebuilding the Empire in any way possible, but I feel that I am no longer capable of commanding so many worthy soldiers. They cannot be asked to lay their lives on the line, to swear allegiance to someone who has been beaten so many times.''

With a precise motion, she coldly and stiffly saluted him, never letting her emerald gaze waver. The stormtroopers stood at attention, drinking in the details.

''But Admiral, I can't accept this. We need you to rebuild—''

''Nonsense, Vice Admiral,'' she said. ''You must be strong. Follow your own convictions. We need an opportunity to recover from such a debacle. We need your strength.''

Daala stood next to him looking long and hard into his eyes. ''You are in command of the Empire now, Pellaeon,'' she said.

She waited rigidly at attention, motionless, until Pellaeon gradually returned her salute.

CORUSCANT

CHAPTER 63

The skies of Coruscant glowed with brilliant signal fires. X-wing fighters dumped clouds of plasma in a diffuse banner high in the twilight. The ionized gases shone with bright colors, spreading out and serving a dual purpose: to celebrate another victory against the Empire, and also to honor those who had died in the recent battles.

For Crix Madine's memorial service, Luke Skywalker waited beside Leia and Han Solo—but his mind was far, far away. He felt empty and cold. The group waited atop the Imperial palace next to a dazzling signal beacon that stabbed up into the atmosphere. The sharp, thin air whipped around them, but he didn't feel it.

Overhead, the X-wing fighters continued to soar, splashing their spectacle across the darkening sky.

See-Threepio, newly polished and gleaming gold under the bright lights, stood proudly beside his counterpart Artoo-Detoo. "Oh Artoo," he said. "It's been the greatest pleasure serving with you again. I wish you didn't have to return to Yavin 4 and assist Master Luke at his Jedi academy."

Artoo whistled and twittered, but Threepio straightened in sudden alarm. "What—*me*? Accompany you to that dense and treacherous jungle? I think not! Here on Coruscant I have many important duties and . . . besides it's so much more civilized."

Artoo gave a low blat of scorn. Chewbacca, standing beside them with his fur neatly combed and washed, groaned something at Threepio. Indignant, the gold protocol droid said, "That will be enough from you, Chewbacca. For your information, I am doing a fine job assisting Mistress Leia in her duties as Chief of State."

Leia looked up, her dark eyes sparkling with unshed tears. An honor guard stood around the upper platform of the immense Imperial palace that looked out upon the towering skylines of the planetwide city. Han remained next to her, troubled but trying to hide it. He placed a comforting arm around Leia's shoulders.

Young Anakin and the twins, Jacen and Jaina, were dressed in stiff and uncomfortable finery, but they behaved themselves, seeming to sense the somber occasion.

As Luke looked at Leia's family, it struck home like a dull knife blade in the heart. He wasn't jealous of Leia and her marriage—he and his sister had very different lives—but he had longed for a similar future with Callista. Only Callista . . .

As two powerful Jedi Knights, they should have been a perfect pair. They could have been deliriously happy, precisely matched—and they would have been, if circumstances hadn't repeatedly conspired against them. Luke's face remained stony, a tired mask that hid his emotions . . . but his inner pain at the loss of Callista was so strong even Leia could sense it. She flinched, looking at him with concern—but she had her own overwhelming duties as Chief of State now. Luke nodded briefly to reassure her.

He felt as if he had been continually denied a facet of his humanity. Had becoming a Jedi forced an unknown choice upon him, that he would forever be blocked from the normal joys and loves other humans encountered? He hadn't realized the cost would be so high.

As Leia stepped to the makeshift podium, the New Republic honor guard snapped to attention, eyes locked forward. Luke glanced at the heavily decorated heroes of the recent Imperial onslaught. His old friend Wedge Antilles stood with new medals pinned to his chest, and beside him the ethereal scientist Qwi Xux blinked her indigo eyes, as if once again amazed to be the center of attention. Admiral Ackbar wore his bright white uniform, riding high as commander of the New Republic fleet.

The X-wings overhead finished their run and streaked off to battle stations in orbit. The glowing displays in the air faded out, sparkling with bright points of fire that gradually dimmed.

Leia began to speak, and dozens of image-recording devices, newsdroids, and Galactic Information Service representatives transmitted her speech to all the worlds in the New Republic.

"We are here to celebrate another victory," Leia said, "and to acknowledge its cost. Once again the Empire has attempted to overthrow the rightful government of the galaxy, and once again they have failed. We will always defeat them, because we have the light on our side."

She looked over at Luke who stared stonily ahead. "This victory has not been without pain, however. Many brave fighters on several wrecked ships have died in their service to the New Republic.

"Two Jedi Knights have fallen, as well. Dorsk 81 sacrificed himself in order to drive back a fleet of Imperial Star Destroyers. His action alone saved the lives of the other Jedi Knights on Yavin 4, who continued to fight until Admiral Ackbar and his reinforcements could arrive.

"Perhaps it is fortunate that Dorsk 81 did not live long enough to learn that his homeworld Khomm was one of the first targets in Admiral Daala's renewed attack. That planet has been devastated, and even now the New Republic is sending aid and reparations in honor of the great sacrifice their kinsman made.

"We also acknowledge the loss of Callista, the Jedi Knight who, though she had lost her powers, still managed to bring about the destruction of the Super Star Destroyer, sending it into the planet Yavin, where we believe she and our nemesis Admiral Daala both perished." Leia paused a moment in somber recollection.

"On another front," she said, turning toward Wedge, "we are happy to report that the Hutts have been prevented from obtaining their own version of the Death Star superlaser, which they would have used to cause untold havoc upon peaceful systems. General Antilles successfully led the attack that scuttled the Darksaber weapon.

"However, this mission, too, has cost us dearly." Leia's voice dropped. "Because he kept a low profile, General Crix Madine was not well known to many of you. He was our Supreme Allied Commander for Intelligence. By working behind the scenes, he claimed more victories than most of us can imagine: accomplishing goals that were not politically possible to pursue in the open. Madine and his crew of commandos sought out the Hutts' hidden weapon and led General Antilles to its site, though Madine's efforts cost him his own life and the lives of his team."

She paused and took a deep breath, shuddering. Luke looked over at her, able to feel the weight of responsibility crashing around his sister. But Leia was strong, and she held up. When she spoke, it seemed as if she were talking to every citizen individually and specifically.

"The New Republic is safe once again, thanks to the selfless efforts of our defenders. We must all continue to add our strength." She swallowed. "And may the Force be with you."

*   *   *

Luke returned to Yavin 4, intending to throw himself entirely into his duties as a Jedi Master—instructing trainees and bringing forth more defenders of the New Republic.

That was his main task now, the remaining purpose of his life.

Out of nostalgia, he and Artoo returned to the jungle moon in a decommissioned X-wing fighter, the type of ship Luke had flown long ago during his initial battles for the Rebel Alliance. When he landed in front of the Great Temple, he saw with a glimmer of warmth in his heart that his Jedi students were busily at work repairing the damage done to the ancient stone structure from the Imperial attack.

Luke clambered out of his X-wing and then used the Force to yank Artoo out of the navigational socket and lower him gently onto the landing grid. The astromech droid had been used as a test object so many times by the Jedi trainees, he was accustomed to being jostled about by invisible hands.

Kyp Durron hurried over to Luke, his dark eyes shadowed from lack of sleep. "Welcome back, Master Skywalker. We knew you'd come soon."

Luke nodded. "I've got to help pick up the pieces here. The search for Jedi Knights continues, no matter what else happens around us."

Kyp nodded soberly. "We made a fine grave for Dorsk 81 out in the jungle," he said uncertainly. "I originally thought we should take him back to Khomm to be buried—"

Luke interrupted, shaking his head, "They have enough of their own dead."

Kyp agreed. "Yes—and I knew him well enough to understand how he felt. Dorsk 81 was a Jedi Knight. He would rather rest here in the place of the Jedi, than be sent back to the homeworld he spent so much time trying to escape. He never fit in there."

Luke looked up into the baleful orange eye of Yavin that filled much of the mist-covered sky. Its storm systems seemed so peaceful, so soft. And yet he knew that the gravity of this giant world had swallowed Callista and Daala and the *Knight Hammer* whole. A shiver ran down his spine, and he hoped for a moment he would hear Callista's voice, see a vision of her face across the planet's surface, a message she sent from beyond.

But it was only his imagination, and no words from Callista were forthcoming.

Tionne came up, her mother-of-pearl eyes shining. She tossed her silvery hair. "The supply ship came while you were gone, Master Skywalker," she said. "Everything is running smoothly again, and we're all working together—but we would achieve better progress under your direction."

Luke forced a smile and looked at the Jedi scholar and loremaster. "You do a fine job yourself, Tionne."

"Oh, I almost forgot," she said, evading the compliment. "The supply shuttle brought a sealed message for you. We put it in your quarters."

Luke frowned. "Who is it from?" he said, expecting more trouble.

Tionne shook her head. "We didn't play it. It's a private message."

"All right," Luke said. "Come on, Artoo. Let's get inside." He gestured in greeting to the other Jedi Knights who continued their training, putting test exercises to work completing reparations to the stone edifice of the temple.

Inside the cool, shadowy corridors of the Massassi pyramid, Luke found the way to his quarters as Artoo rolled along behind him, making occasional whistles and hoots to show his pleasure at being home again.

Luke found a sealed message cylinder on his sleeping pallet. He rolled it on his palm and tried to guess who it might be from, but he could think of no one. He frowned suspiciously, not sure he wanted to know . . . perhaps it was someone expressing unwanted sympathy—and that would only make his loss hurt deeper.

He shucked out of his comfortable flightsuit and

wrapped himself in one of his Jedi robes, feeling the familiarity and the associative power of the Force. Then finally, in his guise of Jedi Master again, he opened the message cylinder, pulled out the data shaft, and inserted the components together so that they played. An image formed in front of him, and Luke gasped.

"Callista!"

Her face looked off into the distance, not seeing him. He couldn't tell how long ago this had been recorded. She seemed weak and haggard, but with a new kind of inner strength.

"Hello, Luke. The first thing you need to know, I suppose, is that I'm not dead. Sorry if I frightened you. There was no way for me to get back. I barely got out of the Super Star Destroyer in one of the last escape pods before the entire ship crashed into Yavin."

She paused, as if contemplating her words, then continued, "After I got away, I drifted. Daala's command-level escape pods had extra propulsion systems. But once I was out of danger, once I escaped, I realized that I could not come back to you—not yet. I'm sorry, Luke.

"The Jedi powers are closer to me now, but they are not yet within my grasp. The wall of the dark side blocks me from them. I'm afraid I'll be tempted again if I work too closely with you, because when I'm with you, Luke, I want *so much* to have my powers back that I'm willing to do anything . . . almost anything. I can't risk that."

"No, Callista," he whispered to her image. "Please."

"I have to go on my own odyssey," she said. "I'm confident that someday I will rediscover my powers. That way I can come back to you on my own terms. I need time, Luke. Just some time. I promise I'll be back—if ever I can prove myself worthy of the great Jedi Master I love."

She swallowed. Her image moved away as if she meant to switch off the recorder, but then she turned back. Her gray eyes were wide and bright and strong. "We will be together in time, Luke." She took a long breath. "And there is a lot of time in the universe."

Her image winked off, and he reached quickly, his fingers brushing the air as if to capture just one more second with her—but Callista was gone.

His heart swelled with inner turmoil, a huge elation that she was not dead after all. Callista remained alive, *alive!*—but he had still lost her, for now. . . .

He stepped outside the Great Temple in the waning afternoon of Yavin 4. The other Jedi Knights moved around him, busy at their activities. He gazed up at the huge orange planet and reached across space with his thoughts, telling Callista of his love and of his hope that her search would someday be successful.

"There is a lot of time in the universe," he echoed, "and we'll be together in time, you and I, Callista."

The new Jedi Knights continued their work, linked together in the Force, and Luke Skywalker went to join them.

ABOUT THE AUTHOR

KEVIN J. ANDERSON's Jedi Academy trilogy—*Jedi Search, Dark Apprentice,* and *Champions of the Force*—spent twenty-two weeks on the *New York Times* bestseller list. He is the author of more than a dozen other novels, including the Nebula Award nominee *Assemblers of Infinity* (written with Doug Beason). His other *Star Wars* projects include three anthologies of short stories and *The Illustrated* Star Wars *Universe,* with artist Ralph McQuarrie. He lives in Northern California.

The World of
STAR WARS Novels

In May 1991, *Star Wars* caused a sensation in the publishing industry with the Bantam release of Timothy Zahn's novel *Heir to the Empire*. For the first time, Lucasfilm Ltd. had authorized new novels that *continued* the famous story told in George Lucas's three block-buster motion pictures: *Star Wars*, *The Empire Strikes Back*, and *Return of the Jedi*. Reader reaction was immediate and tumultuous: *Heir* reached No. 1 on the *New York Times* bestseller list and demonstrated that *Star Wars* lovers were eager for exciting new stories set in this universe, written by leading science fiction authors who shared their passion. Since then, each Bantam *Star Wars* novel has been an instant national bestseller.

Lucasfilm and Bantam decided that future novels in the series would be interconnected: that is, events in one novel would have consequences in the others. You might say that each Bantam *Star Wars* novel, enjoyable on its own, is also part of a much larger tale.

Here is a special look at Bantam's *Star Wars* books, along with excerpts from the more recent novels. Each one is available now wherever Bantam Books are sold.

SHADOWS OF THE EMPIRE
by Steve Perry
**Setting: Between *The Empire Strikes Back*
and *Return of the Jedi***

Here is a very special STAR WARS story dealing with Black Sun, a galaxy-spanning criminal organization that is masterminded by one of the most interesting villains in the STAR WARS universe: Xizor, dark prince of the Falleen. Xizor's chief rival for the favor of Emperor Palpatine is none other than Darth Vader himself—alive and well, and a major character in this story, since it is set during the events of the STAR WARS film trilogy.

In the opening prologue, we revisit a familiar scene from The Empire Strikes Back, and are introduced to our marvelous new bad guy:

He looks like a walking corpse, Xizor thought. *Like a mummified body dead a thousand years. Amazing he is still alive, much less the most powerful man in the galaxy. He isn't even that old; it is more as if something is slowly eating him.*

Xizor stood four meters away from the Emperor, watching as the man who had long ago been Senator Palpatine moved to stand in the holocam field. He imagined he could smell the decay in the Emperor's worn body. Likely that was just some trick of the recycled air, run through dozens of filters to ensure that there was no chance of any poison gas being introduced into it. Filtered the life out of it, perhaps, giving it that dead smell.

The viewer on the other end of the holo-link would see a close-up of the Emperor's head and shoulders, of an age-ravaged face shrouded in the cowl of his dark zeyd-cloth robe. The man on the other end of the transmission, light-years away, would not see Xizor, though Xizor would be able to see him. It was a measure of the Emperor's trust that Xizor was allowed to be here while the conversation took place.

The man on the other end of the transmission—if he could still be called that—

The air swirled inside the Imperial chamber in front of the Emperor, coalesced, and blossomed into the image of a figure down on one knee. A caped humanoid biped dressed in jet black, face hidden under a full helmet and breathing mask:

Darth Vader.

Vader spoke: ''What is thy bidding, my master?''

If Xizor could have hurled a power bolt through time and space to strike Vader dead, he would have done it without blinking. Wishful thinking: Vader was too powerful to attack directly.

''There is a great disturbance in the Force,'' the Emperor said.

''I have felt it,'' Vader said.

''We have a new enemy. Luke Skywalker.''

Skywalker? That had been Vader's name, a long time ago. Who was this person with the same name, someone so powerful as to be worth a conversation between the Emperor and his most loathsome creation? More importantly, why had Xizor's agents not uncovered this before now? Xizor's ire was instant—but cold. No sign of his surprise or anger would show on his imperturbable features. The Falleen did not allow their emotions to burst forth as did many of the inferior species; no, the Falleen ancestry was not fur but scales, not mammalian but reptilian. Not wild but coolly calculating. Such was much better. Much safer.

''Yes, my master,'' Vader continued.

''He could destroy us,'' the Emperor said.

Xizor's attention was riveted upon the Emperor and the holographic image of Vader kneeling on the deck of a ship far away. Here was interesting news indeed. Something the Emperor perceived as a danger to himself? Something the Emperor feared?

"He's just a boy," Vader said. "Obi-Wan can no longer help him."

Obi-Wan. That name Xizor knew. He was among the last of the Jedi Knights, a general. But he'd been dead for decades, hadn't he?

Apparently Xizor's information was wrong if Obi-Wan had been helping someone who was still a boy. His agents were going to be sorry.

Even as Xizor took in the distant image of Vader and the nearness of the Emperor, even as he was aware of the luxury of the Emperor's private and protected chamber at the core of the giant pyramidal palace, he was also able to make a mental note to himself: Somebody's head would roll for the failure to make him aware of all this. Knowledge was power; lack of knowledge was weakness. This was something he could not permit.

The Emperor continued. "The Force is strong with him. The son of Skywalker must not become a Jedi."

Son of Skywalker?

Vader's son! Amazing!

"If he could be turned he would become a powerful ally," Vader said.

There was something in Vader's voice when he said this, something Xizor could not quite put his finger on. Longing? Worry? Hope?

"Yes . . . yes. He would be a great asset," the Emperor said. "Can it be done?"

There was the briefest of pauses. "He will join us or die, master."

Xizor felt the smile, though he did not allow it to show any more than he had allowed his anger play. Ah. Vader wanted Skywalker alive, *that* was what had been in his tone. Yes, he had said that the boy would join them or die, but this latter part was obviously meant only to placate the Emperor. Vader had no intention of killing Skywalker, his own son; that was obvious to one as skilled in reading voices as was Xizor. He had not gotten to be the Dark Prince, Underlord of Black Sun, the largest criminal organization in the galaxy, merely on his formidable good looks. Xizor didn't truly understand the Force that sustained the Emperor and made him and Vader so powerful, save to know that it certainly worked somehow. But he did know that it was something the extinct Jedi had supposedly mastered. And now, apparently, this new player had tapped into it. Vader wanted Skywalker alive, had practically promised the Emperor that he would deliver him alive—and converted.

This was most interesting.

Most interesting indeed.

The Emperor finished his communication and turned back to face him. "Now, where were we, Prince Xizor?"

The Dark Prince smiled. He would attend to the business at hand, but he would not forget the name of Luke Skywalker.

THE TRUCE AT BAKURA by Kathy Tyers
Setting: Immediately after *Return of the Jedi*

The day after his climactic battle with Emperor Palpatine and the sacrifice of his father, Darth Vader, who died saving his life, Luke Skywalker helps recover an Imperial drone ship bearing a startling message intended for the Emperor. It is a distress signal from the far-off Imperial outpost of Bakura, which is under attack by an alien invasion force, the Ssi-ruuk. Leia sees a rescue mission as an opportunity to achieve a diplomatic victory for the Rebel Alliance, even if it means fighting alongside former Imperials. But Luke receives a vision from Obi-Wan Kenobi revealing that the stakes are even higher: the invasion at Bakura threatens everything the Rebels have won at such great cost.

STAR WARS: X-WING
by Michael A. Stackpole
ROGUE SQUADRON
WEDGE'S GAMBLE
THE KRYTOS TRAP
Setting: Two and a half years
after *Return of the Jedi*

Inspired by X-wing, the bestselling computer game from LucasArts Entertainment Co., this exciting series chronicles the further adventures of the most feared and fearless fighting force in the galaxy. A new generation of X-wing pilots, led by Commander Wedge Antilles, is combating the remnants of the Empire still left after the events of the STAR WARS movies. Here are novels full of explosive space action, nonstop adventure, and the special brand of wonder known as STAR WARS.

In this very early scene, young Corellian pilot Corran Horn faces a tough challenge fast enough to get his heart pounding—and this is only a simulation! [P.S.: "Whistler" is Corran's R2 astromech droid]:

The Corellian brought his proton torpedo targeting program up and locked on to the TIE. It tried to break the lock, but turbolaser fire from the *Korolev* boxed it in. Corran's heads-up display went red and he triggered the torpedo. "Scratch one eyeball."

The missile shot straight in at the fighter, but the pilot broke hard to port and away, causing the missile to overshoot the target. *Nice flying!* Corran brought his X-wing over and started down to loop in behind the TIE, but as he did so, the TIE vanished from his forward screen and reappeared in his aft arc. Yanking the stick hard to the right and pulling it back, Corran wrestled the X-wing up and to starboard, then inverted and rolled out to the left.

A laser shot jolted a tremor through the simulator's couch. *Lucky thing I had all shields aft!* Corran reinforced them with energy from his lasers, then evened them out fore and aft. Jinking the fighter right and left, he avoided laser shots coming in from behind, but they all came in far closer than he liked.

He knew Jace had been in the bomber, and Jace was the only pilot in the unit who could have stayed with him. *Except for our leader.* Corran smiled broadly. *Coming to see how good I really am, Commander Antilles? Let me give you a clinic.* "Make sure you're in there solid, Whistler, because we're going for a little ride."

Corran refused to let the R2's moan slow him down. A snap-roll brought the X-wing up on its port wing. Pulling back on the stick yanked the fighter's nose up away from the original line of flight. The TIE stayed with him, then tightened up on the arc to close distance. Corran then rolled another ninety degrees and continued the turn into a dive. Throttling back, Corran hung in the dive for three seconds, then hauled back hard on the stick and cruised up into the TIE fighter's aft.

The X-wing's laser fire missed wide to the right as the TIE cut to the left. Corran kicked his speed up to full and broke with the TIE. He let the X-wing rise above the plane of the break, then put the fighter through a twisting roll that ate up enough time to bring him again into the TIE's rear. The TIE snapped to the right and Corran looped out left.

He watched the tracking display as the distance between them grew to be a kilometer and a half, then slowed. *Fine, you want to go nose to nose? I've got shields and you don't.* If Commander Antilles wanted to commit virtual suicide, Corran was happy to oblige him. He tugged the stick back to his sternum and rolled out in an inversion loop. *Coming at you!*

The two starfighters closed swiftly. Corran centered his foe in the crosshairs and waited for a dead shot. Without shields the TIE fighter would die with one burst, and Corran wanted the kill to be clean. His

HUD flicked green as the TIE juked in and out of the center, then locked green as they closed.

The TIE started firing at maximum range and scored hits. At that distance the lasers did no real damage against the shields, prompting Corran to wonder why Wedge was wasting the energy. Then, as the HUD's green color started to flicker, realization dawned. *The bright bursts on the shields are a distraction to my targeting! I better kill him now!*

Corran tightened down on the trigger button, sending red laser needles stabbing out at the closing TIE fighter. He couldn't tell if he had hit anything. Lights flashed in the cockpit and Whistler started screeching furiously. Corran's main monitor went black, his shields were down, and his weapons controls were dead.

The pilot looked left and right. "Where is he, Whistler?"

The monitor in front of him flickered to life and a diagnostic report began to scroll by. Bloodred bordered the damage reports. "Scanners, out; lasers, out; shields, out; engine, out! I'm a wallowing Hutt just hanging here in space."

THE COURTSHIP OF PRINCESS LEIA
by Dave Wolverton
Setting: Four years after *Return of the Jedi*

One of the most interesting developments in Bantam's Star Wars *novels is that in their storyline, Han Solo and Princess Leia start a family. This tale reveals how the couple originally got together. Wishing to strengthen the fledgling New Republic by bringing in powerful allies, Leia opens talks with the Hapes consortium of more than sixty worlds. But the consortium is ruled by the Queen Mother, who, to Han's dismay, wants Leia to marry her son, Prince Isolder. Before this action-packed story is over, Luke will join forces with Isolder against a group of Force-trained "witches" and face a deadly foe.*

Luke stood in a mountain fortress of stone, looking over a plain with a sea of dark forested hills beyond, and a storm rose—a magnificent wind that brought with it towering walls of black clouds and dust, trees hurtling toward him and twisting through the sky. The clouds thundered overhead, filled with purple flames, obliterating all sunlight, and Luke could feel a malevolence hidden in those clouds and knew that they had been raised through the power of the dark side of the Force.

Dust and stones whistled through the air like autumn leaves. Luke tried to hold on to the stone parapet overlooking the plain to keep from being swept from the fortress walls. Winds pounded in his ears like the roar of an ocean, howling.

It was as if a storm of pure dark Force raged over the countryside, and suddenly, amid the towering clouds of darkness that thundered toward him, Luke could hear laughing, the sweet sound of women laughing. He looked above into the dark clouds, and saw the women borne through the air along with the rocks and debris, like motes of dust, laughing. A voice seemed to whisper, "the witches of Dathomir."

HEIR TO THE EMPIRE
DARK FORCE RISING
THE LAST COMMAND
by Timothy Zahn
Setting: Five years after *Return of the Jedi*

This No. 1 bestselling trilogy introduces two legendary forces of evil into the Star Wars literary pantheon. Grand Admiral Thrawn has taken control of the Imperial fleet in the years since the destruction of the Death Star, and the mysterious Joruus C'baoth is a fearsome Jedi Master who has been seduced by the dark side. Han and Leia have now been married for about a year, and as the story begins, she is pregnant with twins. Thrawn's plan is to crush the Rebellion and resurrect the Empire's New Order with C'baoth's help—and in return, the Dark Master will get Han and Leia's Jedi children to mold as he wishes. For as readers of this magnificent trilogy will see, Luke Skywalker is not the last of the old Jedi. He is the first of the new.

The Jedi Academy Trilogy:
JEDI SEARCH
DARK APPRENTICE
CHAMPIONS OF THE FORCE
by Kevin J. Anderson
Setting: Seven years after *Return of the Jedi*

In order to assure the continuation of the Jedi Knights, Luke Skywalker has decided to start a training facility: a Jedi Academy. He will gather Force-sensitive students who show potential as prospective Jedi and serve as their mentor, as Jedi Masters Obi-Wan Kenobi and Yoda did for him. Han and Leia's twins are now toddlers, and there is a third

Jedi child: the infant Anakin, named after Luke and Leia's father. In this trilogy, we discover the existence of a powerful Imperial doomsday weapon, the horrifying Sun Crusher—which will soon become the centerpiece of a titanic struggle between Luke Skywalker and his most brilliant Jedi Academy student, who is delving dangerously into the dark side.

In this scene from the first novel, Jedi Search, *Luke vocalizes his concept of a new Jedi order to a distinguished assembly of New Republic leaders:*

As he descended the long ramp, Luke felt all eyes turn toward him. A hush fell over the assembly. Luke Skywalker, the lone remaining Jedi Master, almost never took part in governmental proceedings.

"I have an important matter to address," he said.

Mon Mothma gave him a soft, mysterious smile and gestured for him to take a central position. "The words of a Jedi Knight are always welcome to the New Republic," she said.

Luke tried not to look pleased. She had provided the perfect opening for him. "In the Old Republic," he said, "Jedi Knights were the protectors and guardians of all. For a thousand generations the Jedi used the powers of the Force to guide, defend, and provide support for the rightful government of worlds—before the dark days of the Empire came, and the Jedi Knights were killed."

He let his words hang, then took another breath. "Now we have a New Republic. The Empire appears to be defeated. We have founded a new government based upon the old, but let us hope we learn from our mistakes. Before, an entire order of Jedi watched over the Republic, offering strength. Now I am the only Jedi Master who remains.

"Without that order of protectors to provide a backbone of strength for the New Republic, can we survive? Will we be able to weather the storms and the difficulties of forging a new union? Until now we have suffered severe struggles—but in the future they will be seen as nothing more than birth pangs."

Before the other senators could disagree with that, Luke continued. "Our people had a common foe in the Empire, and we must not let our defenses lapse just because we have internal problems. More to the point, what will happen when we begin squabbling among ourselves over petty matters? The old Jedi helped to mediate many types of disputes. What if there are no Jedi Knights to protect us in the difficult times ahead?

"My sister is undergoing Jedi training. She has a great deal of skill in the Force. Her three children are also likely candidates to be trained as young Jedi. In recent years I have come to know a woman named

Mara Jade, who is now unifying the smugglers—the former smugglers," he amended, "into an organization that can support the needs of the New Republic. She also has a talent for the Force. I have encountered others in my travels."

Another pause. The audience was listening so far. "But are these the only ones? We already know that the ability to use the Force is passed from generation to generation. Most of the Jedi were killed in the Emperor's purge—but could he possibly have eradicated all of the descendants of those Knights? I myself was unaware of the potential power within me until Obi-Wan Kenobi taught me how to use it. My sister Leia was similarly unaware.

"How many people are abroad in this galaxy who have a comparable strength in the Force, who are potential members of a new order of Jedi Knights, but are unaware of who they are?"

Luke looked at them again. "In my brief search I have already discovered that there are indeed some descendants of former Jedi. I have come here to ask"—he turned to gesture toward Mon Mothma, swept his hands across the people gathered there in the chamber—"for two things.

"First, that the New Republic officially sanction my search for those with a hidden talent for the Force, to seek them out and try to bring them to our service. For this I will need some help."

"And what will you yourself be doing?" Mon Mothma asked, shifting in her robes.

CHILDREN OF THE JEDI
by Barbara Hambly
Setting: Eight years after *Return of the Jedi*

The Star Wars *characters face a menace from the glory days of the Empire when a thirty-year-old automated Imperial Dreadnaught comes to life and begins its grim mission: to gather forces and annihilate a long-forgotten stronghold of Jedi children. When Luke is whisked onboard, he begins to communicate with the brave Jedi Knight who paralyzed the ship decades ago, and gave her life in the process. Now she is part of the vessel, existing in its artificial intelligence core, and guiding Luke through one of the most unusual adventures he has ever had.*

In this scene, Luke discovers that an evil presence is gathering, one that will force him to join the battle:

Like See-Threepio, Nichos Marr sat in the outer room of the suite to which Cray had been assigned, in the power-down mode that was the droid equivalent of rest. Like Threepio, at the sound of Luke's almost noiseless tread he turned his head, aware of his presence.

"Luke?" Cray had equipped him with the most sensitive vocal modulators, and the word was calibrated to a whisper no louder than the rustle of the blueleaves massed outside the windows. He rose, and crossed to where Luke stood, the dull silver of his arms and shoulders a phantom gleam in the stray flickers of light. "What is it?"

"I don't know." They retreated to the small dining area where Luke had earlier probed his mind, and Luke stretched up to pin back a corner of the lamp-sheath, letting a slim triangle of butter-colored light fall on the purple of the vulwood tabletop. "A dream. A premonition, maybe." It was on his lips to ask, *Do you dream?* but he remembered the ghastly, imageless darkness in Nichos's mind, and didn't. He wasn't sure if his pupil was aware of the difference from his human perception and knowledge, aware of just exactly what he'd lost when his consciousness, his self, had been transferred.

In the morning Luke excused himself from the expedition Tomla El had organized with Nichos and Cray to the Falls of Dessiar, one of the places on Ithor most renowned for its beauty and peace. When they left he sought out Umwaw Moolis, and the tall herd leader listened gravely to his less than logical request and promised to put matters in train to fulfill it. Then Luke descended to the House of the Healers, where Drub McKumb lay, sedated far beyond pain but with all the perceptions of agony and nightmare still howling in his mind.

"Kill you!" He heaved himself at the restraints, blue eyes glaring furiously as he groped and scrabbled at Luke with his clawed hands. "It's all poison! I see you! I see the dark light all around you! You're him! You're him!" His back bent like a bow; the sound of his shrieking was like something being ground out of him by an infernal mangle.

Luke had been through the darkest places of the universe and of his own mind, had done and experienced greater evil than perhaps any man had known on the road the Force had dragged him . . . Still, it was hard not to turn away.

"We even tried yarrock on him last night," explained the Healer in charge, a slightly built Ithorian beautifully tabby-striped green and yellow under her simple tabard of purple linen. "But apparently the earlier doses that brought him enough lucidity to reach here from his point of origin oversensitized his system. We'll try again in four or five days."

Luke gazed down into the contorted, grimacing face.

"As you can see," the Healer said, "the internal perception of pain and fear is slowly lessening. It's down to ninety-three percent of what it was when he was first brought in. Not much, I know, but something.''

''Him! *Him! HIM!*'' Foam spattered the old man's stained gray beard.

Who?

''I wouldn't advise attempting any kind of mindlink until it's at least down to fifty percent, Master Skywalker.''

''No,'' said Luke softly.

Kill you all. And, *They are gathering* . . .

''Do you have recordings of everything he's said?''

''Oh, yes.'' The big coppery eyes blinked assent. ''The transcript is available through the monitor cubicle down the hall. We could make nothing of them. Perhaps they will mean something to you.''

They didn't. Luke listened to them all, the incoherent groans and screams, the chewed fragments of words that could be only guessed at, and now and again the clear disjointed cries: ''Solo! Solo! Can you hear me? Children . . . Evil . . . Gathering here . . . Kill you all!''

DARKSABER by Kevin J. Anderson
Setting: Immediately thereafter

Not long after Children of the Jedi, *Luke and Han learn that evil Hutts are building a reconstruction of the original Death Star—and that the Empire is still alive, in the form of Daala, who has joined forces with Pellaeon, former second in command to the feared Grand Admiral Thrawn. In this early scene, Luke has returned to the home of Obi-Wan Kenobi on Tatooine to try and consult a long-gone mentor:*

He stood anxious and alone, feeling like a prodigal son outside the ramshackle, collapsed hut that had once been the home of Obi-Wan Kenobi.

Luke swallowed and stepped forward, his footsteps crunching in the silence. He had not been here in many years. The door had fallen off its hinges; part of the clay front wall had fallen in. Boulders and crumbled adobe jammed the entrance. A pair of small, screeching desert rodents snapped at him and fled for cover; Luke ignored them.

Gingerly, he ducked low and stepped into the home of his first mentor.

Luke stood in the middle of the room breathing deeply, turning around, trying to sense the presence he desperately needed to see. This was the place where Obi-Wan Kenobi had told Luke of the Force. Here, the old man had first given Luke his lightsaber and hinted at the truth about his father, "from a certain point of view," dispelling the diversionary story that Uncle Owen had told, at the same time planting seeds of his own deceptions.

"Ben," he said and closed his eyes, calling out with his mind as well as his voice. He tried to penetrate the invisible walls of the Force and reach to the luminous being of Obi-Wan Kenobi who had visited him numerous times, before saying he could never speak with Luke again.

"Ben, I need you," Luke said. Circumstances had changed. He could think of no other way past the obstacles he faced. Obi-Wan had to answer. It wouldn't take long, but it could give him the key he needed with all his heart.

Luke paused and listened and sensed—

But felt nothing. If he could not summon Obi-Wan's spirit here in the empty dwelling where the old man had lived in exile for so many years, Luke didn't believe he could find his former teacher ever again.

He echoed the words Leia had used more than a decade earlier, beseeching him, "Help me, Obi-Wan Kenobi," Luke whispered, "you're my only hope."

THE CRYSTAL STAR
by Vonda N. McIntyre
Setting: Ten years after *Return of the Jedi*

Leia's three children have been kidnapped. That horrible fact is made worse by Leia's realization that she can no longer sense her children through the Force! While she, Artoo-Detoo, and Chewbacca trail the kidnappers, Luke and Han discover a planet that is suffering strange quantum effects from a nearby star. Slowly freezing into a perfect crystal and disrupting the Force, the star is blunting Luke's power and crippling the Millennium Falcon. *These strands converge in an apocalyptic threat not only to the fate of the New Republic, but to the universe itself.*

The Black Fleet Crisis
BEFORE THE STORM
SHIELD OF LIES
by Michael P. Kube-McDowell
Setting: Twelve years after *Return of the Jedi*

Long after setting up the hard-won New Republic, yesterday's Rebels have become today's administrators and diplomats. But the peace is not to last for long. A restless Luke must journey to his mother's homeworld in a desperate quest to find her people; Lando seizes a mysterious spacecraft with unimaginable weapons of destruction; and waiting in the wings is an horrific battle fleet under the control of a ruthless leader bent on a genocidal war.

Here is an opening scene from Before the Storm:

In the pristine silence of space, the Fifth Battle Group of the New Republic Defense Fleet blossomed over the planet Bessimir like a beautiful, deadly flower.

The formation of capital ships sprang into view with startling suddenness, trailing fire-white wakes of twisted space and bristling with weapons. Angular Star Destroyers guarded fat-hulled fleet carriers, while the assault cruisers, their mirror finishes gleaming, took the point.

A halo of smaller ships appeared at the same time. The fighters among them quickly deployed in a spherical defensive screen. As the Star Destroyers firmed up their formation, their flight decks quickly spawned scores of additional fighters.

At the same time, the carriers and cruisers began to disgorge the bombers, transports, and gunboats they had ferried to the battle. There was no reason to risk the loss of one fully loaded—a lesson the Republic had learned in pain. At Orinda, the commander of the fleet carrier *Endurance* had kept his pilots waiting in the launch bays, to protect the smaller craft from Imperial fire as long as possible. They were still there when *Endurance* took the brunt of a Super Star Destroyer attack and vanished in a ball of metal fire.

Before long more than two hundred warships, large and small, were bearing down on Bessimir and its twin moons. But the terrible, restless power of the armada could be heard and felt only by the ships' crews. The silence of the approach was broken only on the fleet comm channels, which had crackled to life in the first moments with encoded bursts of noise and cryptic ship-to-ship chatter.

At the center of the formation of great vessels was the flagship of the Fifth Battle Group, the fleet carrier *Intrepid*. She was so new from the yards at Hakassi that her corridors still reeked of sealing compound and cleaning solvent. Her huge realspace thruster engines still sang with the high-pitched squeal that the engine crews called "the baby's cry."

It would take more than a year for the mingled scents of the crew to displace the chemical smells from the first impressions of visitors. But after a hundred more hours under way, her engines' vibrations would drop two octaves, to the reassuring thrum of a seasoned thruster bank.

On *Intrepid*'s bridge, a tall Dornean in general's uniform paced along an arc of command stations equipped with large monitors. His eye-folds were swollen and fanned by an unconscious Dornean defensive reflex, and his leathery face was flushed purple by concern. Before the deployment was even a minute old, Etahn A'baht's first command had been bloodied.

The fleet tender *Ahazi* had overshot its jump, coming out of hyperspace too close to Bessimir and too late for its crew to recover from the error. Etahn A'baht watched the bright flare of light in the upper atmosphere from *Intrepid*'s forward viewstation, knowing that it meant six young men were dead.

The Corellian Trilogy:
AMBUSH AT CORELLIA
ASSAULT AT SELONIA
SHOWDOWN AT CENTERPOINT
by Roger MacBride Allen
Setting: Fourteen years after *Return of the Jedi*

This trilogy takes us to Corellia, Han Solo's homeworld, which Han has not visited in quite some time. A trade summit brings Han, Leia, and the children—now developing their own clear personalities and instinctively learning more about their innate skills in the Force—into the middle of a situation that most closely resembles a burning fuse. The Corellian system is on the brink of civil war, there are New Republic intelligence agents on a mysterious mission which even Han does not understand, and worst of all, a fanatical rebel leader has his hands on a superweapon of unimaginable power—and just wait until you find out who that leader is!

Here is an early scene from Ambush *that gives you a wonderful look at the growing Solo children (the twins are Jacen and Jaina, and their little brother is Anakin):*

Anakin plugged the board into the innards of the droid and pressed a button. The droid's black, boxy body shuddered awake, it drew in its wheels to stand up a bit taller, its status lights lit, and it made a sort of triple beep. "That's good," he said, and pushed the button again. The droid's status lights went out, and its body slumped down again. Anakin picked up the next piece, a motivation actuator. He frowned at it as he turned it over in his hands. He shook his head. "That's *not* good," he announced.

"What's not good?" Jaina asked.

"This thing," Anakin said, handing her the actuator. "Can't you *tell*? The insides part is all melty."

Jaina and Jacen exchanged a look. "The outside looks okay," Jaina said, giving the part to her brother. "How can he tell what the *inside* of it looks like? It's sealed shut when they make it."

Anakin, still sitting on the floor, took the device from his brother and frowned at it again. He turned it over and over in his hands, and then held it over his head and looked at it as if he were holding it up to the light. "There," he said, pointing a chubby finger at one point on the unmarked surface. "In there is the bad part." He rearranged himself to sit cross-legged, put the actuator in his lap, and put his right index finger over the "bad" part. "Fix," he said. "Fix." The dark brown outer case of the actuator seemed to glow for a second with an odd blue-red light, but then the glow sputtered out and Anakin pulled his finger away quickly and stuck it in his mouth, as if he had burned it on something.

"Better now?" Jaina asked.

"*Some* better," Anakin said, pulling his finger out of his mouth. "Not *all* better." He took the actuator in his hand and stood up. He opened the access panel on the broken droid and plugged in the actuator. He closed the door and looked expectantly at his older brother and sister.

"Done?" Jaina asked.

"Done," Anakin agreed. "But *I'm* not going to push the button." He backed well away from the droid, sat down on the floor, and folded his arms.

Jacen looked at his sister.

"Not me," she said. "This was your idea."

Jacen stepped forward to the droid, reached out to push the power button from as far away as he could, and then stepped hurriedly back.

Once again, the droid shuddered awake, rattling a bit this time as it did so. It pulled its wheels in, lit its panel lights, and made the same triple beep. But then its holocam eye viewlens wobbled back and forth, and its panel lights dimmed and flared. It rolled backward just a bit, and then recovered itself.

"Good morning, young mistress and masters," it said. "How may I surge you?"

Well, one word wrong, but so what? Jacen grinned and clapped his hands and rubbed them together eagerly. "Good day, droid," he said. They had done it! But what to ask for first? "First tidy up this room," he said. A simple task, and one that ought to serve as a good test of what this droid could do.

Suddenly the droid's overhead access door blew off and there was a flash of light from its interior. A thin plume of smoke drifted out of the droid. Its panel lights flared again, and then the work arm sagged downward. The droid's body, softened by heat, sagged in on itself and drooped to the floor. The floor and walls and ceilings of the playroom were supposed to be fireproof, but nonetheless the floor under the droid darkened a bit, and the ceiling turned black. The ventilators kicked on high automatically, and drew the smoke out of the room. After a moment they shut themselves off, and the room was silent.

The three children stood, every bit as frozen to the spot as the droid was, absolutely stunned. It was Anakin who recovered first. He walked cautiously toward the droid and looked at it carefully, being sure not to get too close or touch it. "*Really* melty now," he announced, and then wandered off to the other side of the room to play with his blocks.

The twins looked at the droid, and then at each other.

"We're dead," Jacen announced, surveying the wreckage.

STAR WARS: TALES FROM THE MOS EISLEY CANTINA
Edited by Kevin J. Anderson

Droids and mutants rule in sixteen scintillating *Star Wars* tales!

In a far corner of the universe, on the small desert planet of Tatooine, there is a dark, nic-i-tain-filled cantina where you can down your favorite intoxicant while listening to the best jizz riffs in the universe. But beware your fellow denizens of this pangalactic watering hole, for they are cut-throats and cutpurses, assassins and troopers, humans and aliens, gangsters and thieves. . .

A Bantam Paperback

0 553 40971 9

STAR WARS: TALES FROM JABBA'S PALACE
Edited by Kevin J. Anderson

Enter the lair of the galaxy's most notorious criminal in nineteen stories from today's masters of science fiction.

In the dusty heat of twin-sunned Tatooine lives the wealthiest gangster in a hundred worlds, master of a vast crime empire and keeper of a vicious, flesh-eating monster for entertainment (and disposal of his enemies). Bloated and sinister, Jabba the Hutt might have made a good joke – if he weren't so dangerous. A cast of soldiers, spies, assassins, scoundrels, bounty hunters, and pleasure seekers have come to his palace, and every visitor to Jabba's grand abode has a story. Some of them may even live to tell it . . .

A Bantam Paperback

0 553 50413 4

STAR WARS: TALES OF THE BOUNTY HUNTERS
Edited by Kevin J. Anderson

Five stories of the galaxy's most ruthless bounty hunters . . . by some of today's finest writers of science fiction.

In a wild and battle-scarred galaxy, assassins, pirates, smugglers, and cut-throats of every description roam at will, fearing only the professional bounty hunters – amoral adventurers who track down the scum of the universe . . . for a fee. When Darth Vader seeks to strike at the heart of the Rebellion by targeting Han Solo and the Millennium Falcon, he calls upon six of the most successful – and feared – hunters, including the merciless Boba Fett. They all have two things in common: lust for profit and contempt for life . . .

A Bantam Paperback

0 553 50471 1

A SELECTION OF SCIENCE FICTION
AND FANTASY TITLES
AVAILABLE FROM BANTAM BOOKS

☐ 40808 9	**STAR WARS: Jedi Search**	*Kevin J. Anderson*	£5.99
☐ 40809 7	**STAR WARS: Dark Apprentice**	*Kevin J. Anderson*	£4.99
☐ 40810 0	**STAR WARS: Champions of the Force**	*Kevin J. Anderson*	£5.99
☐ 40971 9	**STAR WARS: Tales from the Mos Eisley Cantina**	*Kevin J. Anderson (ed.)*	£4.99
☐ 50413 4	**STAR WARS: Tales from Jabba's Palace**	*Kevin J. Anderson (ed.)*	£4.99
☐ 50471 1	**STAR WARS: Tales of the Bounty Hunters**	*Kevin J. Anderson (ed.)*	£4.99
☐ 40880 1	**STAR WARS: Darksaber**	*Kevin J. Anderson*	£5.99
☐ 40488 1	**FORWARD THE FOUNDATION**	*Isaac Asimov*	£4.99
☐ 40069 X	**NEMESIS**	*Isaac Asimov*	£4.99
☐ 50546 7	**STAR WARS: THE PARADISE SNARE**	*A. C. Crispin*	£4.99
☐ 50495 9	**DINOTOPIA LOST**	*Alan Dean Foster*	£4.99
☐ 50492 4	**THE SHIFT**	*George Foy*	£4.99
☐ 40879 8	**STAR WARS: Children of the Jedi**	*Barbara Hambly*	£4.99
☐ 40501 2	**STAINLESS STEEL RAT SINGS THE BLUES**	*Harry Harrison*	£4.99
☐ 50431 2	**STAR WARS: Before the Storm**	*Michael P. Kube-McDowell*	£4.99
☐ 50479 7	**STAR WARS: Shield of Lies**	*Michael P. Kube-McDowell*	£5.99
☐ 50480 0	**STAR WARS: Tyrant's Test**	*Michael P. Kube-McDowell*	£4.99
☐ 50426 6	**SHADOW MOON**	*George Lucas & Chris Claremont*	£4.99
☐ 40881 X	**STAR WARS: Ambush at Corellia**	*Roger MacBride Allen*	£4.99
☐ 40882 8	**STAR WARS: Assault at Selonia**	*Roger MacBride Allen*	£4.99
☐ 40883 6	**STAR WARS: Showdown at Centerpoint**	*Roger MacBride Allen*	£4.99
☐ 40878 X	**STAR WARS: The Crystal Star**	*Vonda McIntyre*	£5.99
☐ 40926 3	**STAR WARS X-Wing 1: Rogue Squadron**	*Michael Stackpole*	£5.99
☐ 40923 9	**STAR WARS X-Wing 2: Wedge's Gamble**	*Michael Stackpole*	£4.99
☐ 40925 5	**STAR WARS X-Wing 3: The Krytos Trap**	*Michael Stackpole*	£4.99
☐ 40924 7	**STAR WARS X-Wing 4: The Bacta War**	*Michael Stackpole*	£4.99
☐ 50596 3	**STAR WARS: The Truce at Bakura**	*Kathy Tyers*	£4.99
☐ 50492 4	**HONOR AMONG ENEMIES**	*David Weber*	£4.99
☐ 40807 0	**STAR WARS: The Courtship of Princess Leia**	*Dave Wolverton*	£4.99
☐ 40471 7	**STAR WARS: Heir to the Empire**	*Timothy Zahn*	£5.99
☐ 40442 5	**STAR WARS: Dark Force Rising**	*Timothy Zahn*	£4.99
☐ 40443 1	**STAR WARS: The Last Command**	*Timothy Zahn*	£4.99
☐ 40853 4	**CONQUERORS' PRIDE**	*Timothy Zahn*	£4.99
☐ 40854 2	**CONQUERORS' HERITAGE**	*Timothy Zahn*	£4.99
☐ 40855 0	**CONQUERORS' LEGACY**	*Timothy Zahn*	£4.99